# Fat Man Blues

## Richard Wall

Also by Richard Wall:
Evel Knievel and The Fat Elvis Diner
Five Pairs of Shorts

# Red's

Red's was a juke-joint in Clarksdale, Mississippi, just across the tracks from the Ground Zero Blues Club. On the third night that I went in, the place was empty; except for Red, who was engrossed in a newspaper, and an obese black man I'd never seen before who was scribbling in a notebook at a table next to the stage, necking Tanqueray from the bottle and in a world that only he could see.

I walked up to the bar. Red looked up, nodded at me, produced a bottle of Sam Adams and then carried on reading.

"I'm a King Bee" by Slim Harpo was playing on the juke-box; I placed a five-dollar bill on the bar and sipped my beer to the hypnotic swamp-blues vibe.

Slim Harpo stopped singing and the juke-box fell silent. The fat man lifted his massive head and blinked at me slowly.

"Y'all dig the blues, White Boy?" he said.

I said that I did.

The fat man grunted. "I 'member one time, Muddy Waters stopped by here, stood 'sac'ly where you standin' now. Man that cat could play."

He gave three hefty chuckles, took another drink and then belched. "What are y'all doin' here?"

I told him I was following the blues trail and was stopping in Clarksdale for a few nights.

"Jus' another white boy wants t' play the blues, huh?"

I shrugged.

"Where's yo' accent from?"

I told him it was from England.

1

"Well," he said. "This heyah's what the blues is now. Blues is fo' white folks, but it ain't the real blues. I knows where the real blues is, ain't that right, Red?"

Red didn't look up but his head moved slightly. It could have been a nod.

"Come over heyah, son," said the fat man.

I walked over.

Up close he reeked of booze and body odour; beads of sweat covered his bald head, and the black t-shirt stretched across his huge bulk and black sweat pants that encased massive thighs were covered in stains that I didn't want to think about. He cleared his throat and blinked slowly as he fought to salvage discarded words from his gin-soaked vocabulary.

"See," he said. "They's a place where the blues is still like it was." He leaned closer. "I can show yo' that place, if yo' of a mind?"

I said maybe and asked him his name.

The fat man blinked at me, his eyes glazing as he processed this, and then said, "I'll get back to yo' on that."

He stood up, wavered unsteadily and then left the bar through a door at the back of the room.

I returned to the bar and asked Red who that was. He didn't look up from his newspaper.

"Tha's Fat Man," he growled. "An' tha's all I'm sayin'."

True to his word, Red remained silent. I stayed for another beer and then said goodnight.

Fat Man appeared from an alley at the side of the building.

"So, yo' wan' see this place where the blues is at?"

I wondered what sort of scam was about to be played. Maybe he was a hustler for another club?

"Ain't no scam," he said. "An' I ain't no hustler. This place I knows, it ain't no club, but is jus' the sort o' place yo' need to see. Blues is wid y'all."

I asked him what he meant.

"I saw yo' diggin' Slim Harpo," he said. "Yo' heyah cos' yo' woman gone an' yo' feelin' low down. Yo' got the sickness. Yo' got the blues sho' nuff."

I asked him how the hell he knew all that.

"Yo' wearin' a weddin' band but yo' been heyah three nights on yo' own, hittin' the booze an' diggin' the blues. Yo' got a dark aura, kinda sickly. Somethin' bad be hangin' wid yo'."

I said I had to go. Fat Man stepped in front of me. "Hear me, White Boy," he said. "I knows a place yo' would 'preciate. I'm talkin' Charley Patton, Robert Johnson, Willie Brown."

Now I was certain he was drunk. I reminded him that they were all dead.

He winked. "Maybe they is, maybe they ain't. Maybe yo' ain't far behind 'em. An' I ain't drunk, I jus' been drinkin'. We gon' talk again soon."

I stepped around him and walked back into town.

# Holly Ridge

Several drinks later I was sitting on the bed in the apartment I'd rented above the Ground Zero Blues Club, staring at my phone as it swam in and out of focus. I dialled her number and for a long time my thumb hovered over the green icon, then the realisation kicked in and I pressed cancel. Rose was gone.

I replayed the conversation with Fat Man. I was intrigued about what he meant by the real blues. Clearly he was off his head on God only knew what, but would I take him up on his offer?

The jury was still out.

I woke up twice with raging night sweats that I put down to the amount I'd drunk - you can fool all of the people some of the time. I was on a countdown and the next morning I was fifty years and five days old.

I took my hangover to breakfast - it was the least I could do - but it took several refills of coffee to persuade it to leave.

I wandered out into the bright morning sunshine and explored the streets of Clarksdale.

Some time later I found myself standing next to my car in the parking lot of Ground Zero. A cloud passed over the sun and I shivered at the sudden drop in temperature. I got into the car and drove out of town.

Highway 61 was quiet as I headed south, the sun glinting off pools of water that littered the rich, fertile, dark grey soil, serving as a reminder that the delta is nothing more than a playground for the sleeping giant that is the Mississippi River.

As the flat landscape of endless cotton fields flowed beneath the sapphire Mississippi sky, I felt enveloped in a calmness that had been missing for a long time.

Twenty-five miles south of Clarksdale, give or take, is a town called Leland. Here I headed east for five miles on Highway 82 and then turned north.

Holly Ridge is a quarter of a mile stretch of about a dozen houses, a cotton gin, a derelict wooden church and an acre of dilapidated graveyard. It was deserted when I stopped and got out of the car.

This was my second visit and I knew where to go.

I walked fifty feet from the road to a plot at the edge of the graveyard and stood for a long time reading and re-reading the inscription on the grey headstone:

*Charley Patton*

*April 1891 - April 28 1934*

*The voice of the Delta*

*The foremost performer of early*

*Mississippi blues whose songs became*

*cornerstones of American music*

Scattered around the grave were coins of many nations, guitar picks and plastic flowers. Mementoes left by visitors in deference to a mixed race singer who stood five foot five inches tall, weighed a hundred and fifty-five pounds and yet whose voice could be heard five-hundred yards away.

By all accounts, Mister Patton liked to party hard and next to the headstone someone had left a large glass bottle, half-filled with a dark brown liquid that the sun-bleached label proclaimed to be Bulleit Bourbon.

It didn't seem out of place.

"Oh, he liked to party hard, sho' nuff."

I was lost in reverie and physically startled at Fat Man's voice. He walked from behind me to stand next to the headstone.

I looked around. Mine was the only car I could see.

I asked him where the hell he'd come from. Instead of answering he stooped, picked up the bottle, unscrewed the cap and took a large swig, spilling bourbon down his t-shirt and adding to the stains I'd seen the night before. Wiping his mouth with the back of his hand, he grinned and offered the bottle to me.

I shook my head and asked him if he was following me.

Instead of answering he took several long pulls from the bottle, his throat working noisily as he guzzled the dark liquor.

I turned away from the sound and stared towards the old church. According to a book I'd read, Charley Patton used to preach there.

Fat Man belched. "Some say he knew he's took bad, knew his time was short, started to repent all his high livin'. Tha's why he took up preachin', coverin' all 'ventualities, you might say."

By my reckoning, Fat Man had been chugging bourbon for the best part of a minute or so. His eyes took on the liquid shine of a wet brain and booze dripped from his chin. In one movement he replaced the cap and returned the bottle next to the stone.

It took me a few seconds to realise that the level of bourbon hadn't dropped an inch from when I first arrived.

Fat Man chuckled. "I always was whatchoo might call a glass half-full kinda guy."

I looked around, tried to hide my nervousness.

"No need to be scared, White Boy," he said. "Time enough fo' that later."

I asked him who he was, where he'd come from and what he wanted with me.

"Who I am, where I'm from, they jus' incidentals," he said. "Don' mean nothin' in the grand scheme o' things. What I want witchoo? Well now, tha's an interesting question."

He leaned his vast bulk against Charley Patton's headstone and then caught the look on my face. "Ain't no sacrilege," he said. "Ain't nothin' but a stone with a bit o' writin'." He cupped his ear and inclined his head towards the ground. "An' I don' heyah no complainin'."

Fat Man grinned and then reached into his pocket, pulling out a packet of Lucky Strikes and a book of matches. He lit a cigarette, drew deeply on it and blew out a cloud of blue smoke.

"Well now," he said. "Heyah, we all is."

He took another drag. "I'm heyah cos I think yo' not gettin' the full benefit of what a feller like me can offer the discernin' blues tourist."

I said that I had no idea what he was talking about.

He smoked at me for a while, took a final drag of the Lucky Strike, ground the butt into the dirt with his shoe then looked up.

"Yo' plays the gittar back home."

It was a statement, not a question. I asked him how he knew so much about me.

"Don' matter 'how', jus' is. Yo' play the gittar fo' yo' self, but deep down, in yo' quiet time, yo' dreams of playin' slide gittar in a bar, an' havin' all the wimmins shoutin' an' hollerin' fo' mo' of yo' playin'."

I said nothing.

"Ain' nothin' to be 'shamed of. Ever' man deserves a little vanity now an' then."

He lit another cigarette.

"An' sometime's yo' dream yo' playin' yo' gittar with Charley Patton, Son House or Willie Brown."

I could feel myself blushing.

"Ain' nothin' wrong with that neither. Imagination's a powerful force. Can be what drives a man. In his mind, a man can do most anythin'; make his self richer than a king, get his self a beautiful woman, drive his self a fancy car, play the gittar in a Delta juke-joint. Make hell outta heaven an' heaven outta hell. Yessuh, inside the mind of a man can be a wondrous place."

He paused. "A lost paradise, yo' might say."

Chuckling to himself, he blew out more smoke.

"But in yo' mind, hearin' the blues and playin' the blues is all the riches yo' strive fo'. Like a itch yo' jus' cain't reach but needs t'scratch real bad. Blues is all yo' thinkin' of right about now. Yo' think blues has got the answer an' tha's the solid truth."

He stopped and I had nothing to say.

"An' then," he said. "Yo' come all the way from England to drive roun' Mississippi takin' pitchers o' buildin's an' statues an' graveyards. Yo' goes into places where they puts a jukebox filled with blues records and calls themselves juke-joints. Ever'one's friendly, aks yo' where yo' from an' 'I love yo' acceyent' then yo' go home an' tell ever'one that yo' seen the blues. That about right?"

I was about to answer when he aimed his Lucky Strike at me.

"But what yo' really wants to see is the real deal. Yo' a purist, yo' wanna see it like it was back in the day; black man stompin' out the blues on a ol' Stella gittar, folks like Charley Patton raisin' hell in a real juke-joint or shotgun shack, drinkin' rotgut whisky, chasing wimmin an' havin' a high ol' time cos they got no desire to work on no cotton plantation."

Fat Man looked me straight in the eye. "What if I said I can show y'all that? Take yo' back to those times?"

I asked how that was possible.

"Tha's jus' detail," he said, and then flashed a grin. "An' we all knows who lives in theyah."

He drew deeply on the cigarette and wreathed his face in smoke as he exhaled. "This ain' no bullshit," he said. "I can do all o' that."

When I asked him what I had to do he waved a dismissive hand. "Thas' jus' mo' detail," he said. "It ain' gon' cost yo' dollar one, jus' a little bit o' yo' time, of no consequence."

He paused. "In the grand scheme o' things."

Fat Man smiled, and it was almost friendly.

"I talked enough fo' today," he said. "Nex' time we meets we can discuss this matter further."

Right then I had no intention of seeing Fat Man again. I just wanted to get away.

"It ain't my intention to make yo' feel uncomfortable," he said. "But time waits fo' no man an' yo' time gettin' impatient, but I'll move on now an' bid yo' good day."

He stood up and walked past me. For a few seconds I stared at Charley Patton's headstone then turned to walk back to the car.

Fat Man was nowhere to be seen.

As I drove, I tried to make sense of our conversation. By the time I reached Clarksdale, I was none the wiser.

# Ground Zero Blues Club

That night I went downstairs for a beer. I got talking to a lawyer, a fellow blues freak who looked like Buddy Holly and told me he'd driven from Oklahoma City to escape his own women troubles. I bought him a beer and he bought me a beer. It's always good to find a like-minded soul and so we commenced on a bar-crawl around Clarksdale. At the end of the night we found ourselves in Bluesberries Café; by day a mom and pop restaurant, by night a modern day juke-joint with makeshift stage and most of the tables and chairs stacked up in the corner.

As we walked in, everyone was dancing to The East River String Band - Eden Brower was owning the stage and channelling Memphis Minnie as she belted out "Me and My Chauffeur Blues".

To the left of the stage, a girl danced alone so I staggered over and introduced myself. She told me her name was Marilyn and that she loved my accent. I told her that I loved hers and that was that. Buddy Holly hung around for a while then said he was leaving. He gave me his business card and we both lied about keeping in touch. Soon after, Marilyn and I went back to my room.

Next morning, while I was in the bathroom, Marilyn left, taking with her my seed and two hundred dollars in twenties that she'd lifted from my wallet. I didn't care, I was shitting blood.

So it began.

I'd been warned to expect this but the speed and ferocity hit me like a train. I was in agony. Simultaneously sweating, puking and crapping, every orifice producing foul, black matter mixed with dark red blood.

11

Cancer patients are often labelled as heroes, fighting the disease with bravery and dignity.

It's not a fight, it's a chemical lottery and I discovered that I'm a whimpering, snivelling coward. By mid-afternoon all dignity had evaporated; I was lying on the floor in a stench-filled bathroom, naked, covered in shit and getting used to the idea that I might actually die right there.

Eventually, the evacuations stopped and despite intense stomach cramps I mustered enough strength to stand and have a shower. Afterwards, I lay on the bed, closed my eyes and tried to come to terms with the pain, pain that had settled to a roaring fire of agony.

This was bad.

"This' bad, sho' nuff."

I looked up to see Fat Man holding a pizza carton.

"You in a bad way, White Boy. Gotcha somethin' go'n ease yo' pain."

He opened the carton to show a large pizza covered in peppers.

"Jalapeño," he said. "Numbs the inside o' yo' gut."

Fat Man placed the carton onto the bed, helped me sit up and then handed me a slice.

"Take small bites."

The jalapeño hit was intense. My lips buzzed, my eyes filled with tears and sweat poured down my face.

"Keep on eatin'," he said.

I was half way through the pizza before the agony began to subside.

"Gotta take 'em ever' day," said Fat Man. "Ever' single day. That is o' course, if tha's the road you wanna travel. It ain't gon' stop wha's happenin' but at least it'll help wit' the pain."

He dragged a wooden chair close to the bed and sat down.

"Ol' gal I know down in New Orlins, she tol' me about usin' jalapeño peppas."

I asked if it was a voodoo remedy.

Fat Man laughed. "Voodoo? Hell no. She read it on Wikipedia. This' the twenty-first century, home-boy."

Despite my burning mouth, the relief I felt was akin to a religious experience. I thanked Fat Man. I couldn't thank him enough.

"Well now," he said. "I ain't no philanthropist. This here's a gesture o' goodwill, a free sample, if you will. Ain't no mo' givin' be' goin' on, no suh. From here on it's stric'ly business."

He stared at me for a few moments. "If I's a gamblin' man I'd lay odds that yo' clock gon' stop in what, coupla months?"

My doctor had said six months at the outside. That was three months ago.

Fat Man grunted. "What happened today, likely gon' happen tomorrow, an' the nex' day an' the day after that. Each time it does it gon' take yo' longer to get back, until one day yo' wake up wishin' you hadn't." He paused. "Maybe it's time to consider yo' options?"

I said I thought my options were somewhat limited.

"Maybe," he said. "Yo' could try and fly back home but I guess in yo' current state they gon' say yo' unfit to fly an' likely won't let yo' near the airplane. Yo' could get treatment here, that might drag things out a tad, ease yo' sufferin' some. But o' course tha's gon' cost a lot o' money, probl'y mo' than yo' got an' I jus' bet y'aint got no medical insurance?"

I said nothing.

"Thas' what I thought. Third option is that yo' do nothin' an' accept the status quo, keep eatin' them peppers and hope the end comes soon an' wid out too much pain. Gotta say, tha's unlikely. Fourth option is that yo' bring about the end yo'self."

He shrugged. "Cain't throw a stone in Miss'ippi without hitting a gun, or yo' could jus' keep it simple and jump in the river. Whichever way you wants to look at it, yo' reachin' the end o' yo' journey an' yo' gonna face it alone. Ain't no one gon' miss yo'. Ain't no one waitin' back home."

Fat Man lit a Lucky Strike, blew smoke rings and then said. "What if I was to suggest another option?"

I said that I was all ears.

"Yo' come with me. I'll take away yo' pain an' show yo' a good time, show yo' things yo' never thought yo'd see."

I asked him how he could do that.

He shrugged. "Don' matter how, just is."

I asked him what I would have to do in return.

"Work fo' me," he said.

I asked what sort of work.

"Research assistant," he said.

I asked what sort of research.

His eyes narrowed, the chair squeaking as he shifted his vast bulk.

"Researchin' the blues. Yo' gets to travel Mississippi, searchin' out an' recordin' real blues singers playin' the blues at juke-joints an' fish-fries an' house-rents an' such."

He leaned forward and stared at me.

"I'm offerin' yo' an alternative to the place you at right now. Leave behind all the pain, all the sickness. Ever'thin'."

His voice softened, took on a hypnotic cadence. "Yo' walk right into the world yo' been readin' about an' dreamin' about fo' half yo' life. Imagine playin' yo' gittar wit' Charley Patton; walkin' the delta roads, bein' at parties like yo' never seen, at juke-joints where Son House and Willie Brown be playin'. Imagine them seein' yo' wid yo' gittar and askin' yo t' play along. An' wimmins, White Boy. Wimmins like yo' won't never believe, all lookin' atchoo an' askin' fo' a song an' they be sayin', 'whatchoo doin' afta' an' 'why donchoo come roun' my shack?'. Good times, White Boy. Better than endin' yo' days convulsin' an' screamin' an' wit' the taste o' yo' own shit that be comin' outta yo' mouth."

He paused just long enough. "Come with me and yo' gets t'leave all this behind. Ever'thin'."

There had to be a catch.

Fat Man leaned back and blew another smoke ring. "Catch is, come with me an' yo' got to leave all this behind. Ever'thin'."

I was about to ask another question when a bayonet of agony tore through my stomach, triggering a convulsion that threw me off of the bed and put me on my knees on the floor. I rolled over and saw Fat Man eyeing me dispassionately.

"I'm guessing yo' wonderin' what I means by leavin' this world," he said. "An' maybe tha's castin' a shadow o' doubt on the proceedin's? Yo' believe in God, White Boy? Is what I'm sayin' at odds wit' the religious teachin's with which yo' been raised? Is that it?"

Fat Man chuckled. "Well lemme tell yo' somethin'. Situations like yo's; folks who started out believin', they gives it up an' the folks who never believed, they starts prayin'. Ain't that a paradox?"

The wooden chair creaked as he tipped it backwards onto two legs. "Lemme tell yo' 'bout religion. See, put two or more men together an' sooner or later a scam gon' be played. Tha's how it is. All through history, men be schemin' and connivin' to get the better of other men, pullin' scams to get they own way. Tha's all religion is, jus' another scam. Ever' damn religion on this planet be started by a man with the sole intention o' slappin' down other men. Keep 'em scared, keep 'em in line. Sacred an' scared, similar lookin' words when they side by side, doncha' think? Religious words - the Bible an' such - they jus' made up stories to keep the ignorant in they place. Ever' writer has an angle, an opinion they wants to get across, message they wants to sell. Men goes to war in the name o' religion. Religious war ain't nothin' more than men battlin' to keep hold o' they own particular scam."

He paused to take a breath. "How you doin' down there White Boy?"

All I could do was moan.

Fat Man took no notice. "An' these religious teachin's they do say that God made man his own image an' made all the creatures that roam the earth. Yes suh, the Lord God made 'em all. Yo' like honey, White Boy? Honey's made by a bee, ever'one knows that. An' the bee's made by the Lord God. God makes the bee, the bee makes honey fo' the man to eat. Tha's enough to make a man believe, right there. Bettah write that down, tha's a natchel miracle. Honey bee's, they ain't all they seems tho'. Honey bee will sting yo' ass, it knows it gon' die but it gon' sting anyway. Yo' ever been stung White Boy? Hurt like a sumbitch. An' when a bee sting yo' it release a smell fo' other bees an' so they lines up t'sting yo' too. Tha's jus' nasty. How we gon' explain that? Bettah call it God's will."

Fat Man lit another cigarette. "Was a honey bee stung that truck driver. A man made in God's own image. Drivin' a truck loaded with 44 tonnes o' gasoline, comin' up to a red light at better'n 40 miles an hour, an' jus' thinkin' about changin' down when in flies mister made-by-God honey bee an' stings the truck driver on the neck. Damned if the truck driver ain't allergic. Anaphylactic reaction they calls it. Man, his right leg goes stiffer than a virgin's dick, pushes down on the gas pedal an' sends his truck barrel-assin' across the intersection. Truck T-bones a car then jackknifes like in a Hollywood movie an' pushes the

16

car right across the road an' into a furniture store. Gasoline pours out o' the truck, car catches fire, gasoline reaches the flames an' BOOM! They say the explosion was heard five miles away. Yo' musta heard it yo'self? An' who yo' think was drivin' the car? Real purty lady, tha's who. Late forties, kinda smartly dressed, drivin' home to see her husband, hopin' he ain't done nothin' on account o' he got the stomach cancer an' she be feelin' guilty cos she had to get outta the house on account she couldn't take no more o' his feelin' low down. Only now all she wants to do is get home an' hold him and tell him s'all gon' be OK. Except she never gets home. No suh, she end up barbecued in a gasoline fireball. An' all because of a little-bitty honey bee. If tha's God' will then he sho' moves in mysterious ways."

Fat Man looked down at me through hooded eyelids. "Well, he ain't the only one."

He stood up, suddenly businesslike. "Whatchoo wannado White Boy, stay heyah, or come along wit me? S'yo choice."

His words sounded like shouting in a wind tunnel. My head span as I tried to process his description of her death. He was right, the explosion shook the house from half a mile away and I didn't even move, I just sat there in the front room with the curtains closed. Rose was ten minutes away. I didn't even notice she wasn't there. Later that evening, local TV showed footage of the aftermath of the crash and in the wreckage I recognised the shape of the burnt out car as being the same model and with the same roof rack as ours. Only then did I put two and two together and try to call her. Then I called the police.

At the time, no one knew why the tanker ran the red light, why would they? The driver was incinerated. And all the time I was in a darkened room feeling sorry for myself. Which is why Rose left in the first place.

My head span.

"Time's a movin', White Boy, I needs t' hear whatchoo wanna do?"

I said it looked like I had no choice.

"No shit, Einstein?" He said. "But I needs to hear yo' tell me. Yo' have to vocalise it. Whatchoo wanna do?

I told Fat Man that I wanted to go with him.

"An' this is yo' decision, made of yo' own free will, with no intimidation, coercion or pressure from anyone else?"

I nodded. Fat Man took a deep breath. "I needs t' hear yo' say it."

When I repeated what he'd said he breathed out heavily. "Now we gettin' somewhere."

He knelt down and placed the palm of his hand against my forehead. A chill shivered through me and I heard myself make a croaking sound and then croaks turned to barks as my body began to heave with violent, stomach-emptying spasms. My throat burned with the taste of secondhand peppers then I screamed as tissue ripped inside me and then something broke loose and forced its way slowly upwards. I gagged and began to choke as it reached and then blocked the back of my throat.

"Shit, things I gotta do."

Fat Man grabbed my jaw, wrenched it open and pushed his hand deep into my mouth. I felt my throat stretch as he forced his fingers inside, got a firm grip and then pulled out a lump of blood-soaked gristle that filled his hand. He stuffed it in his pocket and managed to step away just as a fountain of blood and shit left my body and hit the far wall with the pressure of a fire hose. I retched two or three times until there was nothing left and then gave a final shudder, cleared my throat and spat out the contents. My mouth tasted foul and the room stank, but the pain in my stomach had disappeared. I managed to crawl back onto the bed, got myself into a sitting position and stared at the mess on the floor and on the wall.

Fat Man followed my gaze and chuckled. "I gotta say, I love what yo' done with the place. I guess tha's bettah out than in, huh?" He looked at me. "Thassit, White Boy, yo' purged o' yo' sickness, i's all good from here on in."

I asked him what happens next.

He stood up and for a second his smile terrified me. "Tomorra' night's a full moon," he said. "An' at midnight yo' 'n' me we gon' meet an' finalise a few things. I'll send yo' directions but in the meantime, git yo'self some rest, build up yo' strength."

He closed the lid on the pizza box. "Yo' may wanna eat wha's left a little later, an' there's a beer in the 'frigerator."

I thanked him. He grunted, nodded, turned and walked out of the room. I lay back exhausted and dozed for maybe an hour. When I woke, it took me a while to register that the floor and wall were clean. The mess of blood, vomit and Christ knows what else had disappeared.

I opened the pizza box expecting to see the few remaining cold slices. Instead, inside was a complete pizza, steaming hot and on the table next to the bed stood a bottle of Sol, condensation running down the sides and with a lime stuck in the neck.

Not caring how it got there, I devoured the pizza, washed it down with the beer, and then took a shower. Later, I was almost cheerful as I went downstairs. I had a couple of beers and then wandered around the streets of Clarksdale for a while before returning for an early night.

I dreamed I was back at home. I was standing outside the furniture store, looking across the road to the traffic lights beyond which I could see the fuel tanker heading towards me. As it accelerated through the lights, I saw our car approaching from the right, Rose staring straight ahead; only ten minutes from home. I wanted to scream, to jump into the road, but I was paralyzed.

Instead, my head flicked back and forth like a spectator at a tennis match; car, tanker, car, tanker, car.

I heard the blast of a horn, saw Rose look to her right, heard the beginnings of a scream and then her blood exploded across the windscreen as the car crumpled under the force of the juggernaut. I could smell petrol, saw the lick of flame.

I looked up at the truck, the driver was sitting bolt upright, gripping the steering wheel, rigid arms forcing him back into his seat. His eyes were wide open but unseeing, his face expressionless. Next to him, roaring with laughter, tears pouring down his face as the tanker ploughed into the furniture store, sat Fat Man.

I woke up at midday and despite the dream I felt better than I had for a long time. A pile of crumpled ten and twenty-dollar bills lay on the bedside table and next to me lay Marilyn.

She opened her eyes. "Hey darlin'," she said.

I asked her how she got into the room. She shrugged. "You lookin' pretty good," she said.

"I guess Fat Man took care o' yo' sickness?"

I asked her how she knew that. She shrugged again.

"Whatever Fat Man done, tha's 'gon' cost yo'. Cost yo' big time."

I asked her what she meant.

"You gon' find out," she said.

I said that there were a lot of things I needed to find out.

She smiled.

I asked her where she lived, what she did for a living.

She said, "I'm kinda inbetween jobs an' in a no-fixed abode situation at this time. Tha's why I took yo' money, had to sort out a few things, but I brought most of it back and I'll pay the rest when I get it."

I told her not to worry about it and asked her to tell me more about Fat Man.

"Fat Man does what Fat Man does," she said. "Yo' gotta find out fo' yo'self."

I told her that I was meeting him at midnight. She smiled mysteriously. "Well I guess that's when you'll find out."

We talked some more and then I went to the bathroom.
When I came out, Marilyn was gone.

Nothing surprised me anymore.

I stayed in bed for a while and was thinking about recent events when my phone rang. I pressed answer and Fat Man's face filled the screen.

"White Boy," he said. "Guess yo' feelin' better this mornin' huh? I'ma sendin' yo' directions to our rendezvous tonight. You gots to be there befo' midnight, don' even think o' bein' late."

I said that I would be there and asked if I needed to bring anything.

Fat Man shrugged. "Bring yo' cell phone, tha's all yo' gon' need. Whatever other shitchoo want, tha's up to yo', yo' the one got's to carry it."

I asked him where we were going.

He grinned. "We go'n see the blues, White Boy, jus' like yo' always wanted. This gon' be a new an' excitin' time fo' yo', not to mention kinda lucrative, if things go right. Anyway, I got things t'do. The route gon' be on yo' phone, I'll see yo' later on."

As he disconnected the call, my phone beeped with a new message. I tapped the screen and a map appeared, it took a couple of seconds to stabilize and then showed the marker pin apparently blinking patiently in the street outside.

I closed the map function and sat back on the bed. It had been a long time since I had felt so healthy and this sense of well-being almost outweighed the misgivings that I had whenever Fat Man was around.

Almost.

I was in his debt, with no question that he would demand repayment. What form this would take was anyone's guess and that's what worried me. It seemed that with Fat Man, anything and everything was possible. I thought back to last night's dream. I could recall every detail, like I was actually there; the smell of the petrol, the sound of the explosion; I'd even been able to feel my skin burning from the heat. That was supposed to be impossible in dreams, wasn't it? Either way, it was horrifying to see Rose in that situation.

In the aftermath of the crash, all the right words were said to me: "It would have been quick" and "She wouldn't have felt anything."

But still.

I shook my head to bring myself back to the present and tried not to think of the immediate future.

I suddenly felt tired. I set the alarm on the phone, tapped the music icon and lay back to the soothing sound of "Green River Blues". Last thing I remember was Charley Patton's gravelly voice singing about "goin' where the southern cross' the dog" and then I fell asleep. This time I didn't dream.

# Down At The Crossroads

I woke just before the alarm went off.

Refreshed by sleep but still cloaked with trepidation, I showered and dressed, gathered the cash, picked up my phone and left the apartment.

Fat Man's route took me through Rosedale and then headed south. At 11.30pm, I was about two miles the other side of Beulah, on a deserted Highway 1 when the engine stopped and the car coasted to a halt. As I tried to restart it, my phone buzzed. I looked down and saw that the marker pin was blinking next to a small road leading off the highway.

The car was dead.

I got out, and by the light of a moon that seemed to fill the sky, began walking along a narrow dirt road.

The still night was silent save for my footfalls in the dirt, the sound of my breathing and the pulse pounding in my ears. I passed through a clump of trees, their naked branches raked upwards like skeleton fingers poking out of a grave and as I walked I fought a primal urge to look behind me. Instead, I stared up at the stars and planets strewn across the sky like fragments of a smashed windscreen on black asphalt. In the distance I heard a dog howl and the moan of a freight train and felt a rising sense of dread deep within me. I kept on walking and soon the road snaked to the right, around another clump of trees. I quickened my pace to get past them and came upon a small cemetery, headstones scattered like crooked teeth, just beyond which stood the remains of an abandoned church next to a crossroads.

As I reached the crossroads, I looked at my phone. It told me it was five minutes to midnight and that I had reached my destination.

I looked around. The road I had walked lay behind me, to my right stood the old wooden church. It looked abandoned in every sense of the word, its faded paint bleached white under the glare of the moon.

Above the main door a sign hung askew:

*Mt Zion Baptist Church*

*All Welcome!*

I heard a sound like a coffin lid being prised open. As I looked up, a wooden cross fell from the roof and broke apart on impact.

"Well now, heyah we all is."

Fat Man's appearances no longer startled me, and I was actually relieved to see him.

"Somethin' kinda creepy lookin' 'roun' here, ain't it?"

He'd dressed up for the occasion: dirty white Converse sneakers, black jogging pants that were almost clean and a black t-shirt with the Rolling Stones lips.

"Glad yo' had the courtesy t' be on time," he said.

He looked around, sniffed at the air then turned back to me. "Why you think yo' here?"

I said I was there because we'd made a deal back at Ground Zero.

"A deal yo' say? Tha's a' interestin' choice o' words. Yo' an' me we about t'embark' on a journey, but yo' gotta make it of yo' own free will. Like I say back in yo' room, agree to my terms and yo' sickness be gone forever. If yo' changed yo' mind then say so now an' things goes back to the way they was."

Fat Man paused.

I said nothing.

He grunted. "OK. We at a crossroads at midnight, do I need t' spell out what this' gon' cost yo'?"

I said I thought I had a fair idea.

Fat Man stared hard. "Trust me on this," he said. "Yo' ain't got the first idea."

I repeated the line from a Charley Patton song, "What can I lose, Lord, with the help I got?"

"Ain't that the truth?" He said. "Yo' bring yo' gittar along?"

I said no.

"Yo' wants to play the blues, yo' gon' need a gittar. Take a look behind yo'."

I turned around. One of the gravestones was tilted backwards, propped against it was an acoustic guitar.

I looked back at Fat Man.

"Well, go on," he said. "Gittar ain't gon' come to yo'."

I walked a couple of steps to the gravestone. Moonlight shone on the inscription that read:

*Henry Watson*
*"Travellin Man"*
*1881 - 1934*
*"Singer of the blues"*

"Got his self strung up by a lynch mob," said Fat Man. "Buncha white trash motherfuckers come across the bridge from Arkansas, lookin' fo' trouble. Damn shame, he sho' could pick on the gittar."

He paused. "He knew these crossroads well, too."

I picked up the guitar and plucked the strings.

"Tha's a Gibson Kalamazoo, jus' like Robert Johnson had, need's tunin' tho'. What's yo' pref'rence? Natchel, Spanish or Vestapol?"

Before I could answer, Fat Man said, "Yo' a slide man, right? Ain't too many slide toones in natchel, an' yo' a big fan o' Charley Patton, so I'm guessin' Spanish." He paused, "Yo' DO know the difference 'tween Spanish an' Vestapol?"

I told him Spanish was Open G tuning and Vestapol was Open D.

"Well, tha's a start. Gimme the gittar."

I handed it over. Fat Man put his foot on a gravestone and rested the guitar across his leg. He stared into space for a few seconds then took a deep breath and exhaled slowly.

In the distance I heard the sound of flapping wings and the panicked splashing of an animal running through water.

Then the night fell silent.

Fat Man plucked the first string then twisted the tuning peg. The note hung in the air and I shivered as the moonlight dimmed and blackness enveloped us. Each string he played seemed to make the night darker still and I felt a chill growing inside me, like ice crystals forming around my heart. Soon, nothing else existed, just pitch darkness and the sound of the guitar. When all six were tuned, Fat Man produced a bottleneck from somewhere, placed it in the third finger of his left hand, hit the strings and dragged the slide from the third to the fifth fret. The sound resonated deep within me and I cried out and fell to my knees.

As the notes hung in the air Fat Man placed his hand on my head. "All that was yo's b'long t'me," he growled. "Yo' tied to me now and fo'ever after."

I shuddered beneath his touch, felt a chilled numbness crawl across my chest and then he lifted his hand.

"Deal's done. Ain't no goin' back. Foller me."

Fat Man turned and we walked towards the church. When we reached the steps he stopped and said, "Cain't recall the last time I cast my shadow on a church-house door, 'cept this ain't no church no more; 'historic buildin'' they calls it, means they cain't be knockin' it down, gotta stay jus' as it is, which works fo' us cos this jus' happens t'be one o' th' gateways too."

I asked him where it led.

"To the blues, White Boy, to the blues." He pushed open the door and went in.

Inside, the church consisted of one large room full of broken chairs, roof tiles and litter. A hole in the roof focused a shaft of moonlight onto a door in the opposite wall. Fat Man made his way towards it, grasped the handle then turned back to me.

"Step into my office," he said.

He opened the door and we went into a tiny room containing a table and two chairs. Fat Man nodded towards another door. "On th' other side is where yo' adventure begins. Fo' we do that, we got a coupla parish notices to get through."

He reached beneath the table, produced a large canvas satchel and placed it on top. "Why don't we sit down?" he said.

We sat down.

Fat Man opened the satchel, produced a small video camera and a digital voice recorder and slid them to me across the table. "These the tools o' yo' new trade," he said.

I asked him what new trade.

"Research assistant," he said. "Yo' gon' wander 'roun' the delta, recordin' an' videoin' blues singers. Then, yo' gon' bring the recordin's back to me."

I asked Fat Man where I would find them. I said that I thought that authentic blues players were few and far between these days.

"These days is right," he said. "They ain't no real blues no mo'. But yo' ain't gon' be wanderin' roun' in these days, yo' goin' where the real blues is at."

Once again, I said that I didn't understand.

Fat Man sighed. "Yo know that song by Son House, 'My Black Mama'?"

I said of course.

"Well," he said. "Yo' recall that line 'bout how nobody cain't tell where he goes when he dies?"

I nodded.

"Well the answer lies just th' other side o' that door."

I looked at the door, then back at Fat Man. He nodded.

"Tha's right White Boy. Yo' goin' cross over to th' other side, back to the time o' the blues. Yo' gon' be in th' afterlife in Mississippi aroun' the 1930's."

How was I supposed to respond to that?

Fat Man said, "See, it works like this: Wherever you is when you die, tha's where yo' gon' be when yo' pass over. All the places yo' lived at, ever'where you travelled, ever'one yo' met, tha's all the same on th' other side. All the same 'cept they ain't no time as such, no one gets older, wherever yo' is, tha's where yo' is."

He must have seen the expression on my face.

"Kinda hard t'explain, it'll make sense when yo' get there. Kinda."

My head was reeling. I was about to ask yet another question but Fat Man shook his head. "Plenty o' time fo' yo' questions when we gets t' th' other side. Now, like I say, they ain't no time as such, not as we know it, years pass but nothin' changes, no one gets older or nothin'.

I asked him how long I would be there.

"Long 's it takes," he said. "Kinda open-ended."

He shrugged. "Ain't no big deal."

He reached into the satchel and pulled out a crude map of the state of Mississippi and a notepad that I recognised as the one he was writing in on the night we met in Red's. He caught my look, smiled and opened the pad.

"This here's a list of blues singers and places where they likely gon' be. Yo' can use that as a startin' point, or yo' can freestyle."

He picked up the camera. "I want yo' to take videos wherever yo' can. Yo' ever used one o' these befo'?"

I said that I had.

Fat Man nodded then picked up the voice recorder. "Some folks may not 'gree to bein' filmed. Sound recordin's is jus' as good. Use this as often as you like an' as much as yo' can, try an' get as many songs as yo' can, an' if yo' find anyone famous, see if they written any mo' songs an' try an' get them too."

I stopped him right there and asked him if he really said that I would be meeting blues men who were now famous?

He frowned. "Hell yeah, yo' goin' to Mississippi in the 1930's, tha's where they lived an' died, 'cept fo' Son House, he died in Detroit an' tha's where he lays now, but he still might show up tho'."

I asked if I would see Robert Johnson.

Fat Man shrugged.

"Maybe, I don' know."

He tapped the notebook. "Like I said, this list is where yo' likely find the known blues singers, those already on record. I wantchoo t'keep a look out for new talent, too. Anyone you see you think good enough, I wants you to record 'em. Voice recordin's first, video if you can. Unnerstan'?"

I said I understood.

"OK, then. Th' afterlife is where the spirits reside, but to you they gon' seem like natchel-born folks. As far as yo' concerned, everthin' gon' look the same and be the same as in this world, all yo' five senses gon' be working an' yo' still gon' need to eat, drink 'n' take a shit. Yo' gon' be livin the life of a wanderin' blues man. That means yo' gon' have to fend fo' yo'self in terms of findin' food an' a place t'stay the night. Tha's where yo' gittar gonna help. Keep it simple's the best advice I can give, some o' them parties go on all night, get too fancy yo' gon' wear yo' self out. Play what yo' audience wantchoo t' play, not whatchoo want; they's the ones throwin' nickels atchoo. Yo' keepin' up White Boy?"

I said it was a lot to take in.

"Is what it is," said Fat Man. "Yo' soon get the hang of it."

I looked again at the notepad and asked Fat Man if he knew that I was going to walk into Red's on the night we met?

Fat Man stared at me then his mouth twisted into a secret smile. "Whatchoo think, White Boy?" he said.

I stared back then decided that I wasn't sure what to think.

"Prob'ly best keep it that way," he said. "Too much thinkin' gets in the way o' things. Stops things from bein' done. Is what it is, don' matter how."

I said that, 'it is what it is' didn't really explain much.

"An' yo' ain't in the position to demand an explanation. Probl'y fo' the best if yo' keep remindin' yo' self o' that fact. We clear?"

I said nothing.

"OK then," he said.

He pointed to the satchel. "Inside they's a bottleneck an' about hunnerd dollars cash."

I said that I also had cash in my wallet.

Fat Man took a breath then paused. "Tha's today's money," he said. "The design's all diff'rent. Th' cash in the bag's from the 1930's. Try an' spend yo' money an' yo' gon' get yo'self arrested fo' forgery an' a bed on Parchman Farm."

30

I hadn't thought of that.

"Jus' fo' now, let me do th' thinkin' an' yo' do the doin'."

He put everything back in the satchel and pushed it back towards me.

I asked if there were spare batteries.

"They's a cable in the satchel," he said. "Fits the camera an' recorder. If the batteries get low, plug that into yo' cell phone an' send me a text. Yo' cell phone battery gon' be fine. I'll see t'that."

I didn't bother asking how.

"Well, I think we about done," said Fat Man. "Yo' ready to rock an' roll, White Boy?"

I said I had one more question and asked him if I would meet Rose.

Fat Man considered this. "She ever visit Mississippi?"

I was pretty sure she hadn't.

Fat Man shook his head. "In that case, she ain' likely t'show up."

He stared at me. "We done a deal, White Boy. Yo' forsaken yo' ol' life an' if yo' look deep down inside, yo' find yo' really don' give a shit no mo'." He paused. "That particular luxury been removed, yo' might say."

A few hours earlier, the news that I would never see Rose again would have upset me. Looking into myself, I realised that I felt nothing.

Fat Man raised an eyebrow. "Can we go now?"

I shrugged and said why not.

We stood up. I put the satchel across my shoulder and picked up the guitar.

Daylight and heat flooded into the room as Fat Man opened the door.

"Follow me," he said.

# To A World Unknown

We stepped out onto rough grass and I could hear the sound of low, rhythmic chanting.

"Tha's the sound o' field workers," said Fat Man. "S'all mechanised in yo' world, here it's hunnerds o' people out workin' the land. Welcome t' 1930's Mississippi.

I still didn't believe it. After years of reading every book about blues history that I could get my hands on, every blues song I'd ever listened to, after soaking up every description of the land, the way of life and the people of the Mississippi Delta, here I was at last.

"I wouldn't get too misty-eyed, White Boy," said Fat Man. "Fo'get yo' romantic notions, this ain't heaven, nuh-uh. Jus' cos folks has moved here don' mean they angels. Grudges live on an' those that be fightin' an' carryin' on when they alive, they still the same over here."

"Fat Man, whatcha' doin' heyah?"

I turned to see a misty shape appear at the centre of the crossroads and then materialise into a tall, thin black man with a white painted face. Dreadlocks dangled from beneath a coal-black top hat, around which were looped strings of brightly coloured Mardi Gras beads. A bright red handkerchief draped from the breast pocket of his frock coat and his black trousers were tucked into calf-length alligator boots. He walked with a cane and limped rapidly towards me, leaned in close, sniffed hard and then recoiled.

"Livin' souuuul," he breathed. For a few seconds he stared at me in wonder and then his face distorted as he snarled in Jamaican patois, "Si me now, me name Gabel. Me de keeper o' de crossroads. Dis Gabel's dominion and ya gad na bidness heyah. Dis nod ya time, go baaaaack livin' man, ya na b'long.'

33

He turned to Fat Man. "Ya know da rules, Fat Man. Him a livin' soul, him not meant t' be heyah, take him back."

Fat Man yawned. "White Boy with me, we goin through an' yo' can't stop us."

"Dis not right, Fat Man, ya kno' dat. Him gonna upset de way o' tings."

Gabel shook his head, turned to me and spoke softly, a sad look on his face. "Go back home, living' man. Fat Man gonna bring nuttin' but pain an' trouble. Ain't nuttin over here for you."

Fat Man stepped between us. "Deal's done. White Boy's stayin' an' tha's that."

"Take him back, Fat Man," said Gabel. "Take him back."

Fat Man shook his head. "Ain't gon' happen."

Gabel pointed a bony finger at him. "Ya no good, ya trickster man, ya cheatin' an' ya robbin' an' ya poison ever'ting ya touch. Ya de Babylon, leave dis livin' man alone, gi' 'im back his soul, let 'im on his way. No good come from dis. Jus' once, Fat Man, do de right 'ting."

Fat Man sighed. "We both knows I'ma come an' go as I damn well please. An' today I DO please an' I'ma bring my associate here wid me. He here of his own free will."

A grin crept onto his face and my blood curdled as he clapped me on the back.

Gabel turned to me and shook his head sadly. "Ya make a deal wid de Fat Man, ya gon' lose ever'ting. I hope it wort' it."

His face hardened. "But lissen, livin' soul," he said. "An' lissen good. Whatever he get ya' doin' here, if ya hurt anyone then ya gonna know me wrath, y' get me?"

When I said that I did, Gabel stepped back, gave Fat Man a look of contempt then turned and limped away.

In the daylight, the church and the cemetery had lost all its menace. Fields on either side of the gravel road converged to a point on the horizon and were peppered with black shapes placing handfuls of cotton bolls into huge white sacks.

Fat Man and I began walking and soon the crossroads was far behind us.

"Le's have us a quiz," said Fat Man. "Test yo' general knowledge."

He lit a Lucky Strike.

"First question," he said. "Yo' know where th' Southern' cross the Dog, White Boy?"

I said that he meant the town of Moorhead, where the Southern Railroad used to cross the Yazoo Delta Railroad.

"Ain't 'used to', still does," he said. "This the 1930's remember? OK, question two: why's it called 'the Dog'?"

I said that I'd read that the Yazoo and Delta railway freight trains had the letters Y.D. on the side and locals nicknamed it Yellow Dog.

Fat Man nodded. "Damn, yo' knows yo' stuff."

I asked him why we were going to Moorhead.

"They's a juke-joint there, called the Yeller Dog. I'm a show yo' the ropes there an' then yo' be on yo' way."

I said that I was looking forward to it.

Fat Man grunted. "Well, hang on t' that," he said.

The sun was high in the sky, but despite its warmth I couldn't shake off the chill I'd felt inside me since our encounter at the crossroads.

"That feelin's gon' be with yo' fo' the rest o' yo' time," said Fat Man. "One o' the side effects o' doin' a deal."

We walked on in silence.

Cotton fields stretched as far as the horizon on both sides of the road. It was then that I realised that the singing had stopped and the field workers were standing perfectly still and staring in our direction. It was creepy.

"Don' pay no mind," said Fat Man. "They looking at me. Ain't nothin' gon' happen."

I asked why they were staring at him.

He shrugged. "Folks is like cattle, they easily spooked, especially over here."

I asked why they would be spooked.

Fat Man said nothing.

After a while, dark shapes appeared in the distance. As we drew closer, the shapes became a collection of buildings that became a small town that straddled the gravel road. A 30-foot steel tower held up a water tank with the word "Russett" painted in large letters on the side.

"How yo' doin' with that ol' gittar'?" said Fat Man. "Whatchoo think yo' gon' play?"

I said that I hadn't thought about it.

"Well yo' needs t'think 'bout it soon, we headin' towards a general store, th' owner might give yo' a dollar to sit and play out front. White Boy playin' th' blues, gotta be worth a dollar jus' fo' th' curiosity."

I said that was funny.

"Yo' ever heard of 'Honeyboy' Edwards?" Said Fat Man.

I said of course. He knew Charley Patton, played with Tommy Johnson and said that he was present on the night Robert Johnson was poisoned.

"Tha's right. He used t'say, 'white folks might be able to play th' blues but they sho' cain't sing 'em'. Guess we about t' find out."

We approached Main Street, which comprised a quarter of a mile of dusty road and a dozen or so wooden buildings. The general store was on the left hand side, with a wooden bench outside sheltered by a canvas awning.

Fat Man said, "We go'n stop here an' rest a while, then see if we can hitch a ride on t'Moorhead. Yo' sit down and do yo' stuff, I'll git us coupla sodas."

I rested the guitar against the end of the bench and sat down. I fished around in the satchel, found the bottleneck, slid it over my finger, placed the satchel between my feet and picked up the guitar. I'd never played in public and felt nervous as I held it, but the first strum sounded sweet and as I picked the strings I felt my fingers loosen up and I began to relax.

I began with a random pattern that grew into a riff; then another riff was born that shouted out to the first one, creating a call and response which I kept going through a twelve bar sequence. I'd never played like this, and as I dragged the bottleneck along the strings I created sweet, glorious sounds I'd never heard before. It felt like something was alive inside me. My eyes closed as my fingers ran and the bottleneck danced across the neck, I became aware of a thumping 4/4 beat and realised it was my own feet stamping out the time on the wooden boards. I've no idea how long I had been playing when I became aware of another sound, not one made by me but a metallic chink followed by another and another; I opened my eyes and saw a pile of pennies, nickels and dimes on and around my satchel, in front of me, standing in the street was a crowd of maybe forty to fifty people, with more approaching from both sides.

Fat Man appeared beside me. "Keep playin', White Boy, yo' got 'em in yo' hand."

I felt myself enter that zone that musicians experience, a place where nothing else exists except for the music. I picked up the tempo and launched into 'Bear Creek Hop', an old ragtime number. I looked up to see two or three women dancing at the front; they were followed by two or three more and soon half the crowd had joined in, whooping and cheering to the stop-time beat. I have no idea how long I kept going, I played the tune over and over, felt my confidence growing as I added little flourishes to try and keep it fresh, and then Fat Man's voice filled my head. "Wrap it up son," he said.

I played one more turn-around and then ended the tune. There was brief silence and then the crowd began cheering and whistling, nickels and dimes showered around my feet and I felt elated. My first ever gig!

Fat Man stepped forward. "Tha's all folks, show's over an' there ain't gon' be no' mo' here today but we gon' be at th' Yeller Dog at Moorhead later, if'n one o' yo' kind folks knows someone can' give us a ride?"

As he spoke, the atmosphere chilled. The crowd fell into uneasy silence as faces became sullen and turned away from him. As they began to disperse I put down the guitar and gathered the coins piled around my feet.

Fat Man handed me a bottle of Nehi, which I emptied in seconds. "Damn, White Boy," he said. "Tha's some pretty fancy playin' yo' got goin' on there. Tha's gotta be close to five dollars. Hidin' yo' light under a bushel, yo' might say."

I said that it surprised me, too.

"Well, if yo' can do that t'night, yo' gon' fit in jus' fine 'roun here."

I said that I knew a lot of the old songs but wasn't sure my singing voice would hold up.

Fat Man said, "Looked like yo' jus' got ha'f the town jumpin' with yo' pickin', that ain't bad fo' a White Boy 'roun' here. An' who knows, maybe yo' might pick up a singer 'long th' way."

I said maybe.

"You boys wantin' a lift t'Moorhead?"

I turned towards the voice, it belonged to a white man, about five foot ten, wearing a wide brimmed hat, white shirt and khaki trousers held up by braces that stretched over an enormous stomach. "Name's H.C. Jackson," he said. "I owns the Jackson plantation just outside Moorhead, I'm headin' there now, if'n ya'll wanna come along?"

"Thank y' sir," said Fat Man. "We surely would 'preciate that."

H.C. ignored Fat Man but stared at me for a long time, then smiled and held out his hand. "Didn't catch your name, son." He said.

I told him they called me Hobo John.

His smile remained fixed. "Hobo John, huh? You got a last name to go with that?"

I smiled back and said that I did but I never used it and then I thanked him for the offer of a lift.

He continued staring then pointed to a 1929 Ford pickup. "Well, my truck's just over there, you can ride up front if you want?" He turned to Fat Man, "you won't mind ridin' in the back now, will you, boy?"

I caught the look on Fat Man's face and said that we would both be fine in the back.

H.C. shrugged. "Well OK, if that's whatchoo want, gon' get a mite dusty, tho'."

I picked up the satchel and guitar and we walked across the street and clambered into the back of the pickup.

Fat Man brooded until we were well out of town.

"Las' cracker called me 'boy' died in front o' his family, after he watched me with his wife."

Then his mood changed. "Hobo John?" he laughed, "Where the hell yo' get that name from?"

I said that I didn't like the way that H.C. looked at me and didn't feel like giving my real name. The false name just sort of appeared.

"Well, good thinkin'," he said. "Yo' needs t' keep yo' wits about yo'. He paused and then chuckled. "Hobo John', damn tha's a good name."

H.C. was right about the dust. We were barreling down a gravel road and the old Ford threw up a great cloud in its wake. The truck had had a hard life and Fat Man and I had to hunker down and brace ourselves against the bumps and jolts of its tired suspension.

The sun was going down as we approached the town of Moorhead. H.C. leaned his head of the window. "You folks say yo' goin' to the Yeller Dog?"

Fat Man winked at me. "Tha's right, boss," he shouted.

"Well, I'll take you into town an' drop yo' off."

"Tha's mighty kind o' yo' boss, we in yo' debt."

We stopped on Southern Avenue. Fat Man and I climbed out and I thanked H.C. for the ride.

"No problem," he said. "Glad to help." He looked at Fat Man, and said, "Hey boy, I got a job on my plantation fo' a big feller like you. If'n yo' the kind o' negro that ain' afraid o' hard work, that is?"

Fat Man bowed his head and mumbled. "Thank y' boss. Mighty kind o' yo' t'offer."

"Jus' pop along anytime, boy. Ask for ol' H.C. Well, nice meetin' y'all." H.C. waved, crunching the gearbox as he drove off.

Fat Man spat in the gutter. "Gon' pay a visit t' that dipshit one o' these fine days."

# Moorhead

"Anyway, tha's where we goin'."

Fat Man pointed across the street to a shabby, one-storey brick building standing alone on a weed-strewn lot. It had no windows and stretched back about fifty feet. Above the narrow frontage hung a hand-painted sign that said "*Yeller Dog.*"

"This' where the fun begins," he said. "Ought t' be some good blues playin' tonight. Yeller Dog's a jumpin' place, can get somethin' kinda lively at times, so watch yo' step. We gon' have us some fun, White Boy."

We crossed the street and as we reached the front door, I looked at Fat Man and did a comic double-take. His sneakers, jogging pants and Stones t-shirt had been replaced by leather shoes, an expensive looking suit, crisp white shirt and black tie, topped off with a trilby hat.

"Whatchoo think White Boy? Yo' think I look good?"

But it wasn't just his clothes that had changed, his physique was different too, leaner. He'd shed 70 pounds and looked positively healthy.

He winked. "Thought I better travel incognito tonight. Some folks gets antsy aroun' me an' that ain' gon' help yo' none,"

He pushed open the door.

Inside, the air was thick with cigarette smoke. Fat Man grinned at my expression, pulled out a pack of Lucky Strikes and added to the fug. "Ain' no Surgeon General comin' in here," he said.

He pointed to an empty table near to the stage at the far end of the room. "Yo' grab that; I'll get us a drink."

I wandered over, propped the guitar against the table, hung the satchel over a chair, sat down and looked around.

Three electric lamps hung beneath the nicotine brown ceiling, casting a sickly glow over photographs of black musicians arranged in a line along all four walls. As I worked my way along the blues gallery I noticed Fat Man talking to another customer. They were standing face to face; Fat Man had his hand on the other man's shoulder and was staring intently into his face. I looked back at the pictures and then Fat Man appeared carrying two bottles of Jax beer.

"Whatchoo think o' the place?"

I said it had character.

He set the beer on the table and pulled out a chair.

"This the real deal, White Boy. This where locals come t' have fun. Can get a tad interestin' when the drinks get a flowin' later on."

I glanced over at a nearby table. Four young black men stared at me in silence. Fat Man followed my gaze. "Don' pay no mind," he said. "They ain' gon' start nothin' that yo' don' start first. Jus' be civil an' polite, like yo' 'spec' to be treated yo'self."

I nodded and smiled at them. One of them said something that caused the other three to break out into raucous laughter.

"Tha's good," said Fat Man. "They don' see yo' as no threat, jus' one mo' white-bread in th' wrong part o'town."

He shouted across to them, "This heyah white boy, this Hobo John. He a friend o' mine an' he gon' pick the gittar later on, make y'all dance."

One of them called back, "Long as we' don' got t' dance like no white boy." This made me smile and caused another table load of merriment.

I told Fat Man that I was nervous about playing later on.

"Well then yo' better man the fuck up," he said. "Yo' gon' be hangin' roun' places like this if yo' wants t' meet authentic blues men an' get recordin's and movies. I said I'd show yo' the real ol' blues and it starts right here. Ain' nothin' mo' blues than pickin' the gittar in a juke-joint an' they ain' no juker

42

joint than this here Yeller Dog. Yo' needs t' find out the way things is done, how folks act, s'acly what can go on."

The bar began to fill with customers; black men and women, some had dressed up, and others still wore work clothes. The men pointed suspicious glances and muttered comments in my direction, whilst the women stole fleeting looks at Fat Man.

"Hell, they only human," he grinned.

Soon all the tables were occupied and customers were standing wherever they could.

Just then, the crowd parted and a sharp-dressed young man in a suit and trilby hat and carrying a guitar eased his way to the stage.

He opened the case and took out a National resonator, its steel body sending out flashes of reflective light with every movement as he looped the strap over his head, adjusted it and checked the tuning.

"How y'all doin'?" He shouted. "My name's Blind Charlie Hunter, but I ain' blind no more."

He gave a huge grin. "An' now I'm gonna make y'all dance."

He hit the strings and the sound of the guitar rang out as only a resonator can. As the opening chord died away he began a ragtime pattern that immediately had feet stomping all around the room. The fingers on his right hand blurred as they picked the strings in complex, ever-changing patterns while his thumb kept a steady bass beat. It was so fast that I gave up trying to follow it and just sat back and let the magnificent sounds wash over me.

Fat Man leaned in close. "He ain't bad is he?"

I nodded.

"They ain't no recordin's of him, neither. He one fo' yo' to talk to later on."

I said there was no time like the present, rummaged in my satchel, grabbed the video camera, stood up and strode towards the stage.

Blind Charlie was mesmerising. One tune segued into another and another and another until soon the tiny dance floor was packed with couples getting on down to the ragtime beat and it seemed like the whole place was jumping. I recorded some great footage of him and the crowd, and I was elated to have captured the vibe of an authentic juke-joint, just as it was back in the day.

He finished a song and I stopped filming and returned to my seat.

Fat Man beamed his approval. "I likes yo' work ethic, White Boy," he said. "I think this 'rangement gon' work out jus' fine."

I took a sip of beer and forced a smile. I was beginning to feel nervous about having to follow him and was desperately trying to think of a list of songs to play when the first gunshot rang out.

I heard the discordant TWANG of a bullet hitting metal and then women screaming as the crowd panicked and tried to get to the exit. Two more shots were fired and I ducked down just as the fourth bullet hit the wall behind me.

When I looked up, Fat Man's chair was empty. I looked around for him but all I could see was a forest of legs, all trying to get out of the building. A space cleared and over by the bar I saw a middle-aged man standing with his back to the wall and pointing a .38 Special at Fat Man. On the stage, Blind Charlie was crumpled against the wall, blood pouring from a wound on his forehead. His guitar lay next to him, a large dent in the steel body.

The room was now silent. The dance floor cleared and the bar empty except for a few people standing by the door, they were all watching Fat Man.

"Lower th' gun, motherfucker," he said.

The man shook his head, waved the Smith & Wesson towards Blind Charlie. "He tried foolin' aroun' with my wife," he said.

"Well, he ain't gon' do that no mo', yo' done killed him by the looks, so why donchoo gimme the gun?"

"Nuh uh, no suh, there's two bullets left, one's fo' to finish him off, but I'll gladly let you have both of 'em if yo' come near me."

"Ain't goin' happen," said Fat Man. "Gimme the gun or I'ma gon' take it, an' yo' won't want that."

He took a step forward. The man became agitated. "I'll put a hole in yo," he shouted. "I means it."

"I know yo' do," said Fat Man. "Tha's why I ain't gon' let yo'."

The man levelled the .38, pointed it straight at Fat Man's face. "Don' come no closer, I'll shoot ya, I'm gonna shoot ya!" he screamed.

Fat Man's voiced lowered. "No you won't," he said.

Then he muttered something I couldn't hear.

The man became more agitated and the gun began to waver as a slight tremor grew in his hand. He took a deep breath, tried to force himself to remain calm, but the tremor became a shiver and he began to sweat in his effort to control it. I watched his finger tighten on the trigger and then heard Fat Man mutter something else. The gunman's eyes opened wide with terror and then in one movement he turned the gun towards his own forehead, screamed and then fired.

In the half-empty room, the explosions were deafening and the smell of cordite filled the air. The first shot went through his left eye, causing a crimson eruption from the back of his head. Then the gun moved slightly and his finger jerked a second time, the bullet destroying his right eye and what was left of his face. He tipped back against the wall, smearing a blood-red exclamation mark of pulp, hair and brain matter as he crumpled to the floor.

45

His body collapsed into a sitting position, his lungs forced out one final sigh and then his head dropped forward, exposing the bloody crater of his skull. I stepped closer and nearly retched when I realised that I could see the wall through the holes in his face.

Fat Man stepped forward and stood for a few moments, staring down at the corpse.

And then he turned to me and grinned.

"Well Goddam," he said. "He shot his self in the face. Two shots, one in each eye."

Fat Man shook his head. "Now how 'n the hell yo' s'pose he done that?"

He turned towards the group of people at the far end of the bar. "S'OK, he dead now, shot his self. Y'all saw that, dincha?" There a few nervous nods.

I heard a groan and turned to see Blind Charlie begin to move. He shook his head and then looked around, a dazed expression on his face.

"What the hell happened?" He put his hand to the wound on his forehead then stared at the blood on his fingers. "Goddam, have I been shot?"

He looked down at his guitar. "Moth-er-fucker. Who shot my National? That cost me 65 dollars."

He looked up and saw us standing over the dead gunman. "Who the hell that?" he said. "What the hell been goin' on? Came here t' sing and some cornfield nigga shoots my gittar then shoots me in th' motherfuckin' head."

Fat Man laughed. "Yo' ain' been shot, the bullet hit yo' gittar an' then grazed yo' head, tha's all. Yo' gon be fine." He pointed to the corpse. "He say yo' been messin' wid his woman, got his self kinda agitated and took his own life."

Blind Charlie stood up. "What the fuck? This the first time I set foot in here, an' I'm only here cos they ain' no train tonight. I jus' got in from New

Orlins and got me a fine looking gal in Memphis an' tha's where I'm headed tomorrow. If yo' be think I be slippin' out on her fo' one night with some brown I picked up in a shotgun shack in asswipe, Miss'ippi then yo' weak in th' head. I ain' been messin' wid nobody." He picked up the guitar. "I can't believe they shot my National."

I asked Fat Man what was going to happen now. Would we have to wait for the police?

"P'lice ain' gon' come," he said. "This' take care o' itself."

I asked him what he meant.

"This here, whatchoo think the p'lice gon' do? Man ain' right in the head, went a bit crazy an' ended things in his own way. Jus' a nigger killed his self; he be gone soon an' ain' nobody aroun' to mourn him. Folks here seen what happened. Ain' no one here gon' call th' p'lice."

I said that he went crazy because he thought Blind Charlie was messing with his wife.

Fat Man waved his hand. "Gunman a fool, he ain' got no wife. He wan't thinkin' straight, probl'y drank too much rotgut moonshine. I mean, Goddamn, he done shot his self in the face fo' no good reason. That ain' the actions of someone of sound body and mind."

He shrugged. "This shit happens all th' time in a juke-joint."

I asked Fat Man how he knew the man had no wife.

He stared at me. "Yo' keeps askin' a shitload a questions tha's jus' gon' get yo' no consequence answers. Don' matter how, jus' is. Man's dead now, ain' no one gon' be grievin'. Don' mean nothin'."

We turned towards the sound of a cane tap-tapping on the wooden floor.

"Fat Maaaan', what me tell ya at de crossroads?"

Gabel hobbled towards us. He got close and waved his cane at Fat Man.

47

"Stand aside, me say." Gabel pointed to the dead gunman. "What 'appen here?"

I told Gabel what the gunman had said and then told him what had happened. Gabel sneered at me. "Him got na wife, never had, never will, him a batty man, him look fo' young men fo' his bed. Tha's how he over here. Clarksdale sheriff shoot him when he caught him in bed wid his son."

Fat Man chuckled. "Shot dead in the last life an' shot dead in this'n. Guess he ain' too lucky aroun' guns."

"Ya tink ya de clown, ya tink ya de jester," said Gabel. "Ya gan' get ya's one day Fat Man."

Fat Man shrugged. "All's I know is this feller went crazy, started shootin' the place up, jus' like White Boy said. I intervened to try and talk to him, next thing I knows he done shot his self in the face."

Gabel looked down at the corpse, poked at the gun with his cane and then looked at Fat Man. "Two shots in de face, wid a tirty-eight special, I wonder s'acly what ya said t' him?"

Fat Man winked.

Gabel shook his head in disgust. "Get out, all o' ya. Leave dis man in peace. G'wan, leave dis place, let me attend t' his nex' jo'ney."

I looked around; the juke joint was now empty.

"Livin' man, ya not been here five minutes an' trouble be startin', dis gon' keep on 'less yo' go back and leave dis world in peace."

"Gabel, yo' like a broken recud," said Fat Man. "I already said, White Boy is stayin'." He looked at me, "Yo' ain' ready t'go back yet, ain' that right?"

Fat Man was right. I knew that he'd played a part in what had just happened, of course I did. You don't need to be an expert to know that it was impossible for a man to blow the back of his head off and then pull the trigger a second time. But right at that moment, that knowledge and the shock of

48

witnessing a man kill himself was outweighed by the memory of the agony and suffering I went through the day before I left Ground Zero.

I wasn't ready to go back yet. Just as I had felt at home in the Delta in the 21st century, I felt even more at home in this life and wanted to explore it further. And besides, truth be told, at that moment, nothing felt real. I felt cold inside, disconnected. Aside from shock at the way he died, the man meant nothing to me.

I told Gabel that we had nothing to do with what happened here.

Gabel stared at me in disgust. "Ya tink me stupid?" He tapped his head. "Ya tink me not right in here? Me know what happen. Me know Fat Man playin' his games here. Ya' tink yo' gon' play along wit' him and everyting gon' be ship-shape and shine? Ya foolin' y'self, Fat Man not ya' friend, him not ya' partna. Him playin' wid ya' an when he get tired he toss ya' way like a broken toy."

He suddenly looked tired, defeated. He turned away and waved a dismissive hand. "G'wan, get out me sight, you too Fat Man. It make me sick t' look at ya. Dis place a bad place now an' gon' stay a bad place until ya' leavin'. Jus go."

"What fuckin' ever," said Fat Man.

I picked up my guitar and satchel and followed him out of the door.

Once outside, Fat Man turned to me. "This where we parts our ways fo' 'while. I gots t' go an' see Alabama Charlie, gots some bidness needs takin' care of. Yo' gots everythin' yo' needs. Go out there an' get me some recordin's."

It was getting late and I asked him he knew where I could stay the night. He pointed down the street. "Fo' blocks down, they's a flophouse over on Main Street, called the Frank James hotel. Should get yo' a bed fo' a dollar. Keep an eye on' yo' stuff tho'. Yo' got any questions fo' I go?"

I said I didn't think so.

He nodded. "OK. anytime yo' wan's t'meet up, find yo' any Mount Zion Baptist church and go in thro' the back do' an' sit down an' wait. Them churches is all over the place, they in most all the towns so yo' shouldn't have no trouble findin' one. Yo' got that?"

I said that I did.

"Outstandin'."

Fat Man ambled away, grew indistinct and then vanished.

I looked around and then began to walk in the direction of Main Street. People bustled along the sidewalks and in the street. Traffic comprised mostly carts drawn by mules and a handful of cars. I walked towards a young black man who was selling tamales from a tin drum over an open fire. The smell was heavenly.

I asked him what was in it and how much they cost.

"Pork an' spices," he said. "An' they two fo' a nickel."

I gave him a coin and he handed over two corn husks. I unwrapped one, took a bite and then inhaled it. It was like nothing I'd ever tasted and before I knew it was halfway through the second.

"Damn, mister, yo' sho' hungry."

I gave him the empty husks and wiped my mouth with my hand.

"Yo' want some mo'?"

I asked if I could take a couple for later on. He nodded and wrapped two more in a sheet of newspaper.

I handed over another coin, took the parcel and placed it in my satchel.

He eyed me suspiciously. "Yo ain' from roun' here."

I said he was right, that I was just visiting and looking for blues singers. I pulled out a dollar bill and asked him if he knew of any musicians playing nearby.

He took the bill and shrugged. "They's bars all over, all got gittar pickers. Tomorrow night they's a fish fry about two miles outta town, they always got someone pickin' on the gittar. Yo' could try there."

I thanked him.

His eyes narrowed. "Fish fry's out in the country, tho'. White boy cain' go there by his self, he gon' need someone by his side so folks can see he OK an' make sho' no folks bothers him."

I knew what was coming next and asked him how much he wanted.

"Gimme five dollars an' yo' can tag along wit me."

I said I'd give him two.

"I'll take fo'," he said.

I said three was the limit.

"Three dollars an' yo' buys a jug o' whisky."

I said OK and we agreed to meet back here the next night.

He shook my hand and grinned. "My name's Curtis, pleased t'make yo' acquaintance, suh."

Before I left I described Blind Charlie and asked Curtis if he'd seen him.

"I seen a tall feller with a cut head, a beat up steel gittar an' a face like a bulldog suckin' on a hornet, he went that way."

He pointed in the direction I was headed. "They's another juke-joint 'bout two blocks down, he prob'ly gon' try his luck in there."

I thanked him again and began walking.

I found Blind Charlie, not in a juke-joint but in a wooden shack that sold whisky. He was sitting out front with about half a dozen other drinkers, tuning his guitar and regaling all who would listen about how someone shot his National.

He looked up as I approached him.

"He was there,' he yelled. "That white boy seen all what happened. Tell 'em how that crazy man shot my gittar."

I grabbed an empty chair and sat next to him.

"Man that was some crazy shit," he said. "I don' know what yo' friend said to him at the bar, but that boy went batshit wid that gun. Somethin' kinda strange goin' on, tha's why I got outta there."

I asked him what he meant.

"I came in an' I saw yo' frien' talking to that crazy man at the bar. Nex' thing, I wakes up covered in blood and sees the crazy man dead wit' yo' frien' standin' over him."

I asked him if he heard what they were talking about.

"Well, I walked in an' waited fo' a drink. Crazy guy, he's drunk as shit, he touched yo' frien' on the ass, got his self a good handful. Yo' frien' turn roun' to him, stared to talkin' real soft, like they's sharin' a secret. I thought maybe they gon' be gettin' it on later."

I asked what happened then.

"Well then yo' frien', he got two beers an' took 'em to yo' table."

He paused.

"Say, where is yo' frien' anyhow?"

I said he had to be somewhere.

Blind Charlie shook his head. "Yo know," he said. "He look kinda familiar to me, like I seen him somewhere befo'. What yo' say his name was?"

I said that I hadn't and asked Charlie if his guitar was badly damaged.

He strummed the National. I said that it still sounded sweet and he nodded.

"This' a type O, bought it new in nineteen an' thirty two." He looked at my guitar. "Is that a Gibson?"

I picked it up, placed it across my knee and said that it was.

"What kinda stuff yo' play?"

I said that I played slide and finger picking, mostly in Spanish tuning.

"Maybe you an' me we could play somethin'?"

I said why not.

He played a slow blues turnaround and then said "Whatchoo wanna play?"

I began to play "Walking Blues" by Robert Johnson.
Blind Charlie listened for a couple of seconds and then joined in, adding frills to my twelve-bar blues backbeat.

I made a few mistakes at first but by the time we'd played half a dozen songs a small crowd had grown around us.

As we took a break between songs, the owner of the bar came out and placed an opened bottle of whisky and two glasses on the table. He looked to be in his sixties and had silver hair and a sad, wise expression on his face.

"I'll give y'all a bottle o' whisky an' fo' dollars if y'all play fo' anotha hour."

Blind Charlie said, "If yo' wants to give us whisky, then we sure would appreciate a bottle that ain' been opened, if that ain' too much trouble?"

"Ain' no trouble, if'n y'all gon' play fo' it?" said the owner.

"That we will, suh," said Charlie. "That we will."

The owner took the whisky and returned with a new bottle. He placed it on the table and said, "I'll give y'all the fo' dollars when y'all played fo' anotha hour."

"Tha's right kind o' yo' suh, we really do 'preciate it, we'll have us a glass and commence playin' straight afta."

The owner nodded and disappeared back into the shack.

Blind Charlie opened the whisky, poured two large shots and downed his glass on one gulp.

When he could breathe and his eyes stopped watering, he poured himself another shot.

"Nevah, evah, take a opened bottle o' whisky from nobody," he said. "Mens been killed on accoun' o' that. Ain' nothin' t'slip poison in an' the whisky so strong yo' ain' gon' taste it."

He raised his glass. "Pleased t'make yo' acquaintance, suh."

He downed the whisky in one gulp and gasped once again.

"Goddam, tha's some pow'ful medicine."

I raised mine in return, took a sip and was convinced that the inside of my mouth had been peeled away.

Charlie held out his hand. "I didn't catch yo' name?" He said.

I told him and he grinned and said, "Hobo John? Ain' nevah heard of yo'. But no mind, yo' fancy accent tells me yo' ain' from roun' here." He shrugged. "A man does what a man does, long as he don' trouble Blind Charlie, Blind Charlie ain' go'n trouble him."

I said that worked for me and gasped at another sip of whisky.

Charlie refilled our glasses. "Now, how 'bout we play some mo' blues?"

It felt like closer to two hours before the owner came out. the place was packed and he said, "I'll make it eight dollars fo' anotha hour."

I shook my head, most of the whisky was gone and I could feel it affect my playing. Blind Charlie was grinning behind moist eyes.

"Anotha hour?" he shouted. "Man, I'm a full o' whisky nigga an' I needs my beauty rest. We jus' take the six dollars an' be gon' if yo' please suh."

The old man grinned and handed over four dollar bills. "Nice try, Slim," he said.

Charlie nodded cheerily and handed two dollars to me.

"Yo' pick pretty good fo' a white boy," he said. "I'ma gon' Memphis tomorrow, got me some gittar work in the lobby of the Peabody hotel. Say, why donchoo come along? we cud play t'gether; man, we'd tear that place up."

I thanked him but said I had other plans. I asked him what time he had to leave.

"Think they's a train t' Memphis about noon," he said. "Why you askin'?"

I asked him if he had ever made a record.

He shook his head, "Well now, tha's a story. I almost did. I was on my way t'Jackson t' do jus' that. Hitched me a ride on th' back of pickup truck. Up front was two white boys passin' a whisky bottle back an' forth, lost control o' the pick up and we done crashed. Tha's how come I passed over t' this place."

I said that I was travelling around looking for musicians good enough to make a record.

"Who gon' be doin' the recordin'?"

I said that I would.

"Where yo' gon' do that?"

I said I could record him pretty much anywhere, and that I'd give him twenty dollars and he'd get a share of any sales.

He was silent for a few moments and then said, "When yo' wannna do this?"

I said how about the next morning, before he left for Memphis.

"Well, I guess I could do that, got me a room at the Frank James hotel."

I told him that's where I was headed. "Well then le's go," he said. "We can have us a nightcap."

The Frank James hotel was a down-at-heel three-storey building in the poor part of Moorhead. There were no street lamps along the way and I was glad not to be walking alone.

I booked a room and then Blind Charlie and I drank some more whisky in the bar.

Later, I staggered up to my room, dragged a wooden chair and tipped it under the door handle, stuffed my satchel beneath the mattress and collapsed onto the bed.

I woke next morning with a whisky hangover. After a quick wash I gathered my stuff and made my way to Charlie's room.

He was ready for me and had positioned a chair so that it facing into a corner of the room.

He looked at me proudly. "I been 'sperimentin', see where the best sound is. Sittin' here make the gittar louder."

He narrowed his eyes. "Where yo' recordin' 'quipment at?"

I pulled the voice recorder out of the satchel and showed him.

"What the hell's that?"

I told him it was the best money could buy and gave him a quick demonstration.

"Damn that sounds clear," he said.

He picked up the National, sat down on the chair and began to play.

I recorded five songs, writing details of each one in Fat Man's notebook. I also wrote down his address, which he told me was an apartment just off Beale Street, and said that I would be in touch if I had anything to tell him.

"Yo' ain' gon' stiff me on this?" he said.

I said that he had my word that I wouldn't and we shook hands.

"Train gon' be here soon, I better get goin'," he said. " Yo' sho' yo' don' wan' come t'Memphis? They's plenty o' places we can play, make us some good money."

I said I had to be somewhere else.

We checked out and I walked with him to the station.

On the way I asked him how come he wasn't blind anymore. He didn't reply for a long time and then said, "Done me a deal with someone, long time ago, an' tha's all I'm gonna say."

At the station, the train was already in. Charlie shook my hand again and said, "Good meetin' yo', Hobo John."

I said that I hoped we could get the chance to play again soon.

He nodded. "Hell, yeah. Yo' gotta come t'Memphis, I knows this one-legged picker, name o' Furry Lewis. Man, he crazy. I think yo'd like him."

He gave me a grin and then climbed into the carriage.

I waited until the train disappeared and then I walked away, thinking about the deal Blind Charlie had made and who he'd made it with.

I followed the railroad tracks until I reached the point where they crossed another set of tracks running left to right; the fabled point where the Southern crosses the Dog.

I sat down, ate cold tamales and played my guitar for a while. It seemed like the right thing to do.

As I played, I tried once again to comprehend the fact that I was at the epicentre of blues culture, sitting close to one of its major icons, experiencing it as it was in its heyday and not just as another memorial on the Blues Trail.

I played some more then lay down next to the track, arranged my satchel as a pillow and fell quickly into a dreamless sleep.

# Stella

A low rumble from the earth together with the hum and vibration of the rails dragged me from slumber. The sun was low in the sky and in the distance, almost at the vanishing point where the rails converged I could make out the dark shape of a locomotive approaching beneath a plume of steam, calling out to me with a long, low moan of its whistle.

I stood up and walked back into town.

On a small wooden shack in a side street, a hand-painted sign said "*Coffee here!*"

I walked inside. The place was empty so I sat next to the window, took out Fat Man's notebook and spread his map over the table.

A slim black girl walked over. She looked to be in her late twenties and was wearing a simple blue dress and white apron.

"Mister, yo' sho' yo' in the right place?"

She pointed to the window. It took me a couple of seconds to decipher the crude letters that were painted backwards onto the glass.

Letters that formed two words:

*Coloreds Only*

I asked her if me being there was a problem.

She looked around the room and shrugged. "Ain' nobody here complainin' an' it ain' a problem fo' me. White coin same as black coin fa' as I'm concerned. They ain' no cook yet, so alls we gots is coffee."

I said coffee was fine.

She nodded. "Yo' might wan' sit away from the winda' tho'."

I moved to another table and she brought me a mug of coffee.

"Careful mister," she said. "I made this jus' now an' it be hot."

I took a sip and scalded my tongue.

I opened Fat Man's notebook. He had made two columns; likely blues singers and their probable locations.

As I sipped the coffee, I marked these locations on the map and tried to work out a route that wouldn't stray too far from a Mt Zion Baptist church.

I heard the sound of the door open. I didn't take any notice until I became aware of two skinny, hostile-looking white men staring down at me.

"I think maybe yo' in the wrong place, son," said one. His left eye was milky and opaque and as he spoke I saw several teeth were missing.

The other had a scar running down his right cheek. He nodded. "See, this place's fo' coloreds only. Says so plain as day on th' winda glass."

He glanced at the waitress. "An' she got no business servin' yo'."

I said that it wasn't her fault and that she had asked me to leave.

"Fac' remains yo' drinkin' coffee in a place where yo' don' rightly belong."

The waitress shot me a terrified look when I replied that that was just too bad.

The men looked at one another. "Well, lissen to that fancy-pants accent," said Milk-eye. "Sounds to me like we got us a panty-waist nigga-lover what needs him some learnin'."

Razor face snickered then leaned towards me. "Where exacly yo' from, son?"

I stood up, shoved my chair backwards and then smiled and suggested calmly that he mind his own fucking business.

His face twisted. "Donchoo sass me, son," he hissed. "I'll break yo' like a twig." He leaned in closer and tweaked my nose. "Whatchoo say t' that mister faggoty-pants?"

I pushed his hand away, grabbed the mug and threw the scalding liquid at his face. As he screamed and clawed at his eyes, I turned, lifted the chair and broke it against the side of his head. He staggered sideways and then dropped to his knees, blood pouring from his temple.

Milk-eye roared and as he leapt towards me, I threw a glass sugar dispenser that smashed against his forehead. Momentarily stunned, his face covered in blood syrup, he too dropped to his knees. I upended the table, catching him in his chest and knocking him backwards. I stepped forward, dragged the table clear and then kicked him twice between the legs. I picked up another chair and was about to hit him when he lifted his hand and yelled, "OK, mister, we've had enough."

I stepped back, shaking with adrenaline and exertion. The last fight I'd had was in a school playground, and I came second. In my old life I would go out of my way to avoid trouble of any kind, but right then I felt euphoric and wanted more. I stepped back, held the chair like a baseball hitter and told them to get the fuck out.

They groaned, helped each other to their feet and lurched drunkenly out of the diner.

I put the table back in place, gathered up the map and notebook, apologised to the waitress and asked her how much I owed her.

"Gimme two dollars fo' the chair," she said, and then she grinned. "Coffee's on the house jus' to hear that white boy squeal."

I handed over the bill and offered to clean up for her.

She shook her head. "Tha's OK mister," she said. "I think yo' gon' use yo' time better gettin' yo' ass outta town. They gon' fo' reinforcements an' they gon' be back real soon wid their hoodlum frien's. Tha's how that kind operates."

I asked her what kind.

She stared at me. "The Klan," she said.

When I told her I was meeting someone later who was going to take me to a fish-fry, she frowned.

"Who this fella yo' meetin'?"

I told her about Curtis.

A smile played around her lips as she raised an amused eyebrow. "Curtis? How much he takin' from yo'?"

I smiled and said I beat him down to three dollars and jug of whisky.

"Three dollars? Curtis would a'taken yo' fo' one dollar an' a glass o' whisky."

I asked her how she knew him.

"That fool my brother, tha's how."

I said that he made a mean tamale.

"He don' make nothin', I makes the tamales, he sells 'em an' we shares the cash."

I said it was a small world, introduced myself and offered my hand.

She held it softly and said, "My name's Stella."

I asked her if she was going to the fish fry.

She nodded. "S'at my uncle's place out by Lake Henry. Ain' too far from here." She looked around at the mess and then glanced nervously out of the window.

"Ain' gon' be safe fo' yo' to go out there. I'ma close the cafe an' go roun' th' corner an' fetch my uncle. He got him a pickup truck an' he'll give us a ride. Yo' stay outta sight an' I'll come back fo' yo' in a little while."

We cleared up the mess and then I sat out of sight of the window and watched as Stella locked the door, turned the 'Open' sign to 'Closed' and then left through another door at the back of the building.

As I waited, I made some more notes.

Sometime later I heard the back door open and then Stella's voice.

"S'ok, Mister John, my uncle's out back. He already heard 'bout the trouble an' he come lookin' for me. We got's t'go."

I grabbed my guitar and satchel and followed her out back.

An elderly black man was sitting at the wheel of a 1927 Ford Model T pickup.

"This my uncle Silas," she said.

I shook his hand and he nodded and smiled when I thanked him for his help.

Stella pointed to a pile of cotton sacks in the pickup bed.

"Yo' needs to lie down an' keep yo'self hid til we outta town." said Stella. "It gon' be ten miles an' a bumpy ride, but sho' beat goin' by mule."

I climbed into the back and lay down. Stella arranged the cotton sacks over me.

It was bumpy, all right. Even though the old Ford was only clattering along at a sedate pace, lying down in the back it felt like I was being dragged along on a board.

After what seemed like a week, I heard Stella shout, "We outta town now Mister John."

I climbed out from beneath the sacks, sat up and watched as the town of Moorhead disappeared from view. We were heading east on a gravel road that cut through cotton fields bathed orange in the reflection of the setting sun. In the cab I could see Stella talking with her uncle, then laughing at something he said, her teeth flashing brilliant white against her coffee complexion.

The sun had almost dipped below the horizon when the truck took a left turn and headed north. I stood up to stretch my legs and looked over the cab. In the distance I saw twinkling lights hanging from tree branches. As we drew closer I could make out a wooden shack with lights in the window and a group of people standing around an open fire.

Brakes screeched as the old Ford slowed and then stopped next to the shack, the engine ran on for a few seconds and then fell silent, its clatter replaced by the unmistakable sound of a slide guitar and a voice that I recognised straightaway.

I jumped from the back and picked up my satchel and guitar. Silas climbed out of the cab and I shook his hand, thanking him once again for helping me out.

Silas nodded and then walked away.

I stepped towards the shack. On the porch, sitting on wooden chair was a thin, black man with a shock of hair atop a high forehead. He was playing guitar and singing in a falsetto voice.

"Woke up this morning with whisky on my mind."

Tommy Johnson.

To most blues enthusiasts, Tommy Johnson was right up there with Charley Patton, Robert Johnson and Son House. And here I was standing less than ten feet from him, watching him sing one of his most famous songs.

"He ain' singin' 'bout whisky."

I turned to see Stella standing next to me.

"He singin' about Canned Heat." She nodded towards a glass jar on the floor between Tommy's feet. It was half-filled with a clear liquid.

"An' tha's what he sippin' from in that Mason Jar."

I looked back at Tommy. His eyes had taken on a drunken glaze, his head was rolling and his voice was slurred but his guitar work was accurate and precise.

He finished the song, picked up the jar and drained it.

"I ain' got no squeeze," he yelled. "Someone get me a Goddam drink."

A huge black woman, her hair wrapped in a brightly coloured scarf, appeared from a room at the back. Her voluminous white cotton dress wobbled

64

suggestively as she shuffled towards him and wagged a finger in front of his face.

"Getcho' own Goddam drink," she said. "An' quit yo' Goddam cursin'."

She noticed me, put her hand on her hip and leaned back slightly. "An' who in the hell are yo' wid yo' gittar, an' whatchoo doin' here in my house?"

Stella stepped forward. "He with me," she said. "He ain' from 'roun' here." She turned to me. "This my aunt Annie."

I smiled at Annie and said I was pleased to meet her.

She raised a suspicious eyebrow.

"Ain' nevah had no white man in my house. What yo' bisness here?"

I said Stella had invited me and that I was looking for blues singers to record.

Annie glanced at Tommy Johnson. "Well, I hope yo' can pick on that gittar, cos judgin' by the state o' this no accoun', Sterno drinkin, sumbitch, it ain' likely that he gon' be playin' much mo' tonight."

Tommy Johnson blinked slowly as he formed his words. "Well, I tell yo' what" he said. "I ain' gon' play anotha Goddamn song til' I gets me some mo' squeeze." He turned and stared drunkenly at me. "Yo' got any whisky, White Boy?"

I said that I didn't.

"I see yo' got a fancy gittar, tho'. How about yo' sit down here an en-ter-tain us po'boy negroes while I finds me a drink?"

He stood up, propped his guitar against the chair and staggered past me.

"He been here most o' the afternoon, drinkin' that shit," said Annie. She turned towards me. "Yo' had anythin' t'eat?"

I said not for a few hours.

"Well, we got fried catfish and fried chicken an' we got us a hog roastin'. Yo' welcome t' whatchoo can eat."

I thanked her and said that was very generous of her.

She barked with laughter.

"Generous? I ain' generous. Hell no, yo' gon' have t'play fo' yo' supper." She turned and waddled out of the room.

Stella touched me on the arm. "Yo' git on an' play fo' while an' I'll fix yo' up a plate o' somethin' later."

My mouth went dry and my heart began to pound at the thought of playing. I asked her to give me a few minutes to get warmed up.

I took a long time to check the tuning and practised a few scales before taking the notebook from the satchel. I wrote down a rough playlist, ripped the page out and tore a finger-sized hole near the top and pushed this over one of the tuning pegs.

I was wasting time but couldn't drag it out any longer.

The lights I had seen from the pickup were make-shift lanterns made from coke bottles half filled with kerosene and hung from tree branches. The light from these and from a large fire in front of the shack illuminated the sea of black faces that all turned to stare at me. Conversation died away and their silence hung in the night air.

I cleared my throat and introduced myself, took a deep breath and began with 'Black Mattie' by Robert Belfour. It didn't go well. I fumbled the bass line a few times and made several mistakes. I became more nervous and then someone yelled, "Go home, peckerwood."

This drew laughter from the crowd that did nothing to help my confidence. I was dying up there and then Annie waddled out of the shack.

That's when inspiration hit me.

I abandoned Black Mattie and launched straight into 'My Black Mama' by Son House. Annie was half way down the steps and when I yelled the words:

"Ohhh Black Annie, what's the matter with you,

said that it ain' satisfaction don' matter what I do."

She stopped, turned and looked at me with surprise and then preened herself, waggling her massive hips as she began to strut her stuff.

I could have kissed her. She stepped back up onto the porch and began to dance. The crowd started laughing and then began to cheer as she moved suggestively around me, pulling faces at me and at them. My confidence grew and I played louder and louder, stamping out the beat on the wooden porch. I played both parts of the song and Annie stayed with me all the way through. When I eventually wrapped it up she sat down heavily on the top step to rapturous cheers.

When she regained her breathing she turned to me. "Damn White Boy, tha's gotta be the best recovery since po' Lazarus. Thoughtchoo was gon' die up there. Looks like yo' earned yo' plate o' food."

I thanked her and started to play 'Preachin' Blues', another Son House tune, followed by 'If I Had Possession Over Judgement Day' and 'Come On In My Kitchen' by Robert Johnson.

As I played I noticed a young man carrying a guitar and a bottle of beer, making his way to the front of the crowd. I finished the song and said I was going to take a break. The young man stepped forward shyly.

I asked if he wanted to play.

"Yes suh, if tha's OK, suh."

I said it wasn't my party and that he didn't have to call me 'sir'.

He grinned and stepped up onto the porch.

I stood up, introduced myself and asked him his name.

"My name' Miss'ippi Jack, suh," He said. "But I go by the name o' Jack. Pleased t'make yo' acquaintance."

Stella appeared with a plate of food and some lemonade. I winked at Jack and told him the stage was all his. He sat down and placed the bottle beneath the chair. Stella and I wandered over to a bench beneath the branches of a cypress tree and sat down.

"Yo' played good, tonight," she said.

I thanked her and said that I still found it scary to play in front of an audience.

"Ain' no need be scared," she said. "Half these fools drunk anyhow."

I kept a deadpan face and told her that made me feel a lot better. Stella paused for a moment and then covered her face with both hands in an effort to stifle giggles that grew into peals of laughter. I kept a poker face then looked sideways at her. This set her off again.

Eventually she regained her composure. "Yo' funny, Mister John," she said.

I told her to call me John.

"Where yo' from, John?"

I said I was from England.

"I heard 'bout England, ain' never met anyone who from there, tho'."

She looked at me. "I said befo' that I ain' gon' pry an' here I is askin' yo' where yo' from an' all like that. Wha's yo' business, stays yo' business."

I said that I didn't mind and that it was nice to talk to her. I told her she could ask me anything.

She thought about this. "Well, I jus' wondered what a English white boy be doin' hangin' roun' with black folks in Mississippi?"

I told her I was a big fan of the blues and had always wanted to come to the delta to hear it played in the land where it began.

"The blues? Yo' mean Sat'day night music played by no-good folks who don' wan' work in the fields? Preachers, they calls it the devil's music."

A cold expression flashed across her face and she folded her arms tightly.

"Then again, what preachers say don' mean a good Goddamn t'me."

She seemed to retreat inside herself and stayed silent for a long time.

I didn't know what to say and was beginning to feel awkward when she lifted her head and smiled at me.

"Ain' no point dwellin' on wha's gone."

She sighed heavily. "So, yo' come all this way to find fools playin' the blues. Yo' gon' put 'em on records?"

I said maybe.

"I 'member two white men come aroun' lookin' fo' singers back in the past time. Ol' man an' his son. They drove a big ol' car with machinery in the trunk. Mister John and Mister Alan, tha's they names. Some folks di'nt want to trust no white fella's but they's pleasant enough."

I asked her if she meant John and Alan Lomax.

Stella nodded. "Lomax, tha's right. Spent quite a bit o' time aroun' here."

I told her that John and Alan Lomax were famous and that their work had helped keep old blues music alive.

"Alive," said Stella. "Tha's a interestin' way o' describin' it. How come a English white boy wan's to hear the blues?"

I said that I heard it from some other English white boys who played music that they heard from recordings of Mississippi blues singers that John and Alan Lomax had discovered.

I asked her if she had heard of McKinley Morganfield.

69

She frowned as she thought about this. "I knows some Morganfields lived on Stovall Plantation. They had a kid-boy liked to pick on the gittar. Yo' tellin' me he become famous?"

I said him and a few others.

"Well, Goddam. An' they records made it all the way to England and English boys be lisnen to 'em?"

I said that was about the size of it. I told her that a group of young men listened to the records and went looking for the singers. Those they rediscovered began playing again and earning proper money for their songs. I mentioned Son House, Skip James, Bukka White, Fred McDowell, Furry Lewis.

"Furry Lewis?" she said. "I knowed a Furry Lewis once. He's born in Missi'ippi but lived in Memphis. Lost his leg hoboin' a train, an' that make him a one-legged sumbitch. He sho' was a ladies man, could charm the birds outta the sky."

She smiled and then laughed. "Yo' know what he said once? Friend o' mine ask Furry Lewis how come he never got married. Furry say, 'I don' need to get married, all my friends got wives.'"

I laughed and told her that he became famous.

"An' yo' bought his records?"

I said I had.

She paused. "An' these folks you recordin' now. They gon' get famous?"

I didn't know what to say. It hadn't even occurred to me to ask Fat Man what he would do with the recordings, but I had a pretty good idea that it wouldn't be for the good of the singers.

I said that I couldn't guarantee anything, that I would be passing the recordings on to someone else.

"But they gon' get paid? These singers? Someone gon' pay them?"

I said I was sure something would be sorted out and that if they did become famous they would get all that they were entitled to.

As my words came out I imagined Fat Man listening and shaking with laughter.

"Well I hope yo' do," said Stella. "Seems t'me that blues singers be doin' the work and white boys be gettin' the money."

I said that I would try not to let that happen, not again.

In my mind, Fat Man laughed even louder.

"You lookin' troubled," she said.

I smiled and said I was fine.

The smile she gave me back was beautiful. "I like the way you talks," she said. "Yo' sound like a gentleman an' you ain' like most white folks."

I asked her what she meant.

She frowned. "Most white folks talks past yo', like yo' ain' there. White men, they think they it OK to touch a black girl, like she ain' no account, like she a piece o' meat. They can do pretty much what they wants if they of a mind, an' no one gon' say nothin'."

Stella shook her head. "Tha's bad enough," she said. "But white womens, they can be ten times worse an' not lay a finger on yo'. They see they man looking at a nigga girl an' they know what he thinkin', but they don' say nothin' to the man on account his dick's bigger than his brain, so they be mean an' nasty to the nigga girl. An' fo' why? Nigga girl don' wan' they husband in the first place."

She was silent for a while and then said.

"Plantation boss, his wife took against me on account she caught him lookin' at me one time. I was havin' a baby wid my own man, but I got took sick. I felt the baby die inside me and then the bleedin' started. Plantation boss, he wan's t' call the doctor, but his wife she say doctor too expensive. 'She only

71

a nigga' she say. 'Git the the mule doctor.' Mule doctor come but it too late. Las' thing I see fo' I pass over is the twisted smile on that white bitch, grinnin' in my face cos she thought I's carryin' her man's baby."

Stella's face twisted in contempt. "An' these is folks who went to church ever' week. Dressed up in they finery, givin' a nod to they white friends. Sunday mo'nin' Christians, sayin' one thing an' doin' another.'

She stopped talking and stared into space.

I said I didn't know what to say, but that not all white people were like that. I said that where I came from, things were different.

She sighed. "Well, I s'pose tha's a good thing but it don' mean nothin'. We here now."

She turned to look at me. "I'm sorry fo' soundin' off like that. I know's you a good man, I can feel it. What happened was a long time ago an' I had plenty o' time t' think about it an' t'realise it ain' doin' no one no good by keepin' it around. So I try to put it out my mind and make the best o' what I got. Now how 'bout we talk about somethin' else?"

We strolled back towards the shack.

On the porch, Mississippi Jack was playing "Ragged and Dirty" by Willie Brown, the party goers dancing to the upbeat finger-picking.

"He ain' bad," said Stella. "Maybe yo' can put him on a record?"

I said I was thinking the same thing.

I reached into my satchel and pulled out the video camera. I switched it on and pointed it at Stella.

"Wassatchoo got?" She frowned.

I told her to smile for the camera.

She laughed and covered her face. "Camera? Don' be pointin' no damn camera at me. I ain' no movie star."

I said she could have been and then asked her to give me a big smile and say a few words.

Shyly, she lowered her hands, looked at me and said. "My name's Stella an' we at a fish fry. Now tha's enough so turn that damn thing away from me."

Her smile dazzled me. Reluctantly I switched off the camera, stood up and said that I would be right back.

I stepped closer to the shack and began filming. I panned around the crowd, getting footage of couples blues-dancing, then turned towards Jack.

As if on cue, he changed songs to Charley Patton's 'Screamin' and Hollerin' the Blues', slapping the guitar and stamping his feet to create a rhythm and energy that reached out to the crowd.

Jack grinned as I moved closer with the camera; playing even more flamboyantly, popping the strings as I zoomed in on the guitar. He reached the end of the song and went straight into 'Future Blues' by Willie Brown.

I continued filming, pulling in close until his face filled the screen, capturing the passion that exuded from the young singer as he belted out the lyrics about his girl with a lightnin' smile.

Then I pulled back and focused on his hands. Blues geeks will scrutinise music videos to see how others play, slowing the footage to learn the finger positions, techniques and mannerisms peculiar to that artist and then try and emulate it in the vain hope of sounding like their hero or heroine.

Ask me how I know this.

Jack kept playing for as long as I filmed him. When I thought I had enough footage, I nodded my thanks. Jack winked and then began to wind the song down, ending with a flourish. I panned around to get shots of the crowd cheering and clapping and then switched off the camera.

I turned back to Jack. He had just taken a swig from the bottle and was wiping his mouth.

"This singin' an' playin' be makin' me somethin' kinda dry," he grinned. He swallowed some more beer and then belched.

"Howjoo like that playin'?" He said. "Yo' get whatchoo wanted?"

I said that I did and thanked him. I asked him if he had ever been recorded.

"Made any records, yo' mean?" He shook his head.

"Nuh-uh. I heard they was folks goin' round lookin' for singers but never seemed to be around where they was." He paused and then said. "I reckon I coulda been good enough to make a recordin' though."

I agreed with him, told him he played as well as anyone I'd ever heard live or on record.

He beamed. "Yo' mean that?"

I said of course. Then his smile evaporated.

"Don' make no diff'rence, now, though," he said. "S'all too late fo' me, this the closest I'ma gon' get."

I said maybe not. I said that I could record him, take it away and see if I could get a record made.

"Yo' think yo' could do that? Man, that'd be real swell. Maybe we can talk later?" He emptied the beer bottle and then winked. "Betta git on an' play some mo'."

I said if he could wait a couple of minutes we could do it right there.

Jack frowned. "Say what?"

I took the voice recorder from my satchel, set it on the rail, adjusted the position and pressed record.

"What the hell's that?"

I pressed stop and then replay.

When he heard himself say, "What the hell's that?" Jack's eyes opened wide and he nearly fell off the chair.

I laughed and said he had just been recorded.

"Well Goddam," he said. "An' yo' can make a recud from that little bitty doo-dad?"

I nodded and asked him if was ready there and then.

"Hell yeah," he said. "I'm gon' play 'Little Red Rooster'.

He lifted the guitar and began picking out a slow blues riff that I recognised straightaway.

I asked him if he'd mind if I joined in. Jack grinned and said, "Sho' thing." He continued riffing while I grabbed my guitar and slid my bottleneck over my finger. When I was ready, I began recording and then leaned against the shack, Jack looked up at me and raised an eyebrow. I nodded and then began to play along.

We played four bars and then Jack took a breath and started to sing.

"I got a little red rooster,"

We played it slow, dragging the slide, making the notes cry out. This time I didn't feel nervous, it was more like two friends jamming than a performance for an audience. I'd forgotten the crowd was there until the song ended and they began clapping and cheering.

"Thank y'all," shouted Jack. He pointed to me, "This heyah, Hobo John, he the blackest white boy I ever seen."

He winked and I felt a stupid grin splitting my face.

Jack turned back to the crowd, "I'm a gon' play a few mo' then have me somethin' t' eat."

He started playing a lively ragtime number that made the crowd move their feet. I clapped Jack on his shoulder and whispered that I would be back in a little while. I stepped down from the porch and went in search of Stella.

I found her a short distance away. She was talking to her Uncle Silas and a young man. As I drew closer I recognised the young man was Curtis and lifted my hand.

Stella stood with her back to me and turned when she saw Curtis nod in reply.

"Yo' needs t'hear this," she said.

She turned to Curtis. "Tell him just whatall yo' told me."

Curtis said, "Yo' sho' kicked up a shitstorm, mister."

I asked him what he meant.

"Them two motherfuckers yo' kicked outta the diner, they lookin' fo' yo' an' they meaner than rattlesnakes. They's a whole bunch a Klan gon' be ridin' out tomorra' with the sole intention o' runnin' down yo' white ass."

Stella said, "Curtis don' think they knows where yo' is. He say they come by the diner afta we'd gone and throwed a rock through the winda. No one see'd us gettin' away but it ain' gon' be long fo' they come lookin' fo' us."

I said that I was the one that fought them off, that Stella played no part. I said that they wouldn't be looking for her.

Curtis shook his head, his face grim. "Mister, that ain' the story they tellin'. They sayin' that it weren't just yo'; they sayin' that Stella hit one of 'em upside the head with a piece o' two-by-four, said she came at 'em like a alley cat, like she possessed."

Stella snorted. "Ain' no two-by-four in that place, an' if they was, no way they'd a walked outta there. I'd a broke both they peckerheads. Goddam white trash, who they think they callin' a alley-cat?"

I asked Curtis where he heard this.

He said, "I heard it from the two crackers yo' stomped on. They come down the street with two other white boys an' stopped an' bought some tamales from me. Like mos' white folks they's talkin' aroun' me like I ain' there. I never said nothin' an' then one of 'em, he aksed me if I knowed the waitress from the diner, an aksed me if I'd seen a white boy with a gittar."

I asked Curtis what he said.

"I said 'nuh-uh, suh'. I kep' my eyes down an' played the dumb nigga who knows his place. Then I said I hoped they enjoyed they tamales."

He grinned, and then winked at me. "I gots special tamales I keeps fo' Klan folks."

Silas said. "Well, I guess we can say they don' know that Curtis an' me is her kin. White folks don' much care who a nigger related to. All the same, it prob'ly ain' gon' be long fo' they come a-lookin' 'roun' here."

I said that I was sorry and that if it would be dangerous for me to be around then I'd better leave right away.

Stella turned to face me. "What yo' mean YO' gon' leave right away?" She said. "They lookin' fo' me too. An' where yo' gon' go? Yo' a English white boy on yo' own in a place yo' ain' meant to be. How long fo' yo' think they gon' run yo' ass down? Yo' gon' need somebody watchin' yo' back."

I said that it was me they were really after. I told her she would be safer staying with Silas and Curtis than risk getting caught with me. I said that I couldn't ask anyone to do that.

"That ain' yo' decision," she said and then pointed to Silas and Curtis. "This my family, this all I got. We been talkin' fo' yo' come along. They ain' too happy but they say they cain't stop me if I goes, if it's really what I wan' do."

I stayed silent as I thought about this.

Stella took my hand. "Yo' gon' need somebody with yo' an' I knows places where we can hide that white folks ain' nevah heard of, an' if they did know they'd shit they pants befo' comin' in after us. Trust me John, we gon' be safer together an' Silas say we can take his truck."

I looked at Silas. He nodded and said, "I gots me a twelve gauge and a box o' shells yo' can take." He looked sideways at Stella. "Mind yo', they Klan mu'fuckers be beggin' you to blow off they heads befo' they take on Stella."

Stella turned to Silas and raised an eyebrow. "An yo' ain' too old to be gettin' a good whuppin' fo' we leave."

She turned to me. "I guess tha's settled."

I said I guessed it was and asked her where we would go.

Curtis stepped forward. "Me an Silas, we reckon y'all oughta head up to Clarksdale."

Stella nodded. "I knows some folks up there. We can leave at first light."

I asked if it would be safe to stay here and why we couldn't go right away.

All three stared at me in silence. Then Curtis said. "It ain' a good a idea t'be travellin' at night. He paused. "No suh, y'all gon' be better off waitin' til first light." He glanced at Silas and Stella and then looked away.

I said that I felt like they weren't telling me something and asked what it was.

"They's things that comes out at night," said Stella. "Comes out huntin' fo' folks on they own. People out at night, they be disappearin', gone next mo'nin. Sometime, folks who goes a-lookin' fo' they kin, they might find a little blood or a scrap o' clothing, but mostly they ain' no sign o' where they are or where they been, or that they ever was. Jus' gone."

Silas nodded. "She right," he said. "Whatevah it is, it ain' nothin' earthly. Somtimes yo' hear screamin' an' howlin'. I's a terrible sound, seem to reach down inside here."

Silas punched his chest. "I heard it one time, near got to shit my pants at the sound."

"Well tha's somethin' we all needed t'hear." Said Stella.

Curtis put an arm around the old man. "C'mon, Silas, 'bout time we had us some o' that corn whisky."

As I watched the two men stroll away, I noticed the crowd.

As if on cue, they all moved closer to the fire, some casting fearful looks out towards the darkness that hung ominously on the fringes of the firelight.

Stella followed my gaze and touched my elbow.

"We safe here," she said. "We got strength in numbers an' a fire. An' if'n we be makin' a shitload o' noise, tha's gon' scare off anythin' bad tha's out there." She glanced at me with a playful smile, "Specially if that noise is yo' pickin' yo' gittar."

I laughed and made a grab for her; she squealed at first and then sank into my arms, putting on a childish voice. "Yo' gon' protect little ol' Stella?" She pouted.

I said it was more likely that I would need protecting from her. She smiled and then pushed me gently away. "I think we needs to get us some rest befo' movin' on tomorra mornin'."

I said that was a good idea.

"I'm gon' find aunt Annie," she said. "See if we can get a bed fo' yo'"

She wandered away, leaving me on the outskirts of the crowd.

I turned towards the darkness. The pitch black of the night hung like a veil, a malevolent barrier hiding a multitude of nameless horrors. A creature howled in the distance, its howl answered by another even further away.

A shiver ran up my back and I found myself hurrying towards the company of the party-goers.

Up on the porch, Jack was still hanging in there and playing his heart out. I made my way to the shack, waited until Jack had finished the song and then stepped up beside him and grabbed the digital recorder. The display told me I had captured about 20 minutes of Jack singing and playing.

The music had stopped and Jack appeared beside me. "Yo' got enough there fo' a record?"

I said that I thought I had more than enough.

"Yo' sho' it gon' be good enough?" He said, "They's a lot o' noise with all the cheerin' an' stompin'."

I said that it would be fine and told him not to worry.

"Well now, how 'bout we get us a drink?" He said.

I said I would find us a beer.

"Beer, hell," he said. "I wan's me some o' Annie's corn whisky."

As if on cue Annie appeared carrying a stone jar. Her eyes glistened in the lamp light as she wavered unsteadily.

"Tha's if they's any left," said Jack.

"I got's me plenty o' whisky, best damn whisky they is."

Annie was slurring well. A beatific smile creased her face as she took a hefty swig and then offered the jug to me.

I hesitated, Annie stared, affronted at first and then realisation filtered through.

"This here's my shack," she said. "This ain' no no account barrelhouse an' any drink yo' offered gon' be offered in th' name o' hospitality."

She waved the jug. "This here's corn whisky me an' Silas made in our own still. Corn whisky pure an' simple, ain' nothin' else."

Tipping her head back she lifted the jug and made a show of pouring the whisky straight into her mouth. When it spilled out over her lips, she stopped pouring, swallowed the mouthful and produced a massive belch that enveloped me in liquor fumes.

"Whatchoo think now?" she said.

I said I meant no offence and that I would be glad to try some.

She waved away my apology and thrust the jug towards me.

I took a mouthful and barely held in a gasp as the raw liquor burned my lips, attacked the inside of my mouth and scorched its way down my gullet like drain-cleaner.

I gave the jug to Jack. He too took a hefty swig, his face twisted and he shuddered violently. "Damn tha's harsh." He croaked. "I thinks maybe I'ma stay on the beer." He shuddered again. "Damn, tha's harsh indeed."

"Harsh?" shrieked Annie. "Is yo' some kinda pussy? I made this brew myself. Ain' nobody makes corn whisky like ol' aunt Annie." She grabbed the jug from Jack and waved it towards me. "Yo' gon' be a pussy too, White Boy?"

Bravado forced me to grab the jug, put the neck to my lips and tip it upwards. My lips and mouth were still numb from the first drink and so I managed to swallow a good mouthful before the reaction kicked in again. I swallowed once more and gripped the porch rail, squeezing tight until the waves of nausea passed and I was able to breathe again.

I handed the jug back to Annie and thanked her, my voice barely a whisper.

She stared at me through rheumy eyes, smiled once more then said. "Well, whatchoo think?"

I coughed and cleared my throat and said that I thought it was lively.

It took a few moments for her to process this and then she screamed with laughter. "Lively? Well Goddam, tha's th' first time I heard it called that. Aunt Annie's Lively Liquor." This set her off again and gales of high-pitched laughter filled the air as she rocked back and forth like a kid's wobble-toy, tears pouring down her face as she fought to stay upright.

Someone tapped me on the leg. I looked down to see Tommy Johnson staring up at me through bloodshot eyes.

81

"Whe's my gittar, White Boy?" He rasped. "I'ma ready to play some mo' blues, whatchoo done wid my gittar?"

I said it was safe and went into the back of the shack to fetch it.

When I returned, he was sitting on the chair, a glass jar full of Sterno between his feet.

As he took the guitar I asked if he would mind if I filmed him.

"Yo' mean like makin' a movie?"

I nodded.

"Hell, I don' see why not."

I thanked him and fished the camera out of the satchel.

Once I'd set it up I nodded to him.

Tommy cleared his throat. "This nex' one goin' out's called, Cool Drink o' Water Blues."

He played the intro note-perfect and then started singing.

It seemed the break had done him good. His voice sounded clearer as he launched into his trademark falsetto yodel.

This time I held the camera steady, pulling back just enough to get him in frame. He was sounding good and looking good, considering what he was drinking.

"Alcohol and Jake Blues' came next, followed by 'Big Fat Mamma Blues' and then 'Big Road Blues'.

I was in awe and could feel the stupid grin return. I was standing four feet away from Tommy Johnson, hearing him play the songs that made him famous.

He finished the song, and then spotted Annie staggering past. Looking up at me he winked and then yelled, "I wan's sing a song fo' Annie. Where the hell she at?"

Annie stopped and looked drunkenly at him. "She right here. Whatchoo gon' play fo' me, Mr Sterno drinkin', no-account gittar picker, yo' ain' hardly sober."

Johnny guffawed. "Well I tell yo' what," he said. "I ain' sober but I ain' so drunk I cain' sing a song fo' a lady."

Annie steadied herself against the corner of the shack. "Well, c'mon, Goddamit," she yelled. "I don' hear no singin'."

Tommy winked at me again and began picking out a simple tune. After a few bars of this he started singing about a big fat mama with meat shaking on her bones.

Annie shrieked with laughter, put the whisky jar down and began a clumsy dance.

It was one of those events that could never be planned, orchestrated or choreographed and a moment in time that I never thought in my wildest dreams I would ever witness.

Tommy Johnson sang with a deep, mournful baritone that contrasted with the pretty tune he picked out so delicately on the treble strings.

Annie lifted the hem of her dress and stepped out to the music.

"Tha's what I'm talkin' 'bout," she shouted. "Meat shakin' on these bones."

Cheers erupted from the crowd as she wiggled her massive behind in time with the music. Someone shouted, "Shake that meat, baby."

Annie wiggled her backside even harder. "Yo' know it."

Despite both of them being roaring drunk, Tommy was note perfect and Annie didn't put a foot wrong. It was magical and I was capturing every second on video.

All too soon the moment passed, the song ended and Annie collapsed heavily onto the wooden step, helpless with laughter amidst the cheering of the crowd.

As I switched off the camera, I noticed Tommy watching me as I placed it in the satchel. I was about to say something when Annie staggered over to him. "Well I guess yo' can pick on that gittar. But yo' still a no-account Sterno drinking bum."

He replied by lifting the glass jar in salute then taking a long drink.

Annie turned to me and blinked slowly. "Oh yeah, I f'got t' say. Yo' n' Stella can sleep in Curtis' place over yonder." She pointed to a dimly lit shack about 100 yards away.

"If yo' gon' git any sleep," she cackled.

I actually felt myself blushing as I collected my guitar, stepped off the porch and made my way to Curtis' shack.

Inside the shack was a large bed with a battered cardboard suitcase lying open on top of the frayed patchwork quilt. Stella stood to one side folding clothes and placing them into the case.

She looked up and smiled. "Jus' packin' a change o' clothes."

She pointed to a small room at the rear of the shack. "They's a jug an' a wash bowl out back. I drew some water fo' yo', 'case yo' wan' freshen up some."

I thanked her, placed the guitar and satchel on the bed and walked through.

In the back room, on a small wooden table stood a large tin bowl, a tin jug and a small folded towel. I walked over and removed my shirt.

When I returned to the main room I felt refreshed but also dog-tired.

Stella was sitting up in bed, the patchwork quilt pulled up to her chin. I was shirtless and I saw her scan my body swiftly and then her eyes locked onto mine.

"I think yo' a nice man," she said. "Ain' met too many o' them. Yo' gonna treat me right?"

When I promised that I would, she stared some more then nodded slightly. "We needs t'git some rest," she said. "Why don' yo' turn out that lamp?"

I hung the satchel over a chair, undressed, climbed into bed and felt Stella's arms encircle me, her naked skin soft against mine.

# Klan

I woke up to the sound of hoof beats, heard men shouting, two gunshots and then boots thumping on the wooden porch.

Stella screamed as the door to the shack burst inwards and four white men rushed in and surrounded the bed.

I recognised two of the men as the ones I fought in the diner. I saw them raise their arms, caught a glimpse of the billy-club, felt the thud against my head, heard Stella scream again and then everything switched off.

# Parchman Farm

"Mista John."

Someone was stroking my face.

"Mista John, please wake up. I needs yo' to wake up."

I heard myself groan and could taste blood in my mouth. My head was pounding, the pain increasing as I opened my eyes to a fierce, blinding light.

With my eyes shut, the pounding subsided a little. I tried again, squinting at first until I became accustomed to the brightness.

I was lying on a straw mattress on the bottom of a steel bunk bed.

Stella was kneeling next to me, the side of her face bruised and swollen. She adjusted her ripped, blood-spattered dress but wouldn't look me in the eye.

"I thought you was dead," she whispered. "They's like crazed animals, they took turns hittin' you, I thought you was never gon' wake up."

She looked around and began to cry. "They kilt Curtis and Uncle Silas and..." She broke down, sobbing, "Oh Mista John, we in a bad place, a real bad place."

I tried to sit up. I could feel that my right eye was swollen shut. My tongue discovered gaps where three of my teeth had been and my ribs hurt to breathe.

I looked down. My bare chest and stomach were covered with bruises; I was wearing trousers and shoes but no socks.

"They pulled on yo' pants when they done beatin' on yo'."

I took her hand and saw the bruises on her knuckles, saw flakes of what looked like dried skin beneath each of her nails. I held her hands but she pulled them away when I asked her what they did to her.

"It don' matter," she said. "What's done is done." She paused. "But they ain't done with yo' yet. Tha's how come they brought yo' here."

We were in a prison cell. Three of the walls were whitewashed brick, the fourth the iron bars of the cell door. High up on the wall opposite the door was a barred window about two feet square.

I swung my legs over the bed and, gripping the bunk frame, tried to stand. My head span and for a second I thought I would pass out, then it cleared and I stumbled towards the bars.

Opposite, across a narrow corridor was a mirror image of our cell. It was empty. I pressed my face to the bars and shouted. My words rang in the air and evaporated into silence. I shouted again.

Silence.

I turned and looked around the cell. Stella sat on the lower bunk, hugging her knees to her chest and staring down at her feet. I could see she was lost in pain, retreating fast to a place that I could never reach. I couldn't imagine what she had gone through and I felt helpless inside; the helplessness grew into a smouldering rage that ignited within me like a fireball.

Shouting and screaming I launched myself at the cell door, kicking the bars and trying to shake it open. It didn't budge an inch and the frustration fed my rage until finally I dropped to my knees, aching and sore and exhausted.

"Yo' finished?"

I lifted my head at the sound of Stella's soft voice.

"No use a'hollerin'," she said. "We in Parchman Farm, ain' gon' get outta here lessen we gets let out."

I said that we had to try and that I would think of something. These were words of bravado, nothing more, and both of us knew it.

Stella simply shrugged.

90

I sat with my back to the door, watching her. Even lost in the depths of anguish she was beautiful. Her head lowered and she reentered her own world. Silence rang in my ears.

I must have dozed off because I woke to a door slam followed by footsteps and a liquid, drunken belch.

Milk-eye staggered into view, steadied himself on the door, belched waves of alcohol fumes into the cell and then focused on constructing a sentence.

"Well lookee here, if it ain' the nigger-lover an' his black bitch."

He swayed, regained his balance then grabbed his crotch and yelled. "Hey bitch! I'ma talkin' to yo'. Yo' look up, now. I want's me some mo' o' whatchoo give out yest'day."

I stood up, turned to face him and told him to shut his fucking mouth.

He swung around, his one good eye blinking slowly. "Well now, mister fancy-pants accent, nigger-lover, I'm gon' be a tad busy fo' awhile, why donchoo sit back an' watch th' show."

He turned back to Stella. "Hey bitch, donchoo igno' me, now. Else'n I'ma gon' have t' come in there an' learn yo' what's right."

Stella lifted her head.

Milk-eye grinned. "Tha's mo' like it, getchoo up here on yo' knees, show me yo' purty, wet little mouth. We can do it thro' the bars, jus' yo' an' me this time."

Stella unfolded her legs, stood up and stepped towards the bars.

"Now tha's what I'm talkin' 'bout." His voice became husky. "Le's get it on."

When she didn't move, Milk-eye slammed the bars. "Well c'mon, Goddamit. Git on yo' knees."

"Yo' want my mouth?" Whispered Stella. "Yo' wants to feel my purty wet, mouth? S'at whatchoo want?"

"Yo' got that right."

Her voice became quieter until I could barely make out her words.

"How 'bout I give yo' somethin' special," she said. "Somethin' yo' can remember me by. Yo' wan' me to do somethin' dirty, jus' fo' yo'. Wouldjoo like that, huh?"

"Oh yeah, baby," Milk-eye's words dripped with lust. "Somethin' dirty, that sound real good."

Stella smiled dreamily. "I got somethin' dirty, jus fo' yo', why donchoo drop yo' pants?"

As he fumbled with his belt, Stella hawked from deep in her throat and spat a gob of mucus in his face.

"Tha's all yo' gon' get from me," she hissed. "Yo' peckerhead motherfucker. I didn't give up nothin', yo' white trash frien's took it from me. After they laughed at you cos yo' couldn't get it up."

Milk-eye wiped his face. "Donchoo talk to me like that."

Her eyes blazing in defiance, Stella folded her arms and leaned forward. "Yo' so big, white trash, why donchoo come in here an' git whatchoo want? Cos yo' scared, tha's why. Cos yo' ain' nothin' mo' than a no-account, po' white trash, peckerhead Klan motherfucker. Yo' a honky with a wrinkled rat's dick that yo' cain get up."

Milk-eye was shaking with fury. "Donchoo talk like that, you nigger bitch. I'ma learn yo' how to talk to white folk."

"Yo' ain' gon' learn me nothin', cos yo' ain' man enough. Way yo' acted yes'day, I betchoo ain' never been with no girl. Yo' frien's, they took they turns but yo' was starin' like yo' never seen a woman nekkid."

She stepped back as Milk-eye grasped at her, his hand flailing inches from her face as he snarled through foam-flecked lips, "Yo' shut yo' mouth yo' uppity nigger bitch. I'ma make yo' give me what I want, I'ma make yo' scream like the worthless black whore yo' is."

Stella spat again. "I already said I ain' ever gon' give yo' nothin'." She pointed to her bruised face. "What's took from me took three men t'hold me down. Fo' men 'gainst one woman. Ain' that brave? Aintchoo pow'ful? Four big strong white men takin' what they want an' beatin' down a nigger girl. Well, guess whut? I done stood back up again. I ain' 'fraid o' yo' nor yo' honky frien's. Yo' ain' nothin' mo' than a bitch-ass, sorry lookin' piece o' white trash shit an' they ain' nothin' mo' yo' can do to me."

She stepped back, her eyes widening as, in a single movement of apoplectic rage, Milk-eye reached behind, pulled a revolver from his waistband, and pointed it at her face.

"Anything else yo' wanna say t'me yo' nigga whore?"

Stella reaction was a tiny movement of her head that lifted her chin in imperceptible defiance.

"Yo' think yo' a real man when yo' behind a big gun, 'cept yo' ain't got the balls to pull that trigger."

From my viewpoint, the gun was a good foot inside the cell, Milk-eye's forearm bisected by a steel bar. I caught a slight movement of his trigger finger, could see the knuckle begin to turn white.

Without thinking, I leapt towards him, grasped his wrist, my forward momentum slamming his arm against the bar.

I heard a sound like the crack of a dead branch, the gun clattered to the floor and Milk-eye howled in agony. As I regained my balance my stomach lurched, I was still holding his wrist but his forearm was bent outwards at ninety degrees. Instinctively, I tried to straighten it just as Milk-eye tried to wrench his broken arm back through the bars. I felt a scraping at the point of fracture and then Milk-eye screamed louder as one of the bones tore through the skin, its broken end gristle-white amidst the blood pouring from the wound.

I yanked his arm towards me, forced myself to ignore the way the skin and tendons stretched, tried to blank out the horrific screams as I pulled him close to the bars and tried to frisk him with my free hand, looking for a key, looking for anything that would get us out. Then something exploded, his head disintegrated and he dropped to the floor.

The gunshot left a ringing sound in my ear. In the corner of my eye I saw Stella holding the revolver, a wisp of smoke curling from the barrel as she took aim and fired two more shots. I looked down to see Milk-eye's body jerking as the bullets slammed into his crotch, then I looked back at Stella just in time to scream as she put the gun barrel in her mouth and pulled the trigger.

Steeling myself for yet another gunshot, I actually jumped at the sound of the hammer clicking against the empty chamber. Stella pulled the trigger again and then once more. I stepped forward and gently took the gun from her.

"Shouldn'a shot him the balls."

Her voice was flat, emotionless. She stared through me then shook her head. "Wasted two Goddam bullets I coulda used to fix my own self."

I said that I was glad the gun was empty, said that I knew she'd been hurt but that I would do all I could to help her.

She looked at me and grunted. "Hurt? I ain't hurt. That stuff they did, ain' no more than white folks been doin' to niggers fo' all time. That jus' body stuff, white boys stickin' they dicks where they want til they gets they satisfaction. That don' hurt me none. I jus' tired, I ain' hurt no mo'. I jus' had 'nuff, had 'nuff bein' frightened o' white folk, had 'nuff o' tiltin' my head down an' crossin' the road an' sayin' 'yessuh, nossuh, kiss yo' ass suh'."

I said that not all white people were like that, that the world she knew had changed, things had got better.

She sighed. "I don' care no mo'."

Stella returned the bunk, pulled her knees to her chest and stared at the floor.

Once again, I felt helpless. Kneeling down I reached through the bars, grabbed Milk-eye's legs and dragged his body a little closer to the bars until I could search his pockets.

Empty.

I heard footsteps and looked up into the barrel of a Winchester rifle. At the other end was Razor Face, flanked by two scrawny white men, each with a pistol in their belt.

Razor Face looked down at the remains of Milk-eye then glared at me.

"Gimme one good reason not to blow yo' fuckin' head off."

His voice sounded dangerous, unhinged.

I stood up. Slowly.

"Who kilt him?" he said.

I told him that it was me. I said that I took the gun off him, shot him in the balls, watched him scream like a bitch and beg for mercy before I blew his fucking head off. I also said that he had deserved it because he was a no-good piece of white trash shit and then I asked Razor Face what he thought about that.

Razor Face ground his teeth and took a second to reply, his voice almost silent. "What I think? I think yo' on the wrong end o' this Winchester t' be gettin' so ambitious. Tha's my brother yo' killed, so me 'n' yo' we gon' go someplace an' y'all gon' git some Miss'ippi justice."

Razor Face stepped back and nodded towards Stella. "What's up with her?"

The two men behind him snickered. "Oh I think we knows what's up," said one. "I bet she still plumb tuckered out from the party she give us."

I forced myself not to react. Instead, I took a breath and asked Razor Face where my guitar and satchel was.

His mouth peeled back in a grin. "Yo' gittar? Why, tha's still in the shack where yo' left it, 'long wid yo' clothes an' yo' bag."

I said that I wanted them back.

This provoked more snickering from the other two.

His grin crawled wider as he looked to them and then back at me. "Well, that could be a mite problematic," he said. "See, last time I looked, the shack wid yo' gittar was burnin' like the fourth o' July."

A cruel smile put a crease in his face as he hefted the Winchester.

"Now, bend down real slow n' git me that .38."

I picked up the gun, pressed a lever and flipped out the chamber. His eyes never left it as he reached into the cell and took it from me.

I asked him what was going to happen now.

Snapping the chamber shut, Razor Face stuffed the revolver into his belt. "What's gon' happen is yo' comin' with us. We goin' on a jo'ney." He levelled the rifle at me again. "Now, step back an' stand next to yo' nigga, we gon' come in an' take yo' outta here. We got us some righteous fun lined up fo' yo' later on, but I'ma tell yo' now; don' even think o' tryin' anythin' cos I will shoot yo' right here an' now."

I nodded and stepped backwards then sat next to Stella and put my arm around her, squeezing her slightly.

"Now tha's mo' like it."

Razor Face used his foot to move his brother's body clear of the door then nodded to one of the men who produced a key from his pocket and unlocked the cage door.

"Now, we gon' open the door an' yo' an' her gon' walk out real slow. We unnerstan' one another?"

I nodded and as I helped Stella to her feet, I put my arm around her to guide her and whispered to her that everything would be OK. She didn't respond but walked zombie-like next to me.

Razor Face nodded again and as the door creaked open he made a show of shouldering the Winchester and keeping a steady aim at my head.

With a sneer, the man with the key motioned for us to follow him.

"This way folks," he said. Then his head span towards a sudden commotion at the end of the corridor as a door burst open followed by the rapid tap-tap-tap of a cane.

"Put down ya gun, bloodclot." Gabel's voice was laden with fury, like distant rumbles of thunder before a violent storm.

There was a whistle-crack sound, Razor Face yelped as blood poured from a wound on his cheek then yelped again as a second wound opened up.

Gabel's cane dripped with blood, his menace palpable as he held it to Razor Face's throat.

"Me say put down th' gun, Bumboclot." His eyes glittered as Razor Face handed it over.

Gabel threw the weapon to the ground and then lowered the cane and prodded Milk-eye's body. "'im lucky, 'im a dead," he snarled.

He pointed at the remaining gang members. "All ya bloodclots, ya gwine pay fa ya sins."

Razor Face pointed at me. "What about him, he kilt my brother, he gon' pay fo' his sins, too?"

Gabel stared at Razor Face, "Yu wanna romp wit me? Ya tink me half idiat? Ya tink me know nuttin'?"

He turned to Stella, his voice softening a little. "What ya done here, girl?"

"It weren't her," yelled Razor Face "'He done it, he the one shot my brother, he done tol' me."

Ignoring this, Gabel took Stella's hand, his voice a gentle murmur. "Ya know what happen, now?"

Tears coursed down her face as she sniffed and nodded.
"Everyting happen gotta have consequences," he said. "Ya' done a bad ting, ya know what must be."

"You tellin' me it was that dirty nigger bitch killed my brother?"

Razor Face leapt towards Stella and then dropped screaming to his knees as Gabel's cane blurred and released torrents of blood from deep slash wounds that crisscrossed his face.

Gabel leaned in close, his voice hissing like leaking gas. "Me seen the pure sufferation ya' left behind," he said. "What mi done jus' now, dat jus' de start."

Standing upright, Gabel motioned to the gang. "Get in de cage," he said.

For a second, Razor Face's henchmen paused and looked at each other. Gabel exhaled slowly and tapped his cane on the floor.

"Ya waan' test me?"

The men shuffled into the cell, their faces clouded with terror.

Razor Face remained on his knees; face down, fat drops of blood spattering onto growing pools that surrounded his stooped posture.

"Get in wid dem, bloodclot." Gabel's cane tapped Razor Face on the chin, "G'wan, get in dere wid ya nuh gud bredren."

As Razor Face stood wearily and turned towards the cell, Gabel turned to Stella. "Now girl, dry fi yuh tears an' we tek yuh wey fram here. It be over soon."

I asked Gabel where he was taking her. He looked me up and down. "Dis between me an' her. She know what she done an' now she gotta answer fo' it."

I said that what she did was understandable; anyone would have done the same.

Gabel pointed to Milk-eye's corpse. "Him gan' fo'ever, him don't exist nowhere now. Neva mind wat him did, that serious bidness, serious as ya gan' get, gotta be consequences; she know dat."

I said that wasn't right, I told Gabel what had happened to her.

"Dis nah fi yuh bidness," he said. "Tep oot of de cell, less yuh wan stop 'ere."

Gabel stepped back as I walked out of the cell then turned back to Stella, his voice softening to a near whisper. "Come now, girl," he said. "It time to go."

As Gabel walked her through the cell door, two henchmen stepped forward.

"What 'bout us?" said one

"Yuh stayin' 'ere," said Gabel. "Me gon' come back fi yuh punishment, an' me gon tek me time."

The cell door slammed shut then Gabel stepped forward and gripped one of the bars. I watched as the paint blistered and tendrils of smoke emerged lazily from the keyhole. After a few seconds, Gabel removed his hand.

"Yuh staying inna dere," he said.

I followed Gabel and Stella as he led her outside.

I blinked in the bright sunlight and looked around. We had been inside a bleak, concrete building about a hundred feet long. Above the door a huge sign said "Unit 32". I had read about this place, Unit 32 - Parchman Farm. Otherwise known as Death Row – Mississippi State Penitentiary.

Turning to Gabel, I asked him again where he was taking her.

"Dat nuh yuh bidness," he said.

I said that whatever Stella did was in reaction to the things that the four men had done to her.

Gabel shrugged. "Me dealt wid dem. Now me deal wid her. She kill a man. Ya' know what dat mean?"

I said she killed him because of what he did to her.

Gabel said, "Me de keeper, me gotta try an' keep order. Me not care 'bout why o' what 'appen befo'. She know what she done, she know what gon' 'appen, what 'ave t'appen."

He paused. "Me know who killed who," he said.

Gabel pointed behind me. "Who dat walkin' dis way?"

I looked over my shoulder. There was no one there. When I turned back, Gabel and Stella had vanished.

# Crystal Springs

Two miles south of Parchman Farm stood a Little Zion Baptist Church. Compared to the one I had been in previously, this was in good condition; the wooden clapboards still gleamed brilliant white in the sunshine and everything seemed in good repair.

I walked around to the rear of the building and tried the back door. It was unlocked but I had to shove hard to open it. Inside, the layout was identical to the other church. I walked into the small office, opened the door to the main room and saw that it was empty.

I knew I was taking a chance that being here would achieve anything but I was half-naked and had nowhere else to go. Picking up a folded chair, I placed it against a wall and sat down.

Some time later, I heard a creak as finger of sunlight crept in and spread across the wall as the front door opened wider. I stood up as silhouette appeared.

A very large silhouette.

"White Boy, I gives yo' one task an' it looks like yo' royally fucked it up."

I said it was a long story.

"Long story, huh? Somethin' tell me they ain' no happy endin'."

I told him what had happened since I last saw him.

"Lemme get this right," he said. "Yo' reco'ded me some singers but then lost th' recordin's an' los' yo' gittar?"

I reminded him that all my stuff was taken from me.

"Ain' yo' stuff," he said. "It my stuff an' all I'm seein' is I's down one gittar, one camera an' one state o' the art voice reco'der, not t'mention th' earnin' potential o' th' singers yo' found."

I said that I could find more singers and that he could take what I owed him from any money that was earned. I said that the most important thing was to help Stella.

"Stella? Who in th' hell's Stella?"

I took a deep breath and repeated that part of the story.

Fat Man shook his head. "I ain' hearin' this. Yo' gotcho' self in all this shit cossa a girl?"

As I began to tell him again what had happened to her, he half-stood and smashed his fist on the table.

"I look like I give a shit?"

His head was so close I felt spittle hit my face.

"Yo' was out they on my business; workin' fo' me, s'posed t'be doin' what I tol' yo'. Now all that time an' money's lost cos yo' cain't keep yo' dick in yo' pants an' get's yo' head turned by th' first nigga' pussy that gives yo' a smile."

This time I banged the table.

I told Fat Man that she helped me when two thugs attacked me in the diner, told him that she smuggled me out of town, showed me kindness and hospitality that no white man deserved and gave me access to some of the best authentic blues anyone would ever see, including video footage of Tommy Johnson. I said that her family was killed because of me, that she was gang-raped because of me and that Gabel had taken her away because she took the chance to get revenge on the piece of shit that killed her relatives. I told Fat Man I was going to help her with or without his help and that if he ever called her a nigger pussy again I'd rip out his fucking throat.

Fat Man blinked and then his lips peeled back in a grin.

"Well Goddam," he said. "Looks like White Boy done grown his self a pair."

Fat Man thought for a moment. "Yo' really got film o' Tommy Johnson?"

I nodded.

"THE Tommy Johnson? Big Fat Mama an' all that other stuff?"

I nodded again.

Fat Man sniffed. "Looks like we got us some fixin' t'do. Where yo' say this party at?"

I told him it was somewhere called Lake Henry.

"Hmmm. Tha's a fair way from heyah," he said.

Fat Man shook his head when I asked about Stella.

"She gone," he said. "She gone an' she ain' comin' back."

I said there must be something we could do.

"We gettin' my merchandise, tha's what we gon' do, an' then we both gon' be on our way."

He looked me up and down. "Yo' looks like shit. We needs t' get yo' some clothes."

He pointed towards the small room. "They's a cupboard in there, got some clothes fo' yo'."

I didn't recall seeing one when I first walked in to the church, but I went through anyway. Sure enough, standing in the corner was a tall wooden cupboard. Inside, hanging from a rail was a dark striped suit and a white shirt. On the floor was a trilby hat and a pair of shoes and dark socks.

I didn't bother even thinking about where they came from. I needed a shower, too and my face was throbbing, but beggars can't be choosers. I dressed rapidly and rejoined Fat Man in the main room.

"Well Goddam, look what the cat drug up."

I said I was ready to go.

"Well then le's do it. We goin' out the front."

I followed him through the door and straightaway I knew something was different. It took me a few seconds and then I realised.

The church that I had entered had the front door facing the road. Now the road ran parallel to the building, as if the church had been rotated by ninety degrees.

"These Baptist churches all over Miss'ippi," said Fat Man. "Makes it easy fo' a sinner like me t' get aroun'." He winked at me, "Don' look so' troubled, White Boy, Lake Henry 'about a mile on up the road. We better git some walkin' done."

As we stepped onto the road, I asked Fat Man where he'd been.

"I been down Vegas wit Alabama Charlie, an' don' ask cos I ain' gon' tell ya'."

We walked in silence for about three-quarters of a mile and then Fat Man stopped and pointed over to our left.

On the other side of a cotton field stood a row of trees, just beyond them, three separate plumes of dark smoke rose vertically in the still air.

Fat Man grunted. "I reckons th' party yo' was at was over yonder. Looks like they Klan fuckers torched th' whole Goddam place."

I thought about the fish-fry, about all the people I'd met, the music I'd played, listened to and recorded. I'd heard only three gunshots, but that didn't mean anything. I wondered if anyone else had got hurt.

"Guess we gon' find out," said Fat Man.

About two hundred yards further on, we turned left onto a track. As we approached the tree line, the smell of smoke became stronger. Following the track out of the trees, Fat Man stopped and surveyed what was left of the farm.

I walked around him and saw for myself.

At first I couldn't get my bearings, every shack had been torched; then I saw the tree where Stella and I had talked and the smoking remains of the bonfire. From there I was able to work out the shack that I had slept in.

As I walked towards it something caught my eye. I turned towards the tree and gasped. Hanging from a low branch was the battered corpse of Annie. Her hands and feet were trussed and her head lolled grotesquely to one side, the hangman's noose coated in dried blood from the wound in her throat. In death her body seemed smaller as it swung gently in macabre rhythm with the bodies of Silas and Curtis hanging from another branch.

Fat Man walked past carrying a yard broom; he glanced up at the bodies then turned to me. "Shift yo' ass, White Boy," he snarled. We ain' got time t' be takin' in this pastoral scene of the gallant south."

He shook his head and grunted. "Where yo' shack at?"

Barely able to compose myself, I nodded towards a smoking pile of charred timber. What had once been someone's home had been razed to the ground.

I could feel the heat from ten feet away, but Fat Man strode into the middle, upended the broom and used the handle to sort through the blackened detritus.

I spotted a rake a few feet away, picking it up I got as close as I could and began sifting through the ash.

"Looks like I found yo' gittar." Fat Man showed me a piece of charred wood with brittle strings dangling from blackened tuning pegs. "Ain' goin' be pickin' no toone from that anytime soon." He threw it to one side and continued sifting through the mess. "Where yo' say yo' satchel was?"

I stopped and tried to remember, tried to recall the layout of the shack. I said that I thought that I hung the satchel on the back of a chair and propped the guitar against it.

Fat Man shook his head, "Well, I cain' see nothin' looks like whatchoo was carryin', ain' no melted plastic anywhere's. Yo' sho' tha's where yo' left it? Yo' sho' yo' memory ain' affected by the knock on yo' head o' th' rotgut whisky yo' drunk?"

I said I was positive.

He grunted. "Well, if it was here, it ain' here now. Which means someone grabbed it while yo' was otherwise engaged."

Fat Man thought for a moment, "Is they anybody yo' think mighta been hangin' 'round?"

I said that no one sprang to mind.

"Mother-fucker." He threw the yard broom onto the ash and watched as the bristles smoked, blackened and then burst into flame.

Deep in thought, he stood watching the broom burn away then lifted his head, stared at me and said. "I think I got's me a idea. C'mon."

Fat Man turned and marched towards the Ford pickup. I set off after him and had to run to catch up. I asked him what we were going to do with the bodies.

He shrugged. "Do whatchoo want, ain' nothin' t'do with me."

I said that we couldn't just leave them there.

Fat Man never broke step. "They ain' goin' nowhere an' we got's business t' attend to."

I told him it wasn't right to leave them. I grabbed his arm and said that we should bury them or at least cover them up.

Fat Man whirled, snatched his arm away and grabbed the front of my shirt in a massive fist and dragged me close. "White Boy, I ain' got time fo' this shit an' I'm gettin' jus' a bit sick an' tired o' hearin' yo' bitchin' an' whinin'. Yo' wanna bury 'em, go ahead, I ain' goin' stop yo'."

He released my shirt and jabbed my chest with a fat finger, "All's I cares about is gettin' my stuff back, stuff thatchoo lost. I don' get that back, tha's goin' cost me a lot o' money; an' trus' me on this White Boy, if that happens they goin' be a world o' pain come crashin' roun' yo' ears. We unnerstan' one another?"

He stepped back and scuffed a line between us in the dirt, "This wha's goin' happen. Yo' goin' choose right now whatchoo wanna do. Yo' come with me now, we sort this out an' continya where we left off; o' yo' goes back t' yo' room in Clarksdale an' yo' can sit an' wait alone cryin' fo' yo' momma, thinkin' 'bout what mighta been while the world falls outcho' ass."

Fat Man paused to take a breath. "Think carefully, White Boy, cos' this goin' be th' las' time I'm goin' aks yo'. Whatchoo wanna do?"

What could I say? The fucker had me over a barrel and he knew it.

He nodded. "Tha's what I thought."

Fat Man turned and stomped away.

When he reached the pickup, he leaned into the cab for a second and then went round to the front. He cranked the starter handle once, stepped back as the engine burst into life and had already squeezed his bulk behind the wheel when he yelled, "Get in."

I had to throw myself into the cab. The pickup lurched forwards as Fat Man crunched the gears and I hung on for dear life, the passenger door flying open as he spun the wheel and steered the truck towards the road.

Fat Man turned to me and grinned.

"Now yo' goin' see some drivin'."

I managed to grab the door and slam it shut just as we hit the road.

I'd read somewhere that the Model-T Ford has a top speed of 45 miles per hour. The way Fat Man drove, it felt more like sixty. The engine howled as his huge fist kept the throttle lever wide open. As the pickup roared along the simple gravel road, the skinny tyres threw dust and grit into the air and into the cab while the primitive suspension transferred the impact of every pothole straight to my lower spine.

Shouting to compete with the road noise, I asked Fat Man where we were going.

As if on cue, a road sign came into view. The words 'Crystal Springs 3 Miles' approached fast and then flashed by.

"Tha's where we goin'," yelled Fat Man. "I reckon I knows who got th' satchel."

It was impossible to hold a conversation and it was a relief when we pulled into town and turned onto Main Street.

Fat Man grinned. "Goddam, never knew a T-Model'd go that fast."

Main Street took us right through Crystal Springs and we were almost at the town limits when we turned left at a set of lights and crossed a set of railroad tracks. I'd heard the expression 'the wrong side of the tracks'- now I knew where it came from. As we drove deeper into the neighbourhood, buildings stood in decrepitude, the streets resembling a shanty town.

Pulling over to the side of the road, Fat Man pointed to a tumbledown shack with boarded up windows and a rusty tin roof.

"Tha's where th' son of a bitch live."

Switching off the engine he said, "Le's go an' have us a chat."

Without waiting for a reply, Fat Man opened the door, the truck rocking and lifting as he grunted his way out.

Like every other place on the street, the shack had three steps leading up to a wooden porch that creaked under our combined weight. The torn and rusty screen-door screeched as Fat Man pulled it open and then tried the main door.

It was unlocked and as it swung ajar the light flooded in and a fecal stench crawled out. From inside came the liquid rasp of drunken snoring.

Fat Man pushed the door wide open and we stepped inside.

At the back of the room, sprawled across a filthy armchair, Tommy Johnson lay in a drunken stupor, his feet surrounded by several large empty bottles.

Fat Man grunted. "Drunk his self stupid on Night Train," he said. "Smells like he shit his self too."

Trying to take shallow breaths, I took a look around. Stepping over the bottles I eased past the armchair and pushed open another door into a smaller room at the back. Dust motes hung in the air, illuminated by the sunlit outline of a rectangle in the far wall, like someone had taken a cutting torch to the darkness. I made my way towards the door, opened it and stuck out my head to take in lungfuls of fresh air.

Apart from two broken wooden chairs, a simple table and a stove, the room was empty. I was about to leave when something caught my eye; on the floor, partially hidden behind the door was the strap of the satchel.

I carried it through into the main room. Fat Man was sitting on the porch, his back to me, smoking a Lucky Strike.

"Yo' found yo' bag, then?"

I dragged a wooden chair, sat next to Fat Man and asked him how he knew where to find it.

He shrugged. "Gut feelin'. Ol' Tommy, he one o' th' best pickers they ever was, but he always was a slave t' liquor. Any chance he get t' make a dollar an' step up from drinkin' Sterno, well,"

Fat Man paused and then shrugged again. "Fuck it, tha's what I'd do."

He nodded towards the satchel. "Well, go on, gimme th' bad news. What's he took?"

I opened the satchel. The camera, voice recorder and the cash was gone, but my phone and the notebook remained.

Fat Man was not impressed. "Motha-fucker," he said. "Yo' sho' they ain' nothin' else in there?"

I took out the phone and notebook and as I upended the satchel, a crumpled piece of paper dropped at my feet.

Straightened out, it looked like a hand-written receipt.

"Lemme see that."

I gave it to Fat Man. His eyes narrowed and then he shook his head. "Pawnbrokers," he said. "A disagreeable ol' Kike got a place further on down Main Street."

Handing me the receipt, Fat Man sighed and then lumbered upright. "I ain' got time fo' this shit."

Back in the pickup, I looked at the receipt. It said that the pawnshop had given Tommy the princely sum of $30 in total for the camera and voice recorder.

"Thirty Goddam bucks t'get my own shit back."

A few minutes later we were parked beneath the familiar pawnbrokers sign.

Fat Man pointed to it. "Yo' know what they three balls signify? Two t' one yo' don' get yo' money back."

Inside, protected by a wire mesh screen, a small, bewhiskered elderly man stood behind a counter that spanned the entire room. The wall behind him was covered with rows of shelving that held all manner of tools and household products. To his right a clothes rail held several threadbare men's suits and guitars hung from the ceiling. In front of the old man, a glass cabinet displayed gold and silver jewellery, wristwatches and precious stones.

"Vot can I help you vit', gentlemen?"

Fat Man looked at me. "Yo' got that receipt?"

I handed over the slip, which he turned and showed to the old man.

"Unnerstan' yo' took possession o' these items."

After a cursory glance, the old man stroked his beard and looked at Fat Man.

"I gave money for these items," he said. "But not to you."

He pointed to me. "Or him."

Fat Man sniffed. "Well, they's a theme developin' here, cos th' person yo' took 'em from was not th' rightful owner. See, these items, they b'longs t' me an' was taken without my knowledge o' permission."

The old man stared balefully through rheumy eyes.

"Says you."

Fat Man took a deep breath. "Tha's right, says me. An' I jus' wan's what's rightfully mine an' then we'll be on our way. Now, they's gotta be a price at which we can both meet in some sorta 'greement?"

The old man shrugged. "Sure thing, just gimme thirty bucks."

In my mind's eye I could see the last grains of sand empty from the egg-timer of Fat Man's patience.

I stepped forward and told the old man that we were in a hurry.

The old man shifted his gaze to me. "And dis affects me how? The price is on the slip. Dat's what I gave, an' dats what it gonna cost you."

Fat Man's voice dropped to a steely whisper that lifted hairs on my neck. "Those goods are my fuckin' merchandise," he said. "Any mo' o' yo' bullshit an' I'ma come 'roun there an' take 'em back."

The old man's whiskers lifted in a sneer.

"Vot, you threatening me? Enough vid this, already. I not gonna talk to you no more."

His chin lifted as he folded his arms.

Fat Man stepped backwards. "What th' fuck yo' mean by that?"

"I not sellin' to you. I vont you outta my store."

For a second, Fat Man was speechless. Then he said, "You tellin' us to leave?"

"Just you. I not scared a' no one, an' no one threatens me in my own store."

The old man nodded at me. "You, you can stay."

Just before Fat Man came up to the boil I took him to one side and suggested he let me handle it.

He didn't take it well.

"Yo' think yo' better than me, White Boy? Yo' think I cain't handle a dried up ol' Jew-boy?"

I said we didn't have time to argue and that I'd see him back at the truck.

His punch put a dent in the wire mesh that could have held a basketball. Breathing hard through his nostrils, Fat Man stared at the Jew then turned to me.

"Yo' better get this done, White Boy."

Fat Man turned and left the store with a door slam that shook the building.

Through all of this the old man stared impassively.

I said that it really was our property and we needed it back.

His deadpan expression unfolded with a wink. "I knew that," he said.

I was lost for words.

His eyes wrinkled in a smile. "Dis stuff," he said. "I not seen anything like it before."

He looked around the shop. "You seen the drek I deal with," he said. "Someone comes in vid items like them," he pointed to the receipt. "That gets my attention. Especially when dat someone is so drunk he can't stand up."

He smiled again. "I was vaiting for someone to claim it."

I asked him if the amount on the receipt matched the amount given to the customer.

The old man shrugged. "Call it a holding fee."

I said we'd give him ten dollars for the equipment.

His eyes twinkled. "Twenty five," he said.

I said twelve dollars, he came back with twenty and we settled on fifteen.

As we shook hands I caught sight of something that almost made me gasp. I asked him for a price on some items that I'd spotted.

"Items?" he frowned. "Vot items?"

Ten minutes later, I walked out of the store.

Fat Man was leaning against the truck, smoking a Lucky Strike. I walked over and asked him if he had forty dollars.

"Forty?" he said. "Uncle Kike wanted thirty."

I said I needed another guitar.

Fat Man stared at me. "Yo' tellin' me that not only I gotta pay to get my own shit back, from a Kike that threw me outta his Goddam shop; now I gotta fund yo' fo' another gittar?"

He produced two twenty's from the pocket of his sweatpants.

"Yo' testin' my patience, White Boy." He said. "Be very careful."

I walked back into the shop and returned with the recording equipment, a steel-bodied National guitar and a carefully folded receipt in my back pocket.

I climbed into the truck and sat with the guitar cradled between my knees.

We had driven ten miles out of Crystal Springs before Fat Man spoke.

"Well, least we back on track. I'ma get these recordin's processed an' yo' gon get me some mo' recordin's."

He glanced over at me. "See yo' gotcho'self anutha gittar. Always wanted a National, huh?"

Before I could answer, he shook his head. "White Boys. Spends a fo'choon on on a National an' thinks it makes 'em a bluesman."

He turned to me. "Yo DO realise that all yo' heroes, they's dirt poor and mostly played on gittars they got fo' a dollar-fifty from a Sears-Roebuck catalog?"

He grunted again. "Some of 'em started out by stretchin' a piece o' wire between two nails on the side of a shack an' usin' a knife o' a bottle. Most of 'em could pick a better toone than yo' could ever dream o' gettin' off of that shiny-ass piece o' shit."

I replied that any guitarist in the world would appreciate a 1930s National.

I dragged my thumb across the strings, producing a loud, full-bodied, discordant twang.

Fat Man guffawed. "Ain' even in tune."

Reaching over, he grasped the headstock in his massive fist, held it for a few seconds and then let go.

"Try it now," he said.

This time the G chord sang out and filled the cab of the truck.

When I asked him how he did that, he tapped his nose. "Is what it is," he said.

A thought struck me, if he could tune it like that why make such a big deal at the crossroads?

Fat Man grinned. "Tha's show business, White Boy."

I asked why we'd had to run around to get the recording equipment back.

"Huh? What's yo' point?" He growled.

114

I asked him that if he could tune a guitar simply by holding it, if he could apparently read my mind, or at least know what I was thinking, why he didn't know where to find the recording equipment?

Fat Man shook his head. "I think yo' head in the wrong place," he said. "I think yo' thinkin' 'bout the wrong shit. Yo' needs t'be thinkin' that ever' minute yo' ain't workin', yo' ain't earnin'. We clear on this?"

I said that I was just asking.

"Sometimes yo' aks too many questions. Yo' lose my shit again an' I'ma get Old Testament on yo' natchel white ass."

Sighing, I picked up the camera and checked through the videos. I opened the one I'd taken of Stella, muted the sound and watched her silent movie. I didn't want to hand it over so when the video ended, I deleted it.

By now we were back out in the delta countryside. I sat back and watched the cotton fields roll past. About a mile ahead, I spotted a tiny white box on the side of the road; as we approached it grew into a familiar wooden building.

Fat Man hit the brakes, swung the wheel and parked next to the church. "Here we is."

The pickup rocked like a trawler in rough seas until Fat Man finally broke free.

By the time I'd got myself sorted, he was opening the front door of the church. Fat Man turned and then fished in his pocket. "Gimme the camera an' voice recorder."

I handed them over and with the fluidity of a gunslinger he replaced the memory cards and handed the equipment back. "Yo' carry on searchin' fo' talent. I don' care who o' what yo' reco'd, jus' get me anythin' yo' think yo' white frien's gon' be interested in."

Fat Man stared at me. "An' I don' wanna hear 'bout no mo' distractions."

He turned, entered the church and slammed the door. I flipped the bird as the deadbolt slid into place, heard Fat Man laugh once and then there was silence.

# Travellin' Man

I sat for a long time on the tailgate of the pickup; staring at the broad expanse of cotton bushes that filled the vista as I tried to work out a plan.

"S'cuse me, suh."

Startled, I turned around. At the side of the road, directly in front of me stood a slim, silver-haired old black man carrying a battered guitar case. Patent leather shoes gleamed beneath the turn-ups of immaculate dark suit trousers, and a red handkerchief dangled from the breast pocket of a dark suit jacket beneath which a crisp, white shirt sported a black string tie.

He doffed his trilby, his eyes downcast as he mumbled again, "S'cuse me, suh."

I stood up and said hello.

The old man put down his guitar case, removed his hat and gripped it nervously in both hands. He nodded at the pickup.

"Suh, I's sorry to bother yuh, but, but I's wonderin', suh, if they's any chance of a ride? I been walkin' a mighty long ways an' I sho' would 'preciate it."

I said of course and asked him where he was going.

"Well, suh, I's hopin' t'get t' Clarksdale, but I guess I'll go as far as yo' willin' to take me."

I held out my hand and introduced myself. At first he flinched, then stepped forward nervously. When he touched my hand, he covered his initial gasp with a stage cough.

He stepped back and ran a hand over his silver hair. "Name's Henry Watson, suh." he said. "Folks calls me Travellin' Man."

He grinned shyly when I said I'd heard of him. "'s'at so?" he said. "'magine that."

He lifted the guitar case and walked towards the pickup.

"Is that a National?" He looked at my guitar and then looked at me. "Yo' pick on th' gittar, suh?"

I said that I tried, and told him to stop calling me sir.

He eyed me suspiciously. "Mos' white folks, they likes a nigger to know they place."

I said that this white boy didn't use that word.

Suspicion lingered still.

"An' some white folks, they likes t' say shit like that, make out they friends wit' th' nigger, only fo' nigger to find his self wit' a knife in his back o' a rope round his neck."

He stared at me with lidded eyes. "What sorta white boy you is?"

I shrugged and said I was the sort who liked a quiet life.

He continued to stare at me, his face an impassive mask, and then a grin broke out.

"Please fo'give the ways of an ornery ol' man, I been aroun' some; an' well, yo' know."

I shrugged again.

Travellin' Man hefted his guitar case into the pickup and then touched his throat. "I'm feelin' somethin' kinda parched," he said. "I sho' could do with a drink o' water, fo' we sets off."

I said that I didn't have any.

Travellin' Man nodded at the church. "They's usually a well out back, what they used t' use as baptisin' water."

I followed him around the side of the church to a cast-iron pump with a small wooden bucket hanging from the spout. Travellin' Man placed the bucket on the ground and pumped the handle several times until water gushed out. Once filled, he lifted the bucket, drank deeply and then splashed water over his face. "Somethin' kinda dusty out on they gravel roads," he said.

He watched me carefully as he handed over the bucket; and then relaxed when I took a drink.

Back at the pickup, he said, "What yo' say yo' bidness was?"

I replied that I hadn't said.

"OK, what kinda stuff yo' pick on yo' box?"

I said blues, mostly.

His eyes twinkled. "White boy playin' th' blues in Miss'ippi, huh? Well I be damned. How's that workin' out?"

It seemed to be my day for shrugging.

"I been playin' th' blues my whole existence," he said. "Ever since I's old enough t' hold a gittar. Used t' pick on th' box when I's s'posed be pickin' cotton. My daddy, he used t' whup me ever' day 'til finally one day I whup him back good an' set off down th' road. I didn't ever go back an' I been travellin' ever since."

He stared across the cotton fields. "Yes suh, I travelled through Arkansas, Miss'ippi, Loosiana, Alabama, an' around in Kentucky an' Tennessee; I made me records in New York an' Wisconsin. I travelled on the Greyhound an' on the train when I had money, an' ridin' th' blinds an' hitchin' a ride when I never had none."

He looked back at me. "Yo' play dice, suh?"

I shook my head.

"Maybe I show yo'," he said. "I learned me how to throw them bones an' made me a lots o' money. I play at lumber camps, at fish-fry's, at barrelhouses an' juke-joints. I play at parties an' on the street. I play fo' money an' fo' moonshine." He paused, then chuckled. "Some folks they didn't liked-

ded th' way I throwed them dice, 'how come yo' always' winnin'?', they say. I
say, 'tha's jus' th' way they rollin''."

Travellin' Man winked at me. "I 'member once I played lumber camp
on a Friday night. Tha's th' day they got paid, see, an' I walks in an' sets myself
playin' th' gittar and ever'body's dancin's an' yellin' an' carryin' on. Later on, I
starts throwin' them dice an' makin' like I ain' got one clue wha's goin' on. I
makes three dollars then loses five. 'I had 'nuff' I say. This feller, he stumbles
over; man he's drunker n' shit, an' says, 'how 'bout we throw th' bones a
while?' Long story, short, I hooked him like a big ol' catfish. Took all his wages
includin' th' money he borrowed from his frien'. Once I done that, tha's my
time t' git gone; time fo' ol' Travellin' Man t' leave town."

He laughed long and hard then switched it off and span round to face
me. "Now, how about we stop this fuckin' around and yo' tell me s'acly what
th' fuck yo' doin' here, White boy? How yo' come t' be in this part o' Miss'ippi
an' what th' fuck yo' afta?"

He spat the words with such venom that for a second I was paralyzed.
Then I regrouped and suggested that perhaps he should mind his own fucking
business.

Travellin' Man stepped backwards. "Wait a minute," he said. "I heard
tell of a white boy runnin' round recordin' blues singers. Say he there when a
faggot shot his self in Mo'head; say he whupped him some white trash in a
coffee house; say he at a fish fry where fire broke out an' three niggers got
lynched."

I asked him what else he'd heard.

He looked like he was about to tell me but then changed his mind. "I
hears lotsa things." He said.

He thought for a moment. "Yo' still lookin' at recordin' musicianers?"

I said I might be.

"Whatchoo gon' do wit' th' recordin's yo' gon' make?"

I said I had someone who was interested in them.

"Interested, huh? Whatchoo gon' give anyone yo' makes a recordin' of?"

When I didn't reply, Travellin' Man shook his head. "Yo' thought yo's jus gon' go out an aks folks t'play fo' yo' an' give 'em a smile an' be thankful, an' they gon' say 'yessuh, nosuh lemme suck yo' white dick suh'? 'sat whatchoo thought?"

I stayed silent.

"Shit, White Boy. Yo' ain' gon' last five minutes."

I said I'd done all right up to now.

"Yo' think so? Who yo' got so far?"

As I listed the singers I'd recorded, Travellin' Man inspected his nails. When I'd finished he said, "'sat it? Yo' got some smartass from Memphis, some rookie at a fish-fry an' Tommy Johnson?"

Travellin' Man shook his head. "Yo' ain' found shit, so far, I can show yo' gittar pickers like yo' ain' never seen."

He stabbed the bed of the pickup with his finger. "A hunnerd times better than anythin' yo' seen so far. An' they here now, right here in the Delta."

He wagged the same finger at me when I asked where I could find them.

"Nuh-uh, White Boy. Yo' ain' never gon' find them on yo' own. They plays in places no white face ever been seen, places white folk ain' never heard of. Yo' go lookin' fo' them yo' be lucky if'n yo' gets away wid' just' havin' th' door slammed in yo' face."

He paused for as long as it took the shit-eating grin to crawl across his face.

121

"Yo' gon' need somebody keep them doors open, somebody who gon' show yo' all th' places where a nigger goes fo' a good time, somebody who can show yo' th' way o'things."

He paused. "I be walkin' the Delta all my life an' ever' since afta that. I can show yo' places yo' only ever dreamed of an' no white boy ever seen."

He paused again. "An' now I see I gotcho' undivided attention."

Travellin Man folded his arms. "Tell me I ain' right."

I asked him what it would cost me.

"I wants fifty percent of whatever gets made from ever' recordin' we makes."

I said that I wasn't dealing with royalties, that I was just a middle man.

"An' I don' give a shit, tha's what I want."

I said that was my position, I couldn't guarantee any deal and if he didn't like that then I'd be on my way.

Travellin' Man thought about this and then smiled. "Well now, I think maybe we gettin' off on th' wrong foot. Please fo'give my somewhat ambitious manner. I'm used t' keepin' th' kinda company where a man has t' stay on top o' every situation, y' unnerstan'? I apologise, I don' mean t' confront yo' none. I hope that in time yo' gon' realise that I ain' a unreasonable man. If yo' give me yo' word that when th' time comes, yo' gon' do whatchoo can t' get me a slice o' th' action, then I'll give yo' mine that I'ma show yo' some o' th' best damn blues yo' ever gon' see. Tha's th' 'rrangement I'm proposin'. Whatchoo say, White Boy, is yo' interested in partnerin' up?"

Taking a deep breath, my heart pounded as I said yes.

Travellin' Man spat into his right palm then extended it, his face breaking into a genuine grin as we shook hands.

"OK partner," he said. "I'll drive if tha's OK widjoo?."

122

I wrapped the guitars in sacking and secured them in the pickup bed as best I could. As I climbed into the passenger seat Travellin' Man swung on the starter handle and the old engine coughed into life.

So it began.

# Pops McCoy

As we pulled out onto the road, Travellin' Man said, "My 'riginal plan was we gon' pick up Highway 61 an' head towards Clarksdale." He looked out of the window. "It gon' be dark soon so it look like that ain' gon' happen; but that don' confront us none, see I knows a place we can stop on th' way an' have us some fun."

He leaned over, winked and jabbed my ribs with his elbow. "I know's a rough ol' jook-joint in th' ass-end o'nowhere, characterful yo' might say. They don' see too many white folks an' the gen'ral behaviour ain't whatchoo might call refined."

He burst out laughing. "Shit, it gon be a baptism o' fire fo' all parties concerned, but donchoo worry none. I think yo' gon' enjoy yo'self, they gon' be some lowdown an' dirty blues, cheap whisky an' even cheaper wimmins."

This made him laugh even harder, tears poured down his face as he pounded the steering wheel.

When it came to conversation, Travellin' Man was a force to be reckoned with. He would hold court on any number of subjects, seemingly flitting from thought to thought with no need of any response on my part. After a while I gave up trying to keep up and settled into my own thoughts with only half an ear on Travellin' Man's chatter.

I thought about Stella, wondering where she was and if I would ever see her again. I made a mental note to remind myself to ask Travellin' Man if he knew anything about Gabel. There was no point bringing it up now, he was clearly on a roll, words spilling from his mouth like water from an overfilled bucket.

Dusk was just surrendering to the night when Travellin' Man turned onto a narrow side road. We jolted along the rough surface for about half an hour until the weak headlights pointed out a fork in the dirt track. Travellin' Man swung the wheel to the right and we continued along a trail that bisected a cotton field, the bushes towering over the pickup.

Just as darkness was about to envelop us, pinpricks of light glowing like lit cigarettes appeared about a mile ahead and danced in time with the rattling pickup.

"Tha's where we headed," said Travellin' Man. He glanced fearfully at the void around us. "Ain' a minute too soon neither."

We lurched over potholes and large stones and then skidded to a halt outside of a large, dilapidated wooden shack. I counted about a dozen cars and trucks parked at the side of the shack, with more at the rear. Close to the shack, five stoic mules stood tethered to a hitching post.

Travellin' Man nodded towards them as we got out. "Come sunrise, they' gon' be findin' they own way home with a drunk-ass rider slumped over they neck."

Reaching into the back of the truck he unwrapped the guitars and handed the National to me. "Keep a holda this," he said. "Folks in here, le's jus' say they ain' gon' allow th' small matter of a conscience t' burden they thinking." He nodded towards my satchel, "An' keep yo' eyes on all whatchoo got in there, too."

I nodded and said that was good advice.

Travellin' Man opened his case and took out a wooden Gibson. He paused to stare at it lovingly and then slipped the strap over his shoulder and ran his fingers over the strings to produce a brief glimpse of an arpeggio that rang out into the night.

"Ain' never had a gittar keep itself in tune like this'n. Man that sound so sweet." He gave me a wink. "Yo' gon' see some blues tonight, White Boy."

I followed him towards the shack. The porch was lit by beer bottles containing gasoline and burning rags that dangled from the roof. At the front, two wooden steps led to large green door. As we approached, the door flew open, releasing the bedlam sound of drinking, dancing and music. A man stumbled out and lurched across the porch, paused just long enough to make two gurgling belches and then folded over the wooden rail. Vomit sprayed from his mouth like a fire-hose, arced into the air and then spattered onto the ground, filling the air with the stench of secondhand corn whisky.

Travellin' Man did a nifty sidestep and just managed to avoid being sprayed with puke. He waved at the drunk. "Man tha's gotta make yo' feel better."

The drunk lifted a weak hand and then sprayed the ground again. I counted at least four discharges before we reached the steps, each one preceded with gut-wrenching bark and followed by a foul liquid splatter.

Travellin' Man stopped at the open door, turned towards me, and with a wink said, "Abandon hope all ye who enter here."

I followed him in and was met with a wall of heat, a thick fog of cigarette smoke and the overpowering stench of weeks-unwashed bodies that sweated and writhed on the tiny dance floor.

Travellin' Man grinned with delight at my shocked expression. "They ain' no dress code this evenin'. But don' worry none, yo' soon gets used t'it."

I heard the sound of a guitar and caught glimpses through the crowd of an old, skinny black man on a wooden chair on small stage at the back of the room.

Travellin' Man motioned for us to head towards a wooden bench against the left hand wall and began to push his way through the onlookers at the edge of the dance floor. Dragging the bench forward, we propped the guitars behind it and sat down.

On the stage, the singer pounded his guitar to a song that I didn't recognise. He wore large, thick-glassed spectacles through which his eyes were magnified to cartoon proportions and as he played he would sing a line and then shout a response to himself, throwing in obvious ad-libs and fooling around.

Despite his Magoo-like appearance and comic interludes, he never once took his eyes off the crowd; giving them what they wanted but also playing them like a puppeteer, directing them every now and then to dance in a certain way. His fingers flew across the strings, his feet stamping a beat hard enough to raise dust from between the floorboards. His face contorted and his eyes rolled backwards as he poured every inch of his heart and soul into yelling the blues. Next to his chair stood a bucket on which was painted the word 'Tips'. Every so often, a dancer would step forward and toss in a nickel or a dime.

I became aware of a sea of black faces turning to stare at me, some stopped dancing and glared openly.

"Looks like we might got us a sitchu-ashun developin'."

Two huge black men stood nearby. Travellin' Man pointed to them and then pulled out two dollar bills from his pocket. The two men walked over.

"Whatchoo want?" said one.

Travellin' Man stood up. "Whas yo' name, son?"

"Name's Lucas and this' my brother, Daniel."

"Well, Lucas, this white boy he wid me an' we jus' wants us a good time."

Lucas looked sullenly at me. "He don' b'long here."

"Well, tha's right, sho' nuff," said Travellin' Man. "But here he is an' he jus' wan's t'see how we 'other half lives."

Lucas shrugged. "So?"

"So, it looks like we gon' need a little protecshun fo' th' evenin' an' I got a dollar each that says yo' an' Daniel gon' be interested."

"We maybe gon' do it fo' five dollars each." said Lucas.

Travellin Man shook his head. "Ten dollars? Nuh-uh, I give yo' fo' dollars."

Lucas looked at Daniel then said, "Tell yo what, ol' man, five dollars says that ain' no one gon' botha yo' tonight."

Travellin' Man smiled as he fished extra notes from his pocket. "Yo' learnin', aincha kid?" he said.

Handing the cash to Lucas, Travellin' Man clapped him on the shoulder then sat down. He leaned close to my ear and said, "I'ma win that back off 'em later when they drunk. An' speakin' o' bein' drunk, I'm feelin' somethin' kinda thirsty myself."

With that he stood up and disappeared into the crowd.

At first I felt uncomfortable. It seemed that everyone not dancing was staring at me, and not in a good way. Lucas leaned over. "This ain' no place fo' white folks," he said. "Yo' gon' have t'get used t'all that, but they ain' gon' give yo' no trouble."

I nodded and thanked him just as Travellin' Man re-appeared carrying two brown paper bags. Handing one to me he said, "Corn whisky, first slug gon' tear yo' insides right out, afta that i's all good."

I pulled out the cork and took a sip. It was strong, but not as bad as the moonshine that Annie had fed me. I took another swig without reacting and winked at Travellin Man.

"Well, hell," he said. "Looks like yo' might got some nigger in yo' afta all." He raised his paper bag. "Here's to a lucrative partna'ship."

I nodded and we tapped bottles.

"Now, how 'bout we have us some fun an' watch us some barrelhousin'?"

Onstage, sweat dripped from the old man's face as he delivered a relentless maelstrom of hard-core blues that permeated every pore of my body. Blues is not about which notes or chords are played, or even which song. Blues is a feeling, and right there I was feeling it. Every hair on my body seemed to be standing on end as the old guy poured out emotion onstage with nothing more than a beat-up old guitar, his feet on the boards and the anguish in his voice.

"Tha's Pops McCoy." Travellin' Man's voice brought me back down to earth. "He ain' bad, but I seen better."

He leaned in close. "See, it ain' jus' about th' music; yo' gotta feel the crowd, i's th' crowd yo' playin', not jus' yo' gittar. Yo' know'm sayin'?"

I said that he seemed to be doing a pretty good job from where I was sitting.

"That maybe so," said Travellin' Man. "But yo' a neophyte, wait til yo' been here long enough to see what's what."

Just then a girl in the crowd caught my eye.

I grabbed Travellin' Man's arm and asked him how we could find Gabel.

"Gabel?" he choked. "Whatchoo want wid' that motherfucker?"

I started to give him a brief history lesson but he cut me off. "White Boy, this ain' th' time nor th' place. We come here fo' some blues, barrelhousin', corn liquor and separating po' drunk motherfuckers from they dollars. Maybe we talk later but right now I wan's me a good time."

He lifted his paper bag. "Can I get an Amen?"

Reluctantly I clinked bottles with him.

The performance came to an end, and the old man finished with a power chord and an arm-windmill that Pete Townshend would have been proud of.

The crowd went wild, jumping, cheering and clapping. Pops McCoy stood up and then bowed, his voice hoarse as he rasped, "Gon' be a short break while I gets me some 'freshment, It ain' easy bein' th' po'boy motherfucker gots t' try an' entertain yo' no-good asses."

He stepped offstage and walked towards us. "Travellin' Man," he yelled. "Yo' got that money yo' owe me, yo' low-down motherfucker?"

Travellin' Man kicked an empty chair towards him and gave him the look. "Watch yo' language, nigger, we got us a bona fidee white boy in th' house."

"So I seen, wha's he here fo'?"

"He wan's t'see th' blues, tha's all."

Pops dragged the chair around and sat down. "White boy out in the ass end o'nowhere in the land o' the dead, Mississippi? Jus' here fo' th' blues? Shit, he a long way from home."

So far he hadn't looked at me once.

Travellin' Man winked at me. "'llow me t' introduce y'all. White Boy, this here's Mister Henry McCoy; we calls him 'Pops'." He turned to the old guy. "Pops, this here...damn, what is yo' name? Anyway, White Boy here has travelled from way overseas in England."

Pops lifted his head once.

"White Boy here t' reco'd blues singers," said Travellin' Man. "Even got his self a fancy gittar."

Pops removed his spectacles, wiped them on his shirt, put them back on and grunted. "Maybe he thinks he gon' show us po' niggas how white folks plays th' blues."

Trying to break his ice I said that going by his performance there was nothing anyone could show him.

"Kissin' my black ass ain' gon' getchoo nowhere, White Boy." He finally made eye contact, targeting me with a stare loaded with mistrust. "These niggas yo' gon' be reco'din', 'sacly what they gon' be gettin' outta th' deal?"

Travellin' Man was quick to respond. "They gon' get five dollars up front, tha's whatchoo said, ain't it White Boy?"

He caught me off guard but I covered it by looking around the juke-joint and then saying that it would depend on how good the artist was.

Travellin' Man nodded. "Tha's right, we ain' jus' givin' five dollars to any ol' nigga wid a gittar, they gon' have to audition first."

Pop cackled at this. "An' who gon' be doin' th' auditionin'? A low down crooked gambler an' a fancy pants white boy? What th' fuck y'all think y'all gon' know 'bout whether nigga can pick th' gittar worth a shit?"

When his wheezing laughter had run its course, I said that where I came from, fancy pants white boys knew a lot more about delta blues than he would ever imagine.

"Delta blues, huh? S'at whatchoo call it?"

Pops stared at me. "So, yo' gon' give five dollars, huh? An' what about if a reco'd get made? What kinda cut the musicianer gon' get?"

Travellin' Man stepped in. "White Boy ain' got no control over that we gon' take th' reco'din's an,..."

"I ain' talkin' to yo'."

Travellin' Man fell silent like he'd just been switched off.

Pops turned back to me. "Well? Whatchoo gotta say?"

I told him there was no guarantee that any records would be made or sold and that if the artists accepted the five dollars then that would waive any rights to further royalties. I also said that if a record did get made and sold well, then there might be an opportunity to record the artist again and we might be able to renegotiate another deal.

"No guarantee, no royalties, might be this, might be that." Pops sneered at me. "It sound to me like this another way fo' white man t' fuck a nigga up his ass."

Travellin' Man leaned in close and aimed his finger at Pop's face. "Motherfucker, yo' think I be sittin' here if tha's how it was? Whatchoo think I am? Some white-ass-kissin' Uncle Tom nigga? Fuck yo', McCoy. Yo' don' wanna' get involved then yo' can kiss MY black ass. I brought us all this way so's cos White Boy can see th' real blues fo' his own self. He lookin' fo' th' real deal an' yo' was th' first name come to mind."

He turned to me. "Didn't I say I take yo' t'see Pops McCoy? Ain' that what I said when we met up? 'Ol' Pops McCoy, he the real deal,' tha's what I said. Didn't I say that?"

Struggling to keep a straight face, I made some non-committal noise.

"Damn straight tha's what I said."

Pops stared at Travellin' Man then shook his head. "Yo' finished? I nevah said I ain' interested, I jus' wan' know what th' deal is, tha's all. Make sho' I ain' gon' be ripped off."

He turned to me. "Yo' see me play when yo' came in?"

I nodded.

"Well then how 'bout that fo' my audition?"

I thought about this then suggested that we watch the rest of his set and make a decision then.

"Fair nuff," he said. "But if'n yo' starts t'reco'din' then don' even think o' runnin' off befo' droppin' some cash in that ol' bucket up there."

He was about to say something else when impatient voices began to yell.

"Where th' music at, ol' man?"

"Hey Pops, we come t'hear some blues not t'watch yo' gettin' in on with a white boy."

"Yeah, Pops, get yo' skinny ass back on that chair an' start pickin' on that box. I wan's dance wid my girl, Goddammit."

Pops turned, glared and pointed to each of the hecklers in turn. "Fuck yo', an' fuck yo', an fuck yo'." Then he waved to the rest of the crowd. "An' th' rest of y'all can fuck yo'selves, Pops gon' play when Pops is ready t'play."

The crowd cheered as he stomped back to the stage, picked up his guitar and launched into a blistering one string boogie that transformed the crowd into a writhing, gyrating, sweating mass of bacchanalian revellers.

Travellin' Man nudged me in the ribs. "He can work up a crowd sho' nuff. Watch an' learn, White Boy, he playin' this boogie so's he can rest his voice, he'll do this'n an' then another'n, an' then he'll start singing again. This way he can keep this up all night. Like I say, he ain' bad, an' I think he worth reco'din'. Yo' think yo' white frien's wan' buy his reco'ds? Yo' think he got what it take fo' t'make us a lot o' money?"

I didn't reply or comment on his assumption but asked him how many other blues singers he knew.

"Hell, I knows at least twenty gon' be jus' right fo' whatchoo lookin' fo'. Most of 'em as good as Pops, an' some even better. Hell, White Boy, check out th' folks here, he raisin' up a storm an' they eatin' outta his hand."

Onstage, Pops' right thumb maintained a constant bass-drone on the bottom string, keeping perfect time and complementing the rhythmic, almost trance-inducing stamp of his feet on worn floorboards. Once more, sweat dripped from his contorted face as Pops McCoy lost himself in the performance. I looked around at the crowd; Travellin' Man was right, they were as transfixed as I was. The steady blues beat pulsed through every single of one of them, a pulse that transported them away from the oppressive, humid, sweat-soaked atmosphere of the juke-joint; a pulse generated by a skinny old black man with a cheap wooden guitar.

We had to record him.

Reaching into my satchel, I grabbed the camera and was about to stand up when Travellin' Man grabbed my arm. "Whatchoo got there?"

I told him it was a camera."

Travellin' Man shook his head, "Nuh-uh. Yo' cain' be wanderin' aroun' this crowd. Whyjoo think I paid fo' Lucas an' Daniel?"

When I told him that I wanted to record Pops, he said, "Better if I do it. How yo' make that thing work?"

I showed him the camera and told him what to do.

"An' I 'pose I gotta give him th' cash, too?"

I said that I would pay him back as soon as I could.

Travellin' Man winked at me but he wasn't smiling. That yo' will, White Boy," he said. "That yo' will."

He stood up and wandered off to a point where he could get a good view of the stage without blocking anyone's view.

Pops was still giving his all but nodded as Travellin' Man dropped a handful of notes into the tips bucket, stepped back and surreptitiously filmed the performance.

By now I was buzzing from the music and feeling all the effects of half a bottle of corn whisky. I leaned over to Lucas and asked him where the bathroom was. "Yo' better foller me," he said.

We stood up and I let him lead the way towards a door on the other side of the room. Lucas opened it and shoved me through into a fetid and stinking room about fifteen feet square. The toilet was a filthy wooden seat built around a hole in the ground, upon which sat an old black woman sipping corn whisky as she urinated noisily. In the corner of the room, four men knelt on the floor playing craps. Each throw of the dice was met with yelled obscenities and the exchange of wads of cash, interspersed with the passing back and forth of a large bottle of whisky.

As I watched the dice game, I heard the splashing come to an end followed by the impressive sound of the old lady breaking wind, her prolonged and noisy fart amplified by earthen acoustics.

One of the dice players looked up. "Sheeeit, girl, what the hell yo' be eatin', yo' parents?"

"I cain' help it," yelled the woman. "I jus' seen me a white boy an' I done lost all control."

This reduced her to a toothless cackle as she staggered past me.

I stayed just as long as was necessary, holding my breath and only just making it out of the bathroom without passing out.

Back in the room Pops was still kicking up a storm and Travellin' Man was still filming as we returned to the bench. Daniel nodded and smirked as we sat down. "Yo' get done whatchoo needed in there?"

He laughed when I said it had been an experience.

Pops finished the tune he was playing and paused to take a long swig of whisky from a bottle beneath his chair. Travellin' Man shouldered his way towards me. Handing me the camera he said, "Yo' better check what I done, make sure I got it right."

Playing back the video made me shiver. Travellin' Man had done a good job of filming Pops, and the image was steady and clear. Blues fans across the world would sell their souls for footage like this.

I smiled at the irony and wondered what Fat Man was doing.

"Well? Whatchoo think?"

Travellin' Man beamed when I told him that he had done a great job and that the video was perfect.

"We in business, then? Yo' an' me?"

I said maybe and asked him if he knew there was a crap game going on in the bathroom.

A look of hunger flashed across his eyes. "Yo' jus' been in there?" he said. "Wha's goin' on?"

I said there seemed to be a lot of shouting and a lot of whisky being drunk.

"Tha's good," he said. "Shoutin's good." He reached into his trouser pocket and produced two fine-looking ivory dice. "Maybe give 'em a little while longer an' then me an' my ol' bones, we gon' go in an' make our acquaintance."

Pops resumed playing onstage, thrashing out another instrumental with a driving beat.

Travellin' Man's face lit up when he heard the tune. "This' my favourite," he yelled. "I'll be back, shortly."

He grabbed his guitar and made his way to the stage. Before stepping up, he caught Pops' eye and lifted his guitar. Pops nodded and Travellin' Man slipped the strap over his shoulder and stepped up to join him.

Once more, Pops was delivering the goods, hammering his old guitar and stamping hard enough to make the boards shake.

Watching Pops carefully, Travellin' Man produced a bottleneck, placed it on the third finger of his left hand then positioned his fingers on the neck and strings of his own guitar. By now the place was jumping, the crowd feeding off the music and Pops feeding off the crowd, each absorbing the emotion of the other; building layer upon layer of intensity and pulsing it back and forth.

All eyes fell on Travellin' Man as he counted down to the key change. On the count of two, Pops looked up and nodded, Travellin' Man grinned then leaped into the air, seemingly hanging there for one beat before coming down, simultaneously hitting the boards and launching into his own version of Pops' tune that brought a deafening cheer.

I was astonished at the intensity of the music brought forth from these two old men. Music that reached down and touched a place in the very depth of my being that I knew had changed me forever.

I decided to risk it. Scrabbling for the camera, I shouldered past Lucas and Daniel, found a vantage point and filmed this glorious performance. When the battery light began to blink, I switched to my cell phone.

Both men were lost in the music, each soaked in sweat and each succumbing to an eyeball-rolling, face contorting, trance-like state of their own creation.

The footage I took that night caught Henry 'Pops' McCoy and Henry 'Travellin' Man' Watson playing like a force of nature, a two-man thunderstorm bringing down blues like hailstones.

Pops was the driving force, a steam locomotive powering the blues beat at full throttle and generating a vibe that pummeled everyone within range.

Travellin' Man's bottleneck was a brass siren, seducing everyone with its keening, beseeching sound; bringing forth by turns howls of anguish, murmurs of pleasure and wails of yearning lamentation.

I have no idea how long their session lasted. I remember Pops singing a bunch of songs, each one backed at a respectful distance by Travellin' Man, his playing toned down so as not to upstage Pops. I captured several songs on the voice recorder, my position close to the stage ensuring that the music was not overpowered by the cheering of the crowd, because cheer they did. The music lifted us all, huge jugs of whisky kept us up there. I have no idea where they came from, they just appeared and were passed around; everyone gorging on rotgut moonshine that brimmed out of mouths and spilled over clothing. We were all high on booze and blues. I danced until my legs ached, shouted until I was hoarse. I was wasted, my head pounding from the music, my throat raw and my senses befuddled from the harsh liquor. I needed to lie down, needed to sleep but was unable to move, possessed completely by a blues performance that had reached to my very core.

I have no recollection of how or when it ended. One minute I was standing by the stage and then I woke up on the bench, Lucas slapping my face.

"Yo' 'k, mister?" He said. "I's mighty sorry for slappin' yo' but yo' wouldn't wake up."

I looked around, the stage was empty and the juke-joint was only half-full. I asked Lucas where Pops and Travellin' Man were.

"Travellin' Man, him an' Daniel they in th' bathroom playin' craps an' Pops he outside gettin' his dirt... er, I means gettin' acquainted wid a young gal. Heyah, yo' want some water?"

Lucas handed me a battered tin mug that I emptied with one gulp.

I rubbed my face awake then grabbed my satchel. My phone, camera and voice recorder were safe. Relieved, I stood up and said I needed some fresh air.

At that point, the bathroom door flew open and Travellin' Man burst out.

"White Boy," he yelled. "Grab the gittars, we gots ta get outta here."

Behind him, I saw Daniel blocking the doorway; behind Daniel I saw some angry, drunk faces.

"Lucas, this fo' yo', block th' door behind us."

Travellin' Man grabbed a bunch of dollars from his pocket, handed them to Lucas then sprinted for the front door. Throwing the satchel around my neck I picked up the guitars and followed him.

As we hit the front porch, I heard the door slam behind us. Travellin' Man vaulted the wooden rail, stumbled, scrambled to his feet and then legged it towards the pick up. By the time I reached it the engine was running and Travellin' Man was clambering inside.

"Move yo' ass, White Boy, we gotta leave town."

# Hell Hounds

Somehow, I managed to get myself and both guitars into the cab, barely managing to grab the door as Travellin' Man reversed, turned and then launched the pickup away from the juke-joint.

"Wha's happenin' behind us? Anyone comin' afta' us?"

Craning my neck, I could see some commotion on the front porch; someone throw a rock that came nowhere near us and I cackled hysterically as someone else threw their hat to the ground in frustration.

"Ain' no laughin' matter, White Boy. Is they anyone comin' afta us?"

A small crowd had gathered but I couldn't see any vehicles moving.

"Tha's a close 'un," said Travellin' Man. "Made us a buncha dollars though, them country peckerheads, they so drunk they don' know which way's up. Wha's happenin' back there?"

I looked behind but could see only blackness. I didn't think anyone was following.

Once again the old pickup was being asked to punch above its weight and I braced myself in the cramped cab as we careered along the track at a speed far too fast to react to anything within the range of the ineffectual headlights.

Thankfully, Travellin' Man appeared to realise this and slowed the truck to a more reasonable speed. We approached a junction and turned onto a gravel road that was a blessed relief after the rough track. We drove about another mile when I felt the truck begin to slow.

I asked what was happening.

"Beats me," said Travellin' Man. "Got the throttle wide open."

The old Model T rallied, picked up speed as the revs increased, travelled a few hundred yards further and then backfired with a shotgun-blast that killed the engine. Mortally wounded; the pickup coasted silently to a halt, headlights dimming to extinction like the flickering eyelids of a dying geriatric.

We both got out and as I put the guitars in the pickup bed, Travellin' Man tried to revive the engine, cranking the starter handle several times before staggering away to lean exhausted against the door. I took over and cranked several times more.

Nothing.

Travellin' Man walked around to the fuel tank and unscrewed the cap. I felt the car rock as he shook it back and forth then heard a dull metallic clatter. "Motherfucker, I jus' dropped the Goddam cap." The car shook again, 'I can hear gasoline sloshin' 'round," he said. "Guess the motor's shot."

I looked around. Cotton fields stretched away from both sides of the road, a solid wall of blackness skirting the range of moonlit visibility that extended no more than fifty yards all around us.

"Yo' got any ideas, White Boy?"

I shook my head. Even if I had a set of tools and the faintest idea of what to look for there was not enough light to see what I was doing. I said we could stay where were and wait until daybreak, try and walk to the nearest town or head back to the juke-joint.

Travellin' Man cast a fearful glance at the void beyond the moonlight. "I gotta say, White Boy, they ain' none o'them options grabbin' my attenshun, right now."

He froze. "'the fuck wassat?"

Something rustled in the night, something not very far away.

We listened.

Silence.

Another rustle, the definite sound of foliage being shaken.

I scanned the darkness.

Fear and tension pulsed from Travellin' Man like heat from an infection.

The beginning of a whispered question was cut short by his frantic wave.

Silence.

Another movement.

I could feel my heartbeat in my chest, the pulse in my ears; my breathing became shallow and my senses heightened as my body tuned in to my imagination.

Darkness growing darker, black wall inching nearer.

Another movement, closer this time.

Travellin' Man pointed to a spot about ten feet away, a large cotton bush cloaked in moon shadow. I saw the barest quiver of a boll, the faintest scrit-scrat sound, and then silence.

Then another scrit-scrat, a snuffle, and then,

"MOTHERFUCKER!" Travellin' Man performed a crazy spastic dance, his right leg kicking at something unseen. I heard a soft thud, a high-pitched screech of pain then a dark shape flew through the air. Whatever it was hit the ground and then ran off squealing.

"Motherfuckin' rat ran over my Goddam foot, I jus' about shit my pants."

He stomped the ground again. "An' they's anotha one."

Something large collided with my shin. I looked down and shuddered with revulsion as a rat's tail dragged across my shoe. Several rats appeared from beneath the truck, all with a clear mission to be somewhere else. I looked around, Travellin' Man had stopped shouting and the stillness of the night was filled with screeching as hundreds of rats burst from the cotton field and flowed across the road, covering the ground like blood from a wound. I gripped the side of the truck as I felt rats brushing against my legs and running over and around my feet; their number increasing by the second, the air filled with a high-frequency din and the smell of rat piss.

Above the screeching, something in the dark bayed a long, low-pitched, rolling howl that bellowed dolefully across the blackness of landscape before falling away like a dying air-raid siren. After a heartbeat of silence, the call was answered by another and then another and another until it was impossible to work out where they were coming from.

Travellin' Man looked at me and opened the driver's door. "Get in the truck, White Boy."

When I hesitated his eyes grew wide. "Hellhounds," he yelled. "Get in the Goddam truck."

I had barely closed my door when something slammed into the side of the pickup with the force of a freight train.

"Oh sweet motherfucking Jesus Christ Lawd have mercy." Travellin' Man's knuckles shone white as he gripped the steering wheel, his eyes rolling in terror.

Shrieking like a child as another huge impact shook the truck, he began hyperventilating, panting the words, "Oh shit, oh shit, oh shit."

BANG.

BANG.

BANG.

BANG.

The pickup rocked sideways as sledgehammer blows pummelled the ancient Ford.

All the action was on Travellin' Man's side and by now, he was almost catatonic with terror. I kept shouting at him to tell me what was happening, but then something slammed into the door on my side. I turned towards the impact just as an enormous dog-like creature backed up and launched itself at us. It was immense, like a Rottweiler crossed with a grizzly bear and with a head the size of a V8 engine. The truck shook again and again as the beast cannoned into the side with the force of an explosion.

Travellin' Man was petrified, rocking backwards and forwards.

"Oh sweet Jesus, we gon' die, Hellhounds found us, they gon' rip us apart. Oh sweet motherfuckin' Christ."

The scene outside was terrifying. Inside the cab it was bedlam, the attacks were relentless and I couldn't see any way out of this. The truck was being destroyed.

The beast on my side thundered into the front corner of the cab, bursting the door from its latch and sending a crack racing diagonally across the windscreen. I hung onto the door handle, praying that I could keep it closed as the hound backed up and charged yet again. The collision sprang the bonnet, flapping it upwards like a broken wing. Distracted, the beast leapt towards it, tore it from the truck and tried to kill it in a frenzy of head-shaking that ended with the bonnet flying through the air.

Howling with frustrated blood-lust, the hound attacked the engine, ripping components away and tearing apart the front end in a ferocious onslaught of primeval rage.

I'd never seen such strength and aggression in an animal; the attack lasted several minutes until the hound, panting, its head plastered in oil, backed up, took a breath and launched itself once more at the engine.

I heard the brief hiss of released pressure and caught a whiff of boiling engine coolant. Frantically the beast span away, skittering in circles and shaking its head as it tried to paw scalding liquid from its eyes. Agonized croaks rasped from its ruined throat and then it stumbled and collapsed with a dull, heavy thump, convulsing and retching as the hot poisonous coolant blistered through its body.

BAM

BAM

BAM

Travellin' Man, eyes shut and praying mournfully, was still rocking back and forth as two hellhounds took it turns to maintain a sustained attacked on his side of the truck. Each collision wrought more damage and it was only a matter of time before the cab structure would be demolished. I didn't want to think about what would happen when the hounds reached us.

My back, wrists and hands ached from the exertion of keeping the door shut; despite my efforts, each collision would crack open the door and I would have to pull it back and try to hang on to it.

Two hounds smashed into the truck in a combined assault, I lost my grip and the door flew open. Shrieking in terror I leaned out and grasped the flapping door. As I slammed it shut the updraft of air carried with it the whiff of engine coolant along with another, more acrid smell.

I turned to Travellin' Man; by now he was deep in shock and couldn't comprehend anything. Holding my door with my right hand I searched Travellin' Man's pockets with my left and nearly cried with relief as my fingers closed around not one but two books of matches.

It took three punches to his face to get his attention. His head swivelled slowly around, tears mixing with skeins of drool that hung from his chin as he stared at me with the vacant expression of a lobotomy patient.

I screamed as the windscreen shattered, and then one of the hounds jumped onto the load bed and commenced battering the rear of the cab.

I shouted my plan, but Travellin' Man just stared at me.

Fuck it, shit or bust.

Scared beyond belief, I kicked the door open, jumped from the cab and felt something splash over my foot. Outside, the hounds seemed even larger, their snarls louder and more menacing. Fighting the urge to escape into the darkness, I ran a few steps and then turned.

Snarling, both hellhounds swung their massive heads in my direction as I tore a match from one of the books. Two pairs of eyes fixed me in a death stare as the two beasts, their muscles trembling in anticipation, crouched in readiness to strike.

Praying that I was clear of the gasoline, I struck the match and then shrieked in terror and frustration as it broke in half. Forcing myself to take a deep breath, my hands trembling like a palsy victim; I tore out another match, struck it and shrieked again, this time in delight as the flame burst into life. I lit the match book just as the hounds took off, and threw it into the pool of gasoline just as they were airborne.

I hit the ground just as the vapour ignited in a searing blast of scorched air, engulfing the hellhounds and the pickup in a huge fireball that lit up the night.

Flames licked at my ankles and as I scrabbled dirt over my burning shoes, the air was filled the smell of burning fur and the blood-chilling howls of two beasts in mortal agony.

I almost felt sorry for them as I ran around to the other side of the truck, just in time to see Travellin' Man run screaming from the cab, his back and right arm trailing fire.

I sprinted after him, tackling him to the ground just as the fuel tank ignited with an explosion that sent metal fragments whistling overhead. Travellin' Man was still burning and I rolled him over and over until the flames were extinguished and then half dragged him back towards the fire.

Both hellhounds were dead, their screams long replaced by roaring flames and the crackle of what was left of the blazing truck.

Travellin' Man sat cross-legged, staring vacantly ahead as I checked him over. Luckily, he had no injuries but he was going to need another suit.

He looked defeated.

Patting him on the shoulder I sat next to him and told him we were safe now. I said that the truck would burn for ages and would keep away any other hounds that might be nearby and anyway, it would be daylight soon.

He didn't respond, but just sat there in shocked silence, immobile save for the barely imperceptible rise and fall of his shoulders in time with his coarse, shallow breaths.

So we said nothing and watched the fire.

I was right about the truck. It burned long into the night, the dying of the flames coinciding with the welcome band of grey morning light rising inexorably to spill over the lip of the horizon and rinse away the malevolent darkness.

Travellin' Man hawked from deep in his throat and spat a huge gob of mucus. "White Boy," he said. "We must be the two luckiest motherfuckers they evah was. How'n th' hell we survive that?"

I said I had no idea. Just lucky, I guessed.

"Luck? Ain' no luck."

Turning towards me, he offered his hand. "S' down t' yo, White Boy. Yo' got us outta there; I thought we's near about gone fo'ever."

He shook his head. "We seen th' hellhounds an' we still around t' talk about it, sheeeit. Yo' see the size o' them ugly-ass motherfuckers."

When I asked him where they came from, he turned away.

"From th' other side o' th' darkness," he said. "Tha's where they from."

He stood up, his joints cracking as he stretched and yawned.

"Tha's th' end o' the truck," he said. "An' I guess the gittars is all burned up, too?"

I'd forgotten about them. Standing up, I walked over to the smoking remains of the pickup. A quick look confirmed that there was nothing left worth salvaging, and then something caught my eye.

Travellin' Man saw it too and strode towards a large metallic object lying in the damp black soil of the cotton field.

Yelling a triumphant, "Well god-dam! Musta got blowed in th' air when the gas tank went up." He picked up the National, brushed off the mud, gave it a cursory inspection and then ran his thumb across the strings.

His face split into a huge white-toothed grin as the open G-chord rang out clear as a bell.

"We got us a gittar," he said. "We can still make us some money."

I said that he already made some money and that was how we came to be here.

His grin turned sheepish. "I nevah could walk away from a dice game, White Boy. Yo' knows how it is."

When I asked him how much he'd got away with he grinned again, delved into his jacket pocket and produced a wad of dollar bills.

"Gotta be fifty bucks," he said. "Musta got me some lucky dice," he winked. "Seems they jus' cain' be beat."

I said that he must be right. After all, we managed to outrun a bunch of angry gamblers, escape an attack from hellhounds and survive a gas tank explosion. I said that he must have weighted his dice with some lucky mercury.

Travellin' Man shrugged. "We still got fifty bucks," he said.

I gave up and looked around. In every direction, cotton fields stretched away to meet the rim of the vast upturned bowl painted in flawless cobalt blue that was the early morning Mississippi sky.

149

"Sure is a perty mornin', White Boy."

I asked him if he knew where we were.

"Beats me," he said. "But I thinks we need to keep a'movin' that way."

I looked down at my satchel; it was scorched and covered in mud but everything inside was unmarked.

Taking a final look around and finding nothing worth taking with us, Travellin' Man and I fell into step and walked on down the road.

After a time we reached an intersection with a two-lane highway.

"I knows where we, is," said Travellin' Man. "This here's Highway 61." He pointed to the right. "An' Vicksburg ain' but a few miles that way, we can git us a meal an' git cleaned up."

So we turned right and kept walking.

The deserted highway stretched away from us and on both sides, cotton fields flowing in the opposite direction at a speed that matched our pace.

We walked on in silence.

With its steel body, the resonator was a heavy guitar and Travellin' Man carried it by balancing it on his shoulder and holding the neck to steady it.

I offered to take a turn carrying it but Travellin' Man shook his head.

"Ain' nothin'," he said.

# Medicine Show

Some time later, a small town appeared on the horizon; its arrival coinciding with the sound of hoof beats behind us.

We stopped and turned around to see two emaciated ponies pulling a wagon that looked like a huge wooden box on wheels. It was driven by a small, round white man wearing a dusty suit beneath which a brightly-coloured waistcoat and a once-white shirt were visible. He wore a black bow tie at a jaunty angle and a battered trilby that had clearly seen better days. As he approached, the man stroked his dapper moustache and goatee beard, waved a hand in welcome and slowed the wagon.

"Whoooooaahh dere, bucks."

The ponies lifted their heads and snorted as they brought the wooden cart to a halt.

The man waved again, winked and in a sing-song Irish accent said, "Good mornin' to ye, me fine fellows and unless I'm very much mistaken you'll not be be seein' a finer mornin' today."

His eyes twinkled in a shallow bonhomie that belied the way he sized up Travellin' Man and myself like a hungry cat contemplating a pair of feeding birds.

Jumping down from the driver's seat, he raised his top hat and pointed to the side of his wagon on which were painted the brightly coloured words:

Doctor Fabulous Medicine Show!!!

The man gave a theatrical bow and launched into a flamboyant, arm-waving sales pitch.

"Please allow me to introduce myself," he said. "I am de one, de only, Sean Ignatius O'Flannery, also known as Doctor Fabulous, proprietor of the Doctor Fabulous Medicine Show and purveyor of ..."

A true showman, his arm-waving misdirected us long enough to allow a bottle of dark liquid to appear in his right hand which he then presented to us in the manner of a wine waiter to a connoisseur.

"The Doctor Fabulous patent elixir of love, life, healt' and happiness. Made from de tears of a rattlesnake, dis medicinal compound is most efficacious in every way. Why, jus' one sip of dis nectar will change your life forever. Guaranteed to cure anyting dat ails ye's. If ye's have got it, dis will get rid of it, if ye's have lost it dis will get it back and if ye's never had it den dere's nuttin' I can do for ye's. Also available in tablet form and strike me down if it's not a bargain at only..."

I interrupted by saying that I wasn't buying today.

Dr Fabulous winked and smiled. "Ah, right so," he said. "Ye can't blame a man for trying, sure ye can't."

Pocketing the bottle, he calmed down a little and looked us up and down.

"Sure, ye's bot' look like ye've been hit by lightning and ye're smelling kinda smokey?"

When I told him that our pickup truck had caught fire his eyes narrowed as he listened to me speak.

"Now dat's not an accent from around here," he said.

He gave a thin, shallow smile when I replied that neither was his.

"Dat's as maybe," he said. "But I'm tinking dat maybe you're a long, long way from where yous belong? A fella such as yerself needs to be careful in a place like this."

When I didn't reply, he turned his attention to Travellin' Man.

"And you, me fine black feller, what might your story be?"

Travellin' Man said nothing, his face clouded with suspicion.

"Dat's a fine looking instrument yous are carryin', do ye play?"

Travellin' Man grunted. "Gittar b'longs t' White Boy, but I plays a little."

Dr Fabulous turned back to me and beamed. "Yous play too?" He said. "But dat's marvellous! For was I not tinking jus' now that I could do wid findin' a musicianeer, for to help me drum up a crowd and sell me wonderful product, and strike me pink I happen upon two o'dem."

He looked us up and down.

"And sure, ye's bot' look like you could do wid a little helpin' yourselves."

Stepping backwards, he folded his arms, contemplated us for a few seconds then said, "I'll tell you what I'll do. Yous come along wid me to the next town, play some foine music while I set up me pitch and I'll give ye's a dollar each. How does that sound?"

Travellin' Man looked at me. "Whatchoo think, White Boy?"

I said why not.

Dr Fabulous was ecstatic. "Das just marvellous."

He spat in his palm and then shook hands with us both. "Nuttin' loike completin' a bidness deal forst ting in de mornin. Sets ye's up for the day."

His face split into a beaming smile and for a second his glittering eyes lost their hardness.

"Providence has indeed shined on us all."

Turning to Travellin' Man he said, "Now, ye's don't mind walking along behind do ye? Only de wagon's a bit full of me essentials, dese old nags have seen better days and dere's only room for two of us up front, and it

wouldn't be right for a white feller to be seen walking along wid a darkie ridin'
in style."

I stepped forward and said that he was out of order.

For a brief instant, violence flashed behind his eyes.

"Well now dere's a ting," he said, his voice flat. "An English feller
preachin' to an Irishman about injustice to his fellow man."

I held his stare and said that if Travellin' Man couldn't ride on the cart
then we'd both walk.

The Irishman shrugged. "Suit yerselves."

With that he climbed aboard the cart, snapped the reins and yelled, "Get
on wid ye, ye's lazy pair o' bastards."

As the horses reluctantly took the strain, he turned to us and winked.
"Oim talkin' to dem, not yous."

Travellin' Man and I fell into step behind as the cart rattled on down
the road.

"What he said's right," said Travellin' Man. "Show a nigga favour over
a white man, yo' gon' attract trouble like flies roun' a pile o'shit."

He touched my arm. "I knows why yo' doin' it," he said. "An' I kinda
'preciate it, but it ain't yo' gon' get whupped o' set on fire o' strung up on th'
edge o' town. I ain' gon' be no Uncle Tom an' I ain' gon' be no sport fo' no
white niggas. We clear on that?"

*****

It was mid-morning when we walked into the town square.

Doctor Fabulous tied the horses to a hitching rail then opened a door at
the rear of the cart.

Leaning inside, he removed a large canvas bag, inside of which were
several fist-sized wooden wedges; these he used to brace the wheels. Next, he
pulled out a short ladder. Placing it against the side of the cart, he checked that it

was secure and then once more leaned in and dragged out a wooden box containing about two dozen medicine bottles and smaller bottles of tablets.

Removing a handkerchief from his pocket, Doctor Fabulous removed his trilby, wiped his face, replaced his hat then squinted up at the sky.

"Sure and it's a hot one already."

Turning to face us, he said, "Well now, I tink we're almost ready t'go, all we needs is a crowd. Tink you's two can play us up some punters?"

Travellin' Man shrugged. "Sho' thing, boss."

Turning to me he said, "I done this kinda thing before, yo' mind if'n I use yo' gittar?"

I said of course.

"Dat's marvelous, you's can play on top o' me cart, better dan any stage in any t'eatre in de world. Come on now, me coloured friend, ascend the stairway to heaven, fame and fortune and play us up a strong crowd wid money t' burn."

Travellin' Man clambered up the steps, the cart rocking as he climbed onto the roof. Running his fingers over the strings, he smiled down at me. "She sho' a sweet-soundin' gittar."

Sunlight flashed off the steel guitar as Travellin' Man adjusted the strap over his shoulder and made himself comfortable.

"This here's a song I heard a fella playin' in a jug band one time."

I smiled as he played the first note, a swooping slide on the bass string that made a deep 'whoop' noise which he followed with an intricate finger-picked melody.

His voice rang out clear and strong as he belted out 'I Will Turn Your Money Green', one of my favourite songs by Furry Lewis.

155

I heard a noise behind me and turned to see Doctor Fabulous lift a stone jug to his lips and blow across the open neck, producing a 'whoop' sound that matched Travellin's Man bass slide.

The music was infectious, my foot tapping as I felt myself succumbing once again to the hypnotic power of the blues notes and Travellin' Man's raw, earthy voice.

Glancing around, I saw that a small crowd was gathering around the cart, with more people walking towards us.

Handing the stone jug to me, Doctor Fabulous said, "Here, you's can take over, I have t' get ready for me show."

Travellin' Man finished 'Turn Your Money Green', began playing a catchy melody then looked down at me. "How 'bout K.C. Moan, White Boy?"

I nodded and self-consciously attempted to keep time and blow a clear bass note as he sang, "*I thought I heard that K.C when she blowed, she blowed like my woman's onboard...*"

To my ears I sounded rubbish, but then I glanced up to catch Travellin' Man wink at me with a huge grin. My shyness evaporated and my grin matched his as the music clicked and we got into a vibe.

More and more people appeared around the cart, some dancing to the music, clapping their hands, stamping feet or just nodding appreciatively.

"Tha's right..."

"Blow that jug, White Boy..."

All too soon the song came to an end and Doctor Fabulous looked around and motioned for Travellin' Man to wind up the performance. Travellin' Man nodded then bowed, the crowd applauding as he stepped down from the cart.

Doctor Fabulous mounted the ladder, took centre-stage on the roof of the cart, waited for the crowd to settle and began his pitch.

"Please allow me to introduce myself," he said. "I am de one, de only, Doctor Fabulous, proprietor of the Doctor Fabulous Medicine Show and I'm here to postulate, speculate, communicate and convey the wonders that are many-fold that surround my miracle product like the aura from a heavenly throng. A miracle product so potent, powerful and palliative that medical science has long fought to remove it from the grasp of the common man lest they be found out for de charlatans dat dey are."

He paused to take a breath.

"Good people who have taken the time to stop, gather and listen, you's are exactly the kind of people that I want as customers and it's to you's directly that I'm going to demonstrate in my own inimitable, idiosyncratic, inimaginable and indeniably unique manner, de product that I behold before ye's."

A bottle materialised in his hand. Doctor Fabulous acknowledged the gasp of the crowd with a smile and a nod.

"You's may well gasp," he said. "For you's are de lucky ones. D'ose of you's that have the foresight, the intelligence quotient, the good manners and last but not least the wherewithal to this miraculous and wonderful potion will be the ones that benefit from a long and healthy existence."

Holding the bottle aloft he pointed to the printed label.

"Ladies, gentlemen and others, what I'm holding here is de liquid solution to all of yer dreams. For dis is the one, de only Doctor Fabulous's patent elixir of love, life, healt' and happiness. Ladies and gentlemen, dis marvellous concoction, dis medicinal compound, most efficacious in every way; is fermented from de tears of a rattlesnake, mixed in precise quantities with a secret mixture distilled from the life-giving waters of the great Mississippi river and blessed by a Placebo Indian medicine man. Drink it down or rub it in, jus' one sip or jus' one drop of dis nectar will reap an instant reward. Guaranteed to cure anyting dat ails ye's. If ye's have got it, dis will get rid of it, if ye's have lost it dis will get it back and if ye's never had it den dere's nuttin' I can do for ye's."

Taking a breath, Dr Fabulous misdirected the crowd once again and another, much smaller bottle appeared in his hand.

Acknowledging more gasps with another smile and a nod, he paused to survey the audience and then pointed to the new bottle.

"Now den," he declared. "In de interests of your convenience, for time is indeed money, I've made dis treatment even more versatile."

Pausing for effect, he held the bottle aloft. "By employing the latest medical techniques to compress, compact and compartmentalise dis magical, inspirational recipe into a handy capsule form designed specifically to act directly in the gut and cast out the tapeworm via de natural course o'tings and in a completely pain-free manner. If any of you's have de worms, den one, just one of dese miracle capsules will give dramatic results within 24 hours."

Travellin' Man tapped me on the shoulder. "Don' know boutchoo, White Boy," he said. "But I's hungry an' I ain' gon' hang round listenin' to no snake-oil pitch when they's good eatin' t' be done."

He looked around, then hawked and spat a gob of soot-tinged mucus between his feet.

"Stinkin' o' smoke, tho', we needs us a change o' clothes first."

I said that this was getting to be a habit.

Travellin' Man grinned. "Tha's life on th' road," he said. "Follow me."

Leaving Dr Fabulous extolling the virtues of his miracle product, we threaded our way through the crowd. Travellin' Man led the way as he strolled away from the town square and down a street that began with a few tumbledown wooden storefronts and then became a gravel road bisecting yet more cotton fields as it stretched into the distance.

"Tha's th' place, White Boy."

I followed the direction of Travellin' Man's pointed finger towards a row of coffins propped against the wall of the last building on the street. A hand-made sign nailed above the door read:

*Horace Handley, Mortician.*

Travellin' Man winked. "Ain' no better place to get clothes than from thems as don' need 'em no more."

Before I could answer, he was halfway across the street and striding purposefully towards the store.

By the time I followed him into the building, Travellin' Man was standing at a desk in the corner of a dismal room lined with coffins and talking to a tall, thin, gaunt white man with a shock of white hair, hollowed cheeks, dark patches around his eyes and the look of someone for whom death is a companion.

Travellin' Man turned to me. "This here's Mister Handley, he gon' give us what we needs."

Mr Handley's eyes flickered in my direction, blinked once then glanced over to a coffin leaning against the wall into which I knew I would fit perfectly.

Turning back to Travellin' Man, Mr Handley cleared his throat and in a slow, deep-voiced drawl said, "Y'all can both choose one pair o' suit pants, one suit coat an' one shirt fo' five dollars. Fo' that, I'll throw in a pair o' shoes an' a hat an' y'all can keep what-all's in th' pockets."

Travellin' Man nodded. "They in th' usual place?"

Mr Handley lifted his head imperceptibly.

"This way, White Boy."

Once again I followed Travellin' Man, this time towards a door at the back of the room, beyond which was a smaller room, heavy with the nose-wrinkling smell of ancient body odour and crammed with clothes rails festooned with garments of every description.

As I looked closer, I could see that the clothes were arranged roughly in order of size. Hearing a movement behind me I turned to see Mr Handley staring at me. Once again his eyes flickered up and down and then he pointed to a row of jackets.

"Yo' size starts at the left side o' that rail, suit pants is inside each suit coat an' size ten shoes is over yonder."

I was about to ask how he knew my size when he said, "I been measurin' folks fo'ever. Soon as I seen yo, I knew yo's five-eleven, hunnerd an' fifty pounds, forty-inch chest an' 32 on th' waist and 32-inches on each leg."

Turning to Travellin' Man he said, "Fo' an extra dollar yo' can wash-up out back, looks like yo' both could do wid a little bathin'."

With that he turned and left the room.

"Bidness kinda slow," said Travellin' Man. "Folks don' get buried ovah here."

When I asked him why all the coffins were on display, Travellin' Man shrugged. "Some folks holds on t' what they had befo' they cross over, gives 'em kinda a comfortin' feelin', familiarity an' such."

He picked out a dark, pin-striped jacket, double-breasted with wide lapels and held it against himself.

"This look kinda sharp."

Removing his own jacket he tried it on.

"Whatchoo think, White Boy?"

He reminded me of the photograph of Robert Johnson, and I said that he did indeed look sharp.

This earned me a self-satisfied nod and a muttered, "Damn straight."

A few minutes later we had picked out a change of clothes and carried them through to a large room containing two mortician's slabs and a large stone sink.

Travellin' Man laid out his new clothes on one of the slabs, began to undress and unleashed the rank smell of a body long unwashed. I had a bad feeling that that I smelled the same.

Removing his clothes, he turned towards the sink then stopped at the sound of my gasp.

Every inch of skin on his back was disfigured with raised welts and lumps of ugly scar tissue.

Leaning over the sink, Travellin' Man opened the taps, began scooping water over himself and then reached for a fist-sized bar of carbolic soap. He stayed silent as he rubbed the soap and covered himself in a lather that smelled of coal tar.

When the last of the suds had been rinsed away, Travellin' Man wrapped a towel around his waist and turned towards me.

"Tha's what happen when Black Annie writes her name up an' down yo' back."

I asked him who Black Annie was.

"Ain' a who, it's a what. Black Annie's a short leather strap, used fo' whuppin' convicts. Got me arrested one time, judge sent me down t' th' county farm. Captain there, he took again's me, said I looked t' be kinda ambitious, said I's one uppity nigga, said I needs a lesson an' Black Annie gon' be th' teacher."

Twisting around to show me his back, Travellin' Man said, "Whatchoo seein' there took six hours t' 'chieve. I's forced down an' hog tied on my knees, had th' shirt ripped offa my back an' then th' Cap'n an' his trustees they took turns t' whup my black ass."

I watched his eyes refocus to the middle-distance.

161

"Six hours," he whispered. "Six hours o' screamin' an' hollerin' an' carryin' on like a child; pleadin' fo' mercy then beggin' fo' death. Alls I could see was th' legs o' folk linin' up to take they turns a-whuppin' me. Six hours o' hearin' they grunts an' th' crack o' leather an' th' jokes they's tellin' when they took a rest from whuppin' me to drink rotgut 'shine; hearin' 'em gettin' drunker an' angrier; feelin' splashes o' they sweat an' th' burnin' sun on wha's left o' th' skin on my back."

He turned back to me.

"Jus' cos the cap'n say I looked uppity."

I said I didn't know what to say.

Travellin' Man shrugged. "Ain' nothin' to say. Cain' change wha's done. Don' confront me no mo'. Life in th' south, it ain' all juke-joints an' fish-fries an' blues music - not if yo' a nigga."

He shook his head, brought himself back to the present then wrinkled his nose.

"White Boy, yo' stinkin' like hog-shit on a dead hog. Clean yo' ass up an' then we gon' go somewhere an' git us a good drink an' sump'n t'eat."

His face split into a grin. "Maybe even git yo' some pussy, whatchoo think 'bout that?"

I thought about Stella and turned my face away.

*****

Later, washed and wearing new-old clothes, Travellin' Man and I walked back towards the town square.

A large crowd had gathered around the wagon and Doctor Fabulous seemed to be doing a roaring trade passing bottles of pills to outstretched hands in return for dollar notes or coins that he slipped inside his waistcoat.

"Tape worms my ass," said Travellin' Man.

I asked him what he meant.

162

"He sellin' pills fo' folks thinkin' they got's a tapeworm. Yo' takes one with a glass o' whisky an' th' nex' day it look like tiny worms be fallin' out yo' ass."

When I said that it sounded effective, Travellin' Man grunted.

"Ain' nothin' but cotton thread," he said. "They pills ain' nothin' but flour-paste wid' a few inches o' cotton thread inside. Yo' eats th' flour-paste, flour paste turns t' shit but th' thread carries on' through. Comes out lookin' like a worm covered in shit. Ain' nobody ever gon' look close 'nough to see wha's goin' on."

I shook my head.

"Some folks," scowled Travellin' Man. "They lives they lives, finds they way thro' the world an' then they passes over an' spend th' rest o' they existence in this world an' they still dumber than a Goddam fence-post."

He paused for a second, produced his dice and then winked at me. "Bring 'em on, I say."

Dr Fabulous looked up at the sound of our laughter.

"Well now, look at you's two enjoying a promenade about town wid yer fancy new suits."

Removing his hat, he gave a showman's bow and with twinkle in his eye said, "And Oi have t' say dat ye's bot' look a lot brighter than de last folks t' wear dem clothes."

He winked again. "Gimme a coupla minutes."

He turned back to the crowd. "OK folks, de show's over cos' de wagon's empty. Oi have t' tell ye's dat nowhere else in my travels have I ever sold out of every single product in such a short space o'time. Oi'd like t' tank all of ye's who recognised de efficacious power of de restorative medicament's and palliatives you's have been shown today. Oi've never seen such collective wisdom evidenced in such a manner. Dis must be de smartest town in de whole of Mississippi and oi tink you's should all congratulate yerselves and give yerselves a round of applause."

Dr Fabulous' began clapping, his broad grin so infectious that within seconds everyone in the crowd had joined in. A true showman, he milked the applause for just long enough and then tipped his hat. "Tank you's for yer custom, oi'll be back around here in a few days and oi hope t' see each and everyone of you's then."

With that he turned and busied himself packing away the wagon as the crowd dispersed. When everyone had gone, Travellin' Man cleared his throat, "Quite a show, doc," he said. "I betchoo made yo'self a whole buncha money."

Doctor Fabulous turned around slowly.

"Somet'in' in your voice is tellin' me dat's more dan a polite observation."

Narrowing his eyes he looked Travellin' Man up and down. "Have you got somet'in' on your mind, big fella?"

Travellin' Man shrugged. "I jus' wonderin' if'n yo' was a gamblin' man?"

The Irishman exploded with laughter. "A gamblin' man?"

He fumbled for a handkerchief and wiped his eyes. "A gamblin' man, he says. If you's tink for one moment dat oi'm going up against you an' dem loaded bones of yours, den you's can tink again. Tank's but no tanks, but oi tink oi'll keep me cash to meself."

He chuckled for a long time, his wet eyes sparkling. Finally regaining his composure, his face grew serious; pointing towards the centre of town he said, "If it's gamin' yer after, dere's a roomin' house just along de street dat might just accommodate you. It's called de 'Banty Rooster'."

Smiling at the way Travellin' Man's eyes glittered hungrily, Doctor Fabulous winked and said, "Oi tink it could be an adventurous evening for ye's bot'."

Travellin' Man rubbed his chin. "Banty Rooster, huh?"
He turned to me. "You know, I'm feelin' kinda lucky, White Boy." he said. "Yo' an' me, we jus' come through a whole shitload o' unpleasantness an' yet here we is, still standin' an' lookin' perty damn sharp. I thinks we deserves us a little entertainment an' maybe even a chance t' win us some cash for t' get me a gittar, whatchoo think?"

I shrugged and said that it was up to him. All I wanted right then was a meal and to sleep in a proper bed.

Doctor Fabulous reached into his jacket and produced a bill-fold. Peeling off four five-dollar bills he handed us two bills each and said, "Dere y'go. Yer payment for de show an' a little bit extra."

With that, he tipped his hat and clambered aboard the wagon. Picking up the reins he waved down at us. "And now oi'll bid you's bot' a fond farewell, good luck to ye's bot'."

# The Banty Rooster

The Banty Rooster was in the poor part of town and was a two-storey building that had seen better days. Four windows faced onto the street; two of them were boarded up with slats of wood nailed crudely into place.

"He'p yo' folks?"

On the porch, a wizened old black man creaked on an ancient rocking chair next to a spittoon, the contents of which I didn't want to think about.

"We lookin' fo' a coupla rooms," said Travellin' Man.

The old man eyed me suspiciously, hawked and spat into the metal pot then turned to Travellin' Man.

"How long y'all plannin' on stoppin'?"

Travellin' Man glanced at me and then shrugged. "Jus' one night, maybe two, we don' got no plans."

The old man nodded. "I gots a coupla rooms, ain' nothin' fancy but they gots a mattress an' the bed bugs comes fo' free."

He thought this was the funniest thing in the world and commenced a paroxysm of wheezing laughter that turned rapidly into a fusillade of short barking coughs and ended in a sound like a dead body being dragged over gravel. Gripping the arms of the rocking chair, the old man hunched forwards, his body heaving in time with dark liquid noises that emanated from his throat and culminated in a spectacular gob of dark mucus which landed in the spittoon with a sound that causes nightmares.

After inspecting his handiwork, the old man lifted his head and grinned. Tiny threads of spittle hung from toothless gums and swayed in the rattling breeze of diseased air. "Been waitin' fo' that'n t' come out for near about a week." He said.

167

"Yo' mus' be mighty proud," said Travellin' Man.

Raising himself on skinny, quivering arms, the old man staggered upright and motioned us to follow him.

The front door opened to a single, large room. To the right, a narrow staircase hugged the wall as it ascended towards a dark gloom. The old man headed left towards a bar running half the length of the opposite wall. The floor-space between was taken up with a random scattering of mismatched tables and chairs, all facing in the vague direction of a small stage at the back of the room upon which stood a battered old upright piano.

Reaching the bar, the old man stepped behind and opened a musty old book that lay on the counter. Licking his finger he made a great show of flicking pages then turning the book around to face us.

"Yo' can have rooms One an' Two." He paused, and then leered. "Unless yo' wantin' th' honeymoon suite, that is?" His cackling produced another bout of rasping coughs but thankfully nothing else.

Travellin' Man signed first, picking up the pen he scrawled a crude X next to the old man's finger.

"Yo' sign here," he said pointing to the line below. "Yo' got room Two."

Shrugging at my illegible scrawl, the old man slammed the book shut. "Upstairs on yo' left," he rasped.

Travellin' Man nodded. "Any place we can get sumpen' t'eat?"

The old man shrugged again. "They's a place nex' do', serves chicken wings an' refried beans; ain' nothin' fancy but then this ain' a fancy part o' town."

"Got that right," muttered Travellin' Man.

The old man turned to me. "Yo' don' got much t'say?"

I shrugged and said that when you've got nothing to say it's best to say nothing.

"Ain' from roun' here, neither," he said.

I said that I hear that a lot.

The old man's face crumpled beneath a toothless and enigmatic smile. "Ain't none o'mine," he said.

Next door was a small diner that reeked of stale cooking fat. Travellin' Man selected a booth at the rear and we sat down. Remembering the last time I was in a diner, I asked Travellin' Man if there was likely to be a problem with me being there.

"Beats the hell outta me," he said.

A young black waiter appeared. "Hear yo' got re-fried beans, son?" said Travellin' Man.

"Best damn beans in town," said the waiter.

Travellin' Man grunted. "Give us two plates an' two cold beers."

The waiter returned first with two bottles of Jax and then with two plates of reddish-brown congealed mess served with rice. My initial resentment at Travellin' Man for ordering for me evaporated at the first delicious mouthful and confirmed that looks can indeed be deceiving. I cleared my plate in rapid time and ordered some more.

Travellin' Man nodded. "Pretty good, huh?"

I agreed that it was and he nodded again. "Yo' don' wan' be eatin' no chicken wings," he said.

When I asked him why not, he replied without looking up, "Well, fo' one thing, it ain' chicken."

Later, replete with food and buzzing from beer and tiredness, we made our way to our rooms where, ignoring the stains on the bare mattress, I collapsed onto the metal-framed bed and slept a long, dreamless sleep.

\*\*\*\*\*

I awoke to sunset streaming dark orange light through battered wooden shutters, projecting shadows like prison-bars across the wall.

As I lay there, I reflected on all that had happened so far, the people I had met and the places and events that I'd seen; but it was the things I had done that took centre-stage in my thoughts.

Like I said before, I'd read pretty much every blues reference book ever written, listened to old recordings over and over again, not so much for the music - which is wonderful in its own right - but also for the subtle nuances; the sound of Robert Johnson's bottleneck clattering against the frets of his cheap Stella guitar, Charley Patton's growling ad-libs or the sound of a steam train passing the hotel room in Grafton, Wisconsin where Son House was recording 'Shetland Pony Blues'.

These were nuggets of pure gold, because they opened a window back through the years and granted me the briefest access to a time where recordings were made ad-hoc using rudimentary equipment that captured everything including the music, adding context and imbuing an atmosphere sadly lacking in later, sterile recording environments.

To me, these precious sound bites instilled a yearning to know more about the world surrounding these unique archives. And here I was, apparently living the itinerant life about which I had read and fantasised so much; playing the blues in 1930s Mississippi with some of the very musicians who previously I had listened to on scratchy old 78 records in comfortable, safe, middle-class, Middle-England. I had, it seemed, been given a backstage pass to an ongoing blues gig where everything is played, including the music.

Be careful what you wish for, they say. I had witnessed authentic blues music, but I had also seen people killed. Living the supposed blues life I had been kidnapped and had fought someone who had a gun in their hand. By my own actions I had rescued Travellin' Man and myself from an attack by a pack of monstrous, terrifying beasts. Each encounter with Fat Man and Gabel terrified me, but so far I had stood my ground.

As I lay in that frugal room I reflected on the obvious; it was as if I had become a different person. Everything that I had witnessed and experienced since meeting Fat Man; every single thing, was a million miles away from my previous life, a life that I was finding difficult to recall.

So far, the pace of events had meant living 'in the moment' with little time to pause for reflection. But as I lay on the bare mattress, I realised that I had to concentrate, focus really hard to recreate any memories of my previous life, memories which were becoming indistinct, as if fading gradually from view like a photograph left too long in sunlight.

Meeting Fat Man, it seemed, had been Day Zero for me and everything in my life beforehand was of no consequence. I suppose I should have felt anxiety, regret or sorrow at the slow disappearance of the mental video clips of my life and the loss of those closest to me.

I tried, but in truth I felt nothing. Every second I was in this new life I was reliving the thrill of driving south from Memphis and crossing into Mississippi for the very first time. I was lost; the blues had taken hold of me and I was moving forwards with no thought of anything other than a curiosity about where this odyssey would take me next.

I didn't have to wait long.

A fist hammered on my door. "Yo' 'wake, White Boy?"

I stood up, crossed the room and unlocked the door.

Travellin' Man entered, sporting a wide grin and a wooden acoustic guitar.

"I tol' yo' my bones is lucky." His grin split even wider. "I couldn' sleep so I took me t' wanderin' roun', found me a dice game on th' outskirts o' town.

Won me jus' enough t' git this gittar, but not enough t' git folks riled up. Whatchoo think?"

He thrust it at me then marched over to the window and opened the shutters wide. Dying sunlight flooded the room as I sat on the bed and inspected the guitar. It was a Gibson and it sounded wonderful. I messed about, experimenting with a few blues riffs and then settled into a 12-bar groove.

"Yo' got it, White Boy." I looked up to see Travellin' Man nodding as he reached for my resonator, slipped a bottleneck on his finger and waited for the moment. Soon my clumsy playing was accompanied by the sparse, keening sound that only a National can make.

Once again, all notion of time disappeared as I sat in a dingy, small-town hotel room in Mississippi, making music with one of the best bluesmen never to be recorded as another day died slowly, its blood staining a sky soon to be wiped clean by darkness. All thoughts of everything that had gone before were carried away with the blues. Once again I was 'in the moment' and once again I felt that this was where I belonged.

After I don't know how long, we stopped playing. Travellin' Man shook his head. "Damn, White Boy, yo' gettin' th' blues, sho' nuff. Where in th' hell that come from?"

I shrugged, said that I didn't know.

"Well, hell. We shoulda' recorded that right there. Too late now, tho', th' moment's gone."

He rested my guitar against the wall and took the Gibson from me, cradling it like a new born and caressing the strings and coaxing new melodies into the air.

"Man this sho' is a perty box."

As he played I opened my satchel and took out the recording devices. The video camera and digital voice recorder were completely dead and my phone had barely enough charge to switch on. I rooted about in the satchel, found the cable and connected it between the phone and the camera.

"Whatchoo doin'?" said Travellin' Man.

I told him that I was charging the batteries.

He managed to grunt, "Huh," and then lost interest.

As soon as I connected the cable, a message opened with the word "Battery." I pressed 'Send'. The battery light on the video camera flashed orange a few times and then burned a steady green.

I repeated this for the voice recorder and in a few minutes all three devices were fully charged.

A quick check told me that the memory cards were almost full. I would need to meet up with Fat Man if he wanted me to record any more artists.

Travellin' Man put down the Gibson and stood up. "I almost fo'got," he said. "That ol' timer booked us in here, he say they's a show downstairs later, a singer from outta town, name of Willie Brown, he gon' be playin'. Might be worth yo' recordin'."

I almost fell off the bed. When I asked Travellin' Man if he meant the same Willie Brown who recorded with Son House, he shrugged. "Maybe, I don' know." He paused. "Wait a minute, yo' know I recollect he DID cut a record, somethin' 'bout a train,"

I asked him if he meant 'M&O Blues'.

Travellin' Man snapped his fingers. "M an' O Blues, thassit, tha's th' song."

This was amazing.

Willie Brown played with Charley Patton, Robert Johnson and Son House but recorded only six sides in 1930. There are no photographs of him and only three known copies of his record 'M&O Blues / Future Blues'.

Film footage of Willie Brown would be worth a fortune. I needed to see Fat Man right away.

Travellin' Man told me where he thought the nearest church was but didn't seem at all happy about it.

"Whatchoo wanna know that fo'?"

When I said that I had to meet someone, his face crumpled into a frown.

"'s'at th' same person yo'd jus' left when we hooked up? I recall yo' did'n look none too happy 'bout it."

I shrugged, picked up my satchel, asked him to look after my resonator and said that I wouldn't be long.

It was just going over to darkness when I found the church on a deserted road about a mile outside the town. The place was eerily still, the night air completely silent.

The front door was locked so I trudged around the building just in time to see the rear door swing open of its own accord. Taking a deep breath, I entered the church.

Fat Man was sitting on a wooden chair and seemed to be deep in thought. His massive head was wreathed in a cloud of smoke produced by the huge cigar which he held in a manner that made me think of Winston Churchill. In the darkness, the tip of the cigar described a brief red arc then glowed fiercely red as Fat Man raised it to his lips and took a final draw. Exhaling smoke like the chimney of a power station, he stubbed the cigar into the palm of his hand.

"Yo' like Cuban cigars, White Boy?" He said.

I said that I'd never tried one.

"Well," he said. "I met me a whore in Havana once, she tol' me that a man cain't call his self a man 'lessen he smoked at least one Cuban cigar in his life."

174

When I said that I reckoned I could live with that, Fat Man merely grunted.

"I takes it yo' got somethin' fo' me?" He said.

I removed the memory cards from the camera and voice recorder and handed them to him.

"Hope yo' got me some good stuff, White Boy," he said. "that last stuff, Tommy Johnson an' them other two, they was OK, but I'ma need plenty mo' variety."

He seemed unimpressed when I told him about Pops McCoy. "Who th' hell's that?" he said. "Yo' think he gon' sell?"

I thought about telling him the effect that his performance had had on me, but decided not to waste my time. Instead, I told him that Willie Brown was playing later that night and that I needed more memory cards.

"Willie Brown, huh? Could be some potential there."

Putting the dead cigar in his mouth, Fat Man lumbered to his feet, put the cards that I had given him in one pocket of his filthy jogging pants, produced a handful of cards from the other pocket and handed them to me.

I placed them in my satchel and looked up to see the cigar glowing brightly and Fat Man blowing smoke rings that drifted lazily above his head.

"Only kinda halo y'ever gon' see me wearin'," he said.

I said that I didn't doubt it and asked him how many videos he'd sold.

"I ain' sold any yet," he said. "Website goin' live in a few days, tho'."

Taking another long draw from his cigar, he winked at me. "Donchoo worry, none, White Boy," he said. "Soon as someone buys a video', yo' gon' be th' first one t' know 'bout it."

When I asked him what he meant, Fat Man smiled his smile and blew another smoke ring.

"So, how yo' enjoyin' yo' time in th' land o' th' blues?" He said. "Is it ever' thing yo' expected?"

Something held me back from telling him that it was everything I expected and much, much more. Instead I shrugged and said that so far it had been very interesting.

Fat Man laughed. "Interestin' huh? Well, tha's good. Yo' bettah hope that carries on."

I asked him what he meant by that.

Framing his words with another smoke ring he said, "This' where yo' wanna be, this' where yo' is an' this' where yo' gon' stay. Tha's th' price yo' gon' pay. Fo'ever an' ever, amen."

His words sent a chill that shivered through me, a chill that made me want to be somewhere else.

"Is what it is, White Boy," he said.

Fat Man exhaled through his nose and then sucked hard; igniting the huge cigar in a small flame that burned towards his face like a lit dynamite fuse then disappeared into his mouth with a barely audible hiss.

Fat Man winked again, swallowed the cigar butt then blew out a thin stream of smoke that travelled towards his feet, wrapped itself snakelike around his ankles and then spiralled upwards, encasing his body in coils of swirling tobacco fumes. As the smoke reached his shoulders, Fat Man said, "I believe this concludes our business discussion so I'm gon' say, sayonara, White Boy."

With that he blew one final smoke ring that encircled his head, obscuring him completely.

When the smoke had dissipated, Fat Man was gone.

I reloaded the camera and voice recorder with memory cards and made my way back to the Banty Rooster.

# Anecdotes

As I walked into the bar I saw Travellin' Man sitting at a table with his guitar, half a bottle of White Lightning and two glasses.

"White Boy," He grinned. "I's startin' t'think yo' weren't comin'."

I said I was touched that he had worried about me.

"Didn't say I's worried," he said. "Yo' think I gives a rat's ass what happens to some honky motherfucker?"

I asked him if he meant the same honky motherfucker that dragged him from a burning truck.

"Yo' th' one set th' truck on fire."

When I asked him to remind me why I did that, he stared at me for a long time and then said, "Yo' wanna drink?"

We finished the bottle of White Lightning, started another one and soon my head was buzzing.

I asked Travellin' Man how he'd felt after he'd crossed over.
He thought for a while. "Don' recall thinkin' nothin' profound as such. Was my time t' cross an' that was that. I's never whatchoo call churchified."

He chuckled. "Th' church say th' blues is the devil's music. Well I says a preacher ain' no diff'rent from a bluesman. Ain' neither one of us is happy t'work fo' a livin'."

He paused and gave a short laugh. "Cept I don' go roun' fussin' an' foolin' an' carryin' on tellin' folks how t' live they lives on account I got me some mighty powerful secret. I jus' plays music an' hope folks likes it 'nuff to hand over some coin."

He lifted his glass. "S'all 'bout th' coin, White Boy," he said as he took another sip.

When I asked him what happens when someone gets killed, he drank some more while he thought about it.

"Well," he said. "Th' person what killed yo' gon' follow yo' where ever it is yo' go to. Gabel gon' see t' that, an' only he knows where that is."

Travellin' Man hiccupped then belched. "Why yo' askin', anyhow?"

I just said that I was interested, that was all.

Travellin' Man drained the bottle into our glasses and then staggered to his feet. "I gotta take a piss," he slurred. "Why donchoo git us 'nother bottle." He threw some dollar bills onto the table and stumbled towards the door.

I had to focus on walking a straight line to the bar.

When Travellin' Man returned I filled our glasses, started a voice memo on my phone and asked him where else he had been in this world.

"I been pretty much ever'where I been when I's in th' other world." He said. "I travelled some, goin' where the music took me but I always seemed t'end up wanderin' between Saturday nights, playin' the gittar an' findin' myself in an' out o' trouble. Tha's what happened then an' tha's wha's happenin' now."

I asked him to tell me more about Saturday nights and his face split into a grin.

"Back then, bein' a nigger on a Saturday night, man they weren't nothin' better. Work all week on th' plantation o' in a lumber camp an' gets paid on Saturday. Folks like me turns up an' tha's when the eagle starts to flyin'."

"Th' eagle on a dollar bill, that is. Workin' nigger cain' spend 'em fast enough. Wimmin's an' whisky, tha's all a nigger need sho' nuff."

He took another mouthful of White Lightning. "I mem'er one time in Greenwood, Mississippi. This fella' playin' th' gittar on a street corner, he see me carryin' my box an' he say 'Hey I seen yo' befo', I seen yo playin' that thing.' Jus' like that. I ain' seen him befo' but I smiles an' say, 'yeah, I play some,' an' he say, 'they's a juke-joint in Baptist Town, I'm a playin' there tonight, why donchoo come on over an' play? An' I say, 'sho'. So that night I goes over t'Baptist Town an' I finds this juke-joint an' it's still early but already they's lots o' drinkin' an' carryin' on an' niggers gettin' kinda raucous. Anyhow, I gits t' play some an' it start to gettin' late but I still don' see no sign o' th' feller I met playin' on th' street so I gots t' thinkin' maybe he ain't showed up. I did'n pay no mind right then cos' I'd found me a girl an' she wanted me to take her outside fo' a little fresh air - tha's what she say - so we went outside an' she got a whole lotta fresh air, if yo' knows what I mean, an' tha's where I seen him layin' down 'gainst a tree."

Travellin' Man paused, finished off the White Lightning then said, "All this storytellin' makin' my throat somethin' kinda dry. Why don' yo' make yo'self useful?"

I stopped recording while I went to the bar. Back at the table, I poured Travellin' Man a drink and started a new voice memo.

"Where was I?" He said. " Oh yeah, so I's out back with this girl an we jus' done bein' friendly, yo' know, when I sees this feller up agin a tree, an' he moanin' an' carryin' on an' such 'bout how he don' feel so good. Tha's when I see th' empty whisky bottle lyin' nex' t' him an' I gots t' thinkin', man, he jus' drunk, but he say, 'I feels bad, somethin' wrong wid me,' an then he done throwed up all down his self an' I tell yo, White Boy I ain' never smelt nothin' so bad as that stuff. 'I needs help,' he say, an' so I goes in an' tells th' barman; I says 'theys a feller out back an' he don' look so good, I thinks he needs a doctor.' Barman, he jus' laugh an' say they ain' no doctor gon' come roun' nigger town. I say, 'well, he still needs help. This nigger feelin' bad.' Barman he say, maybe he drunk but I say he in a bad way but he ain' drunk."

Travellin' Man emptied his glass and motioned for another.

"So anyway, barman he send out two men wid me. One of th' men he say, "I knows him an' I knows where he live.' So th' three of us, we pick him up an' carry him back t' where he stayin' an' all the while he moanin' an' dribblin' an' rollin' his eyes an' yo' could see he goin' down real fast. We gets t' this raggedy-assed shotgun shack in a rough end o' town an' we goes in an' lays him down on his bed an' by now he sweatin' an' shoutin' an' carryin' on 'bout his guts bein' on fire an' one o' th' two men he laugh an' say, maybe nex' time he think twice fo' slippin' out with another man's wife. I say 'whatchoo mean?' An' this man say 'whatchoo think I mean?' Then they both done walked out, leavin' me alone wid this sick negro. Well, they weren't nothin' much I could do 'cept git him a drink o' water an' I think that helped him some cos he went right off to sleep."

Travellin' Man stopped talking and stared off into space for a long time. When he spoke again, his voice was softer.

"I did'n have no place t' stay that night an' he had a old couch so I stayed right there. Did'n git much in the way o' sleep on account he kept wakin' an' moanin' an' I kep' gettin' up an' soakin' a rag an' coolin' his head cos his head was like it was burnin' up an' he stayed like that all through th' night an' all through the nex' day an' I stayed cos it did'n seem right t' leave a man so sick as he was. On th' secon' night he quieted down some an' I musta fell to sleep cos he woked me with a scream an' throwed his self outta bed an' started t'crawlin' on all fours, barkin' like a dog an' pukin' an' shittin' his self an' then blood come outta his mouth like water from a pump an' then he rolled over an' kinda shivered for a while, shivered so hard that what teeth he had was clatterin' away like shakin' pebbles in a tin box."

Travellin' Man paused again. "An' then th' shiverin' stopped an' he made a kinda croakin' noise outta his mouth an' then he was dead right there."

There was another long silence.

"Nevah forgot th' date," he said. "Sixteenth day o' August, it was a Wednesday."

It took a few seconds for me to realise what he'd just said. Speaking clearly so that the phone picked up every word I asked him if he could remember the man's name.

The White Lightning had clearly taken hold and Travellin' Man's eyes blinked slowly as he processed my question.

"Sho' I member," he said. "I found out later his name's Johnson, Robert Johnson. On'y a young feller, 'bout twenty-seven o' so."

When I gasped, Travellin' Man looked up. "What, yo' heard o' him?"

I captured a few more anecdotes and then Travellin' Man raised his hand. "I don' wan' talk no mo'," he said.

# Piano Blues

Looking around, I noticed that the room was filling up. Every table was occupied and a crowd had gathered at the bar.

"Show gon' start soon," said Travellin' Man.

As he spoke, a young black woman glided towards us. She wore a long fur coat and a round scarlet bonnet with a rainbow-coloured feather that quivered with every movement. Stopping at our table, she gave a wide, gold-toothed grin. "Well now," she said, "If it ain' ol' Travellin' Man Watson. Yo' gon' buy me a drink, honey?" Her grin turned to a glance of suspicion. "Less'n o'course I's interruptin'?"

I stood up and offered her my seat. For a moment she seemed taken aback, unsure how to respond; then she arched an eyebrow at me. "White Boy givin' up his chair fo' a black gal? That ain' somethin' happnin' ever'day."

She turned to Travellin' Man. "Cat gotcho' tongue? Yo' not speakin' t'me?"

Travellin' Man smiled. "I jus wan' give myself some time, make sho' I ain' dreamin'."

He looked up at me. "White Boy; this' Justine, Justine Cutmore. She plays a mean pianer."

"I see yo' still a silver tongued ol' bastard," she said.

Travellin' Man beamed. "Yo' knows I ain' lyin'."

He nudged me in the ribs. "She used hang around wid anotha gal. Man, they used t' party. Anywhere they's music a'playin, at a juke-joint an' such, Justine an' th' otha' gal; they be there tearin' th' place up dancin' an' carryin' on."

He began to chuckle. "Then one night this pianer player, he s'pose be puttin' on a show, he turn up so drunk he cain' hardly see, so Justine an' this gal, they jump up on stage an' beat the shit outta th' pianer. Played all night, takin' it turns, playin' t'gether. Man that place was jumpin', sho' nuff."

Frowning, he turned to Justine. "What was that otha' gal's name?"

"Louise," she said. "Louise Johnson."

I inhaled a mouthful of beer. When I stopped coughing I asked her if that was the same Louise Johnson that recorded with Charlie Patton and Son House.

Justine frowned. "Howdjoo hear 'bout that?"

I told her that I had recordings of Louise Johnson back home in England.

"England? Yo' kin git them ol' reco'ds in England?" Her eyebrows narrowed. "Is yo' messin' wid me?"

"Nuh-uh," said Travellin' Man. "This boy straight-up. He a big fan o' th' blues. Come all th' way from Englan', jus' like he say."

Louise stepped back and gave me the look. "Is that right? Hell, yo' somethin' diff'rent, White Boy."

I asked if I could buy her a drink.

"Honey," she drawled, "Yo' had me at hello, but if yo' insist, I'll take a whisky."

Travellin' Man raised his hand. "I'll take me one o' them, too."

When I returned Justine was deep in conversation with Travellin' Man. Setting the drinks down I looked around, saw a vacant chair, dragged it to the table and sat down.

"Justine, she gon' be playin' tonight," said Travellin' Man. "She pretty hot on them keys."

He gave a slow wink, "she pretty hot ever' place else she go, too."

She looked at me and gave a mock sigh. "He ain' changed none, he still think he a smooth rider, but I bet he cain' remember th' last time he got him some."

Travellin' Man cackled. "Tha's where yo' wrong, baby, I got lucky on'y th' other night." He winked at me. "Ain' that right, White Boy?"

Justine raised an eyebrow. "Yo' got lucky with a White Boy? Damn, things is worse than I thought."

When we stopped laughing I said that he was telling the truth.

"Where'n th' hell was this?" She said. "They ain' no school roun' here fo' crazy blind bitches."

Travellin' Man sprayed whisky across the table. "Well I tell yo' what," he said. "Girl I met, she wa'n't blind an' she wa'n't crazy, but she was mighty grateful an' she had a ass that would not quit."

Shaking her head, Justine said, "An' I think yo' a whisky drinkin' fool, cain' tell what's real no mo'. Where'n hell yo' gon' meet a gal tha's gon' want whatchoo got?"

Travellin' Man winked. "Ol' juke-joint 'bout five miles outta town an' a couple miles offa th' highway. Me an' White Boy, we had t' git outta there soon afta', drove that ol' Ford truck til it wouldn't drive no mo', an' then…"

His voice trailed away, his smile evaporating as his features set into a hard stare into the middle distance.

After a pause, Justine said, "An' then, what?"

Then she frowned.

"Wait a minute," she said. "This afta'noon I's in a bar 'cross town. Some fool come in talkin' 'bout a old Ford truck they found beat up an' burned out, 'bout a mile from th' highway. Looked like somethin' 'tacked it, somethin' big. Looked like hellhounds, someone said."

Travellin' Man exchanged a look with me, then turned to Justine. "How they know it wus hellhounds?"

She took a long drink of her whisky, rolling it around her tongue before swallowing.

"Th' fool in th' bar, he say that they's tracks all 'roun' the truck an' marks where somethin' big been dragged away, somethin' big, like hellhound big."

Travellin' Man shrugged. "Don' mean nothin'," he said.

The sound of the piano broke into our conversation. A rapid, left-handed arpeggio of pure boogie-woogie rang out, turning all heads toward the stage. Perched on the stool and hammering out the 12-bar groove was the ancient black man who'd signed us into the hotel.

Travellin' Man leaned across. "Yo' might wanna film this, White Boy," he said. "This gon' be good."

I grabbed the camera and made it to the stage in time to see the old guy run his left hand over the keys in a blur while his right hand held a bottle of Jax to his lips. Draining the beer in seconds, he grinned, threw the empty bottle over his shoulder and commenced an onslaught of piano blues that roused a huge cheer from the crowd. He played for about twenty minutes, his body rocking as it transmitted energy through his wrists, hands and fingers to maintain a driving blues-beat of piano riffs, by turns lifting us to dizzying heights of anticipation and holding us there just long enough to feel almost palpable relief at the resolution of the 12-bar sequence.

I stopped filming and returned to the table, sat back in my chair, closed my eyes and tuned into the music. Moments later, sensing movement next to me, I opened them to see Travellin' Man with his head down, finger-snapping the rhythm. I tapped him on his shoulder, he looked up and grinned and nodded at me. I was about to ask him where Justine had gone when I caught a glimpse of her walking towards the stage.

The old man on the piano saw her too. Grinning widely, he segued from boogie-woogie to a slow, lazy tune while he tapped his left foot on the stage in time with her approaching footsteps.

I recognised the tune straightaway and grabbed my camera once again and began recording one a live version of one of my favourite songs.

Justine reached the piano and the old man continued playing as she stopped, smiled and stroked his head then began snapping her fingers in time to the beat of his left foot. After a few bars of the slow blues riff, Justine turned to the face the crowd and began to sing

"Man, slow down, we'll get there..."

My face pulled a grin as wide as the old man's as she breathed her version of 'Walkin' The Blues' by Willie Dixon.

I looked around the bar; everyone stared at the stage as if entranced by the hypnotic beat of footstep and finger snap and the languid piano blues.

When she reached the line, "Man, is it hot today..." she removed her fur coat in a single, fluid movement to reveal a dark blue, knee-length silk dress that clung to her figure and drew whistles from almost every man in the audience.

At the last bar, the old man wound up the piano part and Justine finished the song to rapturous applause.

Bowing deeply, she turned and kissed the old man on the top of his head and helped him up from the stool, the crowd cheering as he demanded another kiss before hobbling offstage.

Applauding him, she turned to the crowd.

"Ain' he handsome?" She yelled. "He must be gettin' some."

At the side of the stage, the old man barked with laughter as Justine sat down at the piano and played a few scales.

"We gon' speed things up, now," she said and launched into a fast piano break with a walking bass line.

"We-eeell, I'm going to Memphis gonna stop at..."

The crowd yelled and cheered at the opening line of Louise Johnson's song, 'On The Wall', jumping to their feet, rushing to the stage and dancing as if their life depended on it.

I turned to Travellin' Man, saw his empty chair and then laughed out loud when I saw him strutting his stuff and clearing a space in the crowd.

No one can dance quite like an old black musician, and Travellin' Man had all the moves. The Lindy Hop, the Slow Drag and even the Electric Slide. The man had fluid joints and I watched in awe as he made the coolest shapes, oozing rhythm from his dead-man's shoes up to the dark trilby that formed part of his dance moves. Tipping his hat at a young lady, he span around, looked up at me and cupped his hands around his mouth. "Whatchoo waitin' fo' White Boy?" he yelled. "Come heya an' I'ma show yo' how t' dance."

So I did, and, in a triumph of enthusiasm over talent, threw myself around the floor like a man possessed while Justine Cutmore rocked the place.

Eventually, even Travellin' Man admitted defeat and we both retired to our table and a welcome pair of beers. Shortly after, Justine finished her set and stood up to raucous cheering and shouting. Walking to centre stage, she waited for the crowd to quieten.

"Thank y'all, y'all are too kind an' I do 'preciate it. Now we gots anotha' musicianer gon' play fo' y'all." Pausing to look to her left she yelled, "Willie Brown, gitcho ass onstage, theys' folks here wan' see yo' play."

I shot to my feet, scrabbled in my satchel for the camera and made my way to the stage just in time to see a shy-looking, rotund black man appear carrying a black Gibson L-00.

I began filming from the moment he stepped onstage, tuned his guitar, mumbled a few shy words and then launched into the familiar walk-down bass line.

"Can't tell my future, I can't tell my past..."

When he finished 'Future Blues' he played 'M&O Blues', 'Grandma Blues', 'Sorry Blues', 'Window Blues' and 'Kicking In My Sleep Blues'.

Any blues anorak worth his or her salt knows that video footage of Willie Brown, singing every song that he was known to have recorded, would be priceless.

Blues historians are divided in their opinion of Willie Brown's talent and his contribution to the music of Charley Patton, Son House and Robert Johnson. All I know is, that night he rocked the joint. I just wish that I had taken the time to appreciate it.

If wishes were horses, beggars would ride.

I woke next morning to the sound of Justine snoring gently next to me. My recollection of the night's events was as sketchy as my hangover was painful. Looking around the room I was relieved to see my resonator guitar and satchel. My head pounding, I reached over and retrieved the recording devices.

While Justine slept I replayed Willie Brown's performance, punching the air with glee at the quality of my footage.

YouTube wouldn't know what hit it.

The bed shifted as she rolled over, blinked heavily then smiled. "Damn, White Boy. Yo' know's what a gal wants an' how t' give it to her. Yo' got any mo' under there?"

As her hands began exploring, I switched off Willie Brown and put down the camera.

It was nearly midday when we ventured downstairs. Travellin' Man was asleep on the stage, surrounded by empty bottles, cradling his guitar and snoring as if his life depended upon it.

Justine shook her head. "Don' hoot wit' th' owls if yo' cain't soar wit' th' eagles."

Turning to me, she kissed me on the cheek. "I gotta go, White Boy, last night was fun. Maybe we see one 'nother again. Who knows?"

I said that I would like that.

Kissing me again, she walked out of the hotel.

From behind the bar a cancerous wheeze evolved into a cackle of laughter. "Looks like somebody got hisse'f some action?"

I shrugged.

On stage, with a sound like a buffalo coughing, Travellin' Man let rip with an elongated fart that rumbled for a full five seconds and released a wall of foul stench that coated everything it touched.

Snorting and mumbling, he crawled awake, pushed himself stiffly to an upright position and surveyed the room and then squinted up at me and rubbed his mouth.

"White Boy," he said. "Yo' look like shit. Shouldn' hoot wit' th' owls if yo' cain't soar wit' th' eagles."

He smacked his lips, spotted a bottle with half an inch of liquor lurking in the bottom and in one movement picked it up and drained it.

"This place stinkin' somethin' kinda bad. How 'bout we git us some breakfast?"

Breakfast turned out to be refried beans and coffee.

When we'd eaten, Travellin' Man drained his mug for the third time and waved it at the waiter who scurried over with a fresh jug.

As his mug was refilled, he burped, picked his teeth then said. "Whas' th' plan, White Boy? Where we goin' next?"

I said that I wasn't sure where we were, but I guessed that anywhere that played music would be good.

"Yo' wants some mo' blues, huh? How 'bouts we goes t' Clarksdale. Plenty goin' on there, bars an' juke-joints an' plantation parties. Yo' ever been t'Clarksdale?"

I said that I had but that was back in the other world.

"Well I'll tell yo' what," he said. "If'n yo' lookin' fo' th' blues, Clarksdale's where it's at. Can get a bit whatchoo might call lively, but tha's where th' blues is sho' nuff."

I said that suited me and asked him how far it was.

"I reckons fifty miles, near 'bout."

A grin peeled his face open.

"Yo' calls yo'self 'Hobo John'," he said. "I betchoo ain' never once had t' ride th' blinds?"

I said that was true.

His grin peeled wider, his eyes glittering. "Well, damn," he said. "Let's go catch us a train."

# Ridin' The Blind

About an hour later, the town was a memory behind us. As we walked, cotton fields stretched away on either side and the dirt track ribboned ahead towards a collection of buildings barely visible in the distance.

"Thas where we headed." Said Travellin' Man. He pointed away to the left, to a white plume on the horizon. "An' thas what we gonna catch."

I squinted, stared at the cloud moving steadily across the horizon.

"Thas our ride to Clarksdale." He began to run. "C'mon."

Arriving at a railroad crossing I looked to my left. The railroad stretched away, the rails converging beneath a barely discernible black shape that grew steadily larger, a plume of steam billowing above it.

A long, low, mournful whistle rang out over the landscape. Travellin' Man pointed in the opposite direction and began to jog along the railroad. "Foller me," he yelled.

Ahead, a set of points sprouted sidings on which stood several deserted carriages. We jogged to the far end and stopped.

"This where we gonna hobo," he panted. "Ol' train go'n stop back there and take on water. When she full she gon' start up again, when she reaches here we go'n run 'longside and climb into a boxcar, catch us a nice easy ride."

He grinned at me. "Th' look on yo' face sayin' yo' ain' sure 'bout any o' this."

I said I'd give it a go.

"Jumpin' a train this way means less chance o' meetin' any bulls." Before I could speak his face twisted. "Bulls is th' railroad security guards," he said. "Buncha nasty motherfuckers. They always be looking to bust some hobos.

Should be OK here, though. Most o'them too fat an' lazy t'wander too far from th' depot."

When I asked him how fast the train would be going, he shrugged.

"They always a little bit faster than a man can run, but donchoo worry none. Jus' do as I do an ever'thing gon' be fine."

The train whistle moaned again, shortly followed by the unmistakeable sound of a locomotive gathering speed. Travellin Man peered around the end of the carriage then turned to me.

"Train gon' be here in a minute, we only gon' get one chance at this, so you gotta do 'sactly what I do, y'hear?"

I nodded.

"OK then. Ol' train go'n come past making a shitload of noise. We gon' stay put 'til the engine goes by, then we gonna start running. Once we get 'longside a boxcar I'm gon' jump in an you gon' follow me."

Travellin Man turned his back and peeked around the carriage. Standing behind him, I could see the railroad tracks begin to hum and vibrate. Locomotive sounds of steel against steel, the hiss of pressurised steam, clanking chains and rattling carriages grew into a physical mass of noise that I felt in my chest. A whistle blast close by made me jump, my heart pounding as the engine came into view.

I stared open-mouthed as it lumbered past. It looked to be at least 20 feet high and 70 feet long. At the front, the cowcatcher, standing eight feet tall, projected out like the upturned prow of a ship. Behind it, huge pistons worked back and forth, steam jetting out as they powered the wheels, pulling the train with steadily increasing momentum.

Travellin Man turned and pushed me behind the carriage. "Don' want the driver t' see us." He said.

The locomotive moved past, followed by the coal truck and then a procession of wooden boxcars.

Staring at the train, Travellin Man reached behind and grabbed me by the shirt, "Get ready White Boy, I think I seen a open boxcar, when I say run you follow me like yo' ass is on fire, y'unnerstan?"

More boxcars trundled past.

"Le's go."

I followed him as he sprinted towards the train and for a few seconds we ran alongside a boxcar then Travellin' Man flung his guitar through the door, jumped onto the metal brake rods that ran beneath the car, grabbed the sides of the door and hauled himself inside.

The train gathered speed and I had to sprint hard to keep level. Inside, Travellin' Man stood at the door. "C'mon White Boy, throw me yo' gittar."

Above all the noise, I heard the resonator twang as it hit the floor of the boxcar. Grabbing the side of the door I stumbled, tried to regain my footing, tried desperately to run but the train was now moving too fast. Dangling helplessly, my feet dragged through gravel, my body swinging and buffeting. I was about to to let go when suddenly I was pulled upwards and into the boxcar.

For a few seconds, I lay exhausted on the wooden floor.

"Well, you sure took yo' own sweet time," Said Travellin' Man.

I sat up, looked down at my scuffed shoes and then thanked him.

"Well, yo' inside an' yo' in one piece," he said. "Whatchoo done jus' then, tha's one way yo' gon' lose a leg. I seen it happen, faster 'n' yo' can blink. Yo' lucky I's here wid yo'."

I said that I couldn't argue with that and that he probably saved my life, or at least my leg.

He shrugged. "Well, tha's our secret."

Shifting myself over to sit by the door, I was about to dangle my legs outside when Travellin' Man yanked me back inside for the second time.

"Tha's th' other way of losing yo' legs. Yo' NEVER ride wid yo' legs outside th' boxcar."

Shaking his head, he stared balefully down at me. "Shit, White Boy," he said. "I think yo' might wanna think 'bout changin' yo' name, cos I has to say, you the worst damn hobo I ever seen."

I said that everyone has to start somewhere.

Travellin' Man looked unconvinced. "I guess," he said.

Swaying to counter the motion of the train, he picked up the Gibson, made his way to the corner of the boxcar, sat against the wall and began to pick out a slow, 12-bar blues riff.

Reaching across, I picked up the resonator and tuned it to Open G. Taking the slide out of my pocket I messed about for a while, playing softly so as not to distract Travellin' Man.

"Play it up, White Boy," he said. "Tha's a Nashnul, Ain' meant t' whisper, Nashnul meant t' shout, sho' nuff."

Suddenly self-conscious, my head went blank and I fumbled about feeling like a fraud.

"Stage fright, huh? Shit happens. Yo' know 'Roll an' Tumble Blues?'"

Smiling to myself, I silently blessed him. 'Roll and Tumble Blues' is a blues staple with an instantly recognisable riff that Robert Johnson used in 'If I Had Possession Over Judgement Day'. Usually one of the first tunes any slide player learns, it sounds like a 'proper' blues song and, best of all, it's easy to play.

Taking a deep breath I dragged the slide up to the 12th fret, the National screaming the intro as I plucked hard on the top strings then dive-bombed to the fifth fret. Looking up, I saw Travellin' Man watching me. He waited for me to complete the sequence then joined in with the Gibson.

"Well I roll an' I tumble,

an' I cried th' whole night long..."

Travellin' Man's voice rang out and once more I laughed in boyish elation. My confidence returned and I attacked the National, my slide clattering off the frets, notes wailing out as I played louder and faster, dragging every ounce of performance out of my beautiful guitar.

Travellin' Man attacked his strings, hammering chords out of the Gibson and singing at the top of his voice.

> *"Well I'm here wid' a White Boy*
> *an' he wished that he's black*
> *Well I'm here wid' a White Boy*
> *an' he sho' wished he's black*
> *White Boy come from England*
> *an' he ain' never goin' back..."*

I laughed louder as Travellin' Man ad-libbed his way through the song, head thrown back and eyes squeezed shut as he howled the lyrics, his playing interspersed with percussive beats on the soundbox. He was in the zone, the place musicians arrive at where everything connects and what pours out is instinctive, not rehearsed.

I wasn't far behind him, I was responding to Travellin' Man, my playing echoing his as we communicated through music, speaking to one another as natural as speech in a conversation.

"Play it good, White Boy."

Keeping the riff going, I bellowed the words to 'If I Had Possession Over Judgement Day' and on and on we went, playing back and forth, both of us lost in the music. Travellin' Man nodding and shaking his head, his face grimacing then relaxing in response to blues tension and then resolution until finally, through unspoken mutual agreement, Travellin' Man walked down the frets for a final turnaround.

We sat for a long time, watching the landscape, each of us playing our thoughts to the hypnotic rhythm of the train.

Travellin' Man broke the silence between us.

"Damn, tha's th' blues, right there," he said.

"White Boy playin' like a righteous black mothafucker."

I thanked him, secretly delighted that our impromptu session had seemingly affected him in the same way that it did me.

It was one of the best moments of my life, bonding with Travellin' Man whilst rattling along in an open boxcar through the Mississippi Delta towards Clarksdale.

I awoke to the squealing of brakes and the slamming jolts of boxcars under deceleration.

Outside, the scenery began to slow. Cotton fields towing buildings in their wake as we approached the outskirts of a town. Travellin' Man pushed himself to a sitting position, scooted to the open doorway and peered out.

"We comin' into th' freight depot at Clarksdale, White Boy; grab yo' stuff."

He peered out once more. "Train gon' slow some more, but we needs t' be off befo' it stops. If'n we gets off in th' depot then we th' bulls might see us."

He winked at me. "Yo' ready t' jump off, White Boy?"

I grabbed my guitar and asked him when.

Winking again, he said, "how 'bout right now?"

In one movement he positioned himself with his back to the doorway, stepped down onto the brake rods then simply stepped off and hit the ground running.

"C'mon White Boy," he yelled.

By now the train had slowed to a crawl. Cautiously, I stepped down onto the brake rod, took a deep breath, stepped off, ran a few steps then went down like a shot buffalo.

Slightly dazed, I looked up at huge metal wheels trundling inches past my face, heard the sound of the train whistle, the sound of squealing brakes and the cackle of hysterical laughter.

Turning around I saw Travellin' Man on his knees, laughing so hard he couldn't breathe.

Standing up, I dusted my self off, picked up my now scuffed resonator and walked back along the track.

Travellin' Man hauled himself upright, tears coursing down his face as he erupted in a fresh bout of near hysteria.

"Damn," he said. "Tha's near 'bout th' funniest thing I ever seen."

Shaking his head, he wiped the tears from his eyes and slapped me on the back.

"White Boy," he said. "Yo' almost a hobo, now. Sho' nuff yo' cain' get on a train on yo' own, an' yo' cain' get off without fallin' on yo' ass but yo' real good at th' ridin' in between." His chuckles swelling into rich bubbling laughter that tumbled out of him, springing forth fresh tears of glee.

I maintained a dignified silence until, finally, he calmed down.

Wiping his eyes once more, he shook his head.

"White Boy," he said. "Yo' priceless, I'ma gon' buy yo' a beer."

As the final boxcar clattered past, Travellin' Man clapped me on the shoulder. "We got's t' go back a ways," he said. "Git us away from th' depot."

# Clarksdale

Fifty yards along the tree-lined railroad track was a crossing. A road sign announced that this was Issaquena Avenue. We turned left and then left again onto Edwards Avenue.

We walked past the freight depot, ahead was a large blue building with Delta Wholesale Hardware Corporation painted in large black letters.

I stopped and looked around. It all looked familiar somehow, but it was a good minute or so before I realised where we were.

"Y'Ok, White Boy?"

I said that I had been here before.

Travellin' Man grunted. "Prob'ly changed some, huh?"

I pointed to the freight depot buildings and told him that was now the Delta Blues museum.

"Blues museum?" He said. "They gots a museum fo' th' blues? What in th' hell they got in there?"

I told him there were lots of old blues stuff on display and even part of the cabin in which Muddy Waters was born.

"Muddy Waters? Who th' hell's that?"

I said that his real name was McKinley Morganfield and he was born and raised in Rolling Fork.

Travellin' Man thought about this.

"Wait a minute," he said. "Yo' tellin' me that they took a shotgun shack from Rollin' Fork an' built it in a museum they made in Clarksdale freight depot?"

I said that was about the size of it.

"Well Goddam," he said.

Silent for a moment, he frowned and then said. "Morganfield, yo' say? Lived in Rollin' Fork?"

I nodded and asked him if he knew of him.

"Ain' never heard of Muddy Waters, but I recalls th' name Morganfield, thinks they maybe worked on Stovall Plantation. I knows a coupla juke-joints out that way. Maybe's we can take a trip that way sometime?"

I said why not.

Travellin' Man nodded towards the depot. "An' this museum," he said. "Who all goes to see that?"

I told him that most of the visitors to Clarksdale that I'd seen were white blues fans who had travelled from all over the world

"Sheeeeeeit," He said.

He paused. "All th' times I's playin', white folks din't wan' nothin' t'do wid th' blues. They all playin' Jimmie Rodgers tunes and callin' th' blues 'nigger music' an' carryin' 'bout th' 'race records' on th' radio. When I's playin', blues was fo' black folks. Now yo' sayin' blues is fo' white folks?"

Travellin' Man stared into space for a long time.

"Sometimes," he said. "White folks turns up at juke-joints, fin' out we gettin' th' biggest crowd an' aks us t' play at they big houses, but they wantin' show tunes an' break downs an' such. Tha's th' only time yo' see a white man roun' a juke-joint. An' now yo' say white folks is comin' from way overseas jus' t' look at a nigger's wooden shack?"

He shook his head again.

"So what's th' negroes listen to?"

I said that everyone listened to all different kinds of music.

"Is black folks still playin' th' blues?"

I thought about this and said that some did but a lot of blues these days is played by white artists.

Travellin' Man put his hand up. "Hold th' train, White Boy," he said, "I thoughtchoo was a one-off, yo' tellin' me they's mo' white folks playin' th' blues, now?" He shook his head.

I told him that since the 1960's, the majority of blues was played by white artists.

"How come?"

I told him what I had read in the history books; that the old blues fell out of favour when blacks gave up the drudgery of a life of sharecropping or working on a plantation and left Mississippi to find better paid work in the factories in Chicago. I said that while they took the blues with them, the music developed and moved on because a lot of the blacks didn't want to be reminded of the bad times in the south.

"So they ain' no black folks playin' th' blues no mo'?"

I said it was complicated, that there were different types of music now.

"Huh," he said. "So what's black kids listening to?"

When I mentioned rap and hip-hop, he just stared blankly.

"Say what?"

I tried another tack. I told him that kids, black and white, listen to songs about stuff that happens everyday, stuff that reaches out to them and that they recognise from their own lives.

"Tha's like th' blues," he said.

I asked him if he'd heard of David 'Honeyboy' Edwards.

"Cain' say I have," he said.

I told him that Honeyboy was a bluesman from Greenwood, played in the 1930s in Mississippi.

"Huh, so what?"

I said that he lived to be 97 and wrote a book about his life. In the book he said, "You see poor black kids hanging around on the street listening to hip-

203

hop, that's what we were like when we were kids, only we had the blues. But we was just the same; we didn't have nothing, we was dangerous."

Travellin' Man considered this. "Dangerous, got that right," he said. "So, this crap music, I wan's t' hear some. Sing me somethin' White boy."

I laughed and said that it wasn't something that I could sing.

'Well gimme an idea," he said. "How they play this stuff, they play a gittar? Harmonica? Fiddle?"

I said the closest thing I could compare it with was a Baptist preacher giving a sermon, but using rhyme.

He didn't seem convinced. "An' what instr'ment they play, when they sing this?"

I thought about trying to explain a drum machine to him, then had a brainwave.

Reaching into my satchel I grabbed my phone, searched the music, found "Drop the World" by Li'l Wayne and Eminem, plugged in the earphones, placed them in Travellin' Man's ears and pressed 'play'.

For 3 minutes and 49 seconds I watched as Travellin' Man's expression shifted from a suspicious frown to wide-eyed disbelief.

When the song ended, Travellin' Man removed the earphones.

"Man, tha' soun' like one angry motherfucker."

I said that a lot of black kids lived an angry life in an angry culture.

"Tha's a black kid, singing that?" he said. "Shit, black kid ac' like that in Missi'ppi, he gon' find his self on th' wrong end of a rope."

Travellin' Man handed back the earphones.

"Then again," he said. "He only sayin' out loud what us ol' timers be thinkin'."

# High Sheriff Blues

The sun was low in the sky as we turned, put the freight depot behind us and walked towards the centre of Clarksdale.

A few minutes later we arrived at the end of a busy street. "How yo' fancy earnin' some cash an' findin' a place t' play and have us some fun tonight?" said Travellin' Man.

I asked him where he had in mind; he stopped and leaned against a storefront.

"Right here," he said. "An' if we good enough, then someone gon' come along an' aks us t' play somewhere later on."

Travellin' Man removed his hat, placed it on the sidewalk and winked at me. "Yo' stan' back fo' a coupla numbers, I'll git us a crowd an' then yo' can join in wid yo' shiny gittar."

After a few moments tuning, he strummed the guitar hard and then launched into a blistering version of 'Screamin' and Hollerin' the blues'.

I stood back and watched as he belted out the old Charley Patton song. Within a few minutes a crowd began to form, filling out the sidewalk and spilling onto the street.

One by one, coins began dropping into his hat. With each one, Travellin' Man responded with a nod and a cheery smile.

Stepping back, I took out my camera and filmed him as he worked the crowd through three songs. Walking around, I panned back and forth, filming from all angles and capturing his playing combined with the spontaneous dancing of his audience.

Soon, the crowd had grown to around a hundred and stretched across the street.

"I want y'all t' move on an' clea-ah this area."

I turned to see two overweight, khaki-clad white men striding towards us, both with stern expressions and both wielding billy-clubs.

"We ain' gon' tell y'all again," yelled the other. "Y'all are obstructin' a public highway, now git on yo' way, an' you," he pointed his club at Travellin' Man, "Yo' stop singin' right now, nigger."

Travellin' Man stopped immediately. As I stepped forward, he glanced at me, warning me off with a minute shake of his head.

Turning to the cop he dropped his gaze. "Yes suh, I din' mean no trouble, suh. Jus' tryin' t'earn me a few dimes."

Reluctantly, the crowd began to thin as people walked away, some casting sullen glances at the policemen.

I looked up to see the other cop staring at me beneath hooded eyelids. "My name's Sheriff Jim Purvis," he drawled. He nodded to the other cop. "An' this is Deputy Marshall Tom Webster."

Slowly he raised his billy-club and levelled it at me. "Now we introduced," he said. "Why donchoo come ovah heyah, son, I want's a talk with y'all."

I stayed still long enough for Travellin' Man to shoot another glare at me.

"I ain't in th' habit of askin' twice, son," said the sheriff. "An' if I gotta come ovah theyah then yo' troubles gon' increase tenfold."

I said that I hadn't done anything.

Sheriff Purves shot a look at his partner and then took a deep breath.

"Son," he said. "Th' only thing tha's keepin' me polite right now is the fact that I can tell from yo' acceyent that yo' ain' from around here. So ahma gon' give yo' th' benefit of th' doubt an' ask you one more time to kindly step ovah heya."

He raised a dangerous smile. "This is a one-time offah."

"Stop fuckin' around, White Boy," hissed Travellin' Man. "Do as th' man says."

I stepped forwards, stopping two paces from the cop.

"Now tha's mo' like it," he said. "Where y'all from, son?"

I said I was from England.

"Y'all a long way from home," he said.

I said that I hear that a lot.

He nodded towards Travellin' Man. "And what is the nature of yo' relationship with that colored feller?"

I said that we were friends.

"Friends, huh?" The sheriff looked me up and down. "Well," he said. "When yo' in my town, yo' might needs t' think carefully about the nature o' the company yo' keep an' especially careful about the friendships yo' cultivate."

I thanked him for his advice and said that I was more than capable of deciding whose company I would keep and that providing I didn't break any laws I didn't think that the police would need to be troubled by me or any of my friends.

I heard Travellin' Man moan. "Goddam, White Boy. Shut the fuck up."

A dangerous smile sneered across the sheriff's face and his words crawled out coated in menace.

"Be very careful, son." He said. "It's only my good nature that's keepin' yo' on the right side of a whole shitload of trouble, an' if I thought that maybe you wasn't takin' me seriously, or maybe bein' disrespectful or maybe you had a notion that anything yo' try and say might mean anything more to me than a cup of horse piss, then I might have to hand you over to Deputy Marshall Webster."

"Please suh," Travellin' Man stepped forward. "Please, suh, he ain' from roun' here an' he don' know the ways o' the south. He don' mean no trouble, he just here to hear th' music tha's all. Him an' me we hooked up cos he likes t' hear th' blues, an' I'ma jus showin' him aroun'. We ain' lookin' t' cause no trouble, just play some music, earn a coupla dimes an' find us a good time. How about we leaves town tonight? Gets outta yo' way? Whatchoo say, sheriff?"

Deputy Webster snickered, took a step forward and kicked Travellin' Man's hat, scattering copper and silver coins across the sidewalk.

"Earn a few dimes, huh?" he said. "Looks mo' like a few dollars t'me. An' looks like yo' done littered the sidewalk, so why donchoo pick up them coins, boy, fo' I arrest yo' an' throw yo' in jail?"

"Please suh," said Travellin' Man.

"I said; pick 'em up, boy."

Terror flashed across Travellin' Man's face as he knelt down and scrabbled the coins back into his hat, his hands trembling as he staggered back to his feet.

"Yes suh," he stammered. "I done picked 'em all up, suh. Ever' last dime."

Enough was enough.

I held up my hands, said I was sorry for my attitude and for any offence that I might have caused. I said that I was out of line and apologised if I was in any way disrespectful to him or his deputy.

The sheriff sniffed and hitched up his pants.

"Yo' shoulda thought of that befo' comin' onto me with yo' bad attitude, son." His eyes shifted to Travellin' Man and then back to me. "Looks like yo' an' yo' uppity nigger done upset my deputy. How yo' think we gon' rectify this unfortunate state of affairs?"

I sighed and asked him what he wanted.

Winking at the sheriff, the deputy stepped towards Travellin' Man.

"Yo' play th' dice, boy?" he said.

"I plays some."

"Yo' hear that sheriff?" Said the deputy. "He plays some."

The sheriff grunted. "Course he plays th' dice, I ain' never met no nigger who ain' spen' time crouched down throwin' them bones."

"Yo' carryin' yo' bones, boy?" The deputy stood nose to nose.

Travellin' Man said nothing.

"Boy, when th' deputy aks yo' a question yo' bettah damn well answer."

"Yes suh."

"Yes suh, what?" The deputy's voice hardened. "Yes suh yo' knows yo' gotta answer when a deputy aksed yo' a question? Or yes suh, yo' carryin' some bones?"

Travellin' Man looked scared.

"Yes suh, I's carryin' me some dice."

The deputy's voice softened. "Course yo' carryin' dice," he said. "An' I'ma bet yo' carryin' mo' than one pair, s'at right?"

Travellin' Man swallowed hard.

"Tha's right, suh."

The deputy nodded. "S'acly what I thought. Why donchoo getcho dice out an' lemme take a look?"

His hands trembling, Travellin' Man searched his jacket and produced six identical dice.

"Well, lookee here, sheriff."

209

"I can see, son."

I asked what was wrong.

The sheriff adjusted his hat and sniffed. "Ain' nothin' wrong, nothin' wrong at all."

He paused. "Less'n one o' more o' them dice is loaded, o' course, an' then this boy could be in a shit load o' trouble."

He turned to the deputy. "Whatchoo reckon, Tom?" he said. "Cos, I'ma bet a pound to a pinch o' dog shit that under close examination they gon' be three sets o' dice in that boy's hand and each set gon' behave differently."

Nodding in agreement, his eyes never leaving Travellin' Man's face, the deputy sniffed.

"I'll take them odds," he said. "I bet this ol' nigger be 'bout as crooked as a box o' fishing hooks."

"Tha's what I'm'a thinkin'," said the sheriff, "I'ma bet my hat that one set ain' loaded, that one set gon' throw six an' one; an' th'other gon' throw three an' four."

The deputy smiled maliciously. "Whatchoo gotta say, boy? Yo' been playin' craps wid loaded dice?"

Travellin' Man's voice was barely a whisper.

"Yes suh."

The deputy nodded. "Made yo'self a whole bunch o' greenbacks, too?"

"I ain' done too bad, suh."

Nodding again, the deputy considered this. "Show us th' cash yo' won, an' don' even think that we ain' gon' search yo' black ass."

"Inside my suit coat," said Travellin' Man. "Left hand side."

"Well now, I'ma gon' put my hand inside and see fo' my self."

Reaching inside Travellin' Man's jacket, the deputy fished around and then produced a wad of dollar bills.

Stepping back he handed the cash to the sheriff.

Sheriff Purvis riffled the notes. "Well Goddam," he said. "This boy got better'n thirty dollars."

He turned to the deputy. "How much is th' fine fo' this misdemeanour, Tom?"

"Oh, I reckons 'bout thirty dollars, near about."

The sheriff folded the notes and stuffed them into his back pocket.

"Tha's s'acly right," he said. "Thirty dollars on th' button."

The deputy cackled when I said that thirty dollars seemed a lot for carrying loaded dice."

"Carryin' loaded dice?" said the sheriff. "Ain' no law 'gainst carryin' loaded dice."

I said that I didn't understand and reminded him that he had said that Travellin' Man would be in trouble.

Both lawmen smirked.

"He gon' be in trouble if'n he gits found out," said the deputy. "Niggers don' take kindly t' bein' chiselled outta they hard earned dimes."

"Damn right," said the sheriff. "This thirty dollars is yo' fine fo' 'structin' a public highway."

He straightened himself up, his grin faded as he stared me in the eye. "Nex' time, I'ma throw yo' ass in jail. This th' south y'all, we gots our own ideas on justice an' by God yo' better bide by our ways an' remember who yo' is an' think 'bout where yo' allegiance lies."

He stepped in close to me.

"I makin' myself clear, son?"

I stared back and said that I got the message.

He stared some more then sniffed, nodded once and stepped backwards.

"C'mon, Tom," he said. "I think justice has been seen t'be done, we'll let these folks go 'bout they business."

Just before they walked away, the sheriff waved a billy club at us. "An' if'n yo' gon' insist on playin' that nigger shit music, then find yo'self a alleyway somewhere. Don' play it where coloreds gon' congregate and intimidate civilised white folk wid they jiggin' an' carryin' on."

Travellin' Man spoke first. "Yes suh, sheriff. Thank y'suh, we gon' be on our way, sho' nuff."

We watched as they walked out of sight then Travellin' Man pocketed the loose change, dusted his hat and set it squarely on his head.

"Damn," he said. "Jim Purvis an' Tom Webster. I never fails t' be surprised at what a mean pair o' motherfuckers they is."

He shrugged. "Still," he said. "Coulda' been worse."

I said that the deputy had stolen thirty dollars from him and asked how it could have been worse.

Travellin' Man looked up and down the street, picked up his guitar, loosened the strings, pushed his hand into the soundbox, produced a brown paper package then grinned at me. "Cos they missed th' hunnerd dollars I stuck in my gittar th' other night."

Stuffing the package into his jacket pocket, his face grew serious.

"That coulda come out a whole lot worse," he said. "They coulda throwed our asses in jail jus' fo' th' sass yo' give th' sheriff."

He shook his head. "What I gotta say t' get yo' t'unnerstan'? Roun' here they's black an' they's white an' if'n th' two meet up then th' black guy gon' come second one way o' 'nother. I plays th' 'yes suh, no suh' Uncle Tom act an' if they dumb motherfuckers, they takes it in, thinkin' they superior. If they dumb an' mean, then nigger in a shitload o' peril."

He took a breath.

"I knows yo' means well, White Boy, but yo' actin' up on my account ain' likely to help no one, least of all me. We in Mississippi. If yo' white yo' got all th' cards an' if yo' black yo' ain' got shit."

His face peeled into a grin. "Less'n yo' got loaded bones."

Snapping his fingers, he gave a small dance of delight.

"Man, yo' see th' look on Tom Webster's when he foun' that thirty dollars. I thought he's 'bout t' come in his pants."

Travellin' Man danced some more.

"How 'bout we go get us a drink?"

Travellin' Man led me across the railroad tracks and down a dusty street. Substantial buildings gave way to dilapidated storefronts and ramshackle huts and it was almost dark when we came to a rough-looking, open-fronted bar. Hurricane lamps barely kept the gloom at bay but gave enough light to show the interior. Ten feet inside, half-hidden in the darkness, an old door rested on two trestles, behind which stood a surly-looking black man wearing a grubby vest beneath grey braces. At an ancient table at the side of the makeshift bar, half a dozen elderly black men played dominoes by candlelight.

"Whatchoo drinkin', White Boy?" said Travellin' Man.

I asked what they had.

"We gots beer, we gots whisky." The sound of the barman's voice made me think of sand paper. I asked for a beer.

"I'll take me a beer, too, an gimme two ceegars."

The barman nodded at Travellin' Man then produced two bottles of Jax and two fat cigars.

"Fifty cents," he rasped.

Travellin' Man produced a leather wallet from which he took a five-dollar bill and laid it on the bar.

"Drinks all round," he beamed.

I said that I hadn't seen the wallet before.

Travellin' Man handed me a cigar, lit his own, took a long draw and exhaled blue smoke.

"Ain' had it long," he grinned. "B'long t' th' deputy."

He chuckled and took another draw. "That ol' bastard, he like a bird's nest on th' ground. Sumbitch oughta known better than git up close an' personal wid Travellin' Man."

Opening the wallet he counted three more fives and four tens.

"Well Goddam," he said. "Sixty dollars. I thinks we's ahead already."

I shook my head, said that I couldn't believe what he'd lifted the deputy's wallet.

Travellin' Man replaced three of the tens and handed the wallet to the barman.

"I ain' seen no wallet," he turned to the barman. "Yo' seen me wid a wallet?"

"I ain' seen nothin'." He lifted an eyebrow in my direction. "This honky cool?"

Travellin' Man nodded. "He ok. He the reason we gots rolled but he means well. He ain' from roun' here, is all."

The barman's head shifted imperceptibly, I took it to be acceptance, but not of me.

"He calls his self Hobo John," said Travellin' Man. "Worse damn hobo I ever seen, I near bust a gut draggin' his ass on th' train then near bust a gut laughin' when he fell off in th' depot."

I rode the outbreak of laughter as Travellin Man lifted the bottles and handed one to me. "Good times, White Boy," he said.

As I took a swig of beer, Travellin' Man turned to the barman. "Ain't been around town fo' a while," he said. "Anythin' goin' on?"

The barman shook his head. "Not much here, Half-Pint probl'y got somethin' happenin' later," he said. "An' I heard they gonna be a country dance at the Dedman Plantation.

Travellin' Man nodded thoughtfully. "Dedman, huh? Now THAT would be somethin' t' see."

He took another swig and then turned to me.

"Dedman Plantation," he said. "Tha's a wild place. Sat'day nights at Dedman, like a Sat'day night in hell. Lot's o' drinkin' an' fightin' an' carryin' on."

He paused. "Ol' Dedman, he th' owner, he say, 'what happen on th' plantation, stay on th' plantation'. Long as niggers turn up fo' work on Monday he don' care much about what-all they done. Nigger end up in jail, ol' Dedman be down the courthouse an' post his bond an' git th' nigger out an' back in th' cotton field sooner n yo' could say it."

Travellin' Man paused again. "I heard tell one time, on a Sat'day night on Dedman back in nineteen an' twenty eight; two fool white boys showed up, come fo' t'listen t' th' music. Anyhow, they got t' drinkin' white whisky an' one started comin' on t' this plantation gal. She don' want none o'him and started yellin' fo' her boyfriend. Nigger turned up an' he an' the white boy started gettin' into it. Ends up, th' nigger shot th' white boy in th' face. Dead right there. Well, suh, tha's a whole box o' bad news jus' been opened up. Anyplace else, yo' even talk back to a white man you' ain' gon' see th' next sunrise. Anyhow, th' other white boy, he goes a runnin' an' a hollerin' up to th' plantation house. Ol' Dedman come out an' when he heard that a white boy been killed, he went down t'th' party wit a shotgun. Soon as he found out his best nigger had done th' killin', he took th' nigger's gun an' tol' him t' git t' bed an' don' come back til' he say so. Then Ol' Dedman, he tell two other men t'pick up th' dead white boy an' go bury him, jus' like that. White boy still livin'

215

he say, 'you cain't bury him, we needs th' sheriff right now.' Ol' Dedman, he put a hand on th' white boy's shoulder an' tell him t' calm down an' everythin' gon' be alright an' t' follow him back t'th' plantation house an' he go'n sort everything out. Few minutes later, they's a shotgun blast an' th'other white boy, he never was seen again."

Travellin' Man snorted when I said that I found it hard to believe that a white plantation owner would defend a black man who had killed a white man.

"Tha's cos yo' don' know nothin' 'bout life down here in Missi'ippi. Ol' Dedman, all he care 'bout is greenback dollar bills. He thought that if'n he got the sheriff in, then he'd lose his best nigger an' lose workin' time fo' all the niggers that seen what happened. Then they's th' town's reaction. White folks hear of a nigger killin' one a they own, fo' yo' know it they's go'n be lynchin's an' burnin' crosses. Yes suh. Ol' Dedman, he figure them two boys go'n be missed sho' nuff, but they weren't nothin' t'place 'em at his plantation on a Saturday night an' none o' his workers go'n care or be fool 'nuff t' say nothin' 'bout two no-account white boys di'nt have nuff sense t'stay wid they own. He figured his way was the best way, get things under control an' back t' normal. Don' be fuckin' 'round with Ol Man Dedman."

We drank some more beer and then Travellin' Man said,

"Lemme aks yo' somethin'," he said. "Cos yo' ain' never tol' me. How come yo' over here?"

Travellin' Man listened, his eyes wide by the time I finished.

"Man, tha's a story," he said. "So yo' di'nt go lookin' fo' Fat Man, he come lookin' fo' yo'?"

When I said that Fat Man just happened to be in Red's when I walked in that night, Travellin' Man shook his head. "Nuh-uh, Fat Man don' HAPPEN t' be nowhere. No suh, he knew you's go'n be in there, tha's why he come afta yo' later on. He had is eye on yo' all 'long. He seen somethin' in yo' that could get him what he wants."

I said that we hadn't met before that night.

"That don' matter none," said Travellin' Man. "Fat Man been playin' his game a looong time. Yo' might not a'met him, nor even seen him but he been there sho' nuff. He go where he goes cos he knows wha's go'n be there when he gits there. He smell th' sickness in yo' like a coyote smell a sick deer, then he make sure he put his self in th' right place t' take yo' down."

Travellin' Man became thoughtful.

"I gotta say White Boy. Fat Man, he strut his stuff an' do his dance cos folks goes t' him. They do's th' askin'. He knows he got what they wants, an' he make sho' they knows that too, plays 'em like pullin' catfish outta th' creek; an' all th' time pushin' up th' price."

Travellin' Man stared at me.

"But I tell you what, this th' first time I hear'd o' him comin' after someone an' pushin' t' sell what he got."

He scratched his chin. "It almost sound like someone gotta lien on him."

I said so what?

"So it mean someone gotta hold over Fat Man," said Travellin' Man. "An' whoever that is, he have t' be one mean-ass motherfucker."

That stopped me dead.

In Travellin' Man's parlance I tried, and failed, to picture a meaner motherfucker than Fat Man. It didn't bear thinking about and I couldn't begin to imagine Fat Man being in hock to anyone.

Travellin' Man looked around the bar. "Ain' much a'nothin' goin' on roun' here," he said. "Le's go see ol' Half-Pint."

217

# Half-Pint

Finishing our beers, we left the bar and Travellin' Man led me through a maze of backstreets. "Less chance o' th' sheriff seein' us," he said.

We stopped at the entrance of an alley.

"This th' place."

Travellin' Man slapped me on the shoulder. "C'mon, White Boy, le's have us some fun."

I followed him into the alley, which ran for about a hundred feet and ended in a single-story building made from sheet-iron and bordered at the front by a wooden porch on which sat five or six black children, all of whom eyed me first with suspicion and then with looks of opportunism.

I stopped Travellin' Man and asked him how the children had passed over.

"Miss'ippi flood," he said. "Nineteen an' twenty-seven. Levee broke and done flooded the whole delta. Nearabout five hunnerd dead, I heard. Wimmins an' children, mostly." He shook his head. "High water everywhere."

He stepped towards the kids.

"White Boy, he wit' me," he said. "So don' none o' yo' even think o' rollin' him."

He pointed to the smallest of the boys, a vaguely familiar-looking urchin dressed in rags.

"Look up at me, son. Yo' Jacob's Davenport's boy aincha?"

The boy nodded but said nothing.

"Whatcho' name? Harry ain' it?"

"Henry," said the boy.

Travellin' Man winked at me. "Henry, tha's what I meant."

He looked around. "Where yo' Pa at?"

Henry pointed towards a green-painted wooden door with a small hatch. "He in there."

Travellin' Man nodded. "An' how long he bin in there?"

Henry shrugged. "Jus' a little afta sundown, I guess."

Travellin' Man turned to me, "That mean he gon' be flyin' high by now."

I asked who he was talking about.

"Jacob Davenport, he the head man in this heyah barrel-house. That mean he in charge o' makin' sho' they ain' no trouble. Trouble is, Ol' Jacob he like his self a drink now an' again, well mostly again an' again, got him a tendency t' get a might ambitious when th' corn liquor gets a hold, which it always do."

Travellin' Man thought for a moment.

"If'n we goes in," he said. "One-a two things go'n happen. One, ol' Jacob go'n be sober an' we go'n have us a quiet night." He paused. "O' two, ol' Jacob gon' be a full-a-whisky sonofabitch, liken t'bust me upside th' head wit a two-by-four."

When I asked why that was likely to happen, Travellin' Man actually looked sheepish. "He think his woman be slippin' out wit me one time."

I asked why he would think that.

Travellin' Man's eyes betrayed him with a furtive glance towards Henry and I burst out laughing when I realised why the boy looked familiar.

"It ain' no laughin' matter," he hissed.

I said that the boy had his eyes.

"Yeah, n' yo' go'n have my fist if'n yo' carry on."

When I asked him if Jacob knew, Travellin' Man took me to one side.

"I don' think he know fo' sho'," he said. "His lady, she say th' kid his, but he def'nly suspicious, an' when he drunk he take agin' me."

Travellin' Man sighed. "Yes suh, he one ornery sumbitch an' that ain' no lie."

I asked him why he'd brought me here.

"Cos he also th' best damn harp player yo' ever gon' see."

Travellin' Man made up his mind.

"C'mon White Boy," he said. "If yo' go'n be a bear, be a grizzly."

Travellin' Man stepped up, rapped on the door then turned and winked at me. Moments later the hatch slid open to reveal a pair of magnified eyes squinting through bottle-thick spectacle lenses.

"Who dat?" squeaked the eyes.

"Well Goddam," said Travellin' Man, "Who 'n th' hell put a blin' ol' fool on th' fron' do'?"

The magnified eyes blinked, widened, and then a high-pitched voice yelled, "Travellin' Man! I thought I smelled yo' stink. Where yo' bin, son?"

Travellin' Man grinned. "Well if yo' open this Goddam do', I'ma tell yo'."

The hatch slammed shut followed by the sound of a chair being scraped across the floor, and then a bolt rattled and the door swung inwards releasing the noise of a raucous party and, as I stepped towards the door, the now-familiar smells of body-odour, cigarette smoke and fried chicken.

A figure stepped from behind the door. The owner of the magnified eyes turned out to be a wrinkled-faced old black man standing three-feet tall if he was an inch.

He looked up at me, blinked owlishly then turned to Travellin' Man. "Dis cracker widjoo?"

Travellin' Man grinned. "White Boy, I want's yo' t'meet Half-Pint Pearson. Half-Pint, this here fella call his self Hobo John, but tha's a whole other story."

Half-Pint blinked at me and then turned back to Travellin' Man.

"I know'd yo's a'comin' tonight. I said, 'Travellin' Man gon' come roun' tonight' tha's jus' what I said. Folks say 'how yo' know that', yo' don' know that?' I jus' say, 'he a'comin'' an' heyah yo' is. Yes suh, sho' nuff, heyah yo' is, jus' like I say."

He nodded in self-affirmation. "Jus' like I say."

"Well now we got that clear," said Travellin' Man. "What all else be happenin'?"

Half-Pint nodded towards the rear of the juke-joint, "Plenty o' whisky an' singin' an' carryin' on. Yes suh, folks gettin' 'cited cos they knows yo's a comin' jus' like I say yo' was."

He turned to look up at me. "I knows yo' a comin' too. But I nivah said nothin' 'bout that. Nivah mentioned no White Boy comin' in heyah, but I knowed, yes suh, but I nivah said."

He paused. "Some things it ain' best t'know till it come upon ya', tha's th' best times t'know right then, when it come upon ya'. Ain' got time t'think, jus' gotta react, yes suh. Tha's honesty, right there. Ain' no time t'plan, gotta react."

His words made me uneasy and I asked him what he meant.

"Whatchoo heyah fo'," he said. "I knows whatchoo heyah fo'."

He shook his head. "An' it ain' right, no suh, yo' come t'take what they got, take all they got an' they ain' nivah git it back. Nuh Uh. That ain' right, an' it gon' cause people be troubled fo' long time. Lonnng, lonnng time. Yes suh, I knows this, jus' like I knows yo's a comin' an cos I knows this I nivah said yo's a comin'. I nivah did say that. No suh."

222

Travellin' Man shook his head.

"Half-Pint," he said. "Yo soun' like yo' swallowed a Gatlin' Gun. I cain' barely git time t' pick out any words yo' sayin', an' when I do pick 'em out they long gone down the road chased by th' thousands o' others that come a tumblin' out aftah."

Half-Pint lifted his head. "I gotsta git my words out quick," he said. "I got lots mo' words t' come an' I needs t' git em' all out fo' my time come. Yes suh, I done counted all my words an' I knows how many come out an' I knows how many left inside. Half-Pint knows this, but Half-Pint gotta know which words t' keep inside an' which words he gon' let out an' when he gon' let 'em out, cos if'n he let out th' wrong words at th' wrong time then folks be knowin' what they got no business be knowin' an' then they gets upset an' tha's when all th' trouble an' caryin' on be happenin'."

Travellin' Man shook his head again. "Well, since we be standin' here yo' got rid o' a shitload o' words sho' nuff, but yo' ain' said nothin' worth shit."

Half-Pint grinned slyly.

"Tha's where yo' wrong, Travellin' Man," he said. "I gotsta get them words out cos t' make room fo' th' important words, they gon' be on they way real soon. Reeeeal soon. Half-Pint knows this," He swung around and pointed at me. "An' White Boy knows it, too. He jus' don' know yet whatall he don' know."

"Well I tell y'all what I knows," said Travellin' Man. "I knows they some words a'comin' outta my mouth, real soon. An' whats mo' I knows 'sacly what they gon' be an' in what order." He paused, "they gon' say, 'git me a bottle a whisky, Goddamit, cos all this tongue waggling be makin' this ol' boy one thirsty-ass nigger."

He pointed to me. "An' White Boy knows that, cos he th' one gon' buy me th' Goddam whisky. C'mon, I seen a table by th' bar."

"I knows yo' gon' say that," said Half-Pint.

Travellin' Man grabbed my arm and dragged me inside.

The joint was packed but at the back there was indeed an empty table. To the left a small stage stood empty, while to the right, the bar was mobbed by noisy drinkers.

Travellin' Man turned to me. "Yo' take th' gittars an' grab that table, I'll git us some whisky. Yo' can pay me back when I sits down."

At the table, I looked around the juke-joint, ignoring again the sideways looks and muttered comments. From the far end of the room came the sharp clack of a pool ball followed by the sound of several balls being pocketed, followed immediately by a roar of disbelief as the victor, a young black man in a sharp suit and a trilby hat, raised his cue in triumph. Grinning wildly, he took dollar bills from some of the crowd that circled the pool table.

A bottle and two short glasses appeared in front of me.

"Tha's 'Eight-Ball'" said Travellin' Man as he sat down. "Biggest hustler they is."

He cracked the top from a bottle of white whisky, filled the glasses, emptied his in one slug, winced and refilled his glass.

Taking a more measured sip, Travellin' Man ran his tongue over his lips then nodded towards the pool game. "Tha's one way o' makin' money," he said. "But it ain' all that. It ain' like playin' th' dice."

When I said that it seemed to me that both games were played with the intention of taking money from unsuspecting punters, Travellin' Man grinned and raised his glass.

"Tha's true, sho' 'nuff," he said. "But yo' know what makes playin' th' bones mo' pref'r'ble than chasin' pool balls roun' a table?"

I was about to reply when another roar erupted from the gloom of the juke-joint, followed by angry shouts and a scuffle that degenerated into a fist fight. I heard the swoosh-crack of a pool cue against someone's head and out of the corner of my eye saw Travellin' Man lunge towards me, his arm outstretched. As I turned I heard another, more sickening crack as Travellin' Man screamed in pain and buried his right hand beneath his left armpit.

"Mother-FUCKER!"

I asked him what had happened. Still wincing he pulled his hand out. It was still holding the pool ball but his little finger was bent outwards at an angle that made me feel sick.

Jumping up, I yelled for someone to get me some ice then looked down to see Travellin' Man lift the whisky bottle with his left hand, take several long pulls, belched whisky fumes and then put the bottle back on the table.

"Numbs th' pain," he croaked.

I asked him if it worked.

"Nuh uh," he said. "Hurts like a motherfucker."

In the corner, the brawling began to spread outwards. I heard more shouting, louder this time and punctuated with the dull thudding impact of a blunt object meeting flesh and bone.

I looked across to see a tall, broad shouldered black man staggering into the melee. His thin face was twisted into a sneer that was accentuated by narrowed, menacing eyes, a pencil-thin moustache and silver goatee beard. Criss-crossed over the top of his dark suit, white shirt and string tie he wore two leather bandoliers loaded with harmonicas.

He was also carrying a short wooden club which he swung indiscriminately.

"Quitcho' nonsense," he yelled. "I'ma start me a graveyard o' my own by bustin' ever one o' yo' motherfucking heads, ever last motherfucking one."

Those fighting ducked out of his reach and made their way out of the brawl until peace was eventually restored.

The tall figure looked around the juke-joint, grinning in drunken arrogance.

His grin froze and began to fade as our eyes met and he headed towards me. Then he saw Travellin' Man, changed course and the dying grin gave way to a scowl.

"Travellin' Man, yo' sonofabitch, whatchoo doin' in my joint? I'm of a mind t'fuck yo' up good."

As he drew close I stepped between them. I told him that Travellin' Man was hurt and needed help.

"He ain' as hurt as he gon' be an if'n yo' think yo' gon' stop me, then yo' wrong, honky."

My heart was pounding as I stepped forward and told him to give it his best shot.

His face twisted as he stepped towards me and started to raise the wooden club. My eyes were locked on his and I was about to swerve out of his reach as the whisky bottle exploded against the side of his head. Blood pouring from his wound, he turned towards the bar just as another bottle hit him in the face and dropped him like a shot buffalo.

I looked around to see Half-Pint clamber down from the bar and scuttle towards us.

"I knowed this gon' happen," he squeaked. "Yes suh, I knowed fo' long time this time gon come. 'Jacob,' I said. 'Yo 'tracts trouble like mule-shit 'tracts flies,'. Tha's what I said, jus' like that."

He turned to Travellin' Man. "How yo' hand, whatchoo done?"

I looked down, Jacob wasn't moving. When I asked Half-Pint if he was just going to leave him there, he shrugged.

"Ol' Jacob, he one ornery sumbitch but he gotta head like a piece o' railroad steel, yes suh. I hit him so many times afore he git used t'it. He gon' lay

226

there fo' while then, he mumble an' cuss some an' then he gon' git up an' be mad fo' while. Yes suh, that what gon happen, sho nuff. I knows this."

He turned back to Travellin' Man. "Lemme see yo' hand."

Travellin' Man placed the pool ball on the table and flexed his right hand. The little finger still pointed outwards and had begun to swell.

"I thinks it broke," muttered Travellin' Man.

"Ain't broke," said Half-Pint. "Tha's s'located, I kin see that, no suh that ain' broke, nuh uh. Half-Pint'a fix that, sho' nuff. Clear offa that table."

He was staring at me so I did what I was told.

"Travellin' Man, yo putcho hand on' th' table, I'ma fix it, fix it real good. White Boy, yo' stand behind Travellin' Man, he might likely get his self a bit lively wid th' pain an' I needs yo' t' hold him if needs be."

Half-Pint picked up the whisky bottle, poured some into a glass and gave it to Travellin' Man. "Drink that in one go," he said.

Before he finished the sentence, the glass was empty. "Goddam, boy," said Half-Pint. "I said drink it, don' breathe it."

He poured another glass.

"Now drink that'n."

Travellin' Man drank.

Half-Pint poured another glass.

"Jus' one mo'."

Travellin' Man emptied the glass.

Half-Pint pointed towards the far end of the juke-joint then winked at me. "Who that over yonder?" He said.

Travellin' Man turned to look then bellowed in pain as Half-Pint grabbed his finger and realigned it with a snap that made me shudder in revulsion.

Grabbing him before he had a chance to react, I hung on as Travellin'
Man writhed in my bear hug, his agony venting in the form of a stream of
imaginative and profane invective. Eventually, the torrent of swearing reduced
to a trickle, then to a steady drip between each panting breath.

"Yo' can let me go, now White Boy." he said.

Someone had placed a glass full of broken ice onto the table, Half-Pint
emptied several lumps into a handkerchief he pulled out from his pocket.

He looked up at Travellin' Man.

"Hol' yo' han' flat on th' table," he said. "An' rest this on th' top.
White Boy'll po' yo' whisky."

Travellin' Man and I did as we were told. When I asked Half-Pint if he
wanted a glass, he shook his head. "I don' drink that shit," he said. "That shit'll
rot yo' gut clean through, jus' like that, yes suh, clean through."

Travellin' Man slugged his booze in one gulp then flexed his right
hand. "Man, that throb like a reg'lar sonofabitch."

"Leas' yo' can move it," said Half-Pint. "Leas' yo' can still play th'
gittar." He paused, then winked, "Yo' cain't play no worse anyhow, even if yo'
had busted yo' finger."

Travellin' Man's response was interrupted by a groan. We looked down
to see Jacob open his eyes and try to sit up.

"Motherfucker." Jacob stopped moving and clutched his head with both
hands. Judging by the damage from being hit by the whisky bottles, I could only
guess at the headache he was going to be suffering.

After a few moments, he moved his head tentatively then stared at the
blood on his hands.

"I done that," said Half-Pint. "I done throwed them bottles atchoo, yes
suh, an' if yo' wants t'make somethin' of it then lets me know, cos I'll surely do

it again. Yo's actin' all out yo' head an' I had t'putchoo down. Hope y'unnerstan' that?"

"All I unnerstan's," said Jacob. "Is that my head bleedin' an' hurtin' like a motherfucker an' when I stands up they's gon be some stompin' be goin' on."

"Well, if it consolate yo' some," said Half-Pint. "Yo' can have them bottles what hit yo' upside th' head an' don' need t' pay me nuthin'. How that sound?"

Jacob grunted.

"One condition," said Half-Pint. "Condition is yo' don' ac' that way no mo', not in my juke-joint, no suh. Ever' time Travellin' Man walk in heyah, yo' starts actin' up an' liken t' fuss an' fight an' it go'n stop. That clear widjoo?"

Jacob lifted his head. If looks could kill, he was facing a life sentence.

"Why donchoo aks him why I does it." He growled.

"Cos' I don' give a shit," said Half-Pint. "This my place an' yo' gon' respec' that o' I'ma kick yo' ass all down th' road. Y'unnerstan'?"

Jacob grunted again.

"I didn' heyah that," said Half-Pint. "I didn' heyah yo' say yo' unnerstan'. You unnerstan' me, Jacob?"

Jacob was clearly not happy, but he nodded, "OK, Goddammit, I unnerstan'."

"Well tha's good," said Half-Pint. "Now, how 'boutchoo folks kiss an' make up an' set 'bout playin' us some blues? Put a smile back on ever' ones faces an' have us a time?"

I asked Travellin' Man if he would be OK to play.

He flexed his hand once more. "I guess," he said. "I don' pick much wit th' pinkie finger anyhow."

Jacob clambered upright, picked up the whisky bottles that had felled him, slammed them onto the table then dragged a chair and sat down.

He looked a mess.

His forehead had grown a lump the size of a goose egg and the side of his head and neck was covered in drying blood.

"Leas' th' bleedin's stopped." Said Half-Pint. "Yo' wan' me t' fetch a towel?"

Jacob said nothing but picked up the handkerchief, emptied the last of the ice fragments into it then held it to his forehead while he glowered at Travellin' Man.

Trying to defuse the situation, I asked him to tell me about his harmonicas.

He continued staring the turned sullenly to me. "Whatchoo wanna know?"

I asked him if they were Hohner Marine Bands.

"Yo' knows 'bout harps?" he asked.

I said that I knew about blues and that I'd read that Marine Bands were probably the most popular choice with blues harp players.

Jacob narrowed his eyes. "What-all harp players yo' know 'bout?"

I mentioned Peg Leg Sam, Memphis Willie.B and Sonny Boy Williamson.

"Yo' knows Sonny Boy?"

I said that I'd read about him and listened to his music.

"John Lee Williamson," he said. "I taught that sonofabitch how 'play when he's a little bitty boy. I knowed him from when we's both livin' in Jackson, Tennessee an' then we hooked up again in Arkansas jus' fo' he went on up t'Chicago."

This was gold dust.

I asked him if he would mind if I recorded him while he told me some more.

He frowned. "Yo' want's t' make a reco'din' o' me?"

"He reco'din' ever'body," said Travellin' Man. "He say he' gon' sell th' reco'din's so that white folks can heyah th' real blues."

Jacob frowned as much as his swollen brow would allow him. "White folks lisnen' t' blues?" he said. "Ain' never heard o' no white folks buyin' no race reco'ds. I thought white folks listened t' Jimmie Rodgers, yodelin' an' shit?"

"Well, it's true," said Travellin' Man. "I been showin' White Boy 'roun' Miss'ippi, learnin' him where all th' good blues at, tha's how come we in here now. He say 'why we comin' in heyah when yo' say all Jacob wanna do is bust yo' in th' head?' An' I say, 'cos Jacob' th' best damn harp player they is.'"

I was getting my voice recorder from the satchel when Jacob nudged me.

"'S'at true?" he said. "Travellin' Man really say that?"

I told him it was and he did.

Jacob grunted. "Ain' never got recorded, though. Yo' think maybe yo' gon record me?"

Before I could answer, Half-Pint leaned forward and thumped the table. "It ain' right what he's doin'. He takin' stuff from folks ain' nivah gon get it back. I knows this, yes suh, he takin' stuff he don' got no bidness takin' an' it go'n end bad, yes suh, it go'n end real bad."

When I said that I didn't understand what he meant, Half-Pint jumped down from his chair and blinked defiantly at me. "Tha's th' trouble, White Boy," he said. "Yo don' unnerstan' an' yo' ain' nivah go'n unnerstan' cos yo' ain' from roun' heyah. No suh, Half-Pint knows who's gon' happen but they ain' no poin' Half-Pint preachin' cos ain' nobody gon' be lisnen' no how."

231

Half-Pint scraped his chair backwards. "I'ma go'n get back on th' do', stop anymo' hoodlums from a comin' in. Yo' folks can do what th' hell yo' want, an' talk 'bout whatchoo want but if'n yo' gon' stay in my juke joint then I wan's heyah some blues bein' played an' t' see folks dancin' an' enoyin' they-selves. An' it better be happenin' soon or I'ma kick all yo' asses out th' do' an' all th way down th' big road. Y'unnerstan' me?"

Even Travellin' Man looked sheepish.

"Anything yo' say, Half-Pint," he said.

Magnified eyes flashed malice at all of us. "I wantchoo on that stage in five minutes, don' make me come back an' remind yo'."

"Half-Pint right," said Jacob. "Time we played us some blues."

We all stood up and Jacob nudged me again. "Maybe you an' me, we can talk some later on? I'll tell yo' 'bout Rice Miller an how I learned him th' harp, too."

When I said that I looked forward to it, Jacob nodded at my resonator. "See yo gotcho self a National," he said. "Thas' a fancy gittar sho' nuff. Where yo' git it?"

His question reminded me of Fat Man and the pawn shop. I was about to answer but he had turned away to stare at Travellin' Man. "Yo' up t'playin'?" he barked.

"Well I'll tell yo' what," said Travellin' Man. "Busted finger o' not I'll play yo' ass offa th' stage."

"'S'at so, ol' man?"

It looked like it was about to kick off again so I stepped between them and said that we'd better play something.

"We?" said Jacob. "Yo' don' think yo' gon' be playin' tonight? This a juke-joint, black folks 'spectin' black music. Whatchoo think yo' gon' play?"

I asked him if he'd heard of Blind Willie Johnson.

"Sho'," he said. "Nigger from Texas, I heard. Yo' knows his stuff?"

By now my bottleneck was on my finger, I had slung my resonator over my shoulder and was tuning it to Open D.

"Whatchoo gon' give 'em, White Boy?" Travellin' Man's eyes were twinkling.

When I said that I thought I'd try 'Nobody's Fault But Mine', Travellin' Man pointed to Jacob. "Yo' heard th' man," he said. "He gon' be playin' in Vestapol, bettah git yo' ass in gear an' try an' keep up."

Travellin' Man turned back to me. "Yo' git on up there, White Boy, I'ma practice some, git my fingers amovin an' then I be along an' show y'all how th' blues oughta be played."

Leaning in close, he winked at me. "Blow this sumbitch away."

As I stepped onto stage, I felt both nervous and elated. Most of the crowd were talking either at the bar or huddled around tables. The last stragglers from the fight had calmed down to name-calling and finger-pointing.

I took a deep breath, hit the strings and simultaneously dragged the bottleneck down to the twelfth fret. I began picking out the beat with my thumb, alternating between the first and third string, each beat louder and stronger and creating a trance-like pulse. People began to take notice as I began the searing melody on the top string, the resonator screaming the tune as I growled at the top of my voice:

*"We-eellll, Well,*
*Nobody's fault but mine*
*Nobody's fault but mine*
*If I don't read it my soul be lost*
*Nobody's fault but mine"*

233

I looked over at Travellin' Man, his eyes closed and his feet stamping as he nodded his head to the beat. Next to him, Jacob stared at me, pulled a harmonica from his bandolier and raised his eyebrow.

I nodded imperceptibly as I did my best to honour the song by one of the finest slide players ever recorded. Jacob wandered across, his swagger nonchalant but his eyes locked onto my guitar as he counted himself in and joined in with a harmonica riff that sounded like it was growling from the very depths of hell.

"Nobody's fault but mine"

The resonator screamed and the harmonica howled and people leaped to their feet and began to fill the space in front of the stage until soon almost everyone in the room was dancing.

Jacob looked cool, mantling his harmonica like a bird of prey over a fresh kill as he cavorted around me, every fibre of his being, every twitch of his performance all focussed into dragging the soul of Blind Willie Johnson back into the room.

Half way through I made a mistake, a bum note followed by rookie timing error that almost threw me, but Jacob was all over it, playing louder and with an exaggerated flourish of stage misdirection but with half an eye on me as if to say, "I got this, but don't do it again."

I didn't and all too soon I was in the closing bars of the song. Jacob swung up close, spinning around and blowing hell out of the harp, as he faced me he raised his eyebrows, stared pointedly at my guitar, nodded twice and then span away. I looked over at Travellin' Man who was winding his arm as if to say keep going.

Panic set in as my mind went completely blank about what to play next. Somehow I managed to keep the slide melody going as I racked my brains; then Jacob charged in and began a blistering solo that had the crowd yelling. After a

234

few bars he spun around again and loomed in close, his eyes flashing a warning at me. I leaned forward and in a hoarse whisper asked him to give me a train whistle. Jacob gave the briefest of nods then span away across the stage, his harp blasting out raw, dirty blues riffs as he covered for me. Out of the corner of my eye I saw him glance over at me, I nodded slightly and his riffs segued seamlessly, first into the sound of a steam train and then into a long, lonely whistle-moan as I launched into the opening bars of 'Special Streamline' by Bukka White.

As I narrated the spoken parts of the song, Jacob kept up a relentless chugging on the harp before screaming along with the slide notes.

"Play that box, White Boy."

I looked over to see Travellin' Man strutting his stuff and getting his cool self on down with two large black women, both of a certain age who seemed to be competing as to who could gyrate closest to him and in the most suggestive manner.

"Tha's what I'm talkin' bout'" he yelled. "Tell ever'body th' news White Boy. Beat on that box an' get that shit down."

So we did. Jacob and I stayed up onstage for another four songs; long enough for Travellin' Man and the two ladies to disappear and for Travellin' Man to return alone but with a shit-eating grin on his face.

"Yo' want I take over?"

I nodded. Jacob was still going strong, playing as if possessed by the music, dancing around the stage oblivious to everything, his cheeks bloating and hollowing as he pushed and pulled the most incredible sounds through the reeds of his harp.

As the final song neared the end I saw Travellin' Man loop his guitar strap over his shoulder, pick a few chords and then stride towards the stage. I played a slow blues walk-down and then introduced Travellin' Man onto the stage.

I turned to see Jacob glowering but Travellin' Man merely shrugged and kicked off with 'Future Blues' by Willie Brown. As his fingers snapped at the strings he caught my eye and gave a sly wink. 'Future Blues' has a quirky rhythm that doesn't lend itself well to harmonica, but Jacob gave it his best shot and only missed the first couple of bars before coming in with a killer riff that complemented Travellin' Man's playing. The moment may have been saved but the look on Jacob's face told me that this wouldn't be the last we heard of it. I walked over and placed my guitar on the table then fished in my satchel for my camera and phone.

I shot footage of Travellin' Man and Jacob and then wandered around the juke-joint, filming as I went, taking in people dancing, lovers kissing and youths playing pool. I did one circuit of the place then returned to the bar, got myself a beer and made my way back to the stage. Travellin' Man was still playing up a storm but Jacob had gone. I filmed some more and then set off once more around the juke joint. In the far corner of the room I saw a group of men squatting facing the wall. As I drew closer I could see they were playing dice and in amongst them sat Jacob, shaking his cupped hand with a flourish before tossing two dice towards the wall.

I couldn't see what had been thrown but a young man squatting next to Jacob shook his head in disbelief as Jacob picked up a fist-full of dollar bills from the floor.

The young man was not happy and tried to stare Jacob down.

"Yo' gots somethin' yo' want's t' say, sport?" Jacob's face hardened with each word that he spat.

If the young man was going to argue, the way his shoulders slumped told me he'd changed his mind. His scowl told another story. Getting to his feet he turned towards me. "Motherfucker switched bones," he said. "I seen him do it."

In an instant, Jacob had leapt to his feet, spun the young man around, grabbed him by the throat and was now pinning him against the wall.

"Yo' needs t' watch yo' mouth, kid. Yo' 'cuse anyone o'cheatin' yo' better be sho' whatchoo gon' do' 'bout it."

As he spoke he was pushing upwards, lifting the youth until he was forced to stand on tiptoes. I saw Jacob's knuckles whiten as he squeezed the lad's throat, heard the rasping croak as the boy tried to plead for his life.

Uncertain what I could do, I stepped forward anyway. Still holding the youth against the wall, Jacob twisted towards me and pushed his finger in my face. "Yo' don' come no closer, honky," he snarled. "Yo' heard him 'cuse me o' cheatin' an' now this 'tween me an' him."

A knife appeared in his free hand.

My heart pounding, I asked him what he was going to say to Gabel.

Jacob sneered, "I ain' gon' kill no one. Jus' fuck him up is all. He gotta be schooled in th' ways o' th' juke house."

I pointed to the wet patch on the boy's crotch and said that he looked like he was quick learner. Jacob looked down just as urine splashed onto his shoe.

"Goddammit, yo' see that? Motherfucker pissed on me."

The young lad dropped to the ground as Jacob stepped back in disgust. I stepped between them and said that it looked like he'd taught the boy a lesson.

Jacob looked like he wanted to take it further but calmed down a little when I said that I wanted to talk to him about Rice Miller.

Still glaring at the boy, he snarled. "Whatchoo wanna know?"

I said that I wanted to hear anything he could tell me.

He turned to face me. "Why yo' so interested in black folks, anyhow?"

Before I could answer he said, "This Miss'ippi, White Boy, folks like us an' folks like yo', we don' get 'long too well."

I said that I wasn't from Mississippi and that where I came from things were different.

Jacob looked me up and down, his face twisted in contempt.

"Different huh?" he said. "I ain' never met a white man I could trust an' I ain' never met a white man didn't try an' beat me down."

I said that I don't know what to say.

He leaned in close, enveloping us in foul breath as his dead eyes locked onto mine.

"They's lotsa things yo' don' know," he said.

I asked him what he meant by that.

"Yo' think that jus' cos yo' hangin' roun' wid a motherfucker like Travellin' Man, that gon' make yo' black 'nuff so a nigger gon' be yo' frien'? Yo' think that jus' cos yo' pick th' gittar an' play th' blues that black folks gon' accept yo'?"

He shook his head. "Shit, White Boy, open yo' eyes, niggers be laughin' at yo' behind yo' back. Yo' a honky tryin' be black, yo' think that folks here gon' accept yo'? Yo' think that we all gotta be grateful cos yo' takin' an interest? Let me tell yo' 'bout that."

He shook his head again. "Yo' ain' nothin' more than a white Uncle Tom. Yo' ain' black an' no one gon' think yo' black. Stick wid yo' own kind, hang 'round wid yo' white bread friends an' live yo' white bread life an' leave th' negro livin' t' negroes. Whatchoo think 'bout that?"

I said that he sounded like a redneck.

Jacob's right arm blurred and I reacted just in time, jerking my head so that the knife-tip merely scratched at my throat. Instinctively my right foot slid backwards as Jacob stepped towards me. His hand blurred again, and again I avoided the blade then saw my chance. Charging forwards, I stooped low, grabbed his crotch and smashed my head into his chest. As I forced him backwards I parried his knife thrust and then hooked my foot behind his ankles and pushed hard. He staggered and a table splintered beneath our combined weight and in the maelstrom of the fight I heard glasses smash and people swearing. Jacob's eyes burned with murderous intent, I managed to grip his knife hand at the wrist but had to let go of his balls to block his left hand grabbing my throat. He wasn't giving up and he was stronger than me. I shifted position and was about to head butt him when everything went black.

I woke up stinking of whisky on a bare mattress in a small room illuminated by the hissing flame of a hurricane lamp.

The back of my head throbbed and my exploratory fingers touched a cloth bandage wound tightly around my skull.

"Wake snake, day's a-breakin', cain't leave yo' fo' five minutes wid out yo' raisin' a bamalong."

Travellin' Man chuckled when I asked him what a bamalong was.

"Bamalong's a fight, mo' of a brawl yo' might say."

His shadow crept and elongated across the wall as he picked up a chair and set it down close to the bed."

He chuckled again. "Yo' got into it wit' ol' Jacob, then?"

I said it was self-defence.

Travellin' Man chuckled some more. "Well, he ain' gon' forget that in a hurry. Ol' Jacob, he got tombstone eyes an' a graveyard smile. Yo' bettah watch yo' back."

I asked how he was.

"Oh, he in the next room," said Travellin' Man. "He carryin' a few mo' wounds than what he walked in with, but tha's th' way o' things. Trouble an' Jacob, they ain' never spent too much time apart."

239

"Then again," he said. "Yo' ain' too far behin'. I hear tell yo' was goin' afta' Jacob like a crazy man, fixin' t' turn him ever' way but loose, right up 'til Half-Pint snuck up an' hit yo' upside th' head with a bottle-a White Lightnin', tha's how come yo' stinkin' like a 'stillery."

My head pounded as I sat up, when it calmed down I looked around the room.

"We in a transom," said Travellin' Man. "One o' th' rooms out back. Usually men pays a dollar to come in here fo' t'be private wid a gal. Half-Pint took two dollars offa me; we spend too much time in here, folks gon' be talkin' 'bout us."

When I said I would settle up with him, Travellin' Man shrugged. "Ain' no big deal."

He dragged the chair closer, a grin spreading across his face. "I hear'd Jacob done called yo' a white Uncle Tom," he said. "First time I heard a nigger say that 'bout a white boy; is that how comes yo' went at him like a tomcat?"

I said it was something like that.

"Huh," said Travellin' Man. "Well, he keep on sayin' shit like that he go'n find his self wid coon-hounds on his track."

He narrowed his eyes at me. "Yo' goin' take this any further?"

I said of course not.

Travellin' Man nodded. "Tha's good," he said, then stood up.

"Yo' needs t' rest yo' head, White Boy. I'ma grab me some sleep then come find yo' when we ready to put one foot in front o' th' other."

After he walked out of the room I remembered reading somewhere that someone with a head injury shouldn't be allowed to sleep. I thought about this for as long as it took to frame the sentence 'what's the worse that can happen?' and then closed my eyes.

# Walkin' Blues

It was probably late morning when we emerged from the juke-joint. I had awoken earlier to Travellin' Man banging on my door. My head was sore but the pounding had calmed down so I removed the bandage.

We walked out of Clarksdale in silence, the landscape changing from quiet residential streets to a dirt road and cotton fields.

Eventually Travellin' Man said, "White Boy, that was some show yo' an' Jacob put on. He might be a ornery motherfucker wid a barrelhouse habit an' blood in his eye but he sho' can blow on that harp."

I said that it was good to play with him but I wished that I'd managed to record him.

Travellin' Man smiled. "Check yo' cam'ra," he said.

Frowning, I reached into the satchel, grabbed the camera, switched it on and selected the latest recording.

For the first few seconds, footage was shaky and I heard Travellin' Man's voice say, "Jus' point this at the white boy on th' stage, I'ma gon' dance wid them two honeys an' then I'ma gon' come back. Don' even think o' runnin' off cos I'll find yo' an' I'll fuck yo' up good."

Another voice said, "Yes sir," and then the picture settled to show me playing and singing as Jacob prowled around me.

I have to admit I was secretly proud of my performance.

"Paid a kid five dollars t' record that fo' yo'," he said. "Woulda done it myself, but I seen two gals in real tight dresses, showin' they shapes at me an' draggin' me t' them like a moth t' a candle."

I said that the footage was amazing and thanked him.

"Ain' nothin'," he said. "When we gets t' Dedman, yo' gon' see some mo' blues; better make sho' yo' got space on that thing."

I said I would then asked him where we were headed.

"We's headed fo' Coahoma Point. Tha's a short little town 'tween here an' Dedman. We gon' grab sumpin' t' eat then cut some heads on th' street."

He looked at me. "Yo' achin' head gon' be up fo' that?"

Putting the camera away I said that it might be if I knew what it meant."

"Cuttin' heads," said Travellin' Man. "Is when yo' is playin' on th' same street as some other motherfucker wid nothin' mo' than a gittar an' high hopes. Yo' set up jus' along th' street an' try n' play better n' he does so yo' can poach his crowd an' git them t' watch yo' not him."

When I asked him how he knew that there would be other singers on the street, he grunted. "Cos Coahoma Point's the nearest town t' Dedman's, an' tha's where ol man Dedman send his boys t' look fo' gittar pickers."

He paused then said, "Ever' nigger wid a gittar gon' be headin' there; an' I tell yo' what, White Boy, when it come t' cuttin' heads, this black man ain' never been beat. So yo' bettah be sho' that if yo' gon' play wid me, an' if'n yo' want's t' get into Dedman's, then yo' gon' have t' stomp down play."

I said that I thought we could just turn up at the plantation.

Travellin' Man shook his head. "Nuh-uh, it don' work like that. Ol' man Dedman he don' 'llow jus' anybody on his plantation. He only wan's th' best players an' th' best singers, cos he wan's as many folks turning up as he can. Yo' don' jus' turn up an' play, yo' gotta be chosen."

Travellin' Man went on, "While yo' was out cold I's talkin' t' a couple o' fellas, they say ever'body talkin' 'bout it, they say ol' man Dedman gon' pay big money."

I asked Travellin' Man what he meant by 'big money'.

"Oh, he pay maybe, ten, fifteen dollars fo' a big name t' play by the Plantation House then five dollars t'play down by the Plantation Store."

When I said that it sounded like a grand gesture for a plantation owner to pay out for a party for the workers, Travellin' Man stopped and stared at me.

"Fo' th' workers?" he said. "He ain' doin' shit fo' th' workers."

I asked him what he meant.

Travellin' Man shook his head.

"I's real simple, White Boy," he said. "He in it t' make money, pure an' simple. See, it breaks down like this: Ol man Dedman, he make corn whisky on th' side, when he makes enough he throws a big Saturday night party, pays out fo' th' best gittar pickers an' then puts his liquor on sale. Saturday night niggers, all they wan's t' do is drink an' dance an' carry on an' get sloppy drunk. An' o' course th' only drink they can get is corn whisky. Whatever he pay out fo' gittar pickers, ol' man Dedman gon' get it back three times over from niggers buyin' his whisky."

Travellin' Man looked at me. "An' then they's folks sellin' food. All kindsa food; tamales, chicken, catfish, cornbread. Food fo' th' soul, y'know wham sayin'? Only th' best food they is. He let folks come along an' sell they food, but they has t' pay him a percentage."

I asked him what to expect from the party at Dedman's.

"Sat'day night in hell," he said. "I already tol' yo' that."

He thought for a while and then said, "Dedman plantation better 'n sixty thousand acres," he said.

"He got hunnerds' o' niggers workin' th' place from cain't see t' cain't see ever' day o' the week. He know that come Saturday, nigger wanna party an' tha's 'xacly what's gon' happen. Now, if'n yo' is easily scared o' offended then yo' betta think twice 'bout turnin' up."

He grunted when I said that I thought I could handle it.

"If'n we gets picked," he said. "We gon' get tol' where t' be an' when an' then collected in a big ol' open-back truck. They probably gon' fill th' truck an' when we gets there, we gon' be told where we gon' play. Best spot is right outside th' plantation house, tha's where th' best food, the best whisky an' th' purtyest wimmens gon' be. Anyplace else after that gon' be goin' down t' th' spot by th' commissary."

He looked sideways at me. "Now yo' gon' ask what th' hell a commissary is."

I said that it was a plantation store where workers could buy food and tools and suchlike.

"Well Goddam," said Travellin' Man. "White Boy DO know something."

He nodded. "But yo' right, an' th' commissary 'bout a mile from th' plantation house and right close t' th' whorehouses an' shacks. Niggers hang round there, they th' lowest o' th' low. They don' want th' fine folks from th' big house seein' them an' th' feelin's kinda mutual."

He paused. "I ain' never got me too much religion, never listened much to no preacher, but Dedman's, that a sinful place an' th' commissary like th' gates t' hell."

Travellin' Man's face looked troubled.

"If'n we gets that spot," he said. "Yo' gots t' watch yo' back, be careful whatchoo yo' say an' who yo' says it to, cos' once yo' in they ain' no rules."

His mood was getting troubled so I asked Travellin' Man if he'd ever met Charley Patton.

"Yeah, I seen him a few times. He a clowny sonofabitch but he sho' can play th' gittar."

Travellin' Man smiled. "I'll tell yo' what," he said. "Good as he was he always made time fo' youngsters startin' out an' he always lookin' fo' new folks

244

t'play 'long wid him. When it come t'music, ol' Charley Patton he used t' keep his head up an' keep a look out fo' what was goin' on. Ain' never seen anyone pick on th' gittar like he could. He spin it 'round, play it upside his head, fool 'round like that but when he say he gon' play somewhere then yo' knows he gon' be there an' he gon' be there all night."

Travellin' Man paused. "I seen him at Dedman's once, yo' could hear him from a mile away nearabout. Man, he had a voice an' he know how t'use it an' he know how t' work up th' crowd an' get 'em jumpin'. He a stomp-down entertainer sho' nuff."

I found myself smiling as I listened to the old bluesman, and then I asked him to tell me more about how he became a musician.

"Well, suh," he said. "I guess I had a choice. See, when I's growin' up, my daddy was a sharecropper on a plantation. Workin' from sun t' sun growin' cotton. I found out early on that it weren't gon' be no life fo' me, then one time we had a man come by pickin' on a gittar. He done some work fo' my daddy an' showed me how t'pick on th' gittar. Well, lemme tell yo', first time I learned me a coupla chords there weren't no stoppin' me an' I pestered my daddy til he got me a old gittar fo' my own. Afta' that, me an' that ol' box was closer than Jesus t' th' cross. Man, I jus' kep' learnin' an' learnin', playin' first fo' th' family then goin' out on my own."

Travellin' Man chuckled. "My daddy, he weren't too pleased wid whatall I's doin' an' he used t' whup me but good; 'specially when he catch me playin' 'stead o' doin' my chores - which was most o' th' time."

I looked across just in time to his expression soften.

"Then one time I done met me a girl an' she treated me nice an' I thought all my dreams had come true. Then she took off an' left me. Man, that got me th' blues sho' nuff."

He turned to me.

"Yo' got th' blues, White Boy. I's deep inside yo' but plain as day. Yo' tap into that when yo' playin', make th' gittar th' voice o' yo' pain an' they ain' nothin' mo' powerful. Man can only play th' blues when th' man got th' blues. Yes suh, tha's a natchel fact."

We stopped beneath the shade of a magnolia tree that dripped with Spanish moss.

Travellin' Man leaned against the trunk and adjusted his guitar.

"When yo' got th' blues," he whispered. "Yo' cry an' yo' cry alone. Yo' don' want no company. Yo' wan' sit down an' concentrate in yo' own mind. Yo' don' wan' no botherin'."

He shook his head. "'Oh I wished they go way', yo' say."

His guitar began to wail and once more I was entranced, once more this old man had captivated me.

I have no idea how long we stopped there beneath that ancient magnolia tree but I remember thinking that I never wanted it to end.

I was spellbound by the sound of his voice, hypnotised by the shifting expressions on his face. It was as if the pain of all human emotion was being channeled through the rich, dark tones of his deep southern accent, the muscle movements beneath his creased ebony skin, the sorrow that welled out of his hooded, yellowy eyes and the cries of anguish that issued forth each time the glinting bottleneck on his third finger slid across the strings of his guitar.

Tears filled my eyes at the raw passion in this impromptu performance. Every dream I'd ever had about experiencing the authentic music of the Mississippi Delta was realised right there by the side of that dirt road.

I loved this old man; loved him for all that he'd shown me and all that he'd taught me, loved him for his patience, his irascibility, his wry humour, dignity and honesty.

His playing and singing reached a natural break and so he stopped. Without speaking I leaned across and touched him on the shoulder. His eyes lifted and connected with mine as he nodded, a wry smile playing at the corners of his mouth.

"Tha's th' blues, White Boy."

We walked on in the silence born of companionship. Ahead of us the dirt road stretched away to a point on the horizon, flanked by cotton fields that glistened with standing water and capped by the deepest blue Mississippi sky. There was no other sound save for our footfalls and looking down I noticed that while my shoes and trouser legs were covered in dust, Travellin' Man's were immaculate. I remembered someone saying the same about Robert Johnson; no matter where he was or where he had been, his clothes were always clean and pressed.

The effects of his performance lingered within me, something unspoken had passed between us and the peace that I felt in the company of Travellin' Man was all-encompassing.

In the distance a small wooden shack was set back from the road. The sun was directly overhead and Travellin' Man stopped, lifted his hat and wiped the sweat from his brow.

"Sho' is a hot 'un today."

I asked him if he was OK.

"I'm OK," he said. "But I think I'ma find me some shade behind that shack yonder, maybe rest awhile, o' get a glass o' water if they's anyone home."

I said that sounded like a plan and we headed towards the shack.

The wooden building looked deserted but as we drew closer the screen door scraped open and a large old black lady wearing a brightly coloured do-rag, a faded cotton print dress and a sour expression appeared on the porch.

"Whatcho' bidness?" she yelled.

Travellin' Man tipped his hat. "Good day, Ma'am," he said. "My friend an' I we jus' walkin' on down th' road an' we both gettin' mighty hot an' wondered if we could dwell awhile in th' shade o' yo' house an' maybe trouble yo' fo' a glass o' lemonade?"

Having seen his track record with females, I was expecting for her to smile and melt at his words.

I wasn't disappointed.

Her expression sweetened instantly and she smiled coyly down at Travellin' Man.

"Yo' wan' some lemonade, honey-chile?"

"Travellin' Man winked. "Yes ma'am, if tha's not too much trouble fo' yo. Maybe I'll come along inside an' help yo' fix it?"

The old lady simpered. "Now yo' stay right down there, I got somethin' prepared jus' fo' yo' an' it won' take me but a minute to bring it on down."

She ran her finger coyly behind her ear. "'sides," she said. "Yo' look like yo' needs t' rest an' cool down some, get yo' strength back."

Travellin' Man nodded graciously. "Ma'am, I's much obliged, I surely am."

As she disappeared inside, Travellin' Man turned and gave me a sly wink. "Watch an' learn, White Boy," he said. I may have t' leave yo' on yo' own fo' while I attends t' some chores inside."

I didn't hear the screen door open or see the old lady come back out. Travellin' Man was joshing me about his forthcoming conquest, his broad smile alight with anticipation when an explosion deafened my left ear, a black hole appeared between his eyes and the top of his head erupted in a red-mist spray of bone and brain matter. His body slumped backwards, smashing his guitar as he slammed against a tree then crumpled to a sitting position. His head dropped forwards and blood gushed from his eyes, nostrils and sagging mouth, soaking his immaculate suit and staining it a deep red from the shoulders to the waist. His right foot tapped and the fingers of his right hand twitched in unison as if in a final performance and then stopped. Travellin' Man's left arm stretched outwards, his bottleneck lying a few feet away.

I looked down and saw that his shoes and trouser cuffs were coated in dust.

His body twitched like a puppet as four more gunshots blasted holes into his chest. My ears rang at the explosions and I remember shrieking in horror at seeing the bullets blowing my friend apart. I looked up, screaming at her to stop. In her hand a ancient Colt .45 revolver exhaled lazy tendrils of blue smoke. Grimacing down at me, her face twisted, eyes burning with insanity, she lifted the pistol.

"It's fo' yo' own good," she screamed. "Is what it is an' it ain' nothin' mo' than that."

Then she put the barrel in her mouth and pulled the trigger. The top of her head exploded into a brief crimson afro as she rocked on her ankles and dropped backwards like a felled tree, her skull making a sickening squelch as it hit the porch.

The silence afterwards was as horrific as the violence just before and for a long time I was unable to move. I just stood there, tears pouring down my face as I stared down at what was left of Travellin' Man.

Eventually I looked up.

On the porch, all I could see were the pink-white soles of the old lady's feet.

The silence was oppressive and I felt as if I was the last person on earth.

I looked down at Travellin' Man, his blood congealing around him. My chest tightened and as I stooped to pick up his bottleneck, I dropped to my knees and bellowed a primal howl of unbridled grief, my body rocking back and forth, my fingers turning the metal tube over and over as I wept for my friend.

I have no idea how long I knelt there but I remember thinking that I couldn't leave him lying on the ground. Still shaking, I wiped the snot from my nose, laid my guitar and satchel on the ground, rose to my feet, stepped over his body and walked around the shack.

At the rear, a crude lean-to roof provided shelter for a few well-worn tools. I picked up a shovel, selected a spot and began to dig.

I had dug maybe a foot down when a voice startled me.

"Livin' soul, everywhere ya' go ya' findin' destruc-shun."

I looked up to see Gabel silhouetted in the sunlight.

I said that I had had no part in this, that I had done nothing to cause this.

"Ya in league wid' Fat Man, dat make ya guilty by association."

His Jamaican patois hung heavy with contempt as he spat words at me.

"Si me now, me said no good come from ya foolishness, now tree' folks dead 'roun' ya. Gone forever."

I said that I was burying my friend and resumed digging.

"Don' turn ya back on me, livin' soul."

I looked up and said again that I was burying my friend and I wasn't going to stop until that was done.

Gabel stared at me and then nodded once.

"Me feel ya pain, livin' soul. Ya friend gone an' ya' grievin' fo' him. But ya not d'only one, ya not alone in ya hurtin'. Hear me when I say that Fat Man gon' pay fa dis an' fa' all else he done, an' if ya' wid him den ya gon' pay too."

I carried on digging.

When I finished the grave I walked around to the front of the shack.

The woman was gone.

Gabel was sitting in a rocking chair on the porch, smoking a huge joint.

He watched in silence as I knelt down, scooped my arms beneath Travellin' Man's body and struggled upright, a fresh sob escaping from me as the remnants of his guitar fell away.

I cradled the old man for a few seconds and then staggered towards the rear of the shack where I found Gabel standing by the hole that I'd dug.

He said nothing when I stepped down into the shallow grave, laid Travellin' Man in his last resting place, smoothed and straightened his clothing and then mumbled a few words. Tears cascading down my face, I stepped up out of the grave and began shovelling earth over Travellin' Man's body.

When I finished, Gabel removed his top hat, placed it over his heart and then back onto his head.

"Ya done a good ting," he said quietly. "When me turn up like dis, me send dem 'way. But ya got love fo' ya' friend. Ya' give respec' an' ting, ya treat ya friend right."

I stared down at the grave.

"Me tink ya' still got goodness inside."

I looked up and said that I really didn't give a shit what he thought.

Gabel tipped his head. "Me feel ya," he said. "Me sayin' dat cos' maybe it not too late t' break away from Fat Man."

Ignoring him, I walked around to the front of the shack and picked up what was left of Travellin' Man's guitar. The main body had taken the brunt of the force and was smashed beyond repair, leaving the guitar in two pieces of firewood connected by the strings. Gripping the neck, I placed my foot on what was left of the body and yanked upwards. The brief tension allowed the strings to sing out for a final time and then with a loud crack the wood splintered and separated.

I wrapped the strings around the neck, took it back to the grave, pushed it into the ground as a head marker and then stood by the graveside, reflecting on Travellin' Man and the time we had spent together. I knew I would never, ever forget him.

After a time I wandered around to the front of the shack. Gabel had returned to the porch, the chair squeaking softly as he rocked gently, the joint hanging from his lips.

I picked up my guitar, slipped Travellin' Man's bottleneck over my finger then sat on the steps of the porch and began to play, my fingers guided by the memory of his words and the sound of his voice.

The shadows had lengthened when I finally stopped playing. I stood up, stretched and turned to see Gabel staring out over the cotton fields

"Ya carryin' his memory, livin' soul," he said.

"Dat a big responsibility, a memory got powerful energy. Ya got ta keep it safe, nurture it, keep it real."

He took a large toke of the joint.

"Travellin' Man part o' ya now," he went on. "Ya become one, he in yo' an' yo' in him. It de way o' tings. Whateva ya' do now, he gon' guide ya, but ya' gotta keep ya respec' fo' him. Listen to him when he speak, he still heyah, still aroun' ya, he jus' not gon' be by ya side. Ya' dig me?"

When I said that I thought that I did, Gabel's top hat nodded.

I asked him where the dead people went.

He shook his head, rattling the bones weaved into his dreadlocks.

"Stuff like dat not fi ya t'know." he said.

He shook his head again when I asked him about Stella. When I pressed him to tell me he took a long toke on the joint, held the smoke for a long time then exhaled slowly.

"Not fi ya t'know," was all he said.

252

I asked him more questions but each one got the same response so I stopped asking and we sat quietly as the sun dipped towards the horizon.

Just before sunset, I heard the chair squeak as Gabel stood up.

"Trouble steppin' closer," he said. "Take my advice livin' soul. Go on back, ot'erwise Fat Man gon' bring ya down."

And then he vanished.

The delta silence felt ominous.

When the sun had risen to begin this day Travellin' Man had been there by my side. Now all I had were memories and every fibre of previous good-feeling had long since disappeared.

I stepped up onto the porch. All that was left of the old woman were the dark stains on the underside of the roof and on the boards where she fell.

I thought about her last words before she pulled the trigger, tried to guide my thoughts around the obvious conclusion, tried not to think of Fat Man directly lest he was somehow tuned in and able to pick up what I was thinking. In truth, that wasn't difficult, since my mind insisted on replaying the horror of what I'd seen. I blinked back tears at the memory as I took a deep breath and considered what to do next.

The landscape darkened and banished any notions I might have had about venturing out alone at night. Crickets began to call as I dragged the screen door open and went inside the shack. A hurricane lamp and a box of matches stood on a shelf by the door. After finally getting it to light I lifted it to illuminate the shack. I was standing in a large room that took up the width of the building; an open door on the far wall gave a glimpse of what looked like a small kitchen area beyond.

The place stank.

In the left side of the room stood a bed with a bare mattress stained with shit and partially covered with a filthy sheet, the corner of which had fallen into a chamber pot that was half-full with piss.

"I always was whatchoo might call a half-full kinda guy."

I whirled at the sound of Fat Man's voice, but the shack was deserted. I stood for a long time, until the silence became deafening and then, skirting the bed, I lifted the lamp to eye level and inspected a shelf that ran along the opposite wall. In the dim glow, various trinkets and odds-and-ends cast strange shadows as I passed along them.

The hurricane lamp hissed as I continued looking around the shack.

It didn't take long. From what I saw the old lady had lived alone in her squalor.

In a cupboard in the kitchen I found a sheet that looked less filthy than anything else in the shack. I walked out onto the porch, sat in the rocking chair, wrapped the sheet around me and thought about Travellin' Man as I stared up at a million stars.

I woke up with a stiff neck and an aching back and choked back my grief at the realisation that Travellin' Man was gone.

Wincing, I stood up and stretched to loosen my stiff joints. I mooched around the shack but found nothing else of any use or value apart from the envelope of cash that had fallen from the remains of Travellin' Man's guitar. Stuffing it in my pocket, I picked up my satchel and guitar, said some words over Travellin' Man's grave and carried on up the road.

# Tom Walker

The sun was high in the sky when I heard the sound of the engine.

I turned to see a cloud of dust billowing up from an old Chevy pick-up barrelling towards me. I stepped to one side, shielding myself from the dust as the pick-up skidded to a halt.

At the wheel was an elderly white man, stick thin with wispy silver hair, a hooked nose and a generous smile.

"How far ya' goin', son?" he said.

When I said that I was heading towards Coahoma Point, he grinned and slapped the side of the door. "Well, she ain't much," he said. "But she'll getcha where you wanna go, so hop in."

I clambered in, cradling my guitar between my knees.

The old man extended his hand, despite his arms being skinny and covered in liver spots, his grip was firm as he looked me in the eye.

"Name's Walker, Tom Walker. What's yours?"

I told him it was Hobo John.

"Hobo John, huh?" he said, his eyes twinkling. "Interesting accent you got there, son. Guess you must hopped more'n a few boxcars to get y'self around these parts?"

I said it was something like that.

"Well," he said. "Wherever you're from and whatever you're name is, welcome t'Miss'ippi."

Gears crunched, the engine revved and the old truck lurched forward, picking up speed until we were flying down the road.

Stones rattled beneath us, the engine roared and the wind howled past the open windows as the old man planted his right foot hard to the floor.

"Some folks finds my drivin' style a might disconcertin'," he yelled. "But see, I got this theory…"

I slammed into the door as he swerved to miss a pothole.

"The faster you go," he bellowed. "The more the truck wants to act like a plane. Of course, it ain't a plane, it ain't never gonna be a plane and it ain't never gonna take off, but it thinks it will and while it keeps trying it's gonna make the ride over these rough roads a little easier for me."

He looked over and gave me a huge wink. "My wife of course, she thinks I'm a crazy old coot and don't never stop reminding me of the fact. I says to her 'well, I may be a crazy old coot but I know what love is."

He winked again. "Her name's Victoria," he shouted. "She set her eyes on me back in eighteen hunnerd and seventy. I didn't think I had a snowball's chance in hell but she told me there and then we was going to marry."

The truck lurched and bounced as we swerved around another pothole.

Tom laughed out loud. "She come after me and she calls ME crazy."

I yelled that he was very lucky.

"That I am," he yelled back. "That I surely am."

We drove on in relative silence as Tom concentrated on the road.

A railroad sign loomed up ahead, to the left I saw a locomotive heading towards the crossing at full speed.

I shouted a warning just as we flew over the crossing, the train so close that I could see the driver's angry face and had to shield my ears against the raucous blare of the whistle.

"That fella drivin' the train and giving us the evil eye, tha's ol' Dan Tucker," shouted Tom. "Riles him up every time I do that."

Tom pointed ahead. "Coahoma Point's about another five miles from here, we should be there soon."

Part of me was relieved that the trip would be over while another part of me welcomed the distraction.

A few minutes later we skidded to a halt in front of the courthouse in the town square of Coahoma Point. Tom extended his hand and squeezed mine like a vice. "Pleasure talking to you, son," he said. "Good luck wherever you're going and with whatever you're doing."

I got out of the pick up; Tom gave me a cheery wave, gunned the engine, crunched the gears and roared off down the street.

# Coahoma Point

Coahoma Point was a bustling town at the edge of the Mississippi river and I followed the blast of a whistle down to the waterfront just in time to see a paddle steamer come alongside.

On the quayside, labourers scurried amongst huge stacks of cotton bales and passengers queued up patiently. As I watched, the huge vessel steered towards the quay, the paddles stopping and then spinning backwards, frothing the water as the steamer slowed and the crew threw lines to men waiting on the shore.

Within minutes, the steamer was tied up alongside with passengers disembarking across the gangway. On the jetty, stevedores manhandled the cotton bales across cargo gangways.

Taking out my camera I recorded the scene, panning across to capture the full majesty of this icon of the Mississippi river being used for what it was designed for and wondered if it was destined to be the same one that I saw back in my old life: tied up permanently at Natchez and being used as a casino.

"Sure is a beauty, is she not?"

I looked around to see a tall, well-dressed black man in a smart suit and homburg hat.

I agreed that she was.

"I'm guessing from your accent, sir," he said. "That you hail from England, might I ask from which region?"

Before I could answer he said, "I'm guessing somewhere in the West?"

When I concurred, he smiled and offered his hand. "My name's Nathaniel Marchant," he said. "I spent some time at Oxford in my youth and was lucky enough to travel around some."

When I shook his hand he stepped back. "Sir, I do hope I'm not intruding," he said.

I said of course not. His face showed relief as he continued.

"Ordinarily I would of course be reticent about approaching a person such as yourself, but I sensed something about you that sets you apart from the usual white person one meets in these parts."

He looked troubled again. "Have I overstepped the mark?"

I assured him that he had not.

"Might I ask what brings you to these parts?" he said.

I told him it was a long story.

"The most interesting ones usually are," he said. "For myself I trained as a lawyer. My family originated from Vicksburg, sharecroppers, apparently, but then my father and mother moved to New York City just after I was born."

Nathaniel smiled wistfully. "Lucky for me they were foresighted enough to search for a better life and when everyone else from the south went to Chicago, they moved to Harlem."

He turned to me. "Have you ever been to Harlem, sir?" he said.

I said that I hadn't.

"When I was growing up," he said. "Harlem was the place to be. My dad had the idea to open a club; so he, my two uncles, my brother and I, we worked all hours to raise enough money to rent a basement just off of 135th Street."

Nathaniel's face lit up. "Let me tell you," he said. "That was the place to be seen. Fats Waller played there, Zora Neale Thurston, Wallace Thurman and Langston Hughes used to drop by." He shook his head, "It was a jumping place alright, A'Lelia Walker used to invite us to parties at The Dark Tower, man…"

His voice tailed off and followed his stare into the middle distance.

After a moment, he said, "I run a small law firm here and I'm on my way to visit a friend of the family." Nathaniel smiled again, "A crazy old coot who drives his pick-up like a man possessed."

He beamed with delight when I asked if he meant Tom Walker.

"You know Mr. Tom?" he said.

I told him the story of my ride in the pick-up and he roared with laughter. "That's him," he said. "He roars around in that old junker like he just stole it. Always been the same."

He shook my hand again. "I'm on my way to see Mr. Tom later, why don't you join us? I'm sure he'll set an extra space for dinner, especially since you two are already old acquaintances."

I thanked him for his offer but said that I had a prior appointment and needed to get to work pretty soon.

Eyeing my guitar, he said, "Might I suggest that you try the corner of 4th and Juniper Street? The roustabouts and stevedores pass by that way heading into town from working on the river. It's pay day today and pickings should be mighty profitable for a musician of talent."

I thanked him for the advice.

"Not at all," he said. "The pleasure, sir, is all mine. Good luck in your ventures later and if I can be of any further assistance then please do not hesitate to holler."

We shook hands and I felt a piece of card pressed against my palm. His fingers gave a final squeeze and then he smiled, turned and strode away.

I looked down and read the business card he had palmed to me:

Nathaniel Marchant
Attorney at Law
Coahoma Point 1962

Putting the card in my satchel, I fished Travellin' Man's bottleneck out of my pocket, placed it over my third finger and went in search of 4th and Juniper.

When I got there, I found that someone had beaten me to it. A young black guitarist was belting out a blues song accompanied by an elderly violinist, and they were bloody good.

I stood for a while, watching them play until I saw the guitarist look at my resonator. A troubled expression flashed across his face and then his playing became more intense.

Travellin' Man's voice appeared in my head.

"Tha's good White Boy, yo' got him runnin' scared."

I stayed for a couple more bars, then smiled at the guitarist and walked on.

I set up my pitch about fifty feet away at the entrance to an alley between two buildings. If I listened carefully I could hear the guitarist and scratch of the violin.

Tuning my guitar I waited for their song to end, took a deep a breath and launched into 'Death Letter Blues', giving it the beans and beating hell out of the resonator as I yelled out the old Son House song.

"Take it easy, White Boy," said the voice in my head. "Yo' gotta be able t'do this all night if yo' have to. Let th' gittar do th' shoutin'."

I looked over to the crowd. A few faces turned towards me but no one moved. Then I heard the guitar and fiddle start up and the faces turned away.

I finished 'Death Letter Blues' and went straight into 'If I had Possession Over Judgement Day', played with a little less desperation. As I warmed up, a couple of passersby stopped to watch, then, as I was nearing the end of the song a few more people stopped to stare at me. It was then that it dawned on me that perhaps not too many white people played street blues to a black audience and that they had gathered out of curiosity.

Whatever. A crowd is a crowd and while they were there I was going to give them a show. As I played the final note of the Robert Johnson song I froze like a statue, stared straight into the eyes of a pretty black girl, counted to four in my head, winked at her and then began the bass-string run down into 'Future Blues' by Willie Brown.

The girl smiled as I sang to her about the woman I love being five feet from the ground. Glancing around I smiled back as I saw that more people were stopping.

'Future Blues' ended and as I thanked the crowd for listening I retuned the guitar from Open G to standard, took the slide off my finger, fished in my pocket for the pick and then dived into the staccato strumming of "Shake it and Break it" by Charley Patton. Immediately, feet began to shuffle and more smiles appeared as part of my small crowd actually began to dance.

"My jelly, my roll, sweet papa doncha' let me fall."

The young girl had a deep voice that belied her slight frame and as she joined in not only did she add a new dimension to my performance, she also allowed me to rest my voice. From dancing in front of me she moved to my side and sang to the onlookers. We played the song twice and then I segued into 'They're Red Hot'. I prayed silent thanks as the girl began to sing, not only knowing the words but also knowing how to work the crowd; gyrating in front of men and then moving to the outskirts, attracting more people to join our audience.

Looking across, I smirked as the other crowd turned their heads then began to disperse and head towards me, leaving the young black musician alone and forlorn. Smiling, I nodded my head in thanks to my new fans as they joined my crowd then felt my smile freeze as they kept on walking, ignoring me completely as they skirted my audience, picked up their step and almost hurried on down the street. The young girl stopped singing and followed, the crowd around me thinning and dispersing like cigarette smoke through an open window.

Then I looked to my right and saw the reason for the crowd's disappearance.

The black guitarist and violinist pressed their backs against the building as a gang of six rough-looking white men passed them and stalked towards me.

Stopping as they reached me, the largest, roughest looking man stepped into my personal space, his face a few inches from mine.

"Yo' like t'play nigger music?" he said.

I said that I liked playing blues.

He spat tobacco juice between my feet. "Nigger music," he repeated. "Makes them ol' jig-a-boos jump around like monkeys."

The gang sniggered. Their mere presence had cleared black people from the street; the fact that I was white didn't make me feel any less threatened.

"Yo' seem to pick on that box purty good, gotch yo'self a good crowd."

I said it was a good crowd until something scared them away.

He spat again and shrugged.

"They'll come back," he said. "Later on they be linin' up t' get in, payin' a nickel each. All them folks an' hunnerds more."

I asked him what he was talking about.

"At the dance later on," he said.

I must have looked stupid because he shook his head.

"At the Dedman Plantation. We lookin' for gittar pickers. Don' see too many white folks playin' nigger music, but yo' seem t'got what they want."

He paused and my heart stopped.

"Yo' wanna play?" he said.

When I asked who else would be playing, he shrugged. "Who ever we finds that we thinks good enough to drum up a crowda dumb negroes an' get 'em all fired up an' thirsty fo' a drink an' a good time in pursuit o' th' debauchin' they all seems partial too."

He stepped back.

"I ain' askin' again," he said. "Yo' wanna play tonight at the Dedman party?"

When I finally stopped babbling and managed to say yes, the man reached into his pocket, pulled out a yellow card and handed it to me.

I turned it over in my hand, it read:

Dedman Party, Saturday Night – Entertainer - Commissary

"Town square at eight o'clock," he said. "A big ol' stake truck gonna pull up jus' outside th' court house. Show that card t' the driver an' climb up on th' back. Keep a'hold of it if yo' wants payin' at th' end."

He looked me up and down and then sniffed.

"O' course," he said. "Yo' gon' be sat up in the back wid a buncha crazy-drunk ol' niggers. But I guess that don' confront yo' none."

I didn't reply, just kept staring at the card.

The man sniffed again.

"Truck ain' gon' wait," he said. "An' it's like to get a might fractious wid folks clamourin' t'get onboard so my advice to you would be to get there early and hop up on the truck soon as yo' like."

When I thanked him, he just nodded and strode on past.

I stood for a while longer, staring at the card, my emotions scrambled.

Minutes earlier I'd been cutting heads on the street, one of the toughest auditions for any blues player, and I'd got through to the next round. This was a big deal and I should have been excited, but right then all I could think about was Travellin' Man.

265

I missed my friend, and his absence burned like an infected wound deep within me. He should have been there by my side; I wanted to share this with him, go to the party with him, get drunk and play some riotous and righteous blues.

Instead, I was alone and, if truth be told, shitting myself at the thought of taking the blues to an audience high on whisky, cocaine, moonshine and looking to party like Monday wasn't going to happen.

So yeah, I was scared. Scared and sad. But there was no way I was going to back out of this.

I played some more and then wandered towards the town square, stopping off at a stall to buy some tamales and a fifth of moonshine.

# Dedman Plantation

The town square was just off the main drag through the town, and dominated by an imposing court house. I got there at a little before eight and a small group of musicians had already gathered, sitting on its stone steps and passing brown paper bags back and forth.

Fortified by the moonshine, I strode towards them. Conversation lulled and I heard mumbled comments as I sat down nearby, could feel their eyes upon me as I tuned up my resonator.

Once more I found comfort in music, playing slow, lazy slide riffs that soothed my trepidation. I was no Travellin' Man but my playing had definitely moved on from the self-conscious and mechanical blues-by-rote that I used to play. Now I could tap into my feelings and let them flow via the keening notes of my beautiful steel resonator.

The more I played the more relaxed I became, even as the square began to fill with more musicians.

"I got's a ticket, who wan's buy my ticket?" A black youth wearing a sharp suit and large flat cap picked his way through the crowd, holding a ticket aloft.

"Who wan's buy my ticket?" He looked down at me. "Yo' needs a ticket, suh?" he asked.

I said I already had one.

"Yo' do?" His eyes narrowed. "Who sold yo' that? This my territo'."

When I said that I got it from cutting heads down by the river, his eyes opened wide.

"Goddam," he said. "They ain' many white folks gets asked t'play at Dedmans. Yo' mus' be somethin' kinda special. If'n yo' fo'give my forwardness."

I smiled and said that I was taught to play by a great man.

He smiled back at me. "No shit? Who's that?"

His face betrayed half a moment of shock before the grin returned.

"Ol' Travellin' Man?" He shook his head. "Man, I ain' seen that ornery ol' bastard in a long time. How's he doin'?"

Hard eyes cut through the mask of easy bonhomie of his words, eyes that were seeking a reaction, searching for information.

I said that Travellin' Man couldn't make it tonight and turned back to my guitar.

"Couldn't make it, huh?"

There was a long pause.

"Well, I guess tha's jus' too bad."

When I looked up again, the boy had gone.

I glanced around, the crowd had grown, the air alive with chattering, shouting, swearing and singing.

A cheer went up as an ancient Chevrolet flatbed truck lumbered into view, crunching gears as it negotiated the square. The cab had no doors and inside a young black kid, wearing overalls and with a cigarette dangling from the corner of his mouth, wrestled with the steering wheel as he brought the truck a halt. Up on the open flat-bed an unsmiling burly white man in a battered slouch hat was holding a baseball bat. As the truck stopped he climbed on top of the cab and banged on the roof with the bat.

The crowd hushed.

"Dedman Plantation," he yelled. "Tickets only on this truck. Tickets only."

He glared at the crowd. "Don' even try an' git aboard this truck lessen yo' has a ticket. Anybody without a ticket gon' get his self a sore head. Consider this yo' first, second an' last warning.

With that he jumped down, walked to the rear of the truck and hooked a small ladder onto the edge of the bed.

I stood up with the rest of the crowd, slung my guitar over my shoulder, checked my satchel and moved towards the truck. As I reached the ladder, I caught the man's eye and waved my ticket.

Nodding once, he reached for my arm and yanked me up the ladder. Taking my ticket, he inspected it, ripped it in two, stuffed one of the halves into his pocket and gave me the other.

"I heard tell we gittin' a white singer," he said. "Whatall tunes yo' gon' play?"

When I said that I played the blues, he shook his head. "Mo' Goddam nigger music," he said. He waved a dismissive hand. "Git on t' the front o' the truck an' find somewhere t' hang onto."

I stood with my back against the cab and watched as musicians, most of them drunk, clambered onto the truck. Soon I was hemmed in, my world narrowing to the close proximity of alcohol-breath, body odour and tobacco smoke.

I was the only white person on the truck and so far no one had acknowledged me or even made eye contact with me. I felt alone in a crowd of people and another layer of desolation settled upon the memory of Travellin' Man. Trying to be strong tonight was going to be hard.

The crowd bustled around me, curses and complaints rang out as somebody tried to shove their way to the front of the truck, and then I heard a familiar voice.

269

"How y'all doin'?" It shouted. "My name's Blind Charlie Hunter, but I ain' blind no more. Sorry fo' th' inconvenience I'm causin' y'all but they's someone on this truck I needs to speak to. 'Scuse me. Beg yo' pardon. Thank y' suh."

A young man in a sharp suit and a trilby hat appeared next to me. He wore a scar over his left eye and was carrying a National steel resonator with a bullet-shaped dent on the sound body.

It took me a couple of seconds but then I remembered the shooting in the Yeller Dog juke-joint.

"I thought it was yo'," he yelled at me. "How y'all doin'?"

He looked around, addressing the crowd, "There I was, playin' on th' stage at th' Yeller Dog, an' all of a sudden, some crazy-ass motherfucker jumps up wavin' a gun, shoots me in the motherfuckin' guitar an' the Goddam bullet hits me in th' head."

He held up the National. "Y'all don' believe me, this here's where the bullet hit my gittar."

Then he pointed to his forehead, "An' this here's where the bullet hit my Goddam head. Shit, I'ma tell y'all I'm lucky t' be standin' here. An' then, AN THEN, the crazy mothafucker shot his self in th' head. Two shots. Y'all ask th' white boy heyah. He's there that night, he see'd it all."

He turned to me. "That was some night, sho' nuff. How yo' been? Watchoo been doin'?"

I said I'd been around, here and there.

He eyed my guitar. "See yo' gotcho'self a National, too. Been playin' much?"

I said I'd played some.

"We had us a time, that night," he said.

I agreed that we did, and that I really enjoyed his show, at the Yeller Dog, right up to the point where he got shot.

He paused for a second then roared with laughter. "Man, that's gotta be th' best review I ever had."

He addressed the crowd again. "Y'all hear that? 'enjoyed my show right up to when I got shot'."

There was silence and then someone said, "When that white boy's around, lotsa folks gets shot."

Blind Charlie, turned back, looked at me strangely then lurched as the truck crunched gears and began to move.

"Folks says lotsa things," he said quietly. "Don' mean nothin'."

I shrugged.

"Say," he said. "Whatall happened about those recordin's we' made?"

I told him that I'd handed them over and that I was hoping to hear something soon.

"Sounds good. Yo' think they gonna sell?"

I said that I was sure they would.

"Le's hope we find out soon."

He smiled. "So, yo' ever been t' a plantation party?"

I said that I hadn't.

He grunted. "Well, it ain' a place fo' the faint hearted but if'n yo' can pick a good tune, folks will fo'give most things - even bein' white. Jus' keep playin'. Whatever happens, whatever yo' see, jus' keep playin'."

I said that sounded like good advice.

"They's gon' be all kinds'a music," he said. "An' all kinds'a carryin' on, jus' find yo'self a spot an' play."

We lurched again as the truck hit a pothole.

"Tell yo' what," he said. "Bit later on some of us gathers together. Them's some o' th' best times. Y'ain' playin' fo' no one nor nothin' but for th' sake o' playin'. If yo' roun' then, then maybe we can get on down?"

I smiled and said that that would be great.

We fell silent as the truck lumbered on. Above us, a canopy of stars filled the immense sky and my thoughts turned to Travellin' Man. The horror of his last moments played out in my head in a constant loop; and while mundane distractions muted the playback, it was always there as a constant reminder.

I also knew that from now on I would have to look for musicians on my own.

The truck pulled off the road onto a narrow track that wound its way through dark trees heavy with Spanish moss and opened out into a wide expanse of ground.

About 300 yards away to the left I could see the rear of a three-storey antebellum-style mansion.

"This th' nigga's road," said Charlie. "On'y white folks 'lowed through th' front gates o' th' big house."

The truck stopped next to three others and as we disembarked, dozens of assorted cars, pickups and buses pulled up, engines revving and horns blaring as they disgorged revellers and musicians into the growing throng.

I looked across to the mansion, lights shone from every room, giving the building the look of a cruise ship and instilling in me pangs of loneliness that I couldn't explain.

Behind me, Blind Charlie grunted. "Ain' nothin' over there fo' th' likes o' us," he said. "Th' action's th' other way, over yonder."

I turned to see the crowd moving in the opposite direction, funnelling along a path lined by burning torches that lead to an area lit by bonfires. A slight breeze blew up, carrying towards us the sounds of revelry and the smells of cooking.

Blind Charlie clapped me on the shoulder. "Le's go play some blues," he said.

We walked across to the path and fell in step with the crowd, shuffling our way towards the epicentre of the gathering, the air growing thick with the smell of bonfire smoke, hamburgers, fried fish, fried chicken and booze.

Blind Charlie sniffed at the air. "I'm 'bout as hungry as all outside," he said. "Could do wid a drink, too, hold my guitar while I get us some chow."

Ahead, a group of people were huddled around a pig roast, the odour of cooked pork strong and delicious. Blind Charlie returned with two plates piled high with pork and okra and smothered in refried beans; two bottles of Jax beer jammed into his waistband. I laid the guitars carefully on the ground between us and devoured my plate in seconds.

Blind Charlie raised his eyebrows. "Goddam, White Boy," he said. "Yo' didn't even come up fo' air."

I looked over and saw that his plate was stacked with crackling and hunks of fat marbled with strips of lean meat. He inhaled a chunk of fat, smacked greasy lips then grinned.

"Eat th' fat an' that give th' whisky somet'in t' chew on," he said. "Yo' kin drink all night long an' don' hardly get drunk n'mo'."

Blind Charlie's eyes shifted to something over my shoulder and as I turned a voice roared,

"Hey'all yo' son's-a-bitches…"

Jacob staggered towards us clutching a bottle in his right hand, then stopped, his body swaying as his liquid eyes struggled to focus. His expression fixed in momentary concentration as a whisky belch rumbled northwards, expelling the stench of secondhand booze into the night air. Smacking his lips he nodded slightly, blinked twice then took a drunken swig from the bottle; oblivious to the liquor that cascaded down his chin and splashed over the harmonica-loaded bandoliers that criss-crossed his chest.

"Time fo' y'all t' git on home," he shouted. "Less'n y'all think yo' can keep up wit' Jacob Davenport."

He took two steps closer then stopped, belched again and fixed me with a glassy stare. "White Boy," he slurred. "'th' fuck yo' doin' here? Why doncho' git yo' ass back t'th' big house an' hang 'roun' wid yo' own kind?"

His bloodshot eyes stared into mine as he raised the bottle to his lips, gulping it noisily and the tilting it vertically to empty the last drops onto his tongue. Jacob hiccupped and the noise marked his transition from drunk to aggressively shit-faced.

The empty bottle whistled past my head and then I felt my lip burst against my teeth and the taste of blood in my mouth. I stepped back as Jacob swung again, watched as the momentum of his off-target punch dragged him in a half circle, tilted him off-balance and keeled him over. His body hit the ground with a dull thump then lay still.

Blind Charlie grabbed my arm. "He don' mean nothin', suh'" he said. "He jus' drunk is all."

He recoiled as I turned to face him, his eyes wide with fear. "Fo'get Jacob, suh," he said. "Ain' no need t' cause no trouble, he shouldna' struck a white boy but he done drunk too much whisky an' he don' know which way's up."

Blind Charlie frowned in disbelief when I said that I wasn't looking to cause any trouble.

"Black man take a swing at a white man, they's always trouble."

I looked down just in time to see Jacob vomit, his stomach contents fountained upwards and then splashed over his chest. As he retched again I laid down the guitars, knelt down and rolled Jacob onto his side. He vomited twice more then fell unconscious, snoring like a diesel engine.

I looked up at Blind Charlie.

"Well, I guess we ain' gon' hear no mo' from him tonight," he said. "How 'bout we take this beer an' drink it some place else?"

We found a table beneath an oak tree festooned with Spanish moss and lit by guttering candles in glass jars.

Blind Charlie pulled the Jax from his waistband and with two deft movements removed the metal caps with his teeth. He handed me a bottle then raised his own to his lips, staring silently into the middle-distance as he took long sips of the beer.

"I seen a nigger rope-drug behind a pick-up, once," he said. "Jus' fo' lookin' sideways at a white man."

He wiped his mouth with the back of his hand. "Here in Miss'ippi," he said. "What Jacob done, yo' coulda' cut off his dick, had him hog-tied an' set on fire an' white folks be linin' up t' buy yo' a drink."

Blind Charlie grunted when I said that I wasn't from Mississippi.

He raised his bottle in salute. "Amen t'that," he said, then drained his beer.

"Yo' ever been in prison, suh?"

I shook my head.

"I done time in the county jail once," he said. "Bust a guy in th' mouth cos he picked up my gittar." Charlie paused for a moment then grunted. "No one tol' me he had two brothers."

He grunted again.

"So, the po-lice come 'long an' took me t'jail. Nex' day I's in th' courthouse, an' th' judge give me 30 days."

He grinned in the candlelight. "Coulda' been worse, some judges they jus' plain nasty."

He reached for his guitar, tuned to Open D, slipped a bottleneck onto his finger, picked out a note that began a slide riff as his right thumb commenced a lazy bass beat.

"I learned this from a one-legged fella' on Beale Street in Memphis," he said.

"Good Mo'nin' Judge, what may be my fine…?"

His mellow voice was slightly louder than a whisper and I sat back and smiled as Blind Charlie riffed a slow version of "Judge Boushay Blues" by Furry Lewis.

What should have been a sublime moment was clouded by the memory of Travellin' Man.

Blind Charlie ended the song, the final notes hanging in the air and then vanishing on the breeze.

"Whatchoo gonna sing?" he said.

I picked up my resonator and said that I had a song that I learned from a one-legged fella' who used to live on Beale Street in Memphis.

Blind Charlie roared with laughter as I began to pick out "I Will Turn Your Money Green," then fell silent as my eyes welled with the tears of recent memories.

When I finished the song I wiped my eyes and drank the remainder of the Jax.

Blind Charlie stared at me and then nodded. "White Boy sho' got th' blues," he said.

He looked around then banged his fist on the table. "Lookit, suh," he said. "Yo' looks like a man got a whole shitload o' troubles but hell, this

Saturday night at th' plantation. It ain' th' time nor place t'be sittin' here mopin' like a coupla turkeys on Christmas Eve."

I stood up and said that he was right.

"Damn right, I'm right," he said. "Le's go git us some fun."

As we walked out from beneath the oak tree, a passing breeze caressed the branches and I shivered in near panic as a frond of Spanish moss stroked my neck. As I brushed it away, the breeze blew stronger then died away, its brief susurrations rising then vanishing like a final, dying breath.

"Follow me, suh," said Blind Charlie. "I think I seen some musicianer folks I knows, we kin git started wid them an' see what happens."

We skirted a crowd of rowdy black youths, walked past food stands that offered enticing aromas of chicken, catfish and tamales; paused at another table to buy four more bottles of Jax and then headed towards a group of women dancing in the light of burning torches. Beyond them, two wooden tables had been pushed together to form a makeshift stage upon which stood young black man with a National guitar playing 'Spanish Fandango', which, as we arrived segued into a ragtime version of 'Bear Creek Hop'. Part way into the tune, he plucked two staccato beats and stamped his heel twice, grinning as the women hopped in time with the music.

Blind Charlie nudged my arm. "Lookit th' way them gals is jumpin'," he said. "Mississippi Jack, he knows how t' git folks a dancin'."

Hearing his name, the realisation hit me and I looked up into the face of the guitarist I'd recorded on the day that I'd met Stella. He caught sight of me and nodded slightly in recognition as he played up to the dancing women, his steel-bodied guitar flashing in the firelight.

"This where all th' good lookin' gals at!"

From behind us came a voice that I recognised and I turned to see the skinny frame of Pops McCoy, his guitar in his right hand and a brown-paper-wrapped bottle in his left.

"Hey White Boy," he yelled. "Las' time I seen yo', yo' was high-tailin' it away in a shit-box T-model Ford, wid a buncha cash stole by a no-good sumbitch wid a pair o' crooked dice."

He took a drink from the brown paper bag, his eyes narrowing as he leaned in close.

"An' speakin' o'cash," he said. "S'acly how much money y'all make from reco'din' me?"

I said that I'd passed the recordings on but didn't know yet how many had been sold.

Pops sniffed, his eyes blinking indignantly. "So yo' don' know, huh?" he said. "Well, when yo' go'n find out?"

Just then, a blistering harmonica riff tore through the conversation and Jacob wandered into our midst, his cheeks hollowing and expanding like a bull-frog, filling the air with raucous blues.

Pops stepped back. "Well Goddam," he yelled. "Hey Jacob, how's your wife and my kids?"

Jacob stopped playing. "Tha's funny, ol' man, I ain' surprised yo' askin' after her. Yo' wife so ugly, her shadow quit."

"Better ugly than fat," said Pops. "An' yo' wife so fat when she hauls ass she gotta make two jo'neys."

Jacob grinned. "Well yo' gotta be happy then, cos' yo' wife so ugly she scare the flies offa shit."

Pops grinned back. "An' yo' wife so fat she broke her arm an' gravy fell out."

"Well that ain' nothing," said Jacob. "Yo' wife so ugly, when she born they named her 'Damn'."

Pops clapped Jacob on the shoulder. "Yo' look like shit, son," he said. "Look like someone done puked down yo' front."

"Had me some bad whisky, 's'all," Jacob gave a dismissive wave. "We gon' stand here runnin' mouths all night o' we go'n play some blues?"

Pops' guitar appeared from nowhere, brass tube glistening dully on his finger as he countered Jacob's harp riffs with heart-wrenching slide notes.

Mississippi Jack nodded. "Tha's right," he said. "Tell us th' news ol' man." He watched Pops play for a couple of bars then joined in with a foot-tapping ragtime break, at the end of his fingers, steel picks flew across the strings, plucking clear, crisp notes that tumbled out of the National and seemed to climb into the air like fireflies.

Blind Charlie joined in, strumming rhythm chords that added a new dimension.

I stood, mesmerised and a little intimidated by the talent that could produce from nowhere such wonderful music. I reached into my satchel for my camera and began filming, circling slowly around the group with occasional pans to take in the growing crowd of revellers that advanced on all sides, drawn to the music like bees to honey.

As I filmed, the murmuration of impromptu sounds swooped and soared and pulsated around me as I breathed in the heady aroma of wood smoke, outdoor food and liquor beneath a canopy of a million stars.

I did close-ups of each of the players, capturing the finger style of Mississippi Jack, the siren scream of Pops' slide and the chords rhythm of Blind Charlie.

I focussed on Jacob just as it all went wrong.

As I zoomed in, capturing the dirt-ingrained contours of his face and the look in his bloodshot eyes of one completely lost in his art, I watched his harmonica giving voice to his soul, raw blues pouring forth with a sound like a steam train.

Jacob span and whirled, his face contorting as he stuttered notes like machine-gun fire, notes that faltered then faded into the air as his jaw slackened then dropped open. His eyes lifted to stare at me then bulged outwards as harmonica notes became viscous gurgles as dark green liquid projected from his mouth.

My camera followed him as he pitched forwards and then rolled onto his back, his body jerking and thrashing with violent spastic movements.

I could only stare as blood gargled from his mouth, poured from his nostrils and ears and streamed from behind eyeballs the size of goose eggs that bulged almost fully out of their sockets.

Jacob stopped thrashing, his arms and legs locking rigid but then his whole body began to shudder to the rising crescendo of an ear-splitting terrorised scream. Blisters began to form; lumps appearing on his face that swelled to the size of a fist, stretching the skin tight as a drum and then erupting a foul-smelling, blood-streaked, glutinous substance with a dull, thick sound that reminded me of porridge boiling in a pan.

What remained of his face contorted in agony and unspeakable fear as his left eyeball rolled out of its socket and slid between the ragged craters of his ruined flesh before coming to rest at the end of the optic nerve, dangling like a botched prison escape.

Swellings and eruptions pulsated across his throat, choking his screams, reducing them to hoarse liquid moans that diminished to faint gurgles that ended in a harsh cackle as Jacob fell still.

Screams, gasps, moans and shocked curses from the onlookers replaced the hellish sounds of Jacob's death.

As I dragged my eyes away from the remains of his corpse, Blind Charlie cannoned into me and then collapsed. Mississippi Jack began to buck and writhe, ending up on his back, his fingers clawing at his face as he howled a monstrous, unearthly scream that lasted an eternity before cutting off like a flicked switch.

Across from me, Pops McCoy dropped to his knees, staring at his left hand as it swelled to twice its size and then burst in an explosion of blood and pus that tore open the flesh to expose muscle, sinews and bone. He looked up at me, hostile eyes locked onto mine as his shattered hand formed into a fist then extended a ragged index finger that pointed straight at me. He held my gaze as monstrous boils rippled his face, ballooning and shifting beneath his skin; held my gaze even as the eruptions lifted his spectacles then coated the lenses with viscous matter.

Defiant to the last, Pops McCoy died in silence, pitching forward and lying face-down in the Mississippi dirt.

I looked up; the crowd had withdrawn a good twenty feet and now stared in shock at the carnage at my feet.

The party sounds that moments earlier had filled the night sky were now replaced by screams from across the entire plantation, screams that eventually, mercifully died away into a silence punctuated by the sound of weeping.

Slowly, heads began to rise and nearby faces turned to stare at me in sullen accusation.

A young woman stepped forward; she was one of the group who had been dancing to Mississippi Jack. She walked a few steps then stopped and pointed at the bodies on the ground.

"Whatcho' done here?" She said. "I seen y'all playin' 'neath that ol' tree fo' yo' come on over here."

She raised her chin. "How come yo' standin' when all these niggas dead?"

I said truthfully that I had no idea.

"Yo' got no idea, huh?" She said. "Well, somethin' goin' on."

Somcone in the crowd shouted, "Damn right."

More shouts.

"White Boy brought him some bad mojo."

"It ain' right, all them folks dead."

"I heard he got Travellin' Man killed."

"Nigga done that he find himself wid a rope roun' his neck."

"I knows where they some rope, how 'bout we lynch this cracker?"

By now I was shit scared and just about ready to run when I heard a familiar voice.

"Yeah, how 'bout we do that?"

The mob fell silent as Fat Man appeared from behind me.

"What yo' say, White Boy?" he winked. "How 'bout we give these folks a taste o' vigilante justice, let 'em get they own back on th' white oppressor, stick it t' th' man. Yo' get my drift?"

Before I could reply he stepped in front of me and faced the crowd.

"Lissen' up, pilgrims," he said. "White Boy ain' got nothin' t' do with whatever went on here, so take yo' rope an' yo' lynchin' ambitions an' move along."

The crowd eyed him sullenly but didn't move.

Fat Man took a Lucky Strike from behind his ear and placed it in the corner of his mouth. Smoke shrouding his head as he spoke.

"I'ma start countin' an' if any o' yo' gawkin' mothafuckers is still aroun' by time I reach five then I'ma strike down upon thee with great vengeance and furious anger."

He paused.

"One."

The hard edge to his voice broke the mood and the crowd backed off, retreating to a safe distance before he reached three.

Fat Man turned to face me. "Samuel L Jackson, th' very best they is," he winked. "When yo' absolutely, positively got t' intimidate every motherfucker in th' room, accept no substitutes."

He drew deeply on the Lucky Strike then flicked it away.

"I gotta tell yo' White Boy," he said. "That stuff yo' been findin' fo' me, it's pure gold, takin' th' music world by storm."

I pointed to the dead bodies at his feet and said that I didn't really give a fuck.

Fat Man stepped back. "Well, tha's too bad," he said. "Cos all yo' work been payin' off. Yo' videos went live jus' today an' been gettin' millions o' hits already, orders fo' DVDs an' downloads is goin' through th' roof. We gon' be rich."

Fat Man frowned when I asked what the musicians would be getting.

"Whatchoo mean?"

I told him to look around, pointed out that all the men I recorded had died horrible deaths.

Fat Man shrugged. "Yeah, tha's a shame," he said. "But yo' know, we gots t' move forward so yo' gon' have t' find some mo' fresh stock. Keep th' momentum, yo' might say."

"Fat Man an' livin' soul, me gettin' sick o' seein' ya."

Gabel walked towards us, stopped at the dead bodies, removed his top hat and bowed his head for a moment.

Replacing his hat he looked up at us.

"What 'appen 'ere?"

From the crowd, a young woman shouted, "White Boy say he ain' got no idea," her mouth twisting as she affected a British accent.

Gabel shook his head. "Me tink me got an idea," he said.

He turned to Fat Man. "Whatcha got t'say 'bout dis?"

Fat Man smirked. "Look like a buncha dead musicianers t' me."

Gabel's bony finger prodded Fat Man in the chest. "Tell me what ya' know."

Fat Man looked down at Gabel's finger then lifted his head and stared hard. "Yo' did not jus' do that," he whispered.

Gabel quivered in fury, dreadlocks swinging as he jabbed harder. "TELL ME."

Fat Man leaned forward, his forehead inches from Gabel's, neither blinked during the stand-off that lasted until a familiar grin began to crawl upwards over Fat Man's face

He stepped back, spreading his arms wide. "What we got here ain' nothin' but a little co-lateral damage," he said. "Shit can happen but they's plenty mo' fish in th' sea, ain' that so, White Boy?"

I asked him what he meant.

"Yo' come afta' me an' I made yo' a fisher o' men," he said. "Ain' that what th' propaganda say?"

"What dis nonsense?" snapped Gabel. "Answer me question. What ya' done t' these men?"

Fat Man's eyes sparkled with delight. "I ain' done nothin'," he said. "White Boy here, he been runnin' errands fo' me, collectin' merchandise an' such."

He lit another Lucky Strike, inhaled deeply then broke out in a paroxysm of coughing, belching out fist-sized clouds of smoke with sound like a locomotive pulling away. The coughing slowed and Fat Man squinted at the cigarette.

"These things gonna kill me," he croaked.

Fat Man cleared his throat, grimacing as he swallowed whatever had broken loose from his sinuses.

"Where was we?" he said. "Oh yeah. I was sayin', White Boy done his self proud by gettin' me some top grade merchandise. Together we been makin' dollars faster n' a meth dealer."

Gabel forced himself to take a deep breath. "What dis gotta do wid dem folks?"

Fat Man winked. "Dem folks is de merchandise."

Gabel looked at me. "What's he mean?" he said.

I said that I had filmed and recorded them and given the files to Fat Man. Cold beads of dread trickled down my spine at the realisation that somehow I was connected to the violent horror that I had witnessed.

By now Fat Man was chuckling. "Damn right," he said. "An' them films an' recordin's, man, they pure gold. Folks on th' other side they cain' get enough. When the films hit YouTube th' lights dimmed 'cross the world when they started downloadin'"

"Films?" said Gable. "Ya' mean like movin' picture shows?"

"Hell yeah," said Fat Man. "Best damn movies y'all ever seen."

Gabel's voice dropped to a whisper. "Fat Man," he said "Ya tellin' me ya been showin' movin' pictures o' souls that have passed over?"

Fat Man shrugged but said nothing.

Gabel turned on me. "An' ya' th' one been takin' these pictures?"

Icy guilt swelled and grew into shame that swirled inside me beneath the full force of Gabel's stare.

"Do ya know what ya done?"

I stammered that I had no idea what was going on.

Gabel stepped closer to me. "A person's soul belongs only in one place. When ya take de picture of a person, ya capture a piece o' de soul. If ya take dat piece away to anotha world, de soul dies."

He nodded towards the bodies. "An' dis what 'appens."

Gabel turned back to me. "Souls got a limited time in de livin' world an' then they move on; can't go back an' de livin' can't follow."

He paused. "If livin' eyes cast over a passed soul, de soul gone forever."

Gabel sighed. "Between ya, ya caused all dis."

I looked over at the remains of the bluesmen and felt mortified that I had been a party to the death of people I thought I was helping. At the core of my guilt and shame, I felt a ball of anger glowing and expanding.

Fat Man yawned.

"Coulda been worse," he said.

I stared at him.

"Don' be givin' me that look, White Boy. Coulda been yo' ol' timer buddy lyin' there."

My head began to buzz inside and I asked him what he meant.

"If'n that crazy bitch had'n'a blown his head off, he'd'a been turned into popcorn jus' like them."

Gabel swung around. "How yo' know 'bout dat?"

Fat Man raised an eyebrow. "Really? How yo' think?"

286

I felt sick as I asked him if he was responsible for Travellin' Man's death.

Fat Man placed a Lucky Strike into his mouth.

"I'ma plead th' Fifth on that." He lit the cigarette then said, "But it was go'n happen one way o' another. I reckons he got th' best he's gonna get."

He blew out a stream of smoke. "Are we done here? Only I got places t'be."

He crooked a finger at me. "C'mon White Boy, gimme whatchoo got in yo' bag an' I'll be on my way."

My hand was shaking as I reached inside the satchel, my fingers trembling as they closed around the camera and released the memory card.

Staring deep into Fat Man's eyes, my heart was thumping as I placed the memory card between my teeth and bit hard.

"What th' fuck?"

I felt a filling dislodge and a tooth crack as I crunched on the card, Fat Man's eyes widening as the plastic splintered with a crack.

Still staring at him, I spat the card into my hand and then broke it in two. I placed one half on my tongue, worked up some saliva and swallowed.

Wincing as the shard scraped the back of my throat, I flicked the other half at Fat Man, catching him on the cheek and then dropping at his feet.

"Are you fucking serious…?"

I said I'd had enough and that he could stick his job.

I delved back in the satchel and removed the memory card from the voice recorder and placed that in my mouth. Another tooth broke as I bit the card clean in two, but the waves of shooting pain felt almost cleansing as I gave Fat Man the finger and swallowed both halves.

"Don' be flyin' too high, yo' sumbitch," he growled. "We got a deal."

I told him to stick his deal up his arse and then I pulled out the camera and broke off every part that could be opened or removed. What was left I threw into the darkness.

I said the deal was over and threw the voice recorder straight at him. I was rewarded with a yelp as it caught him in the eye but then he moved lightning fast and his huge fist launched me backwards. As I lay winded, my face throbbing, Fat Man bent forwards, grabbed me by the throat and lifted me clear of the ground.

"Yo' b'long t' me, yo' sumbitch. Yo' does what I say, when I say it."

Lights flashed around the edges of my vision, I began to choke but managed to tell him to go fuck himself.

"Fat Man, ya do whatcha like wherever ya go, an' ya don' care fo' nobody, but ya knows ya can't kill a livin' soul."

Fat Man squeezed harder and I was on the verge of passing out when I collided with the ground.

As I lay there, rasping air through constricted pipes; Fat Man stood over me, glowering with fists clenched and murder in his eyes.

Finally I could breathe and I managed to pull myself to a sitting position.

Fat Man stepped back then turned away from me.

"Why ya' do this, Fat Man?" said Gabel. "Everywhere ya go ya leave chaos an' pain."

"Tha's cos I'm a scorpion," he said.

Before Gabel could respond, Fat Man whirled around and pointed a finger at me.

"Notwithstanding all this bullshit," he said. "Yo' an' me we made a deal an' unless yo' got some means o' buyin' o'self out then that deal stands an' yo' gotta do what I say." He turned to Gabel, "Ain' that right, Mr. Voodoo Chile?"

Gabel nodded sadly. "Fat Man speakin' de trut'," he said. "Ya made a deal and a deal's whatchya got. Ya want to end that ya both gotta agree a way out."

Fat Man nodded. "Damn right."

I stood up, my throat on fire as I asked him what it would cost.

Fat Man dropped the stub of his cigarette and ground it into the dirt.

"Yo' wants to buy yo' way out?" He said.

I said that I wanted to end the deal, whatever it would take.

He looked me up and down, a contemptuous smile playing around his mouth.

"Shit, White Boy, yo' on th' bones o' yo' ass. How yo' think yo' gon' pay yo' way out?"

His eyes narrowed.

"Fo' we goes any further," he growled. "Yo' backin' outta this deal means yo' forfeits yo' share o' whatever cash gets made from them reco'din's."

I said that I expected that and that my share could go towards paying to end the deal.

"Oh no," he said. "Nuh-uh. That cash is mine, yo' want's t' change th' deal, yo' gotta pay extra on top."

I said again that I wanted out, whatever it took.

Fat Man rubbed his chin as he stared at me through lidded eyes.

"Whatever it takes, huh?" he said.

He thought some more then waved a finger at me.

"Half a million dollars," he said.

I stared at him.

"Tha's what it gonna cost. Half a million dollars an' we through an' yo' gon' end up back in Clarksdale sittin' in yo' own shit while yo' waitin' out whatever time yo' got left."

He winked at me. "Five hunnerd big ones, or you stays here as my bitch."

His face hardened. "An' I gotta say, given yo' attitude right now, if yo' gon' stay as my bitch, then I'ma have to micromanage yo' ass."

He paused. "An' yo' don't want that."

I said that I would get the money.

Fat Man nodded.

"Oh, one mo' thing," he said. "Yo' got a week t' get it."

I stared Fat Man straight in the eyes as I extended my hand, fighting back feelings of revulsion and horror at his touch.

"Damn, White Boy," he said. "Yo' gotta good grip, yo' work out?"

Amidst the chaos and torment that Fat Man transmitted through his hand shake, I realised that I had no idea how to raise the cash.

Fat Man roared with laughter and then dropped my hand.

"See yo' in church," he said.

He turned and lumbered away, disappearing into the crowd.

As I stood there, my head spinning as I tried to formulate a plan, Gabel walked over to stand close to me. "It time fo' ya' t'go," he said.

I lifted my head. Close up, his bloodshot eyes burned like coals against the stark white of his painted face

"Go back t' ya' own world, livin' soul," he said. "Dat where ya b'long."

He looked me up and down, dreadlocks cascading over his thin, bony shoulders as he shook his head.

"Ya got a jinx roun' ya head," he said. "But me don' tink ya' a bad man, ya been misled."

Just then, breaking through the silence like a rock splashing into a millpond, a raucous voice bellowed, "Who all, wan's t' dance again?"

My heart leapt as I recognised the opening chords to "Down the Dirt Road Blues" and a familiar, growling voice singing about going away to a world unknown.

That's when I had the idea.

Turning back to Gabel I said I would go back but I had to ask him something.

"What ya wanna know?" he said.

The words of a garbled explanation tumbled out and when I'd finished he stood in silence for a while.

"An' aftawards ya gon from dis place?"

I said that he had my word.

Gabel nodded. "Do whatya' gotta do, den leave." He raised a warning finger. "See mi now," he said. "No more recordin' an' filmin', leave dese folks be."

I said that I would.

Picking up my resonator I threaded my way through the crowd, heading towards the voice I had listened to thousands of times on scratchy recordings.

I arrived at a small knot of people surrounding a short skinny man with jug ears sitting on a wooden chair. As I made my way to the front, the song ended and a gaunt face lifted towards me. For a brief moment the singer looked me straight in the eyes, nodded once then launched into "Moon Going Down."

Every emotion, every sensation, every event that I'd experienced since making the deal with Fat Man was rolled up, packaged and presented to me in five minutes of performance given by my hero. For those five minutes I forgot all the horror that had gone before because everything I had read about him, every interview I had listened to, it was all true.

The musician truly was a force of nature. He poured every ounce of his energy into entertaining the crowd, spinning the guitar on its end, playing it between his legs and behind his head without missing a note.

I wanted to stay there all night, to drink in every moment of his show but when the song ended, Charley Patton looked up at me.

"Ainchoo got somewhere t'be?" He growled.

I took the hint and made my way off the plantation.

# Return To Crystal Springs

As I stood at the edge of the gravel road, a cloud dimmed the moonlight and intensified the darkness. Behind me, the party was back in full swing and the faint sounds of music and revelry floated towards me.

Alone and with time to think, my imagination began an onslaught of the horrific scenes and images that I had witnessed that night and as I relived those scenes, guilt and shame weaved through the feelings of shock and terror that I felt earlier.

And then a guttural noise shocked me back to the present; the near-silence of the night rent by a spitting, snarling primeval roar.

I wheeled, just as a 1932 Model B Ford skidded to a halt.

"Ain't she a beaut'?"

Tom Walker grinned from behind the steering wheel, then leaned over and opened the passenger door.

"Better get in, son," he said. "Cain't get t' where yo' goin' by standin' still. Put yo' guitar an' yo' bag on the back seat."

As soon as I closed the door, the engine revved and we took off like a rocket.

"The Chevy's my daytime, ve-hickle," he yelled. "This here's my night time ride."

When I asked if it was a Flathead V8 he grinned.

"Yes sir," he said. "With a few, uh, modifications if yo' will. I started out by…"

I interrupted him, apologised and said that I was very tired.

Tom fell silent.

Then I felt bad and said that I had meant no offence.

"None taken," he said. "Guess yo' could do with some sleep. Settle back, son an' we'll git there in a coupla hours."

He throttled back the V8 to a dull roar and I closed my eyes and braced myself for the nightmares.

I must have been more tired than I realised, because the dreams never came. I rubbed my eyes and shifted my position, contorting my neck and stretching my limbs as far as the confines of the car would allow.

Cotton fields, grey in the first light of morning, stretched away on either side of a road so straight that the vanishing point never wavered from the centre of the horizon.

"Yo' sleep good?" said Tom.

Last night's images came flooding back so I nodded and then stared out of the window; not trusting myself to speak.

The Ford slowed as we approached the outskirts of a town and then stopped outside a run down single storey building with a sign that said 'General Store'.

"Don' know about you, son," said Tom. "But I needs a coffee."

When I said that I would stay in the car Tom shook his head. "Well, I cain' let yo' do that, son," he said. "I know this place don' look much but it does serve the best damn coffee in the state an' cinnamon rolls like yo' wouldn' believe, an' I wouldn' feel right sittin' in there indulgin' myself while yo' was sat here dwellin' on things."

He sighed. "Looks like y'all been t'hell in a handcart so why don' yo' come on in an' let th' coffee an' cinnamon rolls do they jobs?"

I opened the door.

Leaning against the car, I stretched properly and looked around.

A porch ran the full length of the double-fronted store, semi-obscured in the shade of the low roof were two wooden benches set either side of the entrance up against the splintered planks that formed the wall.

I looked across the road and stared at a huge wooden building, its roof a patchwork of rusted corrugated iron. A railroad track ran behind the gin and to the right lay an area of grass with a few small trees with tall grass. It all looked familiar but I couldn't place where I'd seen it before.

Looking up the road to my right I saw a small church and as my eyes swung back around to the cotton gin I saw a cluster of grave stones in the far corner of the grassed area.

Realisation hit me like punch in the mouth, confirmed by Tom as he walked past me and stepped up onto the porch.

"Welcome t' Holly Ridge, son," he said. "Yo' comin' in?"

For a second I couldn't move, the last time I'd been here I had spoken to Fat Man next to the grave of the man I'd watched play the night before.

"Well, son?" said Tom. "Y'all gon' allow me t' buy yo' a coffee?"

I followed him into the store.

Inside, the shop extended the full length of the building in a single room packed with merchandise that rose in stacks or dangled from rafters. To the right, sacks of grain propped against a glass display cabinet topped with a polished-wood counter that ran from front to back. Everywhere I looked I could see cartons, cans and boxes of food, Behind the counter the wall was covered with shelves that bowed beneath the weight of canned goods, pots, pans and earthenware jugs.

To the left of the store ran a shorter counter behind which a pinched-face, middle-aged white woman poured coffee for two white men perched on stools. Behind her stood a large copper water boiler and an array of enamel coffee jugs. On the counter jars of cookies lined up next to a glass display containing pastries and rolls.

Tom strolled over and motioned me towards to a stool next to the two men, then smiled and nodded to the woman.

"Good mornin', ma'am," he said. "And how are you this day?"

The woman didn't react beyond, "WhatcanIgetcha?"

Tom kept smiling. "Well, I guess two coffees and two cinnamon rolls would hit the spot, if you please."

The woman lifted her face a fraction then set out two mugs before making up a jug of fresh coffee. As it brewed she took two rolls from the display cabinet, plated them, set them before us, poured thick black liquid into the mugs and set the jug on the counter.

"Y'all want cream an' sugar?"

We didn't, so she nodded once then moved back to the other two customers.

Tom took a huge bite of his cinnamon roll and rolled his eyes as he chewed and swallowed.

"MM-MMMM, that tastes righteous an' that's no lie," he said.

I took a bite and then jumped at the bark of laughter behind me. I turned to see one of the men slapping the other on the shoulder.

"Tha's a good one," he said, wiping a tear from his eye. "Now I gots one fo' you."

He took a sip of coffee then wiped his mouth on his sleeve.

"So," he said. "This nigger gal is expectin' twins an' just before she's due she falls over and knocks herself clean out. When she wakes up, her brother, he standin' there lookin' down at her. Then this nigger gal, she realise she ain't pregnant no more and so she asks her brother where her babies at.

'Oh, they in the other room,' says the brother. 'Yo was asleep so long we didn't know if'n yo' was ever gonna wake up, so I named 'em an' had 'em river baptised'"

The man took another swig of coffee.

"Now," he said. "This nigger gal's brother, he about as smart as a bag of rocks; he couldn't pour water out of a boot with instructions on the heel, so she starts gettin' all uppity.

'Yo named 'em an' had 'em baptised?' she says. 'Well whatchoo name 'em?'

Nigger gal's brother, he sets a shit-eatin' grin on his face an' says, 'Don' you fret, yo' had a little girl an' a little boy. I named the little girl, Denise.'

Nigger gal don' feel so bad now, 'Denise?' she say, 'why tha's a nice name fo' a girl, whatchoo call th' boy?'"

The man paused for another swig of coffee then continued, "Nigger boy, his ol' shit-eatin' grin gets wider as he says, 'I call th' boy De-nephew.'"

The two men roared with laughter, fists pounding on the counter as tears rolled down their faces.

"Denise an' De-nephew," said the other man. "Tha's a good one, where yo' git that 'un?"

Laughter subsided to chuckles then the man said. "Heard that from Hiram at th' Klan meeting th' other night. Damned if I didn't piss my pants."

His friend nodded. "Ol' Hiram, he sho' can tell a good nigger joke."

The man began to chuckle again. "Talkin' o' dumbass niggers, I heard tell they's a bunch upped and died last night up at the Dedman plantation."

"Say what?"

"Tha's what I heard, group a' musicianers. One minute they pickin' on they gittars, playin' that monkey-junk shit they all likes an' th' next thing they

297

all starts rollin' around an' groanin' an' howlin' like dogs, they skin breakin' out an' shit pourin' over they faces like boilin' milk."

The other man shook his head in wonder. "Boilin' niggers," he said. "Damn, I wished I coulda seen that, wonder how that happen'd."

Tom flashed a warning glance but it was too late.

I was quivering with rage but my voice held steady as I told them to shut their redneck mouths.

There was a moment's silence and then the voice behind me.

"Whatchoo jus' say?"

As I stood up Tom leaped to his feet and tried to pull me away. "My friend didn't mean nothin', we been drivin' all night an' he just tired, that's all."

I shook myself free of Tom's grip, turned to face the men and told them to shut their fucking ignorant redneck mouths.

The one nearest was halfway towards me when my right fist cannoned onto his cheek bone and knocked him sideways onto the counter. Stepping forward I grabbed his hair, lifted his head and smashed his face against the edge, threw him to the floor and stamped on his throat.

At the other end of the counter the woman yelled as I hooked my fingers into the other man's mouth, twisted my hand and pulled him off the stool. His head smacked the floor with a thump that shook the room and as he lay there dazed I followed up with a kick to his face and then stamped on his throat until his groans became tortured rasping breaths.

Amidst the chaos of this violence I had never felt so calm. My brain had closed down to one single, primal aim and I knew I was going to kill these two men.

My breathing was steady as I picked the stool up by the legs, steadied myself, and then with all the force I could muster, swung it like an axe towards the man's head.

"That's ENOUGH."

Something pulled me backwards and I turned to see Tom gripping the stool in one hand, his eyes blazing at me.

"You done enough," he said.

I turned back to the two men whimpering on the floor, my foot lashed out and the whimpers turned to fresh cries as I caught the first man in the face.

"Goddamit, you made your point." Tom jerked the stool out of my hand and it was over.

"Yo' dirty, communist, nigger-lovin' sonsabitches."

I looked up to see the woman advancing towards me, her face twisted with venom. "Yo' gonna regret what yo' done here, Mister Fancypants," she said. "You two race-mixers picked on the wrong men. When this gets out you gon' be tarred and feathered and dancin' on the end of a rope."

Tom produced a wallet, took out a five-dollar bill and placed it on the counter.

"Ma'am, we're right sorry about what happened here," he said. "And you have my word that this man won't trouble you again."

Her eyes came alive with spite, her shrill voice laced with poisoned glee, "Fuck off," she hissed. "An' take yo' nigger lover with yo'."

Tom touched my arm, "C'mon, son, I think we'd better git," he said.

"That's right," shrieked the woman. "You git going, an' don't y'all come back. I catch y'all round here again I'm gonna cut off your dicks and stick 'em in your mouths then string y'all up."

She began to cackle, her voice becoming shriller as we walked out. "Nigger lovers gonna be dancin', twitchin' like puppets with their dicks in their mouths."

Tom strode towards the car.

"Get in, Goddammit."

I looked back at the store then climbed into the car.

As we drove off, Tom looked over at me. "You wanna tell me what that was all about?"

I said that I was tired of hearing the N-word.

He smiled. "The N-word? I ain't never heard it described that way."

I said that I didn't find it funny.

"I didn't say it was," he said. "But damn, son; when you among white folks in Mississippi then you damn sure gonna hear it. I ain't sayin' it's right and it ain't a word that I ever use, but facts is facts."

Fat Man's voice echoed in my head. "Is what it is, ain' no mo' than that."

Tom produced a pipe and a pouch of tobacco that he rested on his lap and I watched out of the corner of my eye as, one-handed, he loaded the pipe, tamped the tobacco then struck a match, his cheeks hollowing repeatedly as he drew the flame across the bowl until the pipe smouldered into life.

He cracked open a window and smoke funnelled out as Tom puffed contentedly, one hand on the steering, the other stroking the bowl of the pipe.

He was silent for a long time then said with a chuckle. "Ain't no denyin' it, son. You got a habit o' pissin' off the wrong people, you surely do."

I thought back to what happened the last time I got into a fight and asked Tom what would happen.

Tom shrugged. "Word'll get out," he said. "Some folks'll get riled up and stomp around an' cuss yo' name an' mine 'cross three counties, but I doubt it'll get beyond that."

He chuckled again. "An' it's likely gonna be a while before I can show my face back there for cinnamon rolls."

I said I was sorry about that.

"That don' matter none," he said. "Probably ain' a bad thing. Given the send off we got. Bless her heart, that gal was madder than a wet hen."

A couple of hours later we drove into Crystal Springs and turned onto Main Street, the Ford's brakes squealing as Tom pulled up outside the pawnbrokers.

"Yo' gonna need any help in there, son?"

When I said that I didn't think so, Tom nodded.

"Well then," he said. "I guess this here's where our journey ends."

His huge hand swallowed mine in its iron grip. "I'ma head back, git me some coffee an' then take my ol' pickup for a spin, see if I cain't find me a train engineer to rile up."

His kindly old eyes glistened as we shook hands.

"Good luck, son," he said.

I thanked him for all his help, grabbed my stuff and then climbed out of the car. As I walked towards the shop I heard gears crunch and then the sound of the Ford pulling away.

The doorbell tinkled as I entered and from behind the wire mesh screen the elderly man looked up.

"Vot took you so long?" he said.

I said that I'd been busy.

The old man grumbled incoherently as he grabbed a bunch of keys and unlocked a window-sized section of the wire mesh. As it swung open, he lifted the counter, then opened a door beneath it and ushered me through.

"I got your merchandise back here," he growled.

I put down my guitar and crouched through the opening as the he dragged a corrugated cardboard box from beneath a shelf and pushed it towards me.

He straightened up and dusted his hands. "You been so long it's covered in shmutz, I should charge you extra."

My hands trembled as I lifted a flap and peered into the box.

"It's all there," said the old man. "Just as ve agreed."

He nodded towards the box. "Drag it out into the shop," he said. "I get nervous vid the counter open."

I stooped down, grabbed the box and dragged it backwards with awkward steps. Back in the shop I opened the flap wider and pulled out a piece of paper folded in half. I felt myself grin as I unfolded it and read it several times.

"It's all there," said the old man.

My heart thumped as I folded the paper and slipped it back inside the box.

I nodded and we shook hands.

The old man regarded me through tired eyes.

"Dis business is concluded," he said.

He looked down at the box. "How you gonna transport that? You gotta car, or a mule?"

I hadn't even considered how I was going to carry it all and when I said I had neither, the old man grunted. "Den you gonna have you hands full."

He stared at the box, stared at me then shook his head, "Vait there."

The old man shambled to a dark corner of the shop and began to dismantle a jumbled stack of boxes and household items until finally revealing what looked to me like a wooden tray mounted on four thin, spoked wheels. It resembled a miniature chuck wagon from the Wild West and as the old man dragged it clear of the jumble I could see the name 'No.4 Liberty Coaster' painted in fading letters along the battered wooden sides. It measured probably two feet by one foot and was pulled along by a wooden bar with a T-handle that folded back over the wagon.

The old man dusted his hands once more. "I give you dis for free," he said. "Bubkes. Take it and go quick before I come to my senses."

I lifted the box onto the wagon, shook the old man's hand and as he held the door open for me I picked up the guitar and then wheeled the wagon out of the shop.

The old man followed me out onto the sidewalk and pointed along the street. "There's a church outta town, about three miles that way. Good luck, you gonna need it."

I heard the door close as I turned and set off along the street, the wagon squeaking behind me.

Crystal Springs was quiet that day and I didn't see anyone as I walked out of town.

# Down The Dirt Road Blues

About a mile into the countryside, the wagon lurched in my hand and I heard a dull thump and discordant guitar twang.

I turned around to see the front axle had broken, the wheel lying next to my guitar.

Fixing the wagon was out of the question so I squatted down, manhandled the box onto my right shoulder, reached for the neck of the guitar and rose shakily upright. I began walking again and within less than a hundred yards the box was biting into my shoulder and my right arm began to ache.

As I walked, my mind helped me ignore the pain by constantly reminding me of all the people I had met and replaying the last moments of those at the plantation party.

Every single person I had recorded on video was dead.

I tried to rationalise this but the tiny voice of reason that suggested that I couldn't have known what was to happen was drowned out by the judgmental bellow of my grief-stricken guilt, lambasting me for what I had done.

"No," the tiny voice persisted. "It was Fat Man. He played you all along, took you for a ride and showed you what you wanted to see, gave you everything that you wanted."

If only I'd…

The thought died right there as something inside me shut down. I dropped the guitar and barely had time to wrest the box from my shoulder before I dropped to my knees. I remember staring at the vanishing point of the road, feeling pressure increase in my head and hearing a rushing sound like wind funnelled between buildings; a sound that rose in intensity, volume and pitch

305

before reaching a keening crescendo that exploded into a scream of anger. I remember looking up at the sky as I railed at Fat Man and then seeing the road rushing up towards me, feeling the collision of gravel against my face as my screams turned into huge wracking sobs of apology to Stella, Travellin' Man and everyone else who had suffered because of me.

Eventually, I have no idea of a timescale; the sobbing waned, and then dried up to a sniffle until finally I was done.

Drained, I forced myself to my feet and took stock.

The box stood in the middle of the road, upright and undamaged. My guitar lay nearby; a quick inspection revealed a few more scratches on the body but that too was undamaged.

Picking up the box and then the guitar, I started to walk.

About a mile further on I could see a tumble-down shack and as I drew closer I could hear a crude, single-stringed melody being played.

I drew level with the front of the shack. Even by Delta standards it was in a poor state of repair. Tattered, filthy rags hung behind torn fly-screens that once protected the windows but now were dangling away from the building in strips that reminded me of peeling skin.

The porch had collapsed at one end and at the opposite end, a black woman sat in a broken rocking chair. She looked to be in her late twenties and next to her a small boy of about nine or ten was engrossed in plucking on a length of wire stretched between two nails, using a broken bottle to produce slide notes.

Devoid of expression, the woman watched every move as I paused in front of the shack, rested my guitar against a rotten post and lowered the box from my shoulder.

"Hush child," she said, her eyes never leaving me.

The music ceased as the boy turned around to stare, not at me but at my shiny metal guitar.

I told him that his music sounded great and that I could hear it a long way down the road.

The boy lifted his eyes to meet mine. "Mama says we don't gotta trust no white folks," he said. "'specially not no white men."

"Randolph, hush yo' mouth," the woman's eyes grew wide with fear as she turned to me. "He don' mean nothin', suh," she said. "He jus' a kid."

I told her not to worry, that her boy was probably right and that I wouldn't come any closer.

She didn't seem convinced so I smiled again and said that I was just passing by and needed to rest for a few minutes.

Her eyes moved to the box. "That do look mighty heavy," she said. "Whatchoo carryin'?"

I said that I had to deliver it to someone.

She panned the landscape and then looked back at me. "Mister," she said. "Wherever yo' bin yo' walked a long ways t' git here, an' wherever yo' headed, yo' got a long ways' t'go."

Her eyes narrowed when I told her I was headed for a church. "On'y thing looks like a church roun' here is wha's left standin' half a mile 'cross that cotton field." She pointed on down the road. "They's a track jus' yonder."

I said that was the church that I was headed for.

"Well," she said. "It sho' used t'be a church but they ain' no one bin worshippin' there fo' a looong time."

I stared across the fields, saying nothing.

She shrugged. "Hell, ain't none o'mine," she said. "I getchoo a drink?"

I said that some water would be fine.

"I got's some cola," she said. "O' a bottle o' Nehi. They ain' cold but they ain' well water, neither."

She turned to the boy. "Randolph," she said. "Go fetch that bottle o'cola an' a glass fo' th' gennelman."

Randolph scampered inside and returned with a bottle of Royal Crown and a Mason jar. Holding them carefully as he negotiated the remains of the treacherous wooden steps, he handed them shyly to me then turned and dawdled up to my guitar, staring at it longingly.

I poured the drink into the jar and took long gulps. It was warm but the fizzy sweetness tasted delicious in my parched mouth.

"Randolph, dontchoo touch nothin', that ainchyo' property."

Randolph looked up at his mother. "I's on'y lookin' momma," he wheedled. "It's a real perty gittar."

I belched softly as I finished the drink then handed the jar and bottle to Randolph, thanking him for the drink.

Randolph smiled when I asked him if he liked my guitar. "'s real nice," he said shyly.

His eyes opened wide when I asked him if he would like it. "Fo' real?" he gasped, then whirled around. "Can I momma? Can I have th' gittar?"

His mother's face hardened. "Why yo' wanna give away such a fine gittar?"

I said that I didn't need it where I was going and that it was getting awkward to carry.

"I thoughtchoo's only goin' over that ol' church," she said. "That ain' but a half mile from here."

I said that I would prefer to leave the guitar in good hands.

The woman nodded once but said nothing.

308

I fished in my pocket, called Randolph over and gave him the brass slide.

His eyes widened even more as he turned it over and over. I looked at the woman and said that it would be safer than using a broken bottle.

"Yo' really wan' give yo' gittar 'way?"

I nodded and said that there was no one else who deserved it more.

She looked at Randolph. "Well? what do yo' say t' th' man?"

Randolph beamed. "Thank yo', suh," he said.

I leaned over and picked up the National then squatted down and rested it across my knee. I picked each string and tweaked it into tune then laid it on the ground. Randolph came to squat next me and listened intently as I showed him how to use the brass slide to get the best sound. The guitar was almost as tall as he was but he picked it up and hauled it onto the porch and then disappeared into the shack. Soon after, tentative slide notes began to waft out of the doorway.

I looked at his mother and said that I thought he was a natural.

She smiled wistfully. "So was his poppa," she said.

I said that I had to go and thanked her again for the drink.

"Yo' wan' sumpthin' t'eat?" she said.

I shook my head and said that I needed to be somewhere.

"Well, anotha' time, maybe."

I said maybe, then picked up the box, said goodbye to her and could feel her eyes staring at me as I began walking down the road.

# Crossing Back

I found a tiny, broken-down, clapboard church at the end of a track overgrown with Cordgrass. The door was ajar and dried-out hinges squealed in alarm as I pushed it open.

Inside it was a wooden shell; just four walls, a floor and most of a ceiling. Directly opposite, a narrow door with a broken hinge rested against a rotten frame like a drunk leaning against a wall. As I walked a few paces into the room and lowered the box to the floor, the door pushed open.

"Yah finally doin' de right ting."

Gabel walked towards me, looked down at the box then back at me.

"An' ya say all dis gonna put tings right?"

I said that I was going to try my best to make it happen.

Gabel nodded. "Take ya stuff an' git outta here. Me not wanna see ya' until it ya' time."

Picking up the box, I walked to the door and then turned to say goodbye.

Gabel had vanished, so I turned back and walked through the door.

I found myself outside the church where I had done the deal with Fat Man. The sun was low in the eastern sky, its light reflecting on the contrails of a passenger jet headed towards Memphis.

I hefted the box onto my shoulder, paused at Travellin' Man's headstone, said a few words to the memory of my friend and then started walking.

The car was where I had left it, the keys still in the ignition. That it started first time didn't surprise me, and neither did the fact that my phone was working.

Sitting in the car, I tapped and dragged my fingers across the screen of the phone, made some calls and sent some emails. Communications complete, I put the car in gear and was soon back on Highway 61.

As I drove into Clarksdale, I saw what I was looking for. Swinging the car left into a U-turn I parked outside a glass-fronted building, opposite a sign on the wall that read:

Marchant & Associates - Attorneys at Law since 1935.

Reaching into my satchel I fished around and pulled out a battered business card then got out of the car.

The young black girl sitting at the reception desk looked up as I walked in. Her eyes scanned, processed and judged me in a finger-snap, but she betrayed no emotion as she attached a polite smile.

"May I help you?"

I asked if it was possible to speak to Mr. Marchant.

"Do you have an appointment?"

I said that I didn't but that I really would like to speak with him.

Her chin raised slightly, her eyes once more scanning my clothing. "Mr. Marchant is busy with a client right now," she said. "Perhaps one of our junior associates can help?"

When I asked her if Mr. Marchant was in the building, she paused but before she could reply I handed over the business card and asked her if she could please take it in and show it to him.

The receptionist stood up and nodded towards an armchair.

"Please, take a seat," she said.

Next to the armchair was a water-cooler. As the receptionist walked towards a door at the back of the office, I filled and drank three cups before sitting down. In the comfort of the armchair I suddenly felt old, weary and dirty.

She returned a few minutes later. "Mr. Marchant will see you now," she said.

I walked through the reception area towards the open door of an office. Inside, a tall, distinguished-looking black man rose from his seat. His shiny pate, oxblood loafers, khaki chinos, pristine white polo shirt and faint whiff of expensive cologne were a stark contrast to my shabby attire and I suddenly felt awkward and out of place.

Extending his hand he shook mine in a firm, confident grip. He smiled easily, but caution hunkered down behind his eyes.

"Benjamin Marchant," he said. "Please, come in to my office."

Stepping back, he motioned for me to enter, followed me in and closed the door.

Gesturing for me to sit down, he asked if I would like a coffee and smiled again when I said it would save my life. A few moments later he handed me a china mug with Clarksdale, Mississippi written in large red letters.

"I keep the bone china cups and saucers for those who don't know any better," he winked. "You look like you need it weapons-grade."

As I took the first, welcome sip of the coffee, Benjamin produced an identical mug, brimmed it with steaming black liquid and then sat at his desk.

"How's the coffee?" he said.

I replied that it had indeed saved my life. His smile this time was brief and I could almost see the questions loading up behind his eyes.

He picked up the business card, turned it over between his fingers and then looked directly at me.

"I'm curious to know where you got this?" he said.

I said it was a long story and asked if he was related to the name on the card.

"Nathaniel was my great-uncle," he said. "Came down from New York to set up this law firm with his brother, my grandfather. They say he looked around a few places before settling in Coahoma Point, and then opening this office some years later."

His eyes widened when I dropped the name of Tom Walker, the old family friend who drove a pick up like it was stolen.

"How in th' hell do you know about that?" he said.

I took a deep breath and suggested that he probably wouldn't believe me if I told him.

"OK", he said. "Lets park that for now and you can tell me what it is you think I can do for you."

Producing a large yellow writing pad, he removed the top from a fountain pen and held it inches above the paper.

"First half-hour is free," he said. "After that I'll give you my opinion based on what you tell me and we can discuss what happens next."

We spoke for an hour and quarter, after which he followed me out to the car and examined the contents of the cardboard box.

"I think we can do business," he said. "I was about to send out for sandwiches, how about we go back inside and get some more coffee?"

Later, having demolished a Catfish Po'Boy and drunk my body-weight in Italian coffee, I asked Benjamin what became of Nathaniel.

"Nathaniel died in 1940," he said. "In a night club, down in Natchez."

When I asked him if it was the Rhythm Club, Benjamin raised an eyebrow.

"You know a lot about Mississippi history," he said. "But yes, he was there that night."

Benjamin shook his head. "Awful, awful night," he said. "You know they boarded the windows and locked the back door so no one could sneak in and watch the band. Spanish moss, hanging from the rafters, caught fire and burned the place down. 209 people killed and God knows how many more injured."

I asked what happened to Tom Walker. Benjamin gave a wry smile. "Story has it Ol' Tom was barrel-assing his pickup as usual, spied him a train heading towards a railroad crossing and decided to give chase. They say a tire blew out, Ol' Tom lost control and the train ploughed straight into him."

We spoke some more and then Benjamin finished his sandwich and dabbed at his lips with a napkin.

I stood up and said that I should be going. Benjamin rose with me and gripped my hand. "Thank you for coming in here," he said. "I'll wait to hear from you."

# Buddy Holly

I pulled into Ground Zero parking lot just before lunchtime and took the box upstairs and along the graffiti-covered corridor. At the door to the room I had rented I paused, listened and then tried the handle. Once again, I was unsurprised when the door swung open and inside the apartment it was exactly as I had left it.

Placing the box on the floor, I locked the door, and then undressed and walked into the shower.

Later, dressed in clean, modern clothes, I hefted the box into the bedroom, placed it on the floor and with shaking hands removed its contents one by one and laid them reverentially on the bed.

I dragged a chair towards the bed and sat down, my elbows on my knees, my chin in my hands as I stared in wonder at the treasure I had brought back with me.

Standing up, I reached for my satchel and fumbled inside until I found a crumpled piece of card. I straightened out the card, picked up my phone and dialled a number.

Kyle, the lawyer who looked like Buddy Holly, answered on the third ring.

"Hey, I was just thinking about you," he said. "What's goin' on?"

I told him that I had acquired something that he might be interested in.

"OK," was all that he said.

When I told him it what it was, his Southern politeness held firm. "That sounds great," he said.

I could picture him rolling his eyes; almost hear him framing the sentence that would end the call.

"Email me a picture," he said. "I'll get back to you."

Then he hung up.

I arranged the objects on the bed, photographed them from several angles and then took individual pictures close-up.

I quickly composed a message, attached the images and sent the email.

My phone rang two minutes later.

"And these are real?" said Kyle.

When I confirmed that they were, he dry-whistled.

"Holy shit," he said. "What'all provenance do you have?"

I unfolded the piece of paper and read the words.

"Man, I gotta see this," said Kyle. "I can be in Clarksdale in seven hours."

I said that I would wait for him.

Six and a half hours later there was a bang on my door. I opened it to reveal a tired, dishevelled and agitated Kyle. "Good to see you, man," he said. "I gotta pee, where's your bathroom?"

I grabbed two beers from the fridge and set them on the table. A few minutes later, Kyle emerged, picked up a beer and took a long swallow.

"OK," he said. "I just barrel-assed it from Oklahoma City, an' I'm anxious t' see what-all you got."

I asked him to follow me.

Kyle walked into the bedroom, stopped, looked at the bed, looked back and me and said, "Holy shit."

Laid out on the bed were 22 square-shaped cardboard sleeves. At the centre of each sleeve, a circular cut-out revealed a black label with gold lettering and an image of an eagle clutching the earth in its talons. Beneath the image the words 'Paramount' and 'Electrically Recorded' spanned the label and beneath that was a song title.

Each label bore the name of Charley Patton.

Kyle placed his beer on a bedside table and then wiped his hands on his shirt sleeves.

"Can I pick one up?"

When I told him to go ahead he chose the nearest, held it carefully by the edges and inspected it closely.

"High Water Everywhere, Part 1," he read. "Man, that is a kick-ass song; I can't believe I'm holding it."

He tipped the sleeve and a gleaming black disc slid out and came to rest in the crook of his forefinger.

Light flashed off the 78 rpm record as Kyle tilted it and peered closely to inspect the grooves.

"This looks like it was made yesterday."

His face clouded with suspicion. "You told me this was legit, you gave me your word," he said. "How do I know you ain't had these made."

I showed him the piece of paper that itemised each object and ran my finger down the list, stopping at the reference to the one he was holding.

He looked at the address and date at the top of the page.

"Crystal Springs, that's just south of Jackson," he said. "You telling me these have been in a pawn shop in Crystal Springs since 1934?"

I said not exactly.

Kyle put down the record and picked up another. "Man, I can't believe what you got here…"

His voice tailed off as he stared at the collection and then looked at me.

"How much you want for 'em?"

# Putting Things Right

The next day I drove to Marchant's law firm and saw Kyle standing next to a dark blue Range Rover. I parked the car, checked it was locked and we then both walked into the offices.

Half an hour later and the deal was complete. Hands were shook and then Kyle and I walked outside and transferred the cardboard box from my car to his.

We shook hands again and as he stepped up into his Range Rover, I wished Kyle a safe journey.

His face lit up with a Buddy Holly grin. "You too, mate. Take it easy."

I watched him drive away and then I turned and walked back into Marchant's offices.

Benjamin was standing behind his desk, upon which were arranged several documents and a Montblanc fountain pen.

"OK," he said, motioning me to sit down. "Here is the paperwork you need to read and sign. Once you've done that things will start moving."

He gave me serious look. "Before we get started," he said. This stuff you're asking us to do is going to be a major game-changer for you, are you absolutely sure that this is what you want?"

I replied that I had never been more certain about anything.

Benjamin nodded slightly then removed the cap from the fountain pen and picked up a document. "Well, OK, then," he said. "Why don't we get started?"

When everything was done, Benjamin arranged the documents in a neat pile at the edge of the desk and then stood up.

"I guess there's just one thing left to do," he said. "I'll be right back."

Benjamin returned a few minutes later carrying a black leather attaché case, which he placed on the desk in front of him.

Looking me straight in the eye, he snapped the catches and then opened the lid.

Inside, wrapped in neat bundles, was half a million dollars. I'd never seen this much money outside of a movie and caught my breath at the sight of it.

"I can arrange for someone to escort you if you wish?"

I thanked him but told him that I didn't have far to go.

"Do you want to count it?"

I smiled, said that wouldn't be necessary and shut the case.

Benjamin extended his hand as I stood up.

"What you're doing," he said, "is a noble thing that's going to make a difference to a lot of people."

I smiled again, thanked him for his help, picked up the attaché case containing half a million dollars and walked out onto the street.

# Back at The Crossroads

An hour later, I was about two miles the other side of Beulah, on a deserted Highway 1 when once again the engine stopped and the car coasted to a halt.

In the daylight, the dirt road snaking through the clump of trees seemed benign, but my heart was racing as I walked towards the remains of an abandoned church.

As I reached the crossroads, the rumbling of a straight-eight engine distracted me and I turned to see sunlight flaring from the chrome fender of a bulbous 1950s sedan.

The car growled to halt outside the church, the handbrake ratcheted and then the body rolled on its springs as the driver's door flew open and Fat Man's huge bulk clambered out.

A cigar jutted from the corner of his mouth, held secure between his teeth as his lips peeled back in a triumphant grin.

Fat Man gripped the cigar between his fingers and then waved expansively at the car.

"Whatchoo think o' my automobile, White Boy?" he roared. "Ain' she purty?"

He ran his hand along the hood, his fat fingers caressing the winged ornament.

"Ninteen-Fifty Fo' Pontiac Star Chief," he declared.

"Yo' know what Pontiac stands for?"

When I shook my head, Fat Man winked again, took a long drag on his cigar, his eyes twinkling as he said, "Po' ol' nigger, thinks it's a Cadillac."

323

Fat Man roared with laughter, layers of fat rolling beneath his filthy Keith Richards T-shirt.

"Damn, that never gets old," he wheezed.

I didn't react and Fat Man's laughter stopped like a tap switching off, but the vestiges of a grin remained as he straightened up.

"White folks usually laughs at this point," he said. "Yo' got th' cash?"

I waved the attaché case; Fat Man nodded and then inclined his massive head towards the church. "Shall we?" he said.

I suggested that we could do the deal outside. Fat Man took another long toke on the cigar, stubbed it out in his hands, placed the butt in his pocket and stared upwards as he blew smoke skywards.

"Oh, I think it best we go indoors," he said. "Fo' reasons that will soon become apparent."

Fat Man winked above a dangerous smile. "That ain' a request," he said.

I followed him through the front door, through the church and into the small room opposite.

Fat Man arranged chairs either side of the wooden table and eased his bulk into a sitting position, his eyes glittering as I placed the attaché case between us and opened the lid.

"Half a million big ones," he whispered. "Do I wanna know where yo' got this?"

I said it is what it is.

"Touché, motherfucker."

Fat Man chuckled when I asked him if he wanted to count it. "How long we known each other?" he said. "I ain' go'n count it cos we both know what go'n happen if yo' try an' stiff me."

Almost tenderly Fat Man rang his fingers across the paper money and then lifted a bundle of notes and buried his nose into it.

"Ain' nothin' like the smell o' greenbacks," he said. "Go'n be some happy campers in Vegas tonight."

Placing the wad of notes back inside the case, Fat Man shut the lid, snapped the latches and then sat back, staring at me beneath hooded eyelids.

"Well now," he drawled. "Heyah we all is."

A Lucky Strike appeared between his fingers and then it was in the corner of his mouth, blue smoke trailing lazily upwards and then making patterns as he spoke.

"I want's yo' to know," he said. "Wha's about t' happen ain' go'n give me pleasure none."

Fat Man shook his head. "'s a matter o' fact, I'm kinda disappointed. I had hopes fo' yo' White Boy, high hopes."

He removed the Lucky Strike, tapped ash onto the floor and then ran his tongue behind his lips as he regarded me.

"Yo' an' me, we coulda made a shitload o' money, ten times what we got here."

I shrugged and said that money wasn't everything.

Fat Man grunted. "What fuckin' ever."

He finished the cigarette, crushed it on the corner of the table and then his chair legs scraped across the floor as he stood up.

"An' now we about t' draw a close on th' proceedin's," he said. "Stand up."

At first I didn't move.

"I said, Stand. The Fuck. Up."

I stood.

Fat Man became devoid of all expression, his eyes dead as he reached into the pocket of his filthy jogging bottoms.

What came out made me gag.

Fat Man grinned as he extended his arm, turned his fist palm upwards and opened his fingers to reveal a cancerous tumour the size of a baseball.

Gripped by simultaneous emotions of fear, revulsion and an overwhelming experience of impending loss, I could only stare at the misshapen obscenity cradled in Fat Man's huge hand.

Pink translucent flesh stretched over irregular lumps of fat and cartilage wrapped within a network of veins that in places bulged the flesh outwards. I peered closer, catching a glimpse of partially formed tooth protruding from gristle peppered with tufts of coarse dark hair.

"Ain' she a beauty?"

Fat Man's face had become alive.

"S'grown some since I took it outta yo' mouth," he said. "But tha's th' way o' things. The bigger they gets, th' mo' they feeds, an' th' mo' they feeds, th' sicker yo' gets."

Fat Man hefted the tumour, testing its weight. "Sho' is a heavy sum'bitch," he said. "Gonna take some puttin' back."

Realisation dawned on me and I took an involuntary step backwards.

"'o' course, i's too big t' push back down yo' throat."

Fat Man's grin grew wider.

"Drop yo' pants an' assume th' position."

My body froze, refusing to believe what was about to happen.

"Ain' got all day, son, gotta get this done an' then we be on our way."

When I still didn't move, Fat Man sighed.

"'s too late fo' second thoughts, White Boy," he growled. "An' I'm losin' patience."

I said that there had to be another way.

Fat Man squeezed the tumour and I shuddered as it obtruded between his fingers with the noise of offal being scraped from a carcass.

"Maybe they is," he said. "But this' th' way we gonna do it."

I refused to move, shook my head defiantly and said that it most definitely wasn't going to happen.

Fat Man lost patience.

One moment he was standing opposite me, a second later I was spread-eagled across the table, staring at the tumour in front of me. I felt cool air on my exposed buttocks and then howled as a probing finger pushed roughly inside me.

As I tried to struggle, Fat Man grabbed the back of my head and smashed my face onto the table. I tasted blood in my mouth, and then I heard him hawk his throat, felt his spit hit my body and then I screamed as a second finger found its way in. I felt helpless, helpless and fucking furious and I bellowed that Fat Man was a dirty fucking cunt and that I was going to kill him. My face smashed again onto the table and when I opened my eyes, the tumour had gone and I was being torn apart.

My fury turned to pleading and I begged him to stop, alternately sobbing and screaming at the violation as the abhorrent mass was forced upwards inside of me.

Then I felt Fat Man's hand pushing down between my shoulder blades, his full weight pinned me to the table and then I screamed as in a single, violent movement he withdrew his bunched fist and threw me across the room. My head bounced off the wall and I passed out.

When I awoke, I was lying on the floor, trousers around my ankles. My head ached, my lips felt swollen, my cheekbones felt bruised and my arse felt like it was on fire.

The familiar smell of Lucky Strike tobacco hung in the air and I looked up to see Fat Man picking his nose. Bizarrely, the thought of where his finger had been generated mixed emotions as I wondered what fresh hell was coming next.

Fat Man flicked away whatever he'd dug out of his nose then chain lit another Lucky Strike.

I struggled to my feet, hitched up my trousers and crab-walked gingerly across the room to lean against the wall.

Sitting at the table, Fat Man seemed calmer.

"Th' pain in yo' ass will be gone soon," he said. "Literally and metaphorically. We done here. Yo' back t' where yo' was befo' we made th' deal. I ain' got no hold over yo' an' yo' free t'continue with wha's left o' yo' life."

When I asked Fat Man what he planned to do with the half-million, he shrugged.

"I tol' yo' I been down in Vegas," he said. "Some folks goes kinda crazy when they walks into a casino. They loses all sense o' time an' reason an' befo' they knows it they losin' a whole lot mo'."

Flicking away the dead cigarette, Fat Man drew on the new one and then chuckled asthmatically. "'s funny," he said. "Folks like that, they watch ever'thin' be taken away on th' turn of a card, th' roll of a dice o' where a ball falls in a roulette wheel.

An' each an' every time they always say, 'Man, if I jus' had another hunnerd dollars, I could turn this round'."

The tip of the Lucky Strike glowed fiercely and then Fat Man exhaled a lungful of smoke.

"An' folks in that position, yo'd be surprised what they'd do to get a hold of anotha hunnerd dollars," he paused. "What they'd sell."

He tapped a fat finger on the attaché case. "This here represents five thousand deals with folks like that, tha's five thousand mo' associates o' Fat Man, an' the money from yo' blues recuds gon' make a shitload mo'."

He breathed out more smoke then looked across at me. "An' that equates t' a shitload mo' deals of which yo' coulda had a percentage," he said. "They's gold in them recordin's, royalties gonna be rollin' in fo' a long time."

I said that I sincerely hoped so.

Fat Man's eyes narrowed.

"Whatchoo mean by that?"

I told him that I'd brought back Charley Patton's record collection and sold it for 1.5 million dollars, and that I'd given the million dollars to a lawyer to be distributed equally among the descendants.

"Where th' fuck yo' getta holda Charley Patton's recuds?"

I pulled two twenty dollar bills from my pocket, gave them to Fat Man and thanked him for the loan that he gave me.

Then his frown lifted as realisation dawned, "Well Goddam, yo' bought 'em from Uncle Kike? White Boy, yo' one sneaky motherfucker."

Fat Man frowned, "How yo' get 'em out?" he said. Gabel pretty shit hot when it comes t' protectin' his domain."

I said that Gabel and I had made a deal.

He shook his head in wonder and then chuckled. "Whatever, it don' make a damn bit o' difference. Lawyer gon' make sho' he pocket most o' that million dollars. They ain' gonna be much left for whomsoever crawls outta the woodwork lookin' fo' a handout. Yo' jus' throwed away a million bucks."

I chuckled back and agreed that I'd thought about that and that's why I had chosen a black law firm with a special interest in the rights of black people. I said that's why I'd drawn up a will which bequeathed all my worldly goods to repay the half million I'd used and to fund the cause that I'd set up.

329

I had Fat Man's attention.

"What cause?" he said.

I told him that, under terms of the master recordings copyright the lawyer would be pursuing the claims of the descendants of each and every blues singer to royalties earned from the sale of songs that I recorded.

Fat Man's low, animal cunning went into overdrive; he sat upright, his eyes glinting like a shithouse rat.

"Th' fuck yo' mean, 'master recordin's copyright'?"

I said that when I recorded the singers, I made a note of each recording and claimed copyright for the sound recordings in my name but on their behalf. I said that I had handed over these notes and that the lawyer agreed they were valid evidence of copyright for the sound recording and also for musical composition.

"Bullshit."

I said nothing as Fat Man processed this.

"Yo' was workin' fo' me," he growled. "Recordin's belong t'me."

I shrugged and said that he and I had no written contract of our arrangement, whereas the lawyers seemed to think that my notes provided evidence of the copyright of the performance belonging to the artist and that furthermore they seemed very certain they could recover every cent earned from the sale of recordings in any media and give it to the descendants of the artist.

"Possession's nine tenths o' th' law," said Fat Man.

I agreed that that was true but that it referred to real property, not intellectual property.

Fat Man fell silent, running his tongue around the inside of his cheek as he stared at me.

"Got all th' fuckin' answers, doncha?"

He waved a dismissive hand.

"I don' give a fuck 'bout no lawyers, 's my shit t'sell an' I'ma sell my shit how I want."

I said that I was only telling him what the lawyer had told me.

"Oh yeah? Well fuck yo' an' fuck yo' lawyers, too."

I said nothing.

Fat Man looked troubled as he leaned forward and rested his elbow on the table, tapping a tooth with his thumbnail as he stared into the middle distance.

I waited.

Eventually, his eyes shifted to meet mine.

"These lawyers," he said. "What else they say?"

Smiling inside, I deadpanned my response as I told Fat Man that a cease and desist letter was about to be sent to all his associates in the recording industry.

That did it.

A cold silence cloaked the room as Fat Man's eyes burned with impotent malice. For a few seconds he remained motionless, save for muscles rolling along his jawbone and veins pulsing at his temple. Then his body began to quiver in fury, his face twisting into venomous hatred as he emitted a low rumbling that filled the room like the sound of a distant artillery barrage.

And then he erupted.

Fat Man leapt to his feet and bellowed like a raging Grizzly bear. I dived to one side as the table span through the air like a fighting star and smashed through the wall in an explosion of wood fragments. I covered my head as I saw a chair hit the wall and disintegrate like a Hollywood prop.

Beneath me the floor shook and I looked up to see Fat Man systematically pounding huge holes in the wall. The tired, rotten wood was no match for the fury behind his fists and as he moved around the room a monster punch connected with a supporting post and snapped it like a matchstick.

I heard a creak and felt momentary vertigo as the building lurched and then steadied. By now Fat Man had reached the far corner and made short work of another upright. The crack of released energy sounded like a rifle shot as the corner post gave way followed by a prolonged groan as the roof settled and then more snapping as rotten boards splintered beneath its weight.

The whole building lurched again, walls canting outwards as the roof collapse gained momentum, shafts of sunlight bursting through fresh holes and capturing dust and paint flakes like enemy aircraft in a searchlight beam.

Fat Man was halfway to the next corner when I leapt to my feet and just made it through the door as the roof gave way and the entire church imploded in a huge cloud of dust.

I staggered and tipped backwards, reigniting the fire in my backside as I landed heavily on the other side of a gravestone.

For a few seconds I sat in the roar of post-apocalyptic silence, my fingers tracing the chiselled indents that captured Travellin' Man's name in stone.

My head swam in a brief flashback of our time together and then I heard more wood being splintered and I looked up to see Fat Man emerge from the wreckage of the church.

I could only stare as he stomped towards me, inner thighs chafing with each purposeful step, immense stomach wobbling beneath his filthy, dust-coated T-shirt.

He stopped on the other side of Travellin' Man's gravestone, lit a Lucky Strike and squinted as smoke wreathed his dust-smeared face.

He looked down at me beneath hooded eyelids then aimed a fat finger straight between my eyes.

"This ain' over, White Boy," he said. "Yo' an' me, we go'n dance again."

With that he turned and lumbered towards his car, chain-lighting another Lucky Strike as he clambered into the Pontiac Superchief, fired up the straight-eight engine and span tyres into the distance with the dirty, opening riff of the Stones' "Midnight Rambler" blasting from the speakers.

# End Of The Line

I haven't seen Fat Man since, but I have no doubt that I will.

He took me for a ride and no mistake. I mean, who better to fool a white boy wannabe blues man than a drunken black man in a juke-joint in Clarksdale, Mississippi?

Anyway, by the time I'd returned to my room at the Ground Zero Blues Club the tumour was making up for lost time. That was about a week ago and I haven't been out since. Marilyn tells me that it won't be long, just another few days, maybe a week. Morphine patches manage the pain, but mostly I'm asleep.

Occasionally, like now, the opiate-induced fog of incomprehension lifts to reveal brief moments of clarity like the breeze parting a gas-cloud on some distant battlefield.

Downstairs I can hear a band playing a George Thorogood tune, his trademark song with the intro ripped off from Muddy Waters.

As Howlin' Wolf once sang, I'm goin' down slow. The fog's closing in again and I think this time it's going to stay. I'm ready to go and I'm not scared anymore because, as Fat Man said, "Where yo' is when yo' in this world, tha's where yo' gon' be in the nex' one."

I already know where I'm going. I hope so, anyway. I've got more dues to pay.

The band's getting louder, the singer stuttering the chorus. Just another white boy playin' the blues, but man, that slide guitar, gets me every time.

B-B-B-Bad, Bad to the Bone…

Fat Man. He took me for a ride alright, but what a ride it was.


The End.


335

# Outtake

Deleted scene from The Banty Rooster:


Travellin' Man chuckled, and then grinned. "I never knew a time when I din't have th' blues," he said. "I wrote a song 'bout it, too."

When I asked him to sing it he screwed his eyes up. "Lemme think, how'n th' hell did it go?"

He picked up his guitar, checked the tuning and picked a simple fingerstyle riff as he fought to recall the song.

"Oh yeah, I got it."

As he shifted his chair to clear some space, I reached into my satchel. My fingers closed around my phone and I set it up to record just as Travellin' Man cleared his throat and then mumbled. "This'n called I never knew."

He began to sing in a low, mournful voice.

*I never knew a racehorse that I didn't want to back,*
*I never had a job where I didn't get the sack,*
*I never played a card game, I knew wouldn't lose*
*An' I never knew a time when I couldn't play the blues.*
*I never knew a time when I didn't have a worry*
*I never met a town I didn't leave in a hurry*
*I never found a wrong path that I knew I wouldn't choose*
*An' I never knew a time when I couldn't play the blues.*

Travellin' Man played a different riff then growled, "This here's th' chorus."

*I guess I'm livin' me a life where it seems I'm born to lose*
*It feels jus' like I'm walkin' roun' in someone else's shoes*

337

*It's somethin' that jus happens no matter what I choose*
*I never knew a time that I couldn't play the blues.*

He reverted to the original riff. "This is th' last verse,
*I never met a bar where I didn't stay all night*
*I never knew a time when I didn't start a fight*
*I never met a drink that I knew I could refuse*
*An' I never knew a time when I couldn't play the blues.*

Travellin' Man finished the tune with a flourish.

"Well," he said. "Whatchoo think?"

I said that if that had been recorded it would be a blues classic.

"Well, yo' jus' reco'ded it, dincha?, yo' gon' make me a star?"

I said I would do my best and asked him to tell me about the song.

Putting the guitar to one side he hunched over the table.

"I wrote that in nineteen and thirty-one, nineteenth day of February.
Played it on street corners an' at juke-joints an' fish fries an' such an' folks seem
t'like what I was puttin' down."

He took a drink. "Anyhow, I's in a bar one time an' I heard a feller say,
'yo' know, I never met a drink I could refuse.' An' we all gots t' laughin' cos we
knowed it was right. See, it was a Saturday night an' they ain' any nigger I
knows gon' refuse a drink on a Saturday night. So what that feller said kinda
stuck with me an' I kinda worked it up into that song."

# Acknowledgements

First and foremost I would like to thank my wife Barbara and our amazing friends, Sara & Kyle Sweet. Without you, Fat Man truly would not exist and words cannot begin to express my appreciation for all that you did.

Thank you also to Malvern Writers' Circle – especially Gren Gaskell and Rob Hemming - for your endless support and guidance and for allowing me to read countless excerpts at Circle meetings.

Similarly, thanks to everyone at Writers' Block (you know who you are).

Andy Peters (check out his writing on Amazon) has been a great help, especially when it comes to talking about guitars, and has composed "Riding with the Fat Man" especially for this book.

Ran Walker (check out his writing on Amazon) has been an invaluable and patient source of information regarding black history, black culture in Mississippi and the finer points of southern dialogue. He is also skilled at explaining copyright law to a buffoon. Any inaccuracies are mine.

Eden Brower and Jon Heneghan are known collectively as the East River String Band. Thanks for keeping the old music alive and playing in my head when I was writing. www.eastriverstringband.com is where the magic happens.

Equally, thanks to Lamont "Jack" Pearley for preaching the history of the blues and passing it on to future generations. Check out his website and podcasts at www.talkingabouttheblues.com

Finally, thanks to you for getting this far.

# Reviews

### Evel Knievel & the Fat Elvis Diner

*"This story only takes about 30 mins to read, but it manages to make quite an impression in such a short space of time that it's well worth it. I was still thinking about it a long time after I'd finished..."*

*"A nice tight style, nothing is over described and he holds the attention throughout.*
*Would be very interested in reading more by Richard Wall..."*

*"This is a good, punchy short story... it packs surprising level of emotional resonance - especially for anyone who grew up in 1970s Britain. Neat little twist at the end, too..."*

*"This story is a taste of a great talent, buy it, try it, and you'll tell your grandchildren how you helped discover a wonderful new writer..."*

### Five Pairs of Shorts

*"This writer gets more atmosphere into a thousand words than most writers get into a novel. Five exceptional stories for a few pence. What a bargain and what a wonderful reading pleasure. MORE PLEASE..."*

*"Muscle cars, a box of priceless undiscovered records, a briefcase full of cash and the control room of a nuclear submarine. These are just some of the props in Richard Wall's Five Pairs of Shorts, a collection of ten short stories guaranteed to turn any dreary commute into an edge of the seat experience..."*

*"...stories that seem like they could be the hybrid of Roald Dahl (his adult stories) and Quentin Tarantino. I was particularly fond of a group of stories about a team of criminals who find themselves in the same prison after a job goes south. A situation like that is ripe with conflict, and Wall does not disappoint..."*

16123818R00190

Printed in Great Britain
by Amazon